Praise for *New York Times* bestselling author RaeAnne Thayne

"RaeAnne has a knack for capturing those emotions that come from the heart."
—*RT Book Reviews*

"Romance, vivid characters and a wonderful story…really, who could ask for more?"
—Debbie Macomber, #1 *New York Times* bestselling author, on *Blackberry Summer*

"Plenty of tenderness and Colorado sunshine flavor this pleasant escape."
—*Publishers Weekly* on *Woodrose*

Praise for Caro Carson

"[Caro] Carson's romance is complex, touching and funny. The Texas catastrophe setting awes, the co-stars shine and the morality tale inspires."
—*RT Book Reviews* on *Not Just a Cowboy* (4½ stars)

"[Caro] Carson's romance is a humorous and heartfelt page-turner from the get-go. Her funny, genuinely touching and vibrant narrative sets the perfect pace with just a touch of Texas twang."
—*RT Book Reviews* on *The Bachelor Doctor's Bride*

RaeAnne Thayne finds inspiration in the beautiful northern Utah mountains, where the *New York Times* and *USA TODAY* bestselling author lives with her husband and three children. Her books have won numerous honors, including RITA® Award nominations from Romance Writers of America and a Career Achievement Award from *RT Book Reviews*. RaeAnne loves to hear from readers and can be contacted through her website, www.raeannethayne.com.

Despite a no-nonsense background as a West Point graduate and US Army officer, **Caro Carson** has always treasured the happily-ever-after of a good romance novel. After reading romances no matter where in the world the army sent her, Caro began a career in the pharmaceutical industry. Little did she know the years she spent discussing science with physicians would provide excellent story material for her new career as a romance author. Now Caro is delighted to be living her own happily-ever-after with her husband and two children in the great state of Florida, a location that has saved the coaster-loving theme-park fanatic a fortune on plane tickets.

New York Times **Bestselling Author**

RaeANNE THAYNE

A COLD CREEK SECRET

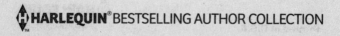
HARLEQUIN® BESTSELLING AUTHOR COLLECTION

ISBN-13: 978-0-373-53781-5

A Cold Creek Secret

Copyright © 2017 by Harlequin Books S.A.

The publisher acknowledges the copyright holders of the individual works as follows:

A Cold Creek Secret
Copyright © 2010 by RaeAnne Thayne

Not Just a Cowboy
Copyright © 2014 by Caro Carson

Recycling programs for this product may not exist in your area.

Printed in U.S.A.

www.Harlequin.com

CONTENTS

Also by RaeAnne Thayne

Harlequin Special Edition

The Cowboys of Cold Creek

HQN Books

Haven Point

Hope's Crossing

Visit the Author Profile page
at Harlequin.com for more titles.

A COLD CREEK SECRET

RaeAnne Thayne

To the wonderful writers of Utah RWA
for your support, encouragement and friendship.

Chapter 1

No matter what exotic parts of the world he visited, Brant Western hadn't forgotten how the cold of a February evening in Idaho could clutch at his lungs with icy claws that refused to let go.

In the past hour, the light snow flurries of the afternoon had turned vicious, intense. The active storm front forecasters had been warning about since he arrived for his mid-tour leave two days earlier had finally started its relentless march across this tiny corner of eastern Idaho toward Wyoming.

Icy flakes spit against his unprotected face with all the force of an Al Asad sandstorm. Somehow they found their way to every exposed surface, even sliding beneath the collar of his heavy shearling-lined ranch coat.

This was the sort of Idaho night made for hunker-

ing down by the fire with a good book and a cup of
hot cocoa.

The picture had undeniable appeal, one of the many
images of home that had sustained him through fierce
firefights and long campaigns and endless nights under
Afghan and Iraqi stars.

After, he reminded himself. When the few cattle at
the Western Sky had been fed and all the horses were
safe and snug in the barn, then he could settle in front
of the fire with the thriller he'd picked up in the airport.

"Come on, Tag. We're almost done, then we can go
home."

His horse, a sturdy buckskin gelding, whinnied as
if he completely understood every word and continued
plodding along the faint outline of a road still visible
under the quickly falling snow.

Brant supposed this was a crazy journey. The hundred head of cows and their calves weren't even his cattle but belonged to a neighbor of the Western Sky who
leased the land while Brant was deployed.

Carson McRaven took good care of his stock. Brant
wouldn't have agreed to the lease if he didn't. But since
the cattle were currently residing on his property, he
felt responsibility toward them.

*Sometimes that sense of obligation could be a gen-
uine pain in the butt,* he acknowledged as he and Tag
finished making sure the warmers in the water troughs
were functioning and turned back toward the house.

They hadn't gone more than a dozen yards when he
saw headlights slicing weakly through the fusillade of
snow, heading toward the ranch far too quickly for these
wintry conditions.

He squinted in the murky twilight. Who did he know

who would be stupid or crazy enough to venture out in this kind of weather?

Easton was the logical choice but he had just talked to her on the phone a half hour earlier, before he had set out on this fool's errand to check the ranch, and she had assured him that after the wedding they had both attended the night before, she was going to bed early with a lingering headache.

He worried about her. He couldn't deny that. Easton hadn't been the same since her aunt, his foster mother, had died of cancer several months earlier. Even longer, really. She hadn't been the sweet, funny girl he'd known and loved most of his life maybe since around the time Guff Winder had died.

Maybe Easton wasn't acting like herself, but he was pretty sure she had the good sense to hunker down at Winder Ranch during a storm like this. If she did venture out, he was pretty sure she was smart enough to slow down when conditions demanded it, especially since he and his foster brothers had drilled that into her head when they taught her to drive.

So if that driver wasn't Easton, who was barreling toward his ranch on the cusp of a ferocious winter storm?

Somebody lost, no doubt. Sometimes these remote canyon roads were difficult to negotiate and the snow could obscure landmarks and address markings. With a sigh, he spurred Tag toward the road to point the wayward traveler in the right direction.

He was just wishing for a decent pair of optics so he could get a better look at who it might be, when the vehicle suddenly went into a slide. He saw it coming as the driver took a curve too fast and he pushed Tag faster, praying he was wrong. But an instant later the driver overcorrected and as Brant held his breath, the vehicle spun out on the icy road.

It was almost like some grisly slow-motion movie, watching it careen over the edge of the road, heading straight for Cold Creek, at the bottom of a maybe five-foot drop.

The vehicle disappeared from view and Brant smacked the reins and dug his heels into the horse's sides, racing as fast as he dared toward the slide-out.

When he reached the creek's edge, he could barely make out in the gathering darkness that the vehicle wasn't quite submerged in the creek but it was a close thing. The SUV had landed on a large granite boulder in the middle of the creek bed, the front end crumpled and the rear wheels still on the bank.

Though he tried not to swear as a habit, he couldn't help hissing out a fierce epithet as he scrambled down from the horse. In February, the creek was only a couple feet deep at most and the current wasn't strong enough to carry off an SUV, but Brant would still have to get wet to get to the vehicle. There was no other way around it.

He heard a faint moan from inside and what sounded, oddly, like a tiny lamb bleating.

"Hang on," he called. "I'll get you out of there in a minute."

Just in the minute or two he had stood surveying the scene and figuring out how to attack the problem, darkness had completely descended and the snow stung at him from every direction. The wind surged around him, taunting and cruel. Even as cold as he was from the storm, he wasn't prepared for the frigid shock of the water through his boots and his lined Wranglers as he waded up to his knees.

He heard that moan again and this time he isolated the sound he had mistaken for a bleating lamb. It was a dog, a tiny one by the sound of it, yipping like crazy.

"Hang on," he called. "Won't take me but a minute and I'll have you out of there, then we can call for help."

When he slogged through the water and finally reached the vehicle, he yanked open the door. The driver was female, in her mid-twenties, maybe. He had a quick impression of wisps of dark curls that looked stark in contrast with her pale, delicate features.

With every passing second, her core temperature would be dropping and he knew he needed to extract her from the SUV and out of the water and the elements before he could completely assess her condition, though it went against every basic tenet of medical training each Army Ranger received, about not moving an injury victim until you knew the extent of injuries.

"Cold," she murmured.

"I know. I'm sorry about that."

He took it as a good sign that she didn't moan or cry out when he scooped her out of the vehicle. If she had broken bones, she wouldn't have been able to hide her discomfort. She didn't say anything at all, just gripped his jacket tightly, her slight body trembling from both the shock and the cold, he guessed.

She wasn't heavy, maybe a hundred and ten pounds, he judged, but carrying her through the ice-crusted water still took every bit of his energy. By the time he reached the bank and headed up the slight slope with her in his arms, he was breathing hard and was pretty sure he couldn't feel his feet anymore.

He'd learned in the early days dealing with combat injuries that the trick to keeping injured men calm was to give as much information as he could about what was going on so they didn't feel completely out of control about what was happening to them. He figured the same technique would work just as well in accident situations. "I'm going to take you back to my place on the horse, okay?"

She nodded and didn't protest when he lifted her onto Tag's back, where she clung tightly to the pommel.

"Hang on now," he said when he was sure she was secure. "I'm going to climb on behind you and then we can get you warm and dry."

When he tried to lift his icy, wet boot into the stirrup, it seemed to weigh as much as the woman had. He had to use all his strength just to raise it that two feet. Just as he shoved it in and prepared to swing the other leg onto the horse, she gasped.

"Simone. My Simone. Please, can you get her?"

He closed his eyes. Simone must be the dog. With the wind howling around them, he couldn't hear the yips anymore and he'd been so focused on the woman that he'd completely forgotten about her dog.

"Are you okay up there for a minute?" he asked, dreading the idea of wading back through that frigid water.

"Yes. Oh, please."

He had survived worse than a little cold water, he reminded himself. Much, much worse.

Returning to the vehicle took him only a moment. In the backseat, he found at least a half-dozen pieces of luggage and a tiny pink dog carrier. The occupant yipped and growled a big show at him.

"You want to stay here?" Brant growled right back. "Because I'd be just great with that."

The dog immediately subsided and under other circumstances he might have smiled at the instant submission, if he wasn't so concerned about getting them all back to the house in one piece. "Yeah, I didn't think so. Come on, let's get you out of here."

As he considered the logistics of things, he realized there was no way he could carry the bulky dog carrier and keep hold of the woman on horseback at the same time, so he unlatched the door of the carrier. A tiny white mound of fur hurtled into his arms.

Not knowing what else to do, he unzipped his coat halfway and shoved the puffball inside then zipped his coat up again, feeling ridiculously grateful none of the men in his company could see him risking hypothermia for six pounds of fuzzy canine.

The woman was still on Tag's back, he was relieved to see when he made his torturous way back through the water, though she seemed to be slumping a little more.

She was dressed in a woefully inadequate pink parka with a fur-lined hood that looked more suited to some fancy après-ski party in Jackson Hole than braving the bitterness of an Idaho blizzard and Brant knew he needed to get them all back to the ranch house ASAP.

"Is she all right?" the woman asked.

What about him? Brant wondered grumpily. He was the one with frostbitten toes. But in answer, he unzipped his coat, where the furry white head popped out. The woman sighed in relief, her delicate features relaxing slightly, and Brant handed the dog up to her.

He caught a glimpse of the little pooch licking her face that looked oddly familiar as he climbed up behind her, but he didn't take time to analyze it as he dug his heels into the horse's side, grateful Tag was one of the strongest, steadiest horses in the small Western Sky stable.

"We'll get you warmed up. I've got a fire in the woodstove at home. Just hang on a few minutes, okay?"

She nodded, slumping back against him, and he curved his arms around her, worried she would slide off.

"Thank you," she murmured, so low he could hardly hear above the moaning of that bitter wind.

He pulled her as close as he could to block the storm as Tag trudged toward home at a hard walk, as fast as Brant dared push him.

"I'm Brant," he said after a few moments. "What's your name?"

She turned her head slightly and he saw dazed confusion in her eyes. "Where are we?" she asked instead of answering him.

He decided not to push her right now. No doubt she was still bemused from the shock of driving her SUV into a creek. "My ranch in eastern Idaho, the Western Sky. The house is just over that hill there."

She nodded slightly and then he felt her slump bonelessly against him.

"Are you still with me?" he asked with concern. When she didn't answer, his arms tightened around her. Out of pure instinct, he grabbed for the dog seconds before she would have dropped it as she slipped into unconsciousness—surely a fatal fall for the little animal from this height. He managed to snag the dog and shove it back into his coat and his arms tightened around the woman as he nudged Tag even faster.

It was a surreal journey, cold and tense and nerve-racking. He didn't see the lights of the ranch house until they had nearly reached it. When he could finally make out the solid shape of the place, Brant was quite certain it was just about the most welcome sight he had ever beheld.

He led the horse to the bottom of the porch steps and dismounted carefully, keeping a hand on the woman so she didn't teeter to the ground.

"Sorry about this, Tag," he murmured to the horse as he lifted the woman's limp form into his arms. "You've been great but I need you to hang on a few more minutes out here in the cold while I take care of our guest and then I can get you into the warm barn. You deserve some extra oats after tonight."

The horse whinnied in response as Brant rushed up the porch steps and into the house. He quickly carried her inside to the family room where, just as he'd promised, the fire he'd built up in the woodstove before he left still sent out plenty of blissful warmth.

She didn't stir when he laid her on the sofa. As he was bent over to unzip her parka so he could check her injuries, the dog wriggled free of the opening of Brant's own coat and landed on her motionless mistress and began licking her face again, where a thin line of blood trickled from a cut just above her eye.

A raspy dog's tongue was apparently enough to jolt her back to at least semiconsciousness. "Simone?" she murmured and her arms slid around the dog, who settled in the crook of her arms happily.

She was soaked through from the snow's onslaught and Brant knew she wouldn't truly warm up until he could get her out of her wet clothing. Beyond that, he had to examine her more closely for broken bones.

"I'm going to get you some dry clothes, okay? I'll be right back."

She opened her eyes again and nodded and he had the oddest sense again that he knew her. She couldn't be from around here. He was almost positive of that, but then he hadn't spent more than a few weeks at a time in Pine Gulch for fifteen years.

The bedroom he stayed in when he was here was one of the two on the main floor and from his duffel he quickly grabbed a sweatshirt and a pair of cutoff sweats that would likely probably drown her, then he returned to the family room.

"I'm going to take off your parka so I can get a better look and make sure you don't have any broken bones, okay?"

She didn't answer and he wondered if she was asleep or had slipped away again. He debated calling the Pine Gulch paramedics, but he hated to do that on a vicious night like tonight unless it was absolutely necessary. He had some medic training and could deal with most basic first aid needs. If she required more than that, he would drive her into town himself.

But he needed to assess her injuries first.

He would rather disarm a suicide bomber with his teeth than undress a semiconscious woman, but he didn't have much choice. He was only doing what had to be done, he reminded himself. Feeling huge and awkward, he pulled off what seemed pretty useless pink fur boots first, then moved the tiny dog from the woman's side to the floor. The dog easily relinquished her guard dog duties and started sniffing around the room to investigate a whole new world full of smells.

Brant unzipped the woman's parka, doing his best to

ignore the soft swell of curves as he pulled the sleeves free, not an easy task since he hadn't been with a woman since before his last deployment. He was only a rescue worker here, he reminded himself. Detached and impersonal.

Her shirt had remained mostly dry under her parka, he was relieved to discover, but her jeans were soaked through and would have to come off.

"Ma'am, you're going to have to get out of your jeans. Do you need my help or can you manage by yourself?"

"Help," she mumbled.

Naturally. He sighed and reached to unfasten the snap and zipper of her jeans. His hands brushed her waist under her soft, blue silk turtleneck. Whether his fingers were cold or whether she was reacting just to the shock of human contact, he didn't know, but she blinked a few times and scrambled away with a little cry.

The tiny dog yipped and abandoned her investigations of the room to trot over and stand protectively over her mistress, teeth bared at him as if a few pounds of fluff would do the trick to deter him.

"You need to get into dry clothes, that's all," he said, using the same calm tone he did with injured soldiers in the field. "I'm not going to hurt you, I swear. You're completely safe here."

She nodded, eyes still not fully open. As he looked at her in the full light, a memory flashed across his brain of her in some barely-there slinky red dress, tossing her dark curls and giving a sultry bedroom look out of half-closed eyes.

Crazy. He had never met the woman before in his life, he could swear to it.

He pulled her jeans off, despising himself for the

little stir of interest when he found her wearing pink lacy high-cut panties.

He swallowed hard. "I'm, uh, going to check for broken bones and then I've got some sweats here we can put on you, okay?"

She nodded and watched him warily from those half-closed eyes as he ran his hands over her legs, trying to pretend she was just another of his teammates. Trouble was, Rangers didn't tend to have silky white skin and luscious curves. Or wear high-cut pink panties.

"Nothing broken that I can tell," he finally said and was relieved when he could pull the faded, voluminous sweats over her legs and hide all that delectable skin.

"Are you a doctor?" she murmured.

"Not even close. I'm in the military, ma'am. Major Brant Western, Company A, 1st Battallion, 75th Ranger Regiment."

She seemed to barely hear him but she still nodded and closed her eyes again when he tucked a blanket from the edge of the sofa around her.

Without his field experience, he might have been alarmed about her state of semiconsciousness, but he'd seen enough soldiers react just this way to a sudden shock—sort of take a little mental vacation—that he wasn't overly concerned. If she was still spacey and out of it when he came back from taking care of Tag, he would get on the horn to Jake Dalton, the only physician in Pine Gulch, and see what he recommended.

He threw a blanket over her. "Ma'am." He spoke loudly and evenly and was rewarded with those eyes opening a little more at him. He was really curious what color they were.

"I need to stable my horse and grab more firewood

in case the power goes out. I've got a feeling we're in for a nasty night. Just rest here with your little puffball and work on warming up, okay?"

After a long moment, she nodded and closed her eyes again.

He knew her somehow and it bothered the hell out of him that he couldn't place how, especially since he usually prided himself on his ironclad memory.

He watched the dog circle around and then settle on her feet again like a little fuzzy slipper. Whoever she was, she had about as much sense as that little dog to go out on a night like tonight. Someone was probably worrying about her. After he took care of Tag, he would try to figure out if she needed to call someone with her whereabouts.

Shoving on his Stetson again, he drew in his last breath of warm air for a while and then headed into the teeth of the storm.

He rushed through taking care of Tag and loaded up as much firewood as he could carry in a load toward the house. He had a feeling he would be back and forth to the woodpile several times during the night and he was grateful his tenant/caretaker Gwen Bianca had been conscientious about making sure enough wood was stockpiled for the winter.

What was he going to do without her? He frowned as one more niggling worry pressed in on him.

Ever since she told him she was buying a house closer to Jackson Hole where she frequently showed her pottery, he had been trying to figure out his options. He was a little preoccupied fighting the Taliban to spend much time worrying about whether a woodpile thousands of miles away had been replenished.

When he returned to the house, he checked on his unexpected guest first thing and found her still sleeping. She wasn't shivering anymore and when he touched her forehead, she didn't seem to be running a fever.

The dog barked a little yippy greeting at him but didn't move from her spot at the woman's feet.

He took off his hat and coat and hung them in the mudroom, then returned to the family room. His touching her forehead—or perhaps the dog's bark—must have awakened her. She was sitting up and this time her eyes were finally wide open.

They were a soft and luscious green, the kind of color he dreamed about during the harsh and desolate Afghan winters, of spring grasses covering the mountains, of hope and growth and life.

She gave him a hesitant smile and his jaw sagged as he finally placed how he knew her.

Holy Mother of God.

The woman on his couch, the one he had dressed in his most disreputable sweats, the woman who had crashed her vehicle into Cold Creek just outside his gates and whose little pink panties he had taken such guilty pleasure in glimpsing, was none other than Mimi frigging Van Hoyt.

A man was staring at her.

Not just any man, either. He was tall, perhaps six-one or two, with short dark hair and blue eyes, powerful muscles and a square, determined sort of jaw. He was just the sort of man who made her most nervous, the kind who didn't look as if they could be swayed by a flirty smile and a sidelong look.

He was staring at her as if she had just sprouted

horns out of the top of her head. She frowned, uncomfortable with his scrutiny though she couldn't have said exactly why.

Her gaze shifted to her surroundings and she discovered she was on a red plaid sofa in a room she didn't recognize, with rather outdated beige flowered wallpaper and a jumble of mismatched furnishings.

She had no clear memory of arriving here, only a vague sense that something was very wrong in her life, that someone was supposed to help her sort everything out. And then she was driving, driving, with snow flying, and a sharp moment of fear.

She looked at the man again, registering that he was extraordinarily handsome in a clean-cut, all-American sort of way.

Had she been looking for him? She blinked, trying to sort through the jumble of her thoughts.

"How are you feeling?" he finally asked. "I couldn't find any broken bones and I think the air bag probably saved you from a nasty bump on the head when you hit the creek."

Creek. She closed her eyes as a memory returned of her hands gripping a steering wheel and a desperate need to reach someone who could help her.

Baby. The baby.

She clutched her hands over her abdomen and made a low sort of moan.

"Here, take it easy. Do you have a stomachache? That could be from the air bag. It's not unusual to bruise a rib or two when one of those things deploys. Do you want me to take you into the clinic in town to check things out?"

She didn't know. She couldn't think, as if every coherent thought in her head had been squirreled away on a high shelf just out of her reach.

She hugged her arms around herself. She had to trust her instincts, since she didn't know what else to do. "No clinic. I don't want to go to the doctor."

He raised one dark eyebrow at that but then shrugged. "Your call. For now, anyway. If you start babbling and speaking in tongues, I'm calling the doctor in Pine Gulch, no matter what you say."

"Fair enough." The baby was fine, she told herself. She wouldn't accept any other alternative. "Where am I?"

"My ranch. The Western Sky. I told you my name before but I'll do it again. I'm Brant Western."

To her surprise, Simone, who usually distrusted everything with a Y chromosome, jumped down from the sofa to sniff at his boots. He picked the dog up and held her, somehow still managing to look ridiculously masculine with a little powder puff in his arms.

Western Sky. Gwen. *That's* where she had been running. Gwen would fix everything, she knew it.

No. This problem was too big for even Gwen to fix.

"I'm Maura Howard," she answered instinctively, using the alias she preferred when she traveled, for security reasons.

"Are you?" he said. *An odd question,* she thought briefly, but she was more concerned with why she was here and not where she wanted to be.

She had visited Gwen's cabin once before but she didn't remember this room. "This isn't Gwen's house."

At once, a certain understanding flashed in blue eyes that reminded her of the ocean near her beach house in Malibu on her favorite stormy afternoons.

"You know Gwen Bianca?"

She nodded. "I need to call her, to let her know I'm here."

"That's not going to do you much good. Gwen's not around."

That set her back and she frowned. "Do you know where she is?"

"Not at the ranch, I'm afraid. Not even in the country, actually. She's at a gallery opening in Milan."

Oh, no. Mimi closed her eyes. How stupid and short-sighted of her, to assume Gwen would be just waiting here to offer help if Mimi ever needed it.

Egocentric, silly, selfish. That was certainly her.

No wonder she preferred being Maura Howard whenever she had the chance.

"Well, Maura." Was it her imagination, or did he stress her name in an unnatural sort of way? "I'm afraid you're not going anywhere tonight. It's too dangerous for you to drive on these snowy roads even if I could manage to go out in the dark and snow to pull your vehicle out of the creek. I'm afraid you're stuck for now."

Oh, what a mess. She wanted to sink back onto the pillows of this comfortable sofa, just close her eyes and slide back into blissful oblivion. But she couldn't very well do that with her host watching her out of those intense blue eyes.

As tough and dangerous as Brant Western looked, she had the strangest assurance that she was safe with him. On the other hand, her instincts hadn't been all that reliable where men where concerned for the past, oh, twenty-six years.

But Simone liked him and that counted for a great deal in her book.

As if sensing the direction of her gaze, he set the dog down. Simone's white furry face looked crestfallen for just a moment, then she jumped back up to Mimi's lap.

"I'm assuming Gwen didn't know you were coming."

"No. I should have called her." Her voice trembled on the words and she fought down the panic and the fear and the whole tangled mess of emotions she'd been fighting since that stark moment in her ob-gyn's office the day before.

Gwen had been her logical refuge as she faced this latest disaster in her life. Mimi's favorite of her father's ex-wives, Gwen had always offered comfort and support through boarding schools and breakups and scandals.

For twenty-four hours, all she had been able to think about was escaping to Gwen, in desperate need of her calm good sense and her unfailing confidence in Mimi. But Gwen wasn't here. She was in Milan right now, just when Mimi needed her most and she felt, ridiculously, as if all the underpinnings of her world were shaking loose.

First driving her car into a creek and now this. It was all too much. She sniffled and made a valiant effort to fight back the tears, but it was too late. The panic swallowed her whole and she started to cry.

Simone licked at her tears and Mimi held the dog closer, burying her face in her fur.

Through her tears, she thought she saw utter horror in her host's eyes. He was an officer in the military, she remembered Gwen telling her. A major, if Mimi wasn't mistaken, in some Special Forces unit.

She had a vague memory of him telling her that. Major Brant Western, Company A, 1st Battallion, 75th Ranger Regiment.

She would have thought a man would have to be a fairly confident, take-charge sort of guy to reach that rank, but Major Western looked completely panicked by her tears. "Hey, come on. Don't cry, um, Maura. It's okay. You'll see. Things will seem better in the morning, I promise. It's not the end of the world. You're safe and dry now and I've even got a guest room you can stay in tonight. We'll get that cut on your eye cleaned up and bandaged."

She swiped at her tears with her sleeve and a moment later he thrust a tissue in her face, which she seized on gratefully. "I can't stay here," she said after she'd calmed a little. "I don't even know you. I passed a guest ranch a few miles back. Hope Springs or something like that. I'll see if they've got availability."

"How are you going to get there?" he asked.

"What do you mean?"

"Your SUV is toast for now and Pine Gulch isn't exactly flush with cab companies. Beside that, the way that wind is blowing and drifting, it's not safe for anybody to be out on the roads. That storm has already piled up seven inches and forecasters are predicting two or three times that before we're done. I promise, you're completely safe staying here. The guest room's even got a lock on the door."

She had a feeling a locked door wouldn't stop him if he set his mind to breaking in somewhere. No doubt this man, with his serious blue eyes and solid strength, could work his way through just about anything—whether a locked door or a woman's good sense.

"Have you eaten?"

"I'm not hungry."

That was certainly true enough. Just the idea of food

made her stomach churn. Ironic that she'd been pregnant for more than ten weeks and hadn't exhibited a single symptom, not the tiniest sign that might have tipped her off. Then the day after she found out she was pregnant, she started with the morning sickness, along with a bone-deep exhaustion. If she had the chance, she thought she could sleep for a week.

"I can't impose on you this way."

He shrugged. "Once you've made a guy wade through a frozen creek twice, what's a little further inconvenience for him? Let me go grab some clean sheets for the bed and we'll get that cut cleaned up and you settled for the night."

She wiped at the tears drying on her features. What choice did she have? She had nowhere else to go. After he left the room, she leaned into the sofa, holding Simone close and soaking in the fire's delicious heat.

Now that she thought of it, this just might be the perfect solution, at least while she tried to wrap her head around the terrifying future.

No one would know where she was. Not her father—as if he'd care. Not Marco, who would care even less. Certainly not the bane of her existence, the paparazzi, who cared only for ratings and circulation numbers.

The world outside that window was a terrifying place. For now she had shelter from that storm out there, and a man who looked more than capable of protecting her from anything that might come along.

She only needed a little breathing space to figure things out and she could find that here as easily as anywhere else.

Only one possible complication occurred to her. She would have to do her best to keep him from calling for a tow when the snow cleared. She knew from experience that people like tow-truck drivers and gas station attendants and restaurant servers were usually the first ones to pick up a phone and call in the tabloids.

She could see the headlines now. Mimi's Ditchscapade with Sexy Rancher.

She couldn't afford that right now. She only needed a few days of quiet and rest. Like that blizzard out there, the media storm that was her life and this latest—and worst—potential scandal would hopefully pass without ever seeing the light of day.

She only needed to figure out a way to stay safe and warm until it did.

Chapter 2

When Brant returned to his living room, he found Maura Howard—aka Mimi Van Hoyt, tabloid princess du jour—gazing into the fire, her features pale and her wide, mobile mouth set into a tense frown.

A few years ago during one of his Iraq deployments, he'd had the misfortune of seeing her one miserable attempt at moviemaking at a showing in the rec hall in Tikrit. He was pretty sure the apparent turmoil she was showing now must be genuine, since her acting skills had been roughly on par with the howler monkey that had enjoyed a bit in the movie.

As long as she didn't cry again, he could handle things. He was ashamed to admit that he could handle a dozen armed insurgents better than a crying woman.

"Everything will seem better in the morning," he promised her. "Once the storm passes over, I can call a tow for your car. I'm sure they can fix it right up in town and send you on your way."

Her hands twisted on her lap and those deep green eyes shifted away from him. In pictures he'd seen of her, he always thought those eyes held a hard, cynical edge, but he could see none of that here.

"I, um, can't really afford a tow right now."

If she hadn't said the words with such a valiant attempt at sincerity in her voice, he would have snorted outright at that blatant whopper. Everybody on the planet who had ever seen a tabloid knew her father was Werner Van Hoyt, real estate mogul, Hollywood producer and megabillionaire. She was a trust fund baby whose sole existence seemed to revolve around attending the hottest parties and being seen with other quasi-celebrities at the hippest clubs until all hours of the day and night.

Did she think he was a complete idiot? The SUV in question was a Mercedes, for heaven's sake.

But if Mimi wanted to pretend to be someone else, who was he to stop her?

"The rental car company should take care of the details. They would probably even send another vehicle for you. Barring that, I'm sure Wylie down at the garage will take a credit card or work out a payment plan with you. But we can cross that bridge once the snow clears. Let's get your face cleaned up so you can get to bed."

She didn't look as if she appreciated any of those options, at least judging by the frustration tightening her features. He had a pretty strong feeling she probably hadn't been thwarted much in her life. It would probably do her a world of good not to get her way once in a while.

He had to bite his lip to keep from smiling. Big shocker there. He hadn't found much of anything amusing since that miserable afternoon three weeks ago in a remote village in Paktika Province.

Longer, come to think of it. His world had felt hollow and dark around the edges since Jo's death in the fall. But somehow Mimi seemed to remind him that life could sometimes be a real kick in the seat.

He had to give her credit for only flinching a little when he cleansed the small cut over her eye and stuck a bandage on it.

"It's a pretty small cut and shouldn't leave a scar."

"Thank you," she said in a subdued voice, then gracefully covered a yawn. "I'm sorry. I've been traveling for several hours and it's been a...stressful day."

"Don't worry about it. Your room is back here. It's nothing fancy but it's comfortable and you've got your own bathroom."

"I hate to ask but, speaking of bathrooms," she said, "Simone could probably use a trip outside."

"Yeah, she has been dancing around for the door for the last few minutes. I'll take her out and try to make sure she doesn't get swallowed by the snow, then bring her in to you."

"Thank you for...everything," she murmured. "Not too many people would take in a complete stranger—and her little dog, too—in the middle of a blizzard."

"Maybe not where you're from. But I would guess just about anybody in Cold Creek Canyon would have done the same."

"Then it must be a lovely place."

"Except in the middle of a February blizzard," he answered. She didn't object when he cupped her elbow to help her down the hall and he tried to store up all the memories. How she smelled of some light citrus-floral, undoubtedly expensive perfume. How her silk turtleneck caressed his fingers. How she was much shorter than he would have guessed, only just reaching his shoulder.

The guys would want to know everything about this surreal interlude and Brant owed it to them to memorize every single detail.

Like the rest of the house, the guest suite was on the shabby side, with aging furniture and peeling wallpaper. But it had a comfortable queen-sized bed, an electric fireplace he'd turned on when he made up the bed and a huge claw-foot tub in the bathroom.

The main house had been mostly empty for the past two years except for his occasional visits between deployments. Since he left Cold Creek a dozen years ago for the military, he had rented the house out sporadically. Gwen Bianca stayed in the small cabin on the property rent-free in exchange for things like keeping the woodpile stocked and the roof from collapsing in.

His last tenants had moved out six months ago and he hadn't bothered to replace them since the rent mostly covered barebones maintenance and county property taxes on the land anyway and was hardly worth the trouble most of the time.

Now that Gwen had announced she was moving away, he didn't know what to do with Western Sky.

"It's not much but you should be warm and comfortable."

"I'll be fine. Thank you again for your hospitality."

"I don't know if this is a warning or an apology in

advance, but I'll be checking on you occasionally in the night."

"Do you think I'm going to run off with your plasma TV?"

He fought another smile, wondering where they were all coming from. "You're welcome to it, if you think you can make a clean getaway on foot in this storm. No. There's a chance you had a head injury. I don't think so but you were in and out of consciousness for a while there. I can't take any chance of missing signs of swelling or unusual behavior."

She sat on the edge of the bed with a startled sort of work. "I appreciate your…diligence, but I'm sure I don't have a brain injury. The air bag protected me."

"I guess you forgot to mention you were a neurologist."

She frowned. "I'm not."

"What are you, then?" he asked, curious as to how she would answer. Heiress? Aimless socialite? Lousy actress?

After a long pause, she forced a smile. "I work for a charitable organization in Los Angeles."

Nice save, he thought. It could very well be true, since she had enough money to rescue half the world.

"Well, unless your charitable organization specializes in self-diagnosing traumatic brain injuries, I'm going to have to err on the side of caution here and stick to the plan of checking on you through the night."

"Don't tell me you're the neurologist now."

"Nope. Just an Army Ranger who's been hit over the head a few too many times in my career. I'll check on you about every hour to make sure your mental status hasn't changed."

"How would you even know if my mental status has changed or not? You just met me."

He laughed out loud at that, a rusty sound that surprised the heck out of him.

"True enough. I guess when you stand on your head and start reciting the Declaration of Independence at four in the morning, I'll be sure to ask if that's normal behavior before I call the doctor."

She almost smiled in return but he sensed she was troubled about more than just her car accident.

None of his concern, he reminded himself. Whatever she was doing in this isolated part of Idaho was her own business.

"I put one of my T-shirts on the bed there for you to sleep in. I'll bring your little purse pooch back after I let her out. Let me know if you need anything else or if you get hungry. The Western Sky isn't a four-star resort but I can probably rustle up some tea and toast."

"Right now I only want to rest."

"Can't blame you there," he answered. "It's been a strange evening all the way around. Come on, pup."

The little dog barked, her black eyes glowing with eagerness in her white fur, and followed him into the hallway.

The wind still howled outside but he managed to find a spot of ground somewhat sheltered by the back patio awning for her to delicately take care of business.

To his relief, the dog didn't seem any more inclined to stay out in the howling storm than he did. She hurried back to where he stood on the steps and he scooped her up and carried her inside, where he dried off her paws with an old towel.

He refused to admit to himself that he was trying to

spare Mimi four cold, wet paws against her when the dog jumped up on her bed.

When he softly knocked on the guest room door, she didn't answer. After a moment, he took the liberty of pushing it open. She was already asleep, her eyes closed, and he set the dog beside her on the bed, thinking she would need the comfort of the familiar if she awoke in a strange place in the middle of the night.

From the dim light in the hallway, he could just make out her high cheekbones and that lush, kissable mouth.

She was even prettier in person, just about the loveliest thing he had ever seen in real life.

She was beautiful and she made him forget the ghosts that haunted him, even if only for a little while. For a guy who only had a week before he had to report back to a war zone, both of those things seemed pretty darn seductive right about now.

Not the most restful sleep she had ever experienced.

At 6:00 a.m., after a night of being awakened several times by the keening wind outside and by her unwilling host insistent on checking her questionable mental status, she awoke to Simone licking her face.

Mimi groaned as her return to consciousness brought with it assorted aches and pains. The sting of the cut on her forehead and the low throb of a headache at the base of her skull were the worst of them. Her shoulder muscles ached, but she had a feeling that was more from the stress of the past two days than from any obvious injury.

She pushed away her assorted complaints to focus on the tiny bichon frise she adored. "Do you need to go outside, sweetie?" she asked.

Instead of leaping from the bed and scampering to the door as she normally would have done, Simone merely yawned, stretched her four paws out, then closed her eyes again.

"I guess not," Mimi answered with a frown at that bit of unusual behavior. Simone usually jumped to go outside first thing after a full night of holding her bladder. Mimi could only hope she hadn't decided to relieve herself somewhere in this strange house.

She looked around the bedroom in the pale light of predawn but couldn't see any obvious signs of a mishap in any corner. What she *did* find was her entire set of luggage piled up inside the door, all five pieces of it, including Simone's carrier.

The sight of them all stunned her and sent a funny little sparkle jumping through her. Somehow in the middle of the raging blizzard, Major Western had gone to the trouble of retrieving every one of them for her.

In the night, more vague recollections had come together in her head and she vividly remembered he had been forced to wade through the ice-crusted creek to reach her after the accident. In order to retrieve her luggage from the SUV, he would have had to venture into that water yet again. She could hardly believe he had done that for her, yet the proof was right there before her eyes in the corner.

No. There had to be some catch. He just seemed entirely too good to be real. The cynical part of her that had been burned by men a few dozen too many times couldn't quite believe anyone would find her worth that much effort.

She pressed a hand to her stomach, to the tiny secret growing there.

"Are you okay in there, kiddo?" she murmured.

She had bought a half-dozen pregnancy books the moment she left the doctor's office but hadn't dared read any of them on the plane, afraid to risk that someone would see through her disguise and tip off the tabloids about her reading choices. Instead, she'd had to be content with a pregnancy week-by-week app on her cell phone, and she had devoured every single word behind her sunglasses on the plane.

At barely eleven weeks, Mimi knew she wasn't far enough along to actually feel the baby move. Maybe in a few more weeks. But that didn't stop her from imagining the little thing swimming around in there.

Something else that didn't feel quite real to her, that in a few months she was going to be a mother. She had only had two days to absorb the stunning news that her brief but intense affair with Marco Mendez had resulted in an unexpected complication.

In only a few days, the provider of half her baby's DNA was marrying another woman. And not just any woman but Jessalyn St. Claire, Hollywood's current favorite leading lady, sweet and cute and universally adored. Marco and Jessalyn. "Messalyn," as the tabloids dubbed the pair of them. The two beautiful, talented, successful people were apparently enamored of each other.

It was a match made in heaven—or their respective publicists' offices. Mimi wasn't sure which.

She only knew that if word leaked out that she was expecting Marco Mendez's baby, Jessalyn would flip out, especially since the timing of Mimi's pregnancy would clearly reveal that they had carried on their affair several months after Marco had proposed to Jessalyn in such a public venue as the Grammy Awards, where he won Best Male Vocalist of the year.

Mimi probed her heart for the devastation she probably should be feeling right about now. For two months, she had been expecting Marco to break off the sham engagement and publicly declare he loved Mimi, as he had privately assured her over and over was his intention.

The declaration never came. She felt like an idiot for ever imagining it would. Worse, when she had gathered up every bit of her courage and whatever vestiges of pride she had left and finally called him to meet her at their secret place after the stunning discovery of her pregnancy, he hadn't reacted at all like she had stupidly hoped.

Arrogant, egocentric, selfish.

She was all those things and more. She had secretly hoped that when Marco found out she was pregnant, he would pull her into his arms and declare he couldn't go through with the marriage now, that he loved her and wanted to spend the rest of his life with her and the child they had created.

She was pathetically stupid.

Instead, his sleek, sexy features had turned bone-white and he had asked her if she'd made an appointment yet to take care of the problem.

When she hesitantly told him she was thinking about keeping the baby, he had become enraged. She had never believed Marco capable of violence until he had stood with veins popping out in his neck, practically foaming at the mouth in that exclusive, secluded house in Topanga Canyon he kept for these little trysts.

He had called her every vile name in the book and some she'd never heard of. By the time he was done, she felt like all those things he called her. Skank. Whore. Bitch.

And worse.

In the end, she'd somehow found the strength to tell him emphatically that keeping the baby or not would be her own decision. If she kept the baby, it would be hers alone and he would relinquish any claim to it. She wanted nothing more to do with him.

If he touched her or threatened her again in any way, she would tell her father, a man both of them knew had the power to decimate careers before he'd taken a sip of his morning soy latte.

She pressed a hand to her tiny baby bump.

"I'm sorry I picked such a jerk to be your daddy," she whispered.

She loved this baby already. The idea of it, innocent and sweet, seemed to wrap around all the empty places in her heart. The only blessing in the whole mess was that she and Marco had, unbelievably, been able to keep their affair a secret thus far.

Oh, maybe a few rumors had been circulating here and there. But she figured if she stayed out of the camera glare at least until the wedding was over and then took an extended trip somewhere quiet, she just might muddle through this whole thing. She had no doubt she could find someone willing to claim paternity for enough money.

Or maybe she would just drop out of sight for the rest of her life, relocate to some isolated place in the world where people had never heard of Mimi Van Hoyt or her more ridiculous antics.

Borneo might be nice. Or she could move in with some friendly indigenous tribe along the Amazon.

Staying with Gwen at least until the wedding was over would have solved her short-term problem, if she hadn't been too blasted shortsighted to pick up the phone first.

Why couldn't she still stay here?

The thought was undeniably enticing. Gwen might not be here but, except for her absence, the ranch still offered all the advantages that had led Mimi to fly out on a snowy February afternoon to find her ex-step-mother. It was isolated and remote, as far from the craziness of a celebrity wedding as Mimi could imagine.

She thought of her host wading through a creek in the middle of a blizzard to retrieve her luggage. He seemed a decent sort of man, with perhaps a bit of a hero complex. Maybe Major Western could be convinced to let her stay just for a few days.

She closed her eyes, daunted by the very idea of asking him. Though she had never had much trouble bending the males of the species to her will—her father being the most glaring exception—she had a feeling Brant Western wouldn't be such an easy sell.

Later. She would wait until the sun was at least up before she worried about it, she decided with a yawn.

When she awoke again, a muted kind of daylight streamed through the curtains and an entirely too male figure was standing beside her bed.

"Morning." Her voice came out sultry and low, more a product of sleepiness than any effort to be sexy, but something flared in his eyes for just a moment, then was gone.

Okay, maybe convincing him she should stay wouldn't be as difficult as she had feared, Mimi thought, hiding a secret smile even as she was a little disappointed he wouldn't present more of a challenge.

"Good morning." His voice was a little more tightly wound than she remembered and she thought his eyes looked tired. From monitoring her all night? she wondered. Or from something else?

"Sorry to wake you but I haven't been in to check on you for a couple of hours. I was just seeing if the dog needed to go out again."

"Did you take her out in the night?"

He nodded. "She's not too crazy about snow."

"Oh, I know. Once in Chamonix she got lost in a snow drift. It was terrifying for both of us."

She shouldn't have said that, she realized at once. Maura Howard wasn't the sort to visit exclusive ski resorts in the Swiss Alps, but Brant didn't seem to blink an eye.

"I'm on my way to take care of the horses. I'll put her out again before I leave and I'll try not to lose her in the snow. How's your head?"

"Better. The rest of me is a little achy but I'll survive. Is it still storming?"

He nodded tersely as she sat up in bed and seemed intent on keeping his gaze fixed on some fixed spot in the distance as if he were standing at attention on parade somewhere. "We've had more than a foot and it's still coming down." He paused. "There's a good chance you might be stuck here another day or two. It's going to take at least that long for the plows to clear us out."

"Oh, no!"

Though secretly relieved, she figured he expected the news to come as a shock, so she tried to employ her glaringly nonexistent acting skills. Then, pouring it on a little thicker, she stretched a little before tucking a wayward curl behind her ear.

She didn't miss the way his pupils flared just a little, even as he pretended not to pay her any attention.

"I'm so sorry to be even more of an inconvenience to you, Major Western."

"Around here I'm plain Brant."

"Brant." It was a strong, masculine name that somehow fit him perfectly.

"Thank you so much for bringing my luggage in. It was so kind of you."

"No big deal. I thought you would feel more comfortable if you had your own things, especially since it looks like you're going to be here another night."

"I feel so foolish. If I'd only called Gwen before showing up on her doorstep like this, you wouldn't be stuck with me now."

"That was a pretty idiotic thing to do," he agreed flatly. "What would have happened to you if you'd slid off in a spot in the canyon that wasn't so close to any houses? You might have been stuck in the storm in your car all night and probably would have frozen to death before anybody found you."

His bluntness grated and she almost glared but at the last minute she remembered she needed his help. Or maybe not. She needed a place to stay, but that didn't necessarily mean she had to stay with *him*.

"I hate imposing on you," she said as another idea suddenly occurred to her, one she couldn't believe she hadn't thought of the night before or this morning when she was mulling over her various options. "What if we called Gwen and asked her if I could stay at her house since she's gone?"

"Great idea," he said, with somewhat humiliating alacrity. "There's only one problem with it. Gwen's furnace went out the day she left. I've got a company coming out to replace it but they can't make it to the ranch until later in the week. With the blizzard, it might even be next week before they come out. Occupied dwellings have precedence in weather like this so I'm afraid you're stuck here until the storm clears."

She tried to look appropriately upset by that news. At least his insistence on that particular point would give her a little breathing room to figure out how she could convince him to let her stay longer.

Four hours later, she was rethinking her entire strategy.

If she had to stay here until Marco's wedding was over, she was very much afraid she would die of boredom.

She had never been very good with dead time. She liked to fill it with friends and shopping and trips to her favorite day spa. Okay, she had spent twenty-six years wading in shallow waters. She had no problem admitting it. She liked having fun and wasn't very good at finding ways to entertain herself.

That particular task seemed especially challenging here at Western Sky. Major Western had very few books—most were in storage near his home base in Georgia, he had told her—and the DVD selection was limited. And of course the satellite television wasn't working because too much snow had collected in the dish, blocking the receiver. Or at least that's the explanation her host provided.

The house wasn't wired to the internet, since he was rarely here and didn't use it much anyway.

She probably could have dashed off some texts and even an email or two on her Smartphone, but she had made the conscious decision to turn it off. For now, she was Maura Howard. It might be a little tough selling that particular story if she had too much contact with the outside world.

Her host had made himself scarce most of the day, busy looking over ranch accounts or bringing in firewood or knocking ice out of the water troughs for the livestock.

She had a feeling he was avoiding her, though she wasn't sure why, which left her with Simone for company.

Brant poked his head into the kitchen just after noon to tell her to help herself to whatever she wanted for lunch but that he had a bit of a crisis at Gwen's cabin with frozen pipes since the furnace wasn't working.

Mimi had settled on a solitary lunch of canned tomato soup that was actually quite tasty. After she washed and dried her bowl, marveling that there was a house in America which actually didn't possess a dishwasher, she returned it to the rather dingy cupboard next to the sink and was suddenly hit by a brainstorm.

This was how she could convince Brant to let her stay.

A brilliant idea, if she did say so herself. Not bad for a shallow girl, she thought some time later as she surveyed the contents of every kitchen cupboard, jumbled on all the countertops.

She stood on a stepladder with a bucket of sudsy

water in front of her as she scoured years of grease and dust from the top of his knotty pine cabinets.

Here was a little known secret the tabloids had never unearthed about Mimi Van Hoyt. They would probably have a field day if anyone ever discovered she liked to houseclean when she was bored or stressed.

Between boarding school stays, her father's long-term housekeeper Gert used to give her little chores to do. Cleaning out a closet, organizing a drawer, polishing silver. Her father probably never would have allowed it if he'd known, but she and Gert had both been very good at keeping secrets from Werner Van Hoyt.

She had never understood why she enjoyed it so much and always been a little ashamed of what she considered a secret vice until one of her more insightful therapists had pointed out those hours spent with Gert at some mundane task or other were among the most consistent of her life. Perhaps cleaning her surroundings was her mental way of creating order out of the chaos that was her life amid her father's multiple marriages and divorces.

Here in Major Western's house, it was simply something to pass the time, she told herself, digging in a little harder on a particularly tough stain.

"What would you be doing?"

Mimi jerked her head around and found Major Western standing in the kitchen doorway watching her with an expression that seemed a complicated mix—somewhere between astonished and appalled.

Simone—exceptional watchdog that she was—awoke at his voice and jumped up from her spot on a half-circle rug by the sink. She yipped an eager greeting while Mimi flushed to the roots of her hair.

"Sorry. I was…bored."

He gave her a skeptical look. "Bored. And so, out of the blue, you decided to wash out my kitchen cabinets."

"Somebody needed to. You wouldn't believe the grime on them."

She winced as soon as the words escaped. Okay, that might not be the most tactful thing to mention to a man she was hoping would keep her around for a few days.

"You've been busy with your Army career, I'm sure," she quickly amended. "I can only imagine how difficult it is to keep a place like this clean when you're not here all the time."

He looked both rueful and embarrassed as he moved farther into the kitchen and started taking off his winter gear.

"I've been renting it out on and off for the last few years and tenants don't exactly keep the place in the best shape. I'm planning on having a crew come in after I return to Afghanistan to clean it all out and whip it into shape before I put it on the market."

She paused her scrubbing, struck both that he had been in Afghanistan and that he would put such a wonderful house on the market. "Why would you sell this place? I can't see much out there except snow right now but I would guess it's a beautiful view. At least Gwen always raves about what inspiration she finds here for her work."

He unbuttoned his soaked coat and she tried not to notice the muscles of his chest that moved under his sweater as he worked his arms out of the sleeves.

"It's long past time."

He was quiet for several moments. "The reality is, I'm only here a few weeks of the year, if that, and it's too hard to take care of the place long-distance, even with your friend Gwen keeping an eye on things for me. Anyway, Gwen's leaving, too. She told me she's buying a house outside Jackson Hole and that just seemed the final straw. I can't even contemplate how daunting it would be to find someone to replace her. Not to mention keeping up with general maintenance like painting the barn."

It was entirely too choice an opportunity to pass up. "This is perfect. I'll help you."

Again that eyebrow crept up as he toed off his winter boots. "You want to paint the barn? I'm afraid that might be a little tough, what with the snow and all."

She frowned. "Not the barn. But this." She pointed with her soapy towel. "The whole place needs a good scrubbing, as I'm sure you're aware."

He stared at her. "Let me get this straight. You're volunteering to clean my house?"

She set the soapy towel back in the bucket and perched on the top rung of the ladder to face him. "Sure, why not?"

"I can think of a few pretty compelling reasons."

She flashed him a quick look, wondering what he meant by that, but she couldn't read anything in his expression.

"The truth is, I need a place to stay for a few days."

"Why?"

"It's a long, boring story."

"Somehow I doubt that," he murmured, looking fascinated.

"Trust me," she said firmly. "I need a place to stay for a few days—let's just leave it at that—and you could use some work done around here to help you ready the place for prospective buyers."

"And you think you can help me do that?"

The skepticism in his voice stung, for reasons she didn't want to examine too carefully. "Believe it or not, I've actually helped a friend stage houses for sale before and I know a little about it. I can help you, I swear. Why shouldn't we both get something we need?"

He leaned against the counter next to the refrigerator and crossed his arms over his chest. As he studied her, she thought she saw doubt, lingering shock and an odd sort of speculation in his eyes.

After a moment he shook his head. "I can't ask you to do that, Ms. Howard."

"You didn't ask. I'm offering."

Five days. That was all she needed to avoid Hollywood's biggest wedding in years. With a little time and distance, she hoped she could figure out what she was going to do with the mess of her life.

"I really do need a place to stay, Major Western."

She thought she saw a softening in the implacable set to his jaw, a tiny waver in his eyes, so she whipped out the big guns. The undefeated, never-fail, invincible option.

She beamed at him, her full-throttle, pour-on-the-charm smile that had made babbling fools out of every male she'd ever wielded it on. "I swear, you'll be so happy with the job I do, you might just decide not to sell."

Though she saw obvious reluctance in his dark eyes, he finally sighed. "A few days. Why not? As long as you don't make any major changes. Just clean things out a little and make the rooms look better. That's all."

Relief coursed through her. Simone, sensing Mimi's excitement, barked happily.

"You won't regret it, I promise."

He shook his head and reached into the refrigerator for a bottled water. In his open, honest expression, she could see he was already sorry. She didn't care, she told herself, ignoring that same little sting under her heart.

Whether he wanted her here or not, somehow she knew that Major Brant Western was too honorable to kick her out after he'd promised she could stay.

Chapter 3

Wh* *hat kind of game was she playing?

That seemed to be the common refrain echoing through his brain when it came to Mimi Van Hoyt. He still hadn't come any closer to figuring her out several hours after their stunning conversation, as they sat at the worn kitchen table eating a cobbled-together dinner of canned stew and peaches.

First she was pretending to be someone else—as if anyone in the world with access to a computer or a television could somehow have been lucky enough to miss her many well-publicized antics. The woman couldn't pick up her newspaper in the morning without a crop of photographers there to chronicle every move and she must think he was either blind or stupid not to figure out who she was.

But that same tabloid darling who apparently didn't

step outside her door without wearing designer clothes had spent the afternoon cleaning every nook and cranny of his kitchen—and doing a pretty good job of it. Not that he was any great judge of cleanliness, having spent most of his adult life on Army bases or in primitive conditions in the field, but he had grown up with Jo Winder as an example and he knew she would have been happy to see the countertops sparkling and the old wood cabinets gleaming with polish.

He wouldn't have believed it if he hadn't seen it himself—Mimi Van Hoyt, lush and elegant, scrubbing the grime away from a worn-out ranch house with no small degree of relish. She seemed as happy with her hands in a bucket of soapy water as he was out on patrol with his M4 in his hands.

She had even sung a little under her breath, for heaven's sake, and he couldn't help wondering why she had dabbled in acting instead of singing since her contralto voice didn't sound half-bad.

That low, throaty voice seemed to slide down his spine like trailing fingers and a few times he'd had to manufacture some obvious excuse to leave the house just to get away from it. He figured he'd hauled enough wood up to the house to last them all week but he couldn't seem to resist returning to the kitchen to watch her.

The woman completely baffled him. He would have expected her to be whining about the lack of entertainment in the cabin, about the enforced confinement, about the endless snow.

At the very least, he would have thought her fingers would be tapping away at some cell phone as she tweeted or whatever it was called, about being trapped in an isolated Idaho ranch with a taciturn stranger.

Instead, she teased her little dog, she took down his curtains and threw them in the washing machine, she organized every ancient cookbook left in the cupboard.

She seemed relentlessly cheerful while the storm continued to bluster outside.

Somehow he was going to have to figure out a way to snap her picture when she wasn't looking. Otherwise, his men would never believe he'd spent his mid-tour leave watching Mimi Van Hoyt scrub grease off his stove vent.

But he was pretty sure a photograph wouldn't show them how lovely she looked, with those huge, deep green eyes and her long inky curls and that bright smile that took over her entire face.

Though he knew it was dangerous, Brant couldn't seem to stop watching her. Having Mimi Van Hoyt flitting around his kitchen in all her splendor was a little overwhelming for a man who hadn't been with a woman in longer than he cared to remember—sort of like shoving a starving man in front of one of those all-you-can-eat buffets in Las Vegas and ordering him to dig in.

He'd had an on-again, off-again relationship with a nurse at one of the field support hospitals in Paktika Province, but his constant deployments hadn't left him much time for anything serious.

Not that he was looking. He would leave that sort of thing to the guys who were good at it, like Quinn seemed to be, though he never would have believed it.

Brant treated the women he dated with great respect but he knew he tended to gravitate toward smart, focused career women who weren't looking for anything more than a little fun and companionship once in a while.

Mimi was something else entirely. He didn't know exactly what, but he couldn't believe he had agreed to let her stay at his ranch for a few days. Hour upon hour of trying to ignore the way her hair just begged to be released from the elastic band holding it back or the way those big green eyes caught the light or how her tight little figure danced around the kitchen as she worked.

He shook his head. Which of the two of them was crazier? Right now, he was willing to say it was a toss-up, though he had a suspicion he just might be edging ahead.

"Would you like more stew?" she asked, as if she were hosting some fancy dinner party instead of dishing up canned Dinty Moore.

"I'm good. Thanks."

Though he knew she had to be accustomed to much fancier meals, she did a credible job with her own bowl of stew. He supposed all that scrubbing and dusting must have worked up an appetite.

"Have you had the ranch for long?" she asked, breaking what had been a comfortable silence. "I'm sorry, I can't remember what you told me the name was."

"The Western Sky. And yeah, it's been in my family for generations. My great-great-grandfather bought the land and built the house in the late 1800s."

"So you were raised here?"

He thought of his miserable childhood and the pain and insecurity of it, and then of the Winders, who had rescued him from it and showed him what home could really be.

Explaining all that to her would be entirely too complicated, even if he were willing to discuss it, so he took the easy way out. "For the most part," he answered, hoping she would leave it at that.

Because he was intensely curious to see how far she would take her alternate identity, he turned the conversation back in her direction. "What about you, Maura? Whereabouts do you call home?"

The vibrant green of her eyes seemed to dim a little and she looked away. "Oh, you know. Here and there. California. For now."

"Oh? Which part of the state, if you don't mind me asking?"

"Southern. The L.A. area."

He didn't really follow entertainment gossip but he thought he read or heard something once about her having two homes not far from each other, one her father's Bel Air estate and the other a Malibu beachhouse.

"Is that where your parents live?"

Her mouth tightened a little and she moved the remaining chunks of stew around in her bowl. "My mom died when I was three, just after my parents divorced. My dad sort of raised me but he…we…moved around a lot."

He had to take a quick sip of soda to keep from snorting at that evasive comment—probably Mimi's way of saying her father had residences across the globe.

"And you said you work for a charitable foundation?"

Her wide, mobile mouth pursed into a frown. "Yes. But you probably wouldn't have heard of it."

"And what sort of things do you do there?" He wasn't sure why he enjoyed baiting her so much but it was the most fun he'd had in a long time.

If nothing else, her presence distracted him from the grim events he had left behind in Afghanistan.

"Oh, you know. This and that. I help with fundraising and…and event planning. That sort of thing."

"I don't see a ring, so I'm assuming you're not married."

If he remembered right, she'd been engaged a few years ago to some minor European royalty but he couldn't remember details, other than he thought the breakup had been messy and had, of course, involved some sort of scandal.

"No. Never. You?"

"Nope. Did you ever tell me how you knew Gwen?"

That, at least, was genuine curiosity and not baiting, since his artistic, eclectic, reclusive tenant didn't seem the sort to hobnob with debutantes.

"She was…friends with my father. Years ago. We've always stayed in touch."

Now *that* was interesting. Apparently Gwen Bianca had a few secrets she'd never divulged in the eight or so years she'd been living at the ranch. A past relationship with Werner Van Hoyt? He would never have suspected.

Mimi finally seemed to tire of his subtle interrogation and while he was still digesting the surprising insight into Gwen, she turned the tables on him.

"So how could you possibly want to sell a piece of beautiful land that's been in your family for generations?"

He shrugged. "I don't know if it's fair to say I *want* to sell."

"So don't. The house might be a little worse for wear but it's not falling down around your ears."

"Not yet, anyway."

"A few more years and you'll be retiring from the military, won't you? You'll need a place to settle then, right?"

He had always planned exactly that. But after a half-dozen close calls in his deployment, he'd come to accept that he probably wouldn't live long enough to retire. He didn't have a death wish by any means but he was also a realist.

Since the ambush a month ago, he'd also begun to formulate another motive, one he didn't feel like sharing with a flighty celebrity who spent more on a pair of shoes than some of his men made in a month of hard combat.

"You don't have any other family who might want to do something with the ranch to keep it in the family?" she pressed.

"No. Just me. I…had a younger brother but he died when we were kids."

As soon as he heard his own words, he wanted to take them back. He never spoke about Curtis or his death. Never.

The twenty-year-old guilt might be an integral piece of him, as much a part of the whole as his blue eyes and the crescent-shaped birthmark on his shoulder, but it was private and personal.

"I'm sorry," she murmured, her eyes mossy green with a compassion he didn't want to see. "What happened?"

He wanted to tell her to mind her own business, but since he had been the one to open that particular doorway into the past, he couldn't very well slam it in her face. "He drowned in the creek when I was eleven and he was nine," he finally said.

"The same creek I crashed into?"

He nodded. "There's not much to it now and it might be a little hard to believe, but it's a far different beast in late spring and early summer during the runoff. You know how your SUV went down a slope about five or six feet? During the runoff, that's all full of fast-moving water. So we were being kids and throwing rocks in the creek, even though we weren't supposed to play around it in the springtime. Curtis got a little too close and the bank gave way. I ran downstream and tried to go in after him but…he slipped past me and I couldn't grab him."

"You could have been killed!"

He should have been. That's what his mother had said once in the middle of a bender. *Better you than my sweet baby,* she had said in that emotionless voice that seemed all the more devastating. He wanted to think she hadn't meant it. Curtis had been the funny, smart, adorable one, while Brant had been big and awkward, far too serious for a kid.

After Curtis's death, what had been a tense home life degenerated to sheer misery. The ranch was falling into chaos, his parents fought all the time and both drank heavily. The fighting and the yelling had been one thing. Then his mother had left them and his father had turned all his anger and grief and bitterness against Brant.

That life might have continued indefinitely until one of two things happened—either he grew large enough to pound back or until the old man killed him. He didn't know which would have happened first because Guff and Jo Winder had stepped in.

He sipped at his soda pop, remembering the events

that had changed his life. He had felt the Winders' scrutiny a few times when he'd been in town with his father and once Guff had even said something to J.D. when his father climbed up his grill about something or other at the farm implement store, but his intervention had only earned Brant a harsher beating when they got home.

Then one day Guff had stopped at the Western Sky to pick up a couple of weaned calves and his visit just happened to coincide with one of J.D.'s bad drunks. Brant had tried to hide the bruises but his T-shirt had ridden up when he'd been helping load one of the calves into the Winder stock trailer.

Guff had taken one look at the welts crisscrossing his back and Brant would never forget the instant fury in his gaze. He had been conditioned over the years to shrink from that kind of anger, but instead of coming after him, Guff had picked up a pitchfork and backed J.D. against the wall.

"You son of a bitch," he had said in a low, terrible voice. "You've lost one son through a terrible accident. How are you going to live with yourself if you lose the other one at your own hand?"

J.D. had blustered and yelled but Guff had kept that pitchfork on him while he turned to Brant. "You know me and my wife, Jo, have taken in a relative, a boy about your age. I think he goes to school with you. Quinn Southerland. We've got plenty of room at Winder Ranch and I swear on the soul of your brother that no one there will ever lift a hand to you. Would you like to come stay with us for a while?"

He had been as dazed and shocked as his father. Part of him had desperately wanted to leave the Western Sky, to get as far away as he could. But even then, he'd known his duty.

"I'd best stay with my dad, sir. He's got no one else."

Guff had studied him for a long moment, tears in his eyes, then he had dropped the pitchfork. While his dad slid down the wall of the barn to sit in a dazed stupor, Guff had hugged Brant hard and he had realized in that moment that it had been two long years since he'd been touched with anything but malice.

"You're a good boy, son," Guff had said. "I know you love your dad, but right now you have to protect him and yourself. If I promise to see your dad gets the help he needs, will you come?"

In the end, he had agreed, though it had been the toughest choice of his young life, much more difficult than Ranger training or his first combat mission.

He had spent those first few months at Winder Ranch consumed with guilt but certain he would be back with his father at Christmas. True to his word, Guff had paid for his dad's rehab and told J.D. he had to stay sober six months before they would trust him with his son again.

J.D. had lasted only a month before he'd bought a bottle of Jack Daniels, consumed most of it, then wandered into the corral with their meanest bull, where he'd been gored to death.

"I'm sorry."

He jerked his mind from the past to find Mimi watching him across the table with that sympathy in those big green eyes. It took him a moment to register that she was still talking about his brother's death that had changed everything.

"Thanks. So, yeah. In answer to your question, I'm the only one left in my family. And since I've been here a total of maybe three weeks in the last five years, it seems foolish to hang on to the place."

She looked as if she didn't agree, which he found odd. Still, after a moment, she shrugged. "It should sell easily, especially if you clear out some of the clutter and maybe put a few fresh coats of paint in some of the rooms."

"I don't want to put too much energy into the house," he said, finishing off the peaches. "The only ones who can afford this kind of acreage these days are, uh, Hollywood types who will probably tear down the house and build their own in its place. That's what's happened to several nearby ranches."

As he expected, she ignored the Hollywood jab. How could she do otherwise without revealing her true identity? "You never know. The house has a rustic kind of charm and some people are looking for that. With a little effort, you can show off the lovely old bones of the house. A small investment now could help you set a nice asking price for both the house and the land."

He stared at her. "I thought you said you worked for a charitable organization. For a minute there, you sounded like a real estate agent."

Her cheeks turned pink. "No. I just watch a lot of late-night TV infomercials. You know the ones. How to make a fortune in real estate."

"A dream of yours, is it?" he asked in what he hoped was a bland tone. "To make a fortune?"

"Of course," she said with a tiny smile. "Who wouldn't want to have a fortune?"

Though her words were light, he thought he sensed a ribbon of bitterness twining through them. Maybe being a trust fund baby wasn't all parties and private jets.

"Anyway, right now I don't need a fortune," she said, in what he knew was a vast understatement. "Only a place to stay for a few days and something to do while I'm here. I'm grateful you've been kind enough to give me both."

Yeah, he was going to have a hell of a story when this was all over.

By the next day, Mimi was beginning to think stripping naked and tap-dancing in front of the paparazzi might be easier in the long run than the chore she'd set in front of herself.

She coughed at the cloud of dust that erupted as she yanked down the old-fashioned gingham curtains in the second bedroom upstairs. Simone sneezed, shaking her fuzzy little head. Her formerly pristine little white poochie was now the washed-out, yellow-gray of fading newsprint.

"You are going to need a serious bath," she told the dog ruefully. "Both of us are, I'm afraid."

Simone yipped and continued sniffing around the corners of the room, her tail wagging a mile a minute.

At least her dog was enjoying this little adventure of theirs. Mimi sighed. She wasn't hating it, it was just a bigger task than she had envisioned the day before.

The house wasn't filthy, exactly, just filled with the sort of grime that settled in homes where no one lived. Her father kept full-time staff at each of his residences but even then, dust tended to collect.

After a full day of cleaning and organizing, she was beginning to fear she had taken on a job too big for her to handle. Performing small housekeeping jobs under Gert's supervision in a well-maintained mansion with a large staff was a much different proposition than cleaning out a house that had been largely empty for the past several years.

She felt as grimy as these curtains and she had to wonder what her friends would say if they could see her now, with her hair covered by a particularly ugly Hermès scarf her latest stepmother had given her for Christmas and her skin covered in the same film as the walls.

This had been one of her more harebrained ideas—and that was saying something, since she'd had more than her share.

A few days ago when she flew from L.A. to Jackson Hole, she had expected to find herself being pampered by Gwen, coddled and taken care of by the one person in the world she counted on to care that she was pregnant and frightened and alone.

Instead, here she was dusting out corners and scrubbing baseboards for a man who had hardly said a halfdozen words to her since dinner the night before.

While the storm raged outside after dinner, he had mostly avoided her until she had fallen asleep on the sofa watching a DVD of a romantic comedy she'd seen twice already. He had rather tersely awakened her after nine and suggested she go sleep where she could stretch out.

This morning, he had been awake and out taking care of the horses and checking Gwen's pipes when Mimi awoke, at least according to the brusque note he'd left propped on the kitchen table.

"Help yourself to food," he had instructed, and Mimi had made a face at the note before grabbing a yogurt and a piece of toast.

That was the sum total of her interaction with another human being all day.

She wouldn't feel sorry for herself. That was the old Mimi. The new Mimi was all about finding her own inner strength, taking care of herself. She was twenty-six years old and going to be a mother in six months, responsible for another human being. It was long past time she took that terrifying step into adulthood.

She wadded up the dingy curtains into a bundle in her arms and was just about to carry them downstairs to the washing machine in the mudroom off the kitchen when she heard the front door open.

"Hey, Brant?" a distinctively feminine voice called out. "You know you've got a Mercedes stuck in your creek?"

Oh, crap. Mimi's arms tightened on the curtains. Despite her best efforts at avoiding the outside world, she supposed it was inevitable that Brant might have a visitor.

Her heart pounded as she backed against the wall, out of sight from the foot of the stairs. What should she do? Hide up here and hope whoever it was just went away? Or take her chances that she could bluff her way through and Brant's visitor wouldn't drive away from the Western Sky and immediately call TMZ?

A moment later, Simone took the choice out of her hands. Before Mimi could even think to stop her, the little dog bulleted out of the bedroom and scampered down the stairs, yipping the whole way.

"Well, hello," Mimi heard the woman say in surprise to the dog. "Where did you come from? Brant? What's going on? Whose car and whose dog?"

Mimi drew in a deep breath, dropped the curtains

into a heap and walked to the landing at the top of the stairs.

"Mine," she called down. "I slid off the road during the storm the night before last. I haven't had a chance to get a tow out here yet to take care of it. And that little bundle of noise is Simone."

The woman was slim and blonde, dressed in bright red snow pants and a heavy matching parka with navy-blue stripes. She looked at the dog and then looked back at Mimi, her jaw sagging. "You're…"

"A mess," Mimi said quickly. "I know. I was cleaning out one of the rooms upstairs and I'm afraid I tangled with some cobwebs."

She walked down the staircase and held out her hand. "I'm Maura Howard," she said firmly.

The other woman finally closed her mouth, though Mimi could see suspicion still clouding her blue eyes.

"I'm Easton. Easton Springhill. I've got a ranch down the canyon a ways." Her gaze narrowed and she tilted her head. "This is going to sound crazy, but has anyone ever told you that you look remarkably like that silly woman in the tabloids? Mimi something or other? The one with all the boyfriends?"

Mimi forced a smile she was far from feeling. "I get it all the time. It's a curse, believe me. Ridiculous, isn't she?"

Easton Springhill snickered a little. "I think she's great."

"Really?"

"Sure. She always makes me laugh. No matter what kind of a lousy day I'm having, I can always be glad at least that I'm not as dumb as a box of rocks."

Mimi kept her smile on by sheer force of will. She

couldn't really be annoyed. She wasn't stupid, but plenty of her choices certainly had been.

"How did you get here?" she asked instead of snapping at the woman. "Has the snow stopped?"

"It seems to be slowing a little bit. The roads still are a mess but that's not a problem with the snowmobile. I figured I'd better make sure Brant has enough essentials to live on. He doesn't always remember to buy everything he needs for the pantry between visits. I brought over a couple of casseroles from my freezer as well as a few staples I thought he might need. Bread, milk, that sort of thing."

"That's thoughtful of you," Mimi murmured, wondering just what sort of relationship they shared. It must be a close one if the other woman felt comfortable just walking into his house without knocking.

Easton continued gazing at Mimi with that same slightly stunned look in her eyes.

"It's uncanny. The resemblance, I mean."

"Even with the layer of grit I'm wearing from scrubbing the walls upstairs?"

Drawing attention to her less than sleek appearance seemed to convince Easton that she couldn't possibly be Mimi Van Hoyt.

"It's none of my business," the other woman said, "but were you on your way here to see Brant when you crashed? You must have been, I guess. I can't imagine why else you would be on Western Sky land."

"Actually, I thought I was coming to see Gwen Bianca, his caretaker," Mimi answered. "My visit was sort of a whim and I didn't call ahead of time or I would have found out she was out of the country."

"Yes, Gwen has a gallery showing in Milan. She's

been working on it for months and was so excited about it."

Her former stepmother had probably told her in one of their occasional phone conversations and Mimi hadn't registered it, maybe because she was a self-absorbed bitch.

She sighed. Past tense. She was turning over a new leaf, right?

"I'm sure Gwen will be so sorry she missed you," Easton said.

"Not as sorry as I am to have missed her, believe me."

"So Brant gave you a place to stay while you wait for her to come back. Isn't that just like him?" She smiled but after a moment it slid away. "Sorry, I'm a little slow today. Back up a minute. If you're a guest of Brant's, why, again, are you covered in grime from scrubbing the walls?"

"I wanted to thank him for his kindness in giving me a place to stay for a few days so I offered to help him out a little."

Easton snickered. "And I actually thought for a minute you were Mimi Van Hoyt. How funny is that?"

Mimi did her best to force a smile. "Hilarious. Not exactly the housecleaning sort, is she?"

Before Easton could answer, the door opened behind them and Brant came into the entry. The open delight on his features when he saw the other woman erased any question that theirs was a close relationship.

"Hey, East!" he said with as close to a genuine smile as Mimi had seen. "I thought I heard a snowmobile."

"Can't sneak up on an Army Ranger, can I?"

"Not on a 600-horsepower Polaris, anyway."

This time he gave a full-fledged grin and Mimi stared. She had thought him handsome before in a clean-cut, no-nonsense sort of way. But when he smiled, he was the kind of gorgeous that curled a woman's toes.

"Any word from the newlyweds?" he asked.

"Tess called me this morning from Costa Rica to thank me again for hosting the wedding on such short notice. She bubbled, you know? I haven't seen her like that since high school."

"I still can't quite believe it." Brant shook his head. "Quinn and the homecoming queen. It boggles my mind."

"I think she's perfect for him."

Since Mimi had no idea whom they were talking about, she thought about edging back up the stairs and returning to her work and leaving them alone, but Easton seemed to have suddenly remembered she was there.

"Sorry, Maura," the other woman said with a rueful smile. "It's rude of us to talk about people you don't know. A good friend was married two days ago. He was able to coordinate the wedding with Brant's leave so Major Western here could stand up with him."

He was home on leave for a very limited time. Mimi suddenly realized the implications of that fact and she felt every bit the ditzy bimbo everybody believed her to be.

Dumber than a box of rocks, isn't that what Easton said?

She must be or she would have realized that perhaps Brant might have had other plans for his limited leave from a war zone. Instead of enjoying rest and relaxation— and possibly more than that with the very lovely woman who had braved a blizzard for him—he was forced to play host to a stranger. Mimi. A self-absorbed liar who was using him to avoid the unpleasant consequences of her own actions.

She felt small and ashamed and would have been tempted to leave right at that moment if her rental vehicle wasn't still stuck in a creek.

She could at least give them a little privacy now, she thought, even though the idea of the yummy Major Western with this woman made her insides twist unpleasantly.

Just a hint of that blasted morning sickness, she told herself.

"I, um, think I'll just go finish up the bedroom upstairs."

Easton held out an arm. "Wait a minute, Maura. Brant, what are you thinking to make a guest scrub your walls? Gwen or I can hire somebody to do that for you, just like we've always done."

"He's not making me," Mimi protested, disliking the note of censure in the other woman's voice. "I offered to help him prepare the house to sell."

Her words distracted Easton but she didn't look any happier about them than she did the idea of Brant's guest helping him with the cleaning.

"You're really serious about selling, then?"

He looked as if he'd rather be somewhere else. "You know it's for the best, East. The place is falling apart. I can't maintain it when I only come once a year. And as much as I appreciate you and Gwen working so hard to help me, she's moving now and you don't need one more burden now that you're on your own at Winder Ranch."

Easton's mouth clamped into a tight line, as if she were ready to cry. "I hate that everything's changing.

If you sell the Western Sky, you won't have any reason to come back."

Feeling excessively like a third wheel, Mimi gave a longing look up the stairs. If she could figure out a way to gracefully escape the two of them without leaving more awkwardness behind, she would.

To her discomfort, Brant folded the woman into his arms, parka and all, and kissed her nose in a tender gesture that had those insides churning again.

"Now you're just being silly," he answered. "You're here. You know I'll always come back for that."

Despite his words, Easton didn't look appeased but she also didn't look as if she wanted to press the issue right now, with "Maura" looking on. "I'd better take off while I still have some daylight. You're going to want to put the food in the fridge."

He tugged the front of her beanie. "Be safe."

"That's my line, Major," she said with a sad sort of smile. "I'll see you again before you ship out."

"Deal."

Her smile widened when she turned to Mimi. "You shouldn't have to work for your room and board. I've got plenty of extra space at my place if you want to bunk there for a few days until Gwen gets back. I'm rattling around out there by myself and wouldn't mind the company at all."

The solution was a logical one, though Mimi was reluctant to take it for reasons she wasn't sure she wanted to examine too closely. "That's very generous of you. But I don't mind the work, really."

Easton looked doubtful. She gave her another long, searching look and she could almost see the other woman thinking how much she looked like, well, herself.

She really hoped Easton didn't say anything to Brant, who just might figure out his houseguest was someone other than she'd claimed.

To her relief, Easton only smiled. "Let me know if you change your mind. It's only a fifteen-minute ride on the Polaris."

"Thank you."

"Call me when you get home so I know you're safe," Brant ordered.

Easton rolled her eyes at him. "I manage by myself three hundred and sixty-five days out of the year, Brant."

"But when I'm here I reserve the right to worry."

"I suppose that's fair since I worry about you every minute of those other three hundred and sixty-five days when you're not."

There was more than just affection between them, Mimi thought as the other woman left. This was a deep, emotional bond.

The realization left her depressed, for reasons she didn't understand.

Chapter 4

Easton left in a swirl of snow and wind and the roar of her powerful snow machine. As Brant closed the door behind her, he couldn't help thinking about the girl she had been, blond braids and freckles and an eager smile as she followed him and Quinn and Cisco around the ranch.

Their foster mother had called them her Four Winds. Like the Four Winds, they had scattered: Quinn Southerland to Seattle, where he ran a shipping company; Cisco Del Norte to Latin America, where he apparently wandered from cantina to cantina doing heaven knows what; and Brant to the Army and five tours of duty in the Middle East in seven years.

Only Easton had stayed. She had been running Winder Ranch for years, even before Jo's death in October.

As much as he still missed Jo, he knew Easton had

it much harder. Her aunt and uncle had raised Easton after her own parents died in a car accident when she was a teenager. Jo had been more than a mother figure to Easton. She had been her best friend and her confidante and he knew Easton had to be terribly lonely without her.

He wished he could make it right but he didn't think the answer was to hang on to his own ranch simply because he knew Easton would be upset when he sold it.

"She's lovely."

He shifted to find Mimi still standing nearby. What surprised him more, he wondered: that he'd forgotten her presence or that she had actually noticed any other woman existed but herself?

Not fair, he admitted with some chagrin. He was judging her purely on her public persona, which so far seemed to be a very different thing than the way she acted away from the cameras.

"She is. Lovely, I mean. And, as usual, she's right to go after me like she did. You shouldn't have to clean for your supper. You're a guest here and I'm not a very good host for allowing you to scrub my walls and clean my toilets."

"Oh, give it a rest, Major. We've been through this."

"It still doesn't seem right."

"Are you saying you think I should take your friend up on her generous offer and stay with her?"

He should agree. He knew it was the proper thing to do and he certainly didn't want Mimi underfoot if she didn't have to be, did he?

But when he opened his mouth to agree and offer to drive her to Winder Ranch on the Western Sky snowmobile, the words seemed to clog in his throat. Despite his better judgment, he didn't want her to go yet. He wasn't quite ready just yet to give up the guilty pleasure of having her here, of watching her in living color.

"It's your call. Either way, you really don't have to clean the house. You can just be a guest. East is right, I can hire somebody to do all this."

"You did hire somebody," she said emphatically. "Me. We made a deal and I'm not going to let you back out of it. If you're sure you want to sell the ranch, I want to help you ready it for the appraisal."

He shouldn't be so relieved, he told himself. But he couldn't help a little inward smile as he headed for the kitchen, shrugging out of his ranch coat as he went. "Well, thanks to East, it looks like we won't starve, even if the blizzard keeps up for days."

"That won't happen, will it?" she asked with wide eyes, though he thought she looked almost relieved at the idea.

He had to wonder again what kind of trouble she might be running away from that she thought his run-down old ranch offered a safe haven. He could only hope it wasn't anything illegal. One of their decorated officers harboring a fugitive might not go over well with the Army brass.

"It's possible for a series of storms to follow one right after the other if we get on the right weather track," he answered as he began putting away the food items Easton had brought over. "When I was a kid, we had one winter where we missed twenty-one days of school because of snow. Storms just kept coming and coming. We spent a miserably short summer that year because of all the make-up days."

She looked so astonished that he couldn't resist needling her. "Did it snow much where you grew up, Ms. Howard?"

She looked blank for only a moment, then quickly recovered. "M-Maura," she said. "I told you I moved around a lot when I was a kid. But never anywhere with this kind of snow. It seems…unreal, somehow."

He definitely agreed with that. Since the moment he'd seen that vehicle head for the creek, he'd somehow slipped into *The Twilight Zone.*

"Well, I guess I'd better do something about dinner. I'll see if I can throw one of these casseroles Easton brought over into the oven."

"I'll go finish up the bedroom I was cleaning."

He nodded and tried not to look too obvious as he watched her move back up the stairs, her powder puff of a dog following closely behind. She had some silky-looking scarf thing over her hair, a sunny yellow T-shirt and a pair of what he was quite certain were designer jeans that hugged her figure.

More than anything, he suddenly wished that she really *was* Maura Howard and not Mimi Van Hoyt. Maura Howard seemed like a nice woman, someone he would enjoy getting to know a little better. Someone who might not mind that he was a rough-edged Army officer with a tumbledown ranch full of bad memories.

Wouldn't it be nice if she could be just a regular woman who worked for an obscure charitable organization and who preferred cuddling in bed during a blizzard to walking the red carpet at a movie premiere?

He was fiercely attracted to Maura Howard or Mimi Van Hoyt or whoever she was. He wanted to tell himself it was just a normal, red-blooded reaction to a beautiful woman, but the more time he spent with her, the more he was beginning to fear it was more than that.

He sighed and headed for the kitchen. It didn't matter how attracted he was to her. Maura Howard might be polite enough to him during this surreal experience they were sharing. But he had a feeling that since he wasn't a movie star or a minor European prince or some jetsetting playboy, Mimi Van Hoyt wouldn't give him the time of day.

They shared a pretty good dinner of some chicken-and-broccoli pasta dish. Or at least he thought it was good. Mimi didn't eat much and she seemed subdued.

"I think I'll go start tackling the second bedroom upstairs," she said.

"Forget it." He spoke in the same implacable tone his men knew better than to question, but Mimi didn't take the hint.

"Why not?"

"Because you've been on your feet cleaning all day and you look exhausted."

She frowned. "Didn't anyone ever tell you it's not polite to tell a woman she looks less than her best?"

"Didn't anyone ever tell *you* it's not wise to argue with a man who knows a dozen ways to kill an enemy combatant with a dinner fork?"

"Why, Major Western, is that a threat or a joke?"

"I'll let you choose."

She smiled, apparently deciding on the latter. "If you're not careful, I might suspect you have a sense of humor."

He shrugged. "I think it's somewhere buried under all that camouflage."

She smiled again and he wanted to soak it in. Given

the fierce attraction that coiled through him like concertina wire, spending the evening with her probably wasn't the greatest of ideas. He had found every excuse he could think of all day to avoid spending any great stretch of time with her, but Brant was suddenly in the mood to live dangerously.

"Would you like to watch a movie? Or I can go out and sweep the snow out of the satellite dish. There's a basketball game I wouldn't mind catching tonight."

"Sure. I like basketball," she answered and he suddenly remembered she had once dated one of the Lakers.

When he returned, she was curled up in one corner of the sofa, looking half-asleep with one of his favorite thrillers open on her lap. She seemed subdued and he thought he saw a shadow of sadness in those mossy green eyes. He wondered again what had brought her fleeing to Gwen in Idaho without making arrangements first, then reminded himself it was none of his business.

Though it was always a tricky operation, sweeping the dish out had done the trick to fix the satellite system and he quickly tuned in to the game he had hoped to watch. After a few moments, Mimi set aside her book and seemed to be engrossed in the game, though he still thought there was a hint of melancholy in her gaze.

In her understated clothes and with her hair back in a simple ponytail, she looked a far cry from the sleek and polished socialite. She looked young and fresh and so beautiful it was all he could do to stay on his side of the sofa, to firmly remember they lived in entirely different worlds.

"You know what would make this perfect?" he asked.

She gave him a curious look and he imagined their definition of perfect probably diverged considerably.

"Popcorn. Buttered popcorn, a fire in the woodstove, a knuckle-biter game on TV and a pretty woman to watch it with me. Do you have any idea how many guys in my entire company would volunteer for latrine duty for a year just for the chance to change places with me right now?"

She smiled a little. "You and your company all apparently have simple tastes, Major."

She was far from simple. He was beginning to think there was far more to Mimi Van Hoyt than a big smile and a lot of flash.

Her silly white dog followed him into the kitchen and lapped at her water and the silver dish of food from the supply Mimi had carried in one of her suitcases.

"Not too much of that water. I don't want Mimi to have to take you out all night," he muttered. The dog yipped at him and wagged her tail and he couldn't help but smile.

The Twilight Zone wasn't necessarily a scary place, just different.

When he returned from the kitchen with two bowls of popcorn, he was relieved to see the score was still tied. He came in just in time to catch a car commercial showing a little nuclear family with a father and mother loading a smiling little toddler into a car seat. Just before they drove away into supposedly happily ever after in their dreamy minivan, the father winked at the toddler, who giggled hard.

Almost instantly, another commercial flashed on, this one for peanut butter, a father and a kid of maybe three sitting together at a kitchen table making sandwiches. The little boy had peanut butter smeared across his mouth and a minute later the camera panned back to the dad, who now had the peanut butter on his cheek where the kid had kissed him.

"Do the advertisers really think all the dads watching the game are going to get right up and make PB and J sandwiches with their kids?" he asked conversationally as he handed her a bowl of popcorn. "With a close game like this, most of them have even forgotten they *have* kids right about now."

To his astonishment, she looked stricken at his words.

"What's the matter?" he asked, trying to figure out what he'd said.

She let out a long breath and manufactured what was obviously a false smile. "Nothing. Nothing at all. Thank you for the popcorn."

She ate very little of it, though, he noticed. And she seemed to have lost most of her interest in the game. After only maybe a quarter of an hour of her picking up a kernel here and there, Simone jumped up and scampered to the door in an obvious signal.

"Don't get up," Mimi said. "I'll put her out."

Simone had made it clear she much preferred going out the back kitchen door. The snow was still deep there but the house's bulk had protected the area from the worst of the snowdrifts.

A few moments later, Mimi returned with the dog in her arms, drying her paws with the towel by the back door he'd reserved for that purpose. "I don't think I can make it to the final buzzer," she said. "I'm just going to maybe take a bath and go to bed."

If he lived to be two hundred, he would never understand women, Brant decided. "How can you leave with a tied score and only two minutes left on the clock?"

She shrugged. "It's been a long day and I was thinking about painting the guest room tomorrow. I found some white paint in the utility room that looks fairly new. You'd be amazed what a coat of white paint can do for a room with the right accessories. Do you mind?"

"I think you're crazy. You know that, don't you?"

"I think you're absolutely right. I must be or I would have gone back with Easton earlier." She still looked upset, but for the life of him, he couldn't figure out why.

"Why didn't you?"

"Excellent question." She pushed her face into the dog's fur to avoid meeting his gaze. "I like this place, as crazy as that sounds. Simone does, too. There's a sort of peace here. I can't explain it."

He had to think there was some truth to that. By rights, he should hate it here. His childhood had been a difficult time for him, filled with anger and conflict and insecurities. During the bad years, he had dreaded coming home on the school bus. Once he had even stayed on, hunched down on the seat with some vague idea of camping out there until the next morning so he wouldn't have to face his father. His plan might have worked if their old driver, Jesse Richards, hadn't discovered him when he parked the bus for the night at his own place down the canyon.

Despite the bad memories of the Western Sky when he was a kid, he had plenty of good ones, too. When he was out on a mission, this was the place he dreamed about.

So maybe everybody was right. Maybe he should reconsider his decision to sell.

He pushed away the thoughts for now.

"It's just a broken-down ranch house," he answered Mimi. "Yeah, you do sound a little crazy."

"Not the boil-a-rabbit-on-your-stove kind, I promise."

"And wouldn't that be exactly the thing the boil-a-rabbit sort would say?"

She smiled that little smile again, but it didn't quite reach her green eyes. "I'm sure a big, tough Army Ranger like you can take care of himself. But don't worry. I won't even know if you lock your door."

She headed toward her bedroom on the other side of the kitchen and Brant briefly wondered what she would do if he followed her in there and gave in to the low hum of desire he'd been trying to ignore all day.

No, crazy or not, he wouldn't be visiting Mimi Van Hoyt's room anytime soon, he thought, and forced himself to turn back to the game, though it took a super-human effort.

He might have been able to stick to his pledge to leave her alone if he hadn't heard her crying.

An hour later, Brant stood outside the guest bedroom listening to the quiet weeping coming from the other side of the door. He hissed out a low curse, though he wasn't quite sure if it was aimed more at her or at himself.

He was a sucker for a crying woman. He always had been—maybe because his mother had so seldom cried.

Paula Western had been a master at containing her emotions. Her reaction after Curtis's death had been to turn into herself and shut him and his father out. Except for that single devastating outburst when she had told him she wished he had been the one to drown instead of his baby brother, she had become an empty husk, void of love or affection or emotions of any kind.

He could vividly remember the first time Easton had

cried after he moved to Winder Ranch. He had been twelve and Easton was nine, a little tomboy with blond braids living with her parents on the ranch, where her dad was the foreman.

One of the barn kittens had been run over by a tractor driven by a ranch hand. They had all seen it happen but had been too far away to prevent the accident. Easton had been inconsolable and Brant well remembered his panicked compulsion to do something, to fix the situation somehow, even though he knew that particular tragedy had been far beyond anyone's control.

Nothing had changed. He was still compelled to try to fix things, as much as he wanted to hide out and pretend he didn't hear her.

"Mi—Maura?" He caught himself just in time before he would have used her real name. "Everything okay in there?"

The low whimpering stopped. "Yes. Everything's fine."

She didn't say anything else and he sighed, wishing like the devil that he were the sort of guy who could just walk away and leave her to her obvious distress. "Are you sure?"

"Fine."

"Because I could swear I heard someone crying in there."

"I, um, was just humming."

She must think he was the dimmest bulb on the shelf.

"Humming? That's really what you're going with here?"

After another pause, she opened the door a crack and he could see her nose was a little pink, her eyes slightly swollen. He had a feeling Mimi was the sort of woman other females loved to hate for a number of reasons, not least of which was how those subtle signs of distress only made her look impossibly lovely, in a fragile, delicate, take-care-of-me sort of way.

She aimed a glare at him that burst that bubble quickly. "Yes. I was humming. What's it to you?"

He raised his hands in the universal sign of surrender. "You're right. Hum yourself to sleep, for all I care. But here, let me get this teardrop that's not really a teardrop."

He stepped forward and touched his thumb to the skin just at the side of her nose with one finger, where one crystalline bead of moisture pooled.

At his touch, her eyes widened, her gaze caught by his. She was warm and soft, the softest thing he'd ever touched in his life. He wanted nothing more than to slide his hand and cup her chin, to explore the curve of her cheekbone and that delicate shell of an ear.

At that single touch, he wanted to keep touching and touching until he'd explored every inch of delectable skin.

She stared at him for a long, drawn-out moment and he could swear he saw a spark of answering awareness in her eyes. Her dark pupils expanded, until the black nearly overpowered the green. He leaned forward just a hair and she caught her breath.

The instant before his mouth would have found hers, reality exploded like a shoulder-fired missile in his head. Kissing her would only make this hunger in his gut all the more painfully intense, only make him more cognizant of what he was missing.

He dropped his hand and forced himself to throttle back.

He thought he saw disappointment flicker in her

eyes, but she stepped away and lowered her eyes. "I'm sorry if I disturbed you. It won't happen again, I promise."

"Does that mean you're done or just that you'll keep your…humming to yourself from now on?"

She didn't answer, just seemed to grip the door that much harder. "Good night, Brant."

He knew it was corny but hearing her say his name in that throaty voice sent heat rippling through his insides.

For a long, protracted moment, he stared at her standing there in a soft, pale green nightgown that only seemed to make her eyes look more vivid. He still wanted to kiss her, with a heat and urgency that shocked him. But he had learned a long time ago that just because he wanted something didn't make it good for him.

Chapter 5

"Are you sure you're going to be okay now? No more…humming?"

Mimi gazed at him, so big and commanding and decent. For one insane moment, she wanted to throw herself against that powerful chest and sob out everything, all the lousy choices she had made that led her to this place up to this moment.

She was appalled at herself for breaking down—and for doing it where she had a potential audience.

It had to be the hormones. She hadn't meant to cry. When Brant had been making popcorn earlier, a promo for one of the entertainment news shows had come on, touting their insider coverage of the fifty-thousand-dollar Vera Wang dress Jessalyn was going to wear in only a few days' time.

She probably would have been just fine with that,

but then in rapid succession during halftime had come two sappy commercials showing sweet-as-cotton-candy interactions of fathers and their children, highlighting even more clearly what she knew her child would have to do without.

Even with that, she might have been able to hold back the crying fest. But after her bath, as she had been pulling a nightgown on she had caught sight of her tiny, barely noticeable baby bump in the mirror and out of nowhere she had been overwhelmed with a combination of fierce joy and abject terror.

She was only hormonal, she reminded herself. That's the reason tears seemed to threaten at the oddest moments these days.

She had never been much of a crier, since she had learned early that her tears had absolutely no effect on Werner Van Hoyt. He would look down his aquiline nose in that slightly bored look he'd perfected, glance at his antique Patek Philippe, and then ask her if she was quite finished yet.

But here was Brant Western, a man she barely knew, showing up at her bedroom door with a slightly panicked but determined look on his face at the sound of her tears. Instead of ignoring her and walking by, as most sane men would probably do when confronted with a strange woman's weeping, he stopped and knocked to ask if she was all right.

Sharing her fears with *someone* would be so comforting, but she couldn't tell him, of course.

She barely knew the man. How could she just blurt out that she'd had an affair with an engaged Grammy winner who was getting married in a few days, that she was now pregnant from said affair, and that she planned to keep the child and raise it on her own, despite the father's strident objections?

Framed so bluntly, it all sounded so stark and sordid. And once she put some of it into words, she was afraid she would blurt out everything. Her identity, Marco's, all the stupid choices that had led her to this moment, and then Major Western would despise her, as well he should.

When he touched her cheek with such tenderness to wipe away the tear she claimed didn't exist, she thought she had seen a spark of male interest in his eyes. But of course she couldn't have. He and the so-beautiful Easton had feelings for each other and Mimi had made a personal vow that she would never allow herself to become involved with another woman's man.

Been there, done that. She'd been the "other woman" only once in her life, with Marco—though she knew rumors said otherwise—and she wasn't about to repeat the experience, no matter how tempting the package.

"I'm fine. Good night, Major."

She closed the door firmly behind her, then leaned against it. As tempting as it was, she couldn't spill everything to Brant. She was on her own now. She couldn't count on anybody but herself.

Not her father, not feckless celebrities who cheated on their betrothed with other feckless celebrities, and certainly not soldiers she barely knew who watched her with quiet blue eyes and offered an entirely too appealing shoulder to cry upon.

The snow was still falling when she awoke the next morning. The light outside her window was murky and pale but she could see through a gap in the curtains that soft flakes continued to drift down.

Maybe the snow would continue to fall and fall and fall and she would never have to return to real life.

She couldn't hide out here forever. Eventually she would have to face the consequences of her decision. Her father would have to know. He would no doubt be gravely disappointed in her. Nothing new there.

She didn't care. She would weather that storm like this old ranch weathered all the Idaho winters.

She touched her abdomen. "We'll tough it out together, kiddo," she said out loud, waking up Simone.

The dog stretched and yawned, then jumped off the bed to the floor and skittered to the door, where she stood wagging her tail insistently in a clear indication of her needs.

Mimi sighed and reached for her robe. She cautiously opened her bedroom door and peered out into the hall. She did *not* want to encounter her host yet this morning, not when she was still so mortified about her emotional breakdown the night before.

To her relief, Brant wasn't anywhere in sight, so she quickly let Simone outside. When she opened the door, she saw that the snow had indeed slowed but the drifts had to be higher than her waist in places.

It would take them days to dig out, she thought happily. Real life could wait at least a few days longer.

She showered quickly after letting Simone back inside and spent only twenty minutes on her hair and makeup, definitely some kind of record. Her stylist Giselle would probably blow a gasket if she caught Mimi with her hair a frizzy mess and wearing only barebones foundation and mascara.

She didn't care. She gazed into the round warped mirror in the bathroom. What did she need with Giselle?

She thought she looked good. She had gained a little weight with the baby but for the first time since she hit adolescence, she thought a little extra weight wasn't necessarily a bad thing on her. It filled in some of the hollows of her features, made her almost lush.

Brant still hadn't returned to the house by the time Mimi finished a quick breakfast, so she headed up to the larger upstairs bedroom.

Now that the snow had begun to clear just a little, she had a fantastic view from up here of the west slope of the Tetons, jagged and raw in the distance. It was a breath-taking vista and she thought that if she owned the ranch, she would make this her bedroom and position her bed looking out so that she could always wake to that view.

She caught her breath at the idea. What if *she* bought the Western Sky? It would be a wonderful place to raise a baby, surrounded by dogs and horses and those mountains.

Once planted, the idea refused to die and as she prepped the room for paint, she had great fun imagining what changes she might make if she had full reign here.

A new kitchen would be at the top of her list. And perhaps she would take that wide porch off the back and screen it in so that she could sit out there on summer evenings while the baby played on the floor.

"You weren't lying about the humming."

Mimi gasped and whirled around to find Brant in the doorway looking tall and gorgeous and completely yummy. How had she missed hearing him come in?

She aimed a glare at Simone for not warning her but the little dog only bared her teeth in her version of an embarrassed smile for slacking on her guard-dog duties.

"I never lie," she lied.

A tiny dimple appeared in the corner of his mouth. "Is that right?"

Just about every word she had said to him since she arrived had either been a half-truth or an outright fib—or had concealed something she hadn't wanted him to know—but she decided to keep that information to herself.

"You must have left the house early. Is everything okay?"

"I was just checking the pipes at Gwen's. So far no breaks in the line. I heard from the furnace company and they're going to try to schedule the job Friday."

"That's good."

"Did you have breakfast?"

"I grabbed a cup of tea and some toast."

"I made fresh coffee."

"I saw it." And she had craved some desperately but she had read in one of those secret pregnancy books that she should avoid caffeine during the pregnancy. She had also read to avoid oil-based paints. To her relief, the cans she found were all water-based.

Funny how there was nothing in the books about avoiding gorgeous soldiers with wide shoulders and elusive smiles. He looked tired, she thought. But then, his eyes had looked tired since she arrived.

"I saw the snow seems to have eased a little bit," she said.

"Some. According to the forecast, it should snow until mid-morning and then we can start the fun of digging out."

"That's a relief, I'm sure."

"I don't know if I'd say that but at least we'll be able to get your car fixed."

She wasn't convinced that was something to stick in the positive column. "When do you have to report back to the Army?"

"Tuesday."

"Less than a week. Oh, Brant, I'm so sorry. You've had to spend your entire free time playing host to a guest you hadn't expected and don't want. It was supremely selfish of me to intrude like this, to just assume I wouldn't be in the way. You have only a few days to call your own and I ruined everything for you."

To her deep mortification, her throat swelled with tears and she again cursed the pregnancy hormones.

He tilted his head, studying her with a puzzled sort of concern. "Please don't start humming again."

She managed a watery laugh and focused on thinking about baby names until she was calmer. "I'm sorry. I'll spare you that, at least."

He was silent for a moment to give her a chance to compose herself, a small courtesy she found touching and thoughtful.

"You've already been busy this morning," he said.

"I think I'm just about ready to start painting."

"Do you need some help?"

She should just tell him now and push him out the door. But it was his house, after all. If he wanted to spend his limited leave with a paintbrush in his hand, how could she possibly stop him?

"You've lucked out. I've already done the hardest part, the prep work. I'm just about ready to start painting." She held up the angled brush she'd found with the paint supplies in the storage room. "Do you want to roll or cut in the edges?"

"I'm assuming that by the sound of it, cutting in the

edges takes some skill with a paintbrush, which is something I'm sorry to say I don't possess. I think I should be able to handle a roller without any major catastrophes."

She smiled and handed him the paint roller she had also found in the utility room. "Just remember that you offered."

He seemed to be wading deeper and deeper into The Twilight Zone.

An hour later, Brant finished rolling paint on the last section of wall and stood back to survey the work.

Mimi stood on a ladder, her arms above her head as she angled the brush carefully to keep the paint away from the ceiling and trim.

Who would have guessed that Mimi Van Hoyt even knew how to hold a paintbrush, forget about how to wield it so expertly. When in her pampered life would she possibly have had the opportunity to paint a room? He would have thought her father hired teams of high-priced designers for projects like this.

The woman was a complete mystery to him. He wanted to ask what she was *really* doing in Cold Creek Canyon. Who or what was she running from? What was behind that little glimmer of sadness he sometimes caught in her eyes, those tears she hadn't been at all successful in hiding the night before?

At this point, he was going to have to come right out and ask her since all his subtle attempts to extract information had led him to dead end after dead end.

No matter what he asked or how he asked it, she somehow deflected every question, until he had no clearer idea what she might be doing there than he had when she showed up.

He had questioned hardened enemy combatants who weren't as adept at avoiding the truth as Mimi Van Hoyt.

He found her fascinating. Everything about her, from the way she nibbled on her bottom lip while she concentrated on a tricky corner to the way she focused completely on his face when he was talking to the lush curves that gave him entirely inappropriate ideas when she was climbing up and down the ladder.

Nobody would ever believe she was actually here in his ramshackle house, with her curly dark hair tied back in a ponytail and a tiny spray of paint splattering her cheek like white freckles.

He couldn't quite believe it—nor was he particularly thrilled about the way he couldn't seem to stop watching her.

At least for the last hour, she had completely distracted him from the pain and guilt that seemed to follow him everywhere.

"You were right," he said a moment later as he slid the roller back into the tray.

"I was? About what?" She sounded as surprised as if she'd spent her entire existence being told otherwise.

"About the paint. I'm amazed at what a difference a simple whitewash can make. It looks like a whole new room."

"Wait until we put the second coat up. I was thinking I'll move the furniture around a little bit to take advantage of that stellar view. If you angle the bed a little, the first thing your guests will see are those mountains out there. And what do you think about moving that watercolor that's in the hallway where it's too dark to be appreciated? It would fit right there on the south wall."

He gave her a careful look. "You're into this, aren't you?"

She blinked at him from her perch atop the ladder. "What?"

"Giving new life to this old place."

She looked taken aback at first, and then slowly considering as she climbed down the ladder. "I do enjoy it," she said, wiping her hands on a rag. "I told you I've done it before. A friend of mine from school flips houses in L.A. and she sometimes lets me help her stage the place for an open house."

"In between your charity work." He must have missed the paparazzi coverage of her renovating an old house.

"This is just a hobby. You know. For fun."

Before he had become acquainted with her these past few days, he would have thought her whole life was about having fun. After spending a little time in her company, he wasn't so sure. He had a feeling life hadn't been the smooth sail for Mimi that people seemed to think.

"Marisa calls me whenever she needs another set of hands. It gets me out of my routine, you know? A change of pace."

"Have you thought about doing this as a career? Staging houses, I mean?"

"I couldn't!" she exclaimed. "I don't know the first thing about what I'm doing."

"That hasn't stopped you here."

She gazed at him, her eyes a deep, startled green. "You really think I could?"

"Why not?"

"Why not." She looked rather dazed by the idea and he wondered just what he might have unleashed.

"I never thought… I mean, I'm always glad to help Marisa. We always have a good time, but that's just her telling me what to do."

"You don't have anybody telling you what to do here. How to place the furniture or hang the pictures or whatever."

"You're right." She smiled then, that radiant smile he couldn't get enough of, the one the public seemed to adore. "That is a really interesting idea, Major. I'm going to have to give it some thought."

He managed a smile in return, even though his insides were jumping around like sand fleas.

"You've got a little bit of paint on your nose."

"Where?"

"Not so much a smudge as a few tiny splatters. You look like you've got white freckles."

Color rose along her cheekbones, making the spots stand out in stark relief, much to his astonishment. She took the cloth, found a clean corner, and started dabbing at her face, but in completely the wrong spot.

If the idea of her exploring the possibility of going into the real estate business was a good one, this ranked right up there on the opposite side of the spectrum. It was a phenomenally dangerous impulse but Brant couldn't seem to stop himself from stepping forward and taking the cloth from her hands.

"No. Here. Let me."

He dabbed along the side of her nose and then just along the angled ridge of her cheekbone.

His fingers brushed her skin as they had the night before and he heard her sharp intake of breath, but he was too busy fighting back his own fierce hunger to cup her face in his hands and press his mouth fiercely to hers.

A smart man would turn around and walk out of the room. No, a smart man would just keep on going until he'd put another zip code between himself and a dangerous woman like Mimi Van Hoyt.

But right now he didn't feel very smart. He suddenly ached to taste her, just once. She was a soft, beautiful woman and he was a hardened soldier who had been far too long without much sweetness in his life.

Years from now, when he saw her in the newstands, looking polished and beautiful and worlds away from his life, he could remember how their worlds had once intersected just for a moment.

He stepped forward and lowered his head. One kiss, he told himself. What could possibly be the harm?

She tasted sweet and sensual at the same time, like deep, rich chocolate drizzled over vanilla ice cream.

For a good ten seconds, she stood frozen like a spear of ice as his mouth moved over hers. At first, she didn't exactly respond but she didn't jerk away in outrage, either. As he deepened the kiss, she seemed to give a little shiver, her hands gripping his shirt, and he felt the seductive slide of her tongue against his. And then she was kissing him with as much wild heat as he could have ever dreamed.

He was hard in an instant. How could he not be? She was soft and warm and the most beautiful woman he'd ever seen in his life and she was right here in his arms, kissing him like she never wanted him to stop.

Chapter 6

She was sinking, sinking, sinking.

For long, wondrous moments, Mimi let herself be carried away on the slow, leisurely current of this delicious attraction. His mouth was firm and determined on hers and he was big and solid and muscled and she just wanted to nestle against him and stay here forever.

Gradually, a tiny hint of reason began to flutter cautiously through her, like a tiny moth unfurling its wings for the first time.

She wanted so much to ignore it, to swat at the annoying little thing until it disappeared. In his arms she could be Maura Howard, someone good and decent. Someone much better than she was.

She wanted to stay right here in his arms. For now, the only important thing was the two of them and this delicious heat between them, sliding around and through her like a ribbon of river cutting through a steep canyon.

Brant kissed like a man who put a great deal of thought and energy into it. He seemed to know just how to dance his mouth across hers, just where to slide that tongue.

She wrapped her arms around his back, soaking in the solid strength of his muscles and the scent of him, of laundry soap and some sort of sage and cedar aftershave and the underlying sharpness of paint around them.

More than anything, she wanted to stay in this room kissing him while the snow drifted down in lazy flakes outside. But that annoying moth of a conscience continued to flutter at the edge of her thoughts until she couldn't ignore it any longer.

Easton. Brant had feelings for his beautiful neighbor, with the sleek blond hair and the big blue eyes.

He belonged to someone else and Mimi had no right to kiss him like this. She couldn't do this again. She *wouldn't*. She had just spent three terrible, guilt-ridden months in a furtive relationship with a man who was committed to someone else.

She had believed Marco when he told her his engagement with Jessalyn was just for show, that he didn't love her, that he would figure out a way to break things off before the wedding.

She had known, somewhere deep inside, that he was lying to her, but she had been too caught up in the thrill of the moment and had ignored the voice of reason.

She couldn't ignore it now.

She was going to be someone's mother in six months. Wasn't it past time that she became someone she could like and respect? Tangling tongues with a man whose heart belonged to someone else didn't seem the way to achieve that particular goal.

She closed her eyes, fighting the part of her that just wanted to hang on tight to Brant, to absorb a little of his strength.

No. She needed to stand on her own, to find her own strength.

"Stop."

To her grave chagrin, instead of sounding tough and determined, the word came out a tiny squeak, one she wasn't sure he even heard.

She drew in a breath and tried again.

"Stop!" The second time, the word came out over-loud, especially in the quiet bedroom, and Brant froze.

After a long moment, he groaned and wrenched his mouth away and for a long moment they stood bare inches apart, their breathing heavy and their gazes locked.

The raw hunger in his eyes sent an answering throb humming through her. She was so very tempted to smash that little moth of conscience under her shoes and just plunge back into the heat of his arms. But if she couldn't find the strength to do the right thing now, however was she going to stand up against her father and all the others who would have a problem with her pregnancy?

"I don't want this." Her voice wobbled a little but it still held a note of determination. "Not with you."

She saw disbelief and even a little hurt in his eyes before he shuttered his expression. After another moment, he stepped away. "Apparently I misread some kind of sign."

She closed her eyes so she didn't reveal to him that

he had misread *nothing*. She had wanted him to kiss her, had craved it desperately.

If she hadn't listened to that blasted fledgling conscience, she would still be wrapped around him. The shame of just how much she still wanted to ignore it turned her voice sharper than she had intended.

"Why would you just jump to the conclusion that I'm the sort of woman who would start tangling tongues with someone she barely knows?"

He gave her a long look. "I don't know. Maybe because that's just what you *did?*"

Her mouth tightened and she opted to go on the offensive. "You took me by surprise and didn't give me a chance to react. I was too stunned to push you away."

"So your hands in my hair and your tongue in my mouth, that was just you being stunned?"

She glared. "I did not come to Idaho to start something with some soldier just trying to hit on anybody warm and willing while he's home on leave."

She immediately regretted the words, especially when his color rose and his jaw tightened. He suddenly looked rough and hardened, every inch a warrior. Not a wise move, taunting a man who lived a dangerous life she couldn't even imagine, especially when she was alone here at his ranch and completely at his mercy.

Easton was the only person who knew for certain where she was, she suddenly realized.

He wouldn't hurt her, she told herself, though the hard anger in his eyes wasn't an encouraging sign.

"Well, you're obviously not willing," he said in a lethally soft voice. "And not particularly warm, either, when it comes to that. My mistake."

She had wounded him, she realized, by implying

any woman would do as well as the next one. For a moment, she wanted to apologize, but then she remembered Easton and the obvious affection between the two of them and she glared right back at him.

"Now that we know where we stand, I'm going to go out and check on the horses and see if I can start clearing away some of the snow yet."

The sooner you leave, the better. He didn't say the words but she caught the subtext anyway.

After he stalked out of the room, she eased onto the edge of the bed, to the slick plastic she had found to protect the furnishings in the room from the paint.

She had never been kissed like that, with such fierce concentration, such raw intensity. She touched a finger to her lips and closed her eyes, reliving the heat and wonder of it.

After a long moment, she opened her eyes and slid from the bed with a crackle of plastic. Enough. She had to get back to work and forget the past few moments ever happened, though she had a feeling that was going to be a harder task than scrubbing every inch of his old house.

Brant didn't come inside at all for lunch, something that left her feeling both grateful and guilty—grateful for the space and distance between them right now but guilty over the idea of him going hungry. She could hear the rumble of some sort of heavy machinery outside, and once she had peeked out the window and saw him on a powerful-looking tractor pushing snow with smooth, practiced motions.

Simone jumped up on a chair near the window in

the kitchen and watched Brant on the tractor as if she'd never seen anything quite so fascinating.

Mimi knew just how her dog felt. She sighed and dumped the rest of her sandwich into the garbage.

The second coat in the bedroom took her less than an hour since she didn't need to be as precise around the edges. He still hadn't returned to the house by the time she finished cleaning up the brushes and the roller and returning the paint supplies to the utility room. After she finished, she realized she was exhausted, another of those little pregnancy joys.

A small nap was definitely in order, she decided, before she tackled the upstairs bathroom.

When she awoke, she was astonished to see she had slept for two hours and the light outside her bedroom was pale with late-afternoon sun.

Some days back in L.A., she wouldn't even get up until two or three in the afternoon so she could go clubbing all night. She couldn't go back to that world, ever. She didn't want to, even if everything hadn't changed with that simple pregnancy test.

That world, the endless quest for fun and excitement, had all seemed so vital. Now she could clearly see how very empty her life had been.

She was twenty-six years old and didn't know the first thing about responsibility. She had somehow squeaked her way to a degree in public relations and marketing from UCLA, probably because her father had donated a large sum to the university, but she had no idea what to do with her education.

She thought of Brant's suggestion that she consider staging houses. Real estate. Mimi shook her head. Maybe she had inherited more from her father than green eyes and a temper. Still, it was exciting to think about the possibilities.

Her stomach rumbled a bit and she realized the two bites of sandwich she'd eaten at lunch just weren't enough now that she was eating for two and had to consider things like folic acid and calcium intake.

She took a little extra care in the bathroom with her hair and makeup then stood at the mirror for a long moment, wary of walking out into the kitchen and facing Brant again.

Their easy companionship of the morning while they had worked together painting seemed a long time ago and she wasn't looking forward to the tension she feared would tug between them now that they'd kissed.

She couldn't hide out here in the bathroom hugging an old-fashioned bowl sink forever, she reminded herself. She could handle whatever challenges life threw at her, even in the form of a mouthwatering man who gave her entirely inappropriate ideas.

She opened the door to her bedroom and heard him in the kitchen before she saw him. He was talking on the phone and though she didn't intend to eavesdrop, she couldn't help but hear his words.

"I know I told you I would try to make it down for a few days, Abby, but this has been a bear of a storm and there have been…complications at the ranch."

Abby? Yet another woman? She frowned. The man did get around. But then, he'd been in the Middle East for several months and she imagined dating opportunities weren't exactly thick on the ground there.

Mimi frowned as she suddenly realized *she* was the complication he was talking about at the ranch that made it difficult for him to leave to visit his apparently endless string of honeys.

"Yeah, I understand," Brant was saying. "I'm sorry things haven't worked out like I planned. But I'm still flying out of Salt Lake City and my flight doesn't leave until late Tuesday. What if I come down in the morning and spend the day before I have to be at the airport? A short visit is better than nothing."

He was quiet as Abby, whoever she was, must have responded. "Yeah," he said after a moment. "I know, sweetheart. It's not fair. I hate it, too."

His voice sounded not regretful in the way of a man breaking a date but tight, almost bleak.

"Yeah, I'll call you. Hugs to the girls from me. Love you."

After a long moment of silence from the kitchen, Mimi tried to walk nonchalantly into the room. She didn't know what she expected to see but it wasn't the strong and capable Brant Western sitting at the kitchen table with her dog in his lap, his features tight with pain and a sorrow she couldn't begin to guess at.

She froze in the doorway, not quite sure how to react to the sight of his obvious turmoil. She would have slipped back down the hall to her bedroom before he caught sight of her but Simone barked and scampered off his lap, bounding into her arms.

By the time she had picked up her dog and given the requisite love, as inconvenient as the distraction was, Brant had schooled his features.

He could tell she had heard, she realized, as he moved away from the table and dumped the dregs of his coffee mug into the sink. She didn't think it was an accident that he avoided her gaze.

He obviously wanted to pretend nothing was wrong but she had never been very good at keeping her mouth shut, even when she knew darn well it was a mistake to speak.

"Having girlfriend trouble?"

He looked baffled. "Girlfriend?"

"On the phone. I heard the tail end of your conversation."

His eyes widened and he stared at his phone and then back at Mimi. "Abby? No! She's not... We're not..."

He looked aghast at the very idea and Mimi shrugged, knowing she shouldn't be so relieved. One girlfriend was enough. "None of my business. You just seemed upset. That was the logical conclusion."

"Well, you were wrong."

"Oh?"

He narrowed his gaze at her and she saw anger there and something deeper, something dark and almost anguished. "Abby is smart and warm and lovely, but she isn't my girlfriend. She's the widow of one of my men."

"Oh." Her small exclamation sounded unusually loud in the sudden hush of the kitchen. "My mistake."

"Right." He paused. "Ty Rigby was a damn good soldier. He was killed three weeks ago in an ambush, along with two other of my most trusted men."

She stood frozen as the words poured out of him like thick, ugly sludge. "As we were fighting to keep him from bleeding to death, he asked me to watch out for his wife and his two little girls. I'm doing a hell of a job, aren't I?"

"Oh, Brant. I'm so sorry." The words seemed painfully inadequate as she saw the torment in his eyes, the weight of responsibility in him.

She thought of her life, the shopping and the gossip and the parties. While he was risking his life and watching his friends die, she was complaining about eye shadow and the new girl who did her pedicures all wrong and how some restaurant had taken her favorite thing off the menu.

"Bad enough that Abby has lost her husband, but now she's facing financial problems. She's probably going to lose the house. She doesn't have a college degree and even with Ty's death benefits, it's going to be a real struggle for her to make it the next few years while the kids are little."

Mimi sank into a chair, her mind racing as she tried to figure out how she could fix things for the poor woman without revealing that she had more money than she could ever spend in a hundred lifetimes.

"Why doesn't she come here?" she suddenly suggested. "You've got a house that sits empty all the time. She could bring her kids and take care of the house in exchange for rent. It's the perfect solution!"

He looked astonished and rather impressed. "I actually had the same idea," he admitted. "I offered it to her but Abby's a proud woman and she refused. Besides that, her family and Ty's are in Utah and she doesn't want to leave that support cushion right now. She'll probably go live with her parents until she can get back on her feet. She won't be homeless. But she won't have her husband, either."

His voice was grim, desolate, and Mimi chewed her lip, disgusted with herself for the angry thoughts she'd had about him earlier.

"That's the reason I was thinking about selling the ranch. I thought maybe I could, I don't know, maybe set up a trust or something to help. I guess you'd know more about that, since you work for a charitable foundation, right?"

She opened her mouth to respond, wondering why he used such a harsh, goading tone, but he didn't give her a chance.

"It's a crazy idea," he went on. "But I feel really helpless about the whole thing."

"And responsible?" she guessed.

He scraped his chair back from the table and stood quickly. "I need to head back out and see if I can at least finish clearing out the driveway. I don't know if I'll be back inside before it gets dark out there so go ahead and find what you want for dinner. I just ate a late lunch so I won't be hungry for a while."

"Okay." She forced a smile but he was already heading to the mudroom and didn't turn back around.

What had she said that hit such a hot button? she wondered as he stalked from the kitchen.

Why couldn't he have just kept his big mouth shut?

Brant stomped outside into the bitterly cold afternoon, shoving on his work gloves as he went.

Mimi didn't give a rat's rear end about a bunch of soldiers in a world thousands of miles away from her pampered existence. She had more important things to think about, like her next movie premiere.

A woman like her couldn't possibly understand the gritty, hazardous irrevocability of his world. So why had he told her? The words had just bubbled out and he hadn't been able to stop them.

She hadn't reacted quite as he might have guessed. He had seen shock in her eyes, certainly, but also an unexpected empathy. For a moment, he had wanted to spew all of it to her. His pain and his guilt and the grief for his friends.

Somehow it was only too easy to forget who she was when they were alone here at the ranch. He almost couldn't believe the woman who teased him and scrubbed his walls and spent the morning painting his spare bedroom was the same flighty, shallow publicity-hungry ditz the tabloids seemed so enamored with.

She had kissed him with passion and an urgent heat and then she had pushed him away, accusing him of being some sex-starved bastard putting the moves on any woman who breathed at him.

That had stung, he admitted. And absolutely wasn't true. He had kissed her because he hadn't been able to think about anything else all morning long as they worked together painting the room.

He didn't know what to think of her. Which was the mask and which was the real woman?

None of his business, he reminded himself as he started the tractor, which sputtered to life with a low rumble. In a few days, he would be returning to duty and she would be Gwen Bianca's problem. He would never see her again and this strange interlude would simply be a story for him to tell his men on boring transports.

That was what he wanted, right? So why did the thought of never seeing her again leave him feeling as cold and empty as the February sky?

Chapter 7

The room looked fantastic, if she did say so herself.

An hour after Brant left in such a hurry to return to the endless task of shoveling snow, Mimi stood on the second to top rung of the stepladder in the newly painted bedroom, trying to rehang the curtains.

Lucky for her the paint had been fast-drying so she could start the fun process of returning the furnishings and really making a difference in the room.

The new coat of paint had brightened the room considerably, making everything look fresh and cheerful. She had found a lovely deep blue crazy quilt in the linen closet and decided to use that as the focal point of the room.

On the top shelf of the bedroom closet, she had unearthed a goldmine of dusty antique bottles of various sizes and shapes in deep jewel tones, including several in a blue that nearly identically matched the quilt. She washed them out with dish soap and water and set them along the frame of the double-paned windows, where they glowed as they caught the pale afternoon light.

She had hung the same now-clean curtains but decided they needed something extra. A further search of the attic found a length of fabric in a pale blue, long enough to use as a graceful swag above the other drapes.

It would be a small change, maybe, but sometimes tiny changes had the power to rock the world. Just look at her pregnancy.

Okay, it had rocked *her* world. But wasn't that enough for now?

She reached to arrange a fold that wasn't quite even and she wasn't exactly sure what happened next. She must have leaned just a few inches too far, upsetting her balance, or perhaps the ladder tilted on an uneven spot on the carpet at just the moment she was off-kilter.

Whatever happened, one moment she was reaching across the window to adjust the curtain, the next she was tumbling down, taking the fabric and a few of the antique bottles with her.

She hit the ground, her gasp frozen in her throat as her lungs froze at the impact.

Even as she panicked and fought to catch her breath, pain screamed out from her right side and she realized she must have banged against the small square table she had situated beneath the window to be used as a writing desk.

Simone barked and rushed toward her, her little body wriggling and her black eyes wide with concern. She licked at Mimi's face and the action of that tiny wet tongue on her skin seemed to jolt her lungs back to action, for some strange reason.

She lay on the floor, focusing only on inhaling and exhaling for several long moments before she dared move to scoop the anxious dog against her.

She hurt everywhere.

Her head, her side, the wrist that she had instinctively thrown out to catch her fall.

Several shards of broken glass from the bottles were embedded in her palm and blood dropped onto the carpet until she pulled it across her chest so it could drip on her shirt.

At the movement, a heavy cramp suddenly spasmed across her lower stomach and then another, so intense, she had to curl up. For several endless moments, she couldn't think past the sudden raw, consuming panic.

No. Oh, please. Dear God, no.

"You're okay, kiddo," she whispered, her words a ragged whimper. "You're all right. I'm sorry. I'm so sorry. It was an accident."

Her abdomen cramped again, a rippling wave that took what was left of her breath.

Simone whined, snuggling closer, and Mimi clung to her.

She couldn't lose this baby. Not after she had reached the monumental decision that she wanted it so very desperately. She needed help. A doctor. She had to find Brant. He would help her. Oh, why hadn't she asked for his cell phone number?

Through her panic, she heard a steady rumble outside. The tractor. He must be plowing closer to the house.

Though the very magnitude of the task overwhelmed

her, she knew she had to somehow make her way down the stairs and out into the bitter cold to attract Brant's attention so he could help her.

The next few moments were a blur of pain and fear as she made her way slowly through the house, one painful step at a time.

By the time she reached the front door, she was breathing hard and soaked with sweat from the effort. Her abdomen had cramped twice more and she'd had to stop each time as the pain washed over and through her.

Finally she reached the front door. When she staggered to it and yanked it open, Simone raced out and off the porch, barking furiously on the shoveled sidewalk.

The dog's urgent call for attention might have been more effective if she wasn't a tiny white dog standing amid all that snow, but Mimi still appreciated the effort. She moved to the edge of the porch and grabbed the nearest column as the cold sucked at her bones.

The tractor had an enclosed cab and she knew he wouldn't hear her yelling over the machine's noise, so she waved her uninjured arm as much as she could, blood dripping from her other hand to fall in stark contrast to the snow.

After what felt like the longest moments of her life, her efforts finally paid off. Brant caught sight of her and shut off the tractor. Mimi didn't think she had ever heard a sweeter sound than the sudden silence, and she knew she had never felt such relief when Brant leaped from the tractor and raced toward her, faster than she would have believed possible.

"You're bleeding. What happened?"

"I fell…off the ladder." She could barely squeeze

the words out through her fear. "The baby. Oh, please, I…need a doctor."

He stared at her. "Baby? Baby! You're pregnant?"

She gave a tiny nod, all she could manage, and an instant later he scooped her into his arms and carried her back into the house.

"I'm cramping. It started right after I fell. Oh, please. I don't want to lose my baby. Please help me, Brant."

His face looked carved in granite as he carried her to the family room and laid her gently on the sofa. The fire's warmth soaked into her, warming her from the chill of the outside air, but it did nothing for the iciness in her heart.

"Let me call Jake Dalton and see what we should do."

We. Why had she never realized what vast comfort could be contained in the simple word?

He covered her with the throw from the back of the couch and Simone snuggled against her. Mimi closed her eyes, grateful beyond words that he was a strong, determined, take-charge man, since she barely had a coherent thought in her head beyond her terror.

"Maggie," Brant said urgently into the phone, "this is Brant Western. Yes. I was calling for Jake but you can help me out here. I've got someone staying at my ranch who just fell off a stepladder. She's pregnant and she says she's cramping. What should we do?"

He was quiet for a moment, listening to something on the other end, then he turned to Mimi. "How far along are you?" he asked Mimi. Though she could still see the shock in his eyes, she recognized he was no stranger at adjusting to the unexpected.

"Eleven weeks," she answered. "That's what the doctor said anyway."

He relayed the information to this Maggie person, paused a moment, then turned back to Mimi.

"What about, uh, bleeding?"

If she weren't so terrified she might have smiled at this sign of his discomfort at the intimacy of their discussion. Instead, she only shook her head.

"Negative," he answered into the phone, a look of obvious relief on his features.

"I'll get her there," he said after a moment, his words sounding like a solemn vow. "I can't guarantee how long it will take us to get down the canyon, but we'll make it as soon as we can. Yeah. Okay. Thanks, Mag. See you."

He hung up and turned back to Mimi. "Maggie Dalton is the nurse practitioner at the clinic. Her husband is the town doctor. She thinks it's best to have an ultrasound and check everything out. Are you up for a ride to town?"

"Anything, as long as they can help me. Can we make it through the snow?"

"One of the ranch pickups has a plow. I can't promise you the most comfortable ride you've ever had and it might take us some time, but we'll get there."

"Thank you." Her abdomen cramped again and she folded both arms around it and gave a little moan.

His eyes reflected something close to panic. "Hang on," he said. "You're going to have to give me a couple minutes to get the truck out of the garage and drive it up here. Just wait here and I'll come help you outside."

She nodded and hugged Simone to her, praying fiercely the entire time he was gone. It was probably only five minutes or so but each second seemed endless.

When he returned, he spent another few moments

putting a reluctant Simone in her crate and helping Mimi into her coat, and then before she quite realized what he intended, he scooped her into his arms and carried her outside to an aging blue pickup truck with an extended cab.

"I would suggest you lie down on the backseat but, with the snowy conditions, you're going to need to wear your seat belt and you can't do that lying down. I'm sorry."

"It's fine. Just go."

As soon as she was settled, he backed the truck up and headed down the driveway at a rapid clip. She might have been nervous at his speed under the current conditions, but he drove with confident skill, so she decided to just close her eyes and continue praying.

He didn't speak until they had turned off the access road to the Western Sky and onto the main canyon road.

"Why didn't you tell me you were pregnant?"

Despite her fear, she bristled at the accusatory note in his voice. "Maybe because I didn't think it was any of your business."

"You made it my business when you showed up at my ranch, giving me some cock-and-bull story about needing a place to stay for a few days. Dammit, Mimi. If I'd known you were pregnant, I never would have worked you so hard."

She stared at him, her mouth open. Mimi. He'd called her Mimi.

"I thought it was a joke," he said, his voice disgusted. "Some funny story I could tell my men when I went back to my unit. Mimi Van Hoyt scrubbing my cobwebs and painting my spare bedroom."

"I'm not..."

"Cut the crap. We both know who you are."

A muscle flexed in his jaw and his eyes blazed and she gauged suddenly that he was furious with her.

"You…knew all along?"

"Of course I knew! I'm not an idiot, despite what you apparently think. And yeah, I might have been living in a cave in the desert on and off for the last few years, but you were a little hard to miss whenever I did resurface."

She thought of all her ridiculous efforts to conceal her identity, all the half-truths and the outright prevarications, and her face burned with embarrassment. All for nothing. He had known, probably from the moment she crashed her car.

What must he have thought of her?

That didn't matter, she reminded herself. The important thing right now was doing all she could to save her baby.

"Why all the subterfuge?" he asked. "Why not just call one of your father's people to rescue you the minute you woke up after your accident and found yourself on the ranch? Instead, just about the first words out of your mouth were lies and they just kept coming."

She let out a breath. "You wouldn't understand."

"Not if you don't explain it to me, *Maura*."

She made a face at his deliberate emphasis on the false name she'd given him. "Haven't you ever wanted to be someone else for a while? Maura Howard is safe. Ordinary. Just a nice woman living her nice comfortable life in anonymity. She hasn't made a total disaster of her life."

She hadn't meant to add that last part but it seemed particularly appropriate right now as she fought to save her baby.

"Why here? Why were you running to Gwen?"

"I needed a place away from the limelight for a while and the idea of escaping to Gwen's just felt right. I only found out myself about the baby the day before I arrived and I needed time to…come to terms with everything."

"So you decided to pretend to be someone else and worm your way into me letting you stay at the ranch."

That just about summed it out. "Yes," she admitted. "But whether I'm Mimi or Maura doesn't matter. I don't want to lose my baby."

"I'll do what I can to make sure you don't," he said.

Though he still seemed angry with her, after a long moment, he reached across the cab of the old pickup and folded her hand inside his much larger one.

Despite everything, her embarrassment and her anger that he had let her dig herself into a deeper hole of lies, she felt immensely comforted by the solid, corporeal reassurance of her hand in his.

He couldn't remember a more white-knuckle driving experience, counting the times he'd had to drive a Humvee down a precarious cliffside goat trail in the pitch-black wearing night-vision goggles that cut his peripheral view to nothing.

The road in Cold Creek Canyon had been plowed but was still icy and dangerous around the curves.

He could handle the road conditions. He'd been driving in snow since he was fourteen. But he'd never driven through snow with this abject fear in his gut. Every time Mimi caught her breath beside him at a bump or a sharp turn in the road, he wanted to just pull over and call for heli transport to take her to the nearest level-one trauma center, five hours away in Salt Lake City.

Though he knew he needed to keep both hands on the wheel because of the driving conditions—and he did for the most part—every once in a while he could sense her panic and fear start to break through her tight control and he couldn't resist reaching over and squeezing her fingers.

"Hang in there. We're almost there," he said.

She gave him a grateful look as she clung tight to his fingers.

By the time he reached the small medical clinic in Pine Gulch, his shoulders were knotted and he ached all over as if he had just finished hauling seventy pounds of gear on a fifty-mile march.

The parking lot and sidewalks of the clinic had been plowed already, he was relieved to see. Brant parked the truck near the entrance then hurried around to Mimi's side and scooped her out.

"I can walk," she murmured.

"Shut up and let me do this," he snapped, not at all in the mood to argue with her.

She raised an eyebrow but said nothing as he carefully made his way to the double front doors. Before he could thrust them open, Maggie Cruz Dalton appeared, pushing an empty wheelchair.

"I was watching for you," Maggie said, her features so calm and serene that a little of his panic naturally ebbed away.

She smiled at them both, though her attention was mostly fixed on Mimi, as he set her into the wheelchair. "I'm Maggie Dalton, Ms. Van Hoyt. My husband, Jake, is the town doctor and he'll be in to look at you as soon as we get you settled in an exam room."

Mimi shot Brant an accusing look as Maggie used

her name instead of the whole Maura Howard alias, but he merely shrugged.

He wouldn't let her make him feel guilty for telling the Daltons the truth. He had called Maggie back when he went to get the pickup truck, after it occurred to him it was only fair and right to warn them their impending patient might require somewhat complicated security measures.

"We've cleared the waiting area and we'll get you back into an exam room right away," Maggie said.

"I... Thank you."

Mimi looked a little bit lost and a whole lot overwhelmed and he fought the urge to haul her back into his arms and promise her everything would be okay.

He was way, way out of his depth in this whole situation and felt completely inept and very male. If he had his preference, he would head over to The Bandito for a stiff drink while he waited, but he didn't think mentioning that right about now would earn him points with either Maggie or Mimi.

"I'll, um, just hang out here," Brant said.

He tried to pull his hand free from Mimi's grasp but she wouldn't let go and they tussled a little as Maggie pushed her down the hall toward an exam room.

"Would you feel better if you had someone familiar with you?" Maggie asked.

"Yes," Mimi admitted softly.

No, Brant wanted to say, horrified. *Hell* no.

But how could he just walk away when she apparently was in desperate need of a friendly face. "Do you want me to stay with you?" He voiced the obvious.

"You don't have to," she said in a small voice, and he sighed, giving up the liquor fantasy altogether.

"Sure, if that would make you feel better."

He was uncomfortably aware of the speculative glances Maggie was sending him. He glared at her, dreading the interrogation in store for him after all this.

He'd always had a tender spot in his heart for Magdalena Cruz Dalton, in part because of the courage she had shown when, as a former Army nurse, she had been injured in a bomb blast in the Middle East and lost her leg below the knee.

He had never seen her in action in her capacity as a nurse and he had to admit he was even more impressed when he witnessed her calming demeanor toward Mimi.

At the exam room, she turned to him. "Brant, please wait here in the hall while I help our patient change into a gown and get her settled."

How about the waiting room? Or the parking lot? Or back at the Western Sky?

"Sure," he said instead.

He leaned against the wall and was thinking how surreal this all was, when Maggie came out of the room a few moments later, closing the door behind her.

"You can go back in now."

"Do I have to?" he muttered, and she gave him a long look.

"You don't have to answer because it's none of my business. But I have to ask. Just out of curiosity, how on earth did Mimi Van Hoyt come to be threatening a miscarriage at the Western Sky?"

"It's a long story."

"And a fascinating one, I'm sure."

He sighed. "She's a friend of Gwen's, apparently, and she didn't know Gwen was in Europe. She came out to see her and ended up with me instead."

"So you're not the father."

He glared. "No! I just met the woman three days ago. I only gave her a place to stay while we waited out the storm."

"I'm guessing there's more to the story than that."

"No." *Except I've held her and kissed her until I couldn't see straight.* "Really, I barely know her."

"Be that as it may, it looks like you're her only support right now since Gwen's out of the country. It's good she has someone."

He would rather that someone be any other soul on earth except him, but Brant was determined to do his best to help her. He owed her, especially since it was his fault she was in that exam room right now. If he hadn't gone along with her deception—if he had admitted from the first day that he knew who she was instead of finding unexpected humor in watching her pretend to be someone else—she would not be in this situation. She would have been at one of the high-priced hotels in Jackson Hole sipping lattes in her fluffy pink designer boots instead of hanging curtains and falling off ladders in his spare bedroom.

His fault. He sighed. Just one more thing for which he bore responsibility. He had a feeling that one of these days the weight of all the guilt piled on top of him just might bury him.

Through the next twenty minutes, Mimi didn't let go of his hand. She clung to him while Maggie drew blood and checked her blood pressure. She wouldn't even let him leave when Jake Dalton came in to do an exam, though he was at least allowed to wait behind a little curtain near her head and away from the action, wishing like hell he was somewhere else.

When Jake was finished, he had Maggie hook a band with a monitor on it across Mimi's stomach and a moment later, a steady pulsing sound filled the exam room.

At the sound, the tension seemed to whoosh out of Mimi like a surveillance balloon shot through with mortar fire.

"That's the heartbeat, right?" she said, her famous green eyes bright with excitement and wonder and the echo of her fear.

"That's the heartbeat." Jake Dalton smiled at her, that winsome smile he shared with his two brothers, the one that managed to charm just about any woman in view of it. Mimi didn't seem to be an exception. Since the moment the Pine Gulch physician had come into the exam room, she had visibly relaxed, as if Jake could make everything right again.

Brant supposed that was a good technique for a doctor, to be able to inspire such trust in his patients.

"I'm happy to report that, despite your cramping, the heartbeat sounds strong and healthy," Jake said.

Mimi made a sound of relief mingled with a little sob and tightened her hand on Brant's. He squeezed back, wondering again how the real Mimi could seem so very different from her flighty, ditzy public persona.

"If it's all right with you," Jake went on, "I'd still like to do an ultrasound to get a little better look and check everything out."

"Whatever you think best."

"I can wait outside if you want," Brant offered.

She shook her head. "I'd like you to come," she said. "If you don't mind."

"Sure," he answered. What else could he say?

So he sat beside her while Jake covered her stomach with gel and then moved the ultrasound sensor over her. Brant couldn't seem to move his gaze from the monitor and the various mysterious shapes there, intrigued despite himself by the process and by that little alien-looking shape with a big head and tiny fingers.

Mimi looked enthralled. "Can you tell what it is?" she asked.

"Not yet. A few more weeks," Jake replied. After a few more moments, he set down the wand and handed her a huge pile of paper towels to wipe off all the goop.

"You haven't miscarried, despite the cramping. I can't say it's not still a possibility, but right now your baby is alive and appears to be healthy."

Mimi exhaled a long breath and squeezed Brant's fingers. "Oh, thank you, Dr. Dalton. Thank you so much."

Jake smiled. "I didn't do anything but check things out. I want you to come back immediately if you have more cramping or spotting."

"Of course."

"And I don't know what your travel plans are, but I would feel better if you stay put for now. In fact, I would recommend limited bed rest for at least a few days. That means you can get up to move from room to room, but not much more than that. Can you swing that?"

She pulled her hand away and didn't look at Brant. "I don't… It's not right for me to impose on Major Western more than I already have. Perhaps I could check into a motel in the area."

Brant frowned. "Stop right there. You're staying at the Western Sky."

He was invested in this now. No way was he going to sit by and let her fight to save her baby without him.

"When do you have to report back?" Maggie asked him.

"My flight leaves Tuesday." He could request an additional few days of emergency leave but he and Maggie both knew he wouldn't get it, not for these circumstances.

"She can stay with me until I have to take off," he said. "If she still needs bed rest after that, she can stay with Easton at Winder Ranch."

For some strange reason, Mimi didn't look exactly thrilled at that idea, which he found odd. Everybody liked Easton.

"Or with us," Maggie said. "We've got plenty of room. Don't worry, we'll find a place for you, Ms. Van Hoyt."

"Thank you," she said, with a fairly good rendition of her usual radiant smile.

She hadn't moved her slim hands from her abdomen since he'd found her standing so frightened and pale on the front porch. By all appearances, it looked as if Mimi was excited about this baby.

Who was the father? he wondered, trying to rack his brain to see if he had remembered seeing her with some special date in the tabloids lately. He hadn't paid enough attention to really care but now he wanted to run over to the grocery store and buy every copy of the gossip rags off the stands.

One kiss, no matter how earthshaking, didn't give him the right to be jealous, he reminded himself.

"Just take it easy, eat healthy foods and drink plenty

of fluids," Jake was saying. "I'd like to see you again on Friday. I'll see if I can swing out to the Western Sky."

"Thank you. Both of you," she said to the doctor as he and Maggie headed out of the room. Brant rose to leave with them in order to give her privacy to dress, but he didn't move away from the exam table as a new thought occurred to him.

"Do you need help getting dressed? I can send Maggie back in."

"I think I can handle it. Thank you." She paused and, just before he reached the door, she gripped his fingers again. "Thank you so much for everything, Brant. I don't know what I would have done if you hadn't been here with me."

She wouldn't have been hurt in the first place if not for him.

"You would have been fine. I think you're tougher than you think, Mimi."

"I'm not," she said, but as he left, he thought she looked intrigued at the idea.

Tough or not, Mimi must have been completely exhausted from the stress of the afternoon. By the time he drove the short distance from the clinic to the mouth of Cold Creek Canyon, she was asleep, curled up beside him with her cheek resting against the worn upholstery.

Even though the return trip to the ranch lacked the urgency that had pushed him so hard to drive a little faster than conditions warranted on the way to town, the drive home seemed shorter somehow. Maybe because his stomach wasn't a knot of nerves this time.

At twilight, the canyon seemed spectacularly beautiful, with the mountains looming in the distance and the dark shadows of the Douglas fir a bold contrast to the pure, blinding white of the snow.

When he passed Hope Springs, he saw Nate Cavazos clearing snow from his neighbor's driveway with his tractor, headlights beaming. He lifted a hand in the customary wave and Nate smiled and waved back.

He loved that about Pine Gulch. That sense of community, of being part of something bigger. Shoveling out your neighbor's driveway, casseroles and chicken soup on your doorstep when you were sick, helping anybody in need just because you can.

He remembered when Curtis drowned, the outpouring of support for his parents. Some of the men in town had helped his dad put in his crops that year when he'd been too stunned to do it, then had been there throughout the haying season to help him cut and bale when he was too drunk to bring in his own crop.

It had been that same sense of community, he supposed, that had impelled Guff Winder to keep an eye out for his neighbor's son and then to step in and take care of business when he saw things weren't right.

Maybe that's why he was so conflicted about selling the ranch. He loved it here and found something deeply compelling about being tied to a place, something that wasn't just about geography.

Would he lose that if he sold the ranch?

He would always be connected to Pine Gulch and Cold Creek Canyon through Easton. She and Quinn and Cisco were his family, all he had, and nothing would ever change that. But he had to admit that Easton was right. If he sold the ranch, nothing would be the same.

When he reached the house, he turned off the engine of the big truck and glanced in the fading light at his passenger.

He wasn't crazy about this protective mode that seemed to take over him when he was around her, something that made no rational sense.

Why should he feel any sense of obligation toward the woman? She had more money and resources at her disposal than he could even imagine, enough to probably contract a small private army of her own.

She probably had a dozen houses around the world where she could be recuperating right now. Paris. London. New York. So why was she determined to hide out in Podunk eastern Idaho with him?

Was she escaping her father? The baby's father? The paparazzi? Or all of the above?

Whatever it was, he knew damn well he ought to just let her deal with her own troubles. But at this point, he knew it was far too late for him to step back.

"Mimi, we're home," he said, after allowing himself only a few more moments' indulgence to just look at her.

Her big, long-lashed green eyes blinked sleepily at him as she hovered on the edge of consciousness.

"I'm…sorry," she said with a yawn. "I fell asleep. How rude of me."

"To sleep when your body demanded it? That's not rude. If there's one thing any soldier understands, it's the value of sleeping whenever you can steal the chance."

He moved around the truck and opened the door for her. "Come on, let's get you inside," he said as he scooped her small, curvy weight into his arms.

"You don't have to carry me," she protested. "Dr. Dalton never said I couldn't walk."

He ignored her objection—just as he tried to ignore how warm and feminine and sweet smelling she was in his arms.

"I would hate for you to fall out here. It's still slick."

"What if *you* fall?"

He knew he shouldn't enjoy the way her body slid against his chest when he shrugged. "Then I'll figure out how to hit the ground first so I spare you the brunt of it."

"Could you really do that?"

He smiled a little at the disbelief in her eyes. "I have no idea. But since I'm not going to slip, we won't have to find out, will we?"

For some reason she was staring at his mouth and his smile slid away.

"Don't stop," she murmured.

"I'm only opening the door," he said. "I was planning to set you down on the sofa in the family room by the fire."

"I meant, don't stop smiling. You're far less terrifying when you smile."

Terrifying? She was afraid of him? After he had just spent a deeply uncomfortable afternoon holding her hand in a doctor's office?

His gaze met hers and suddenly he remembered the kiss between them, the softness of her mouth and the way her hands had curled into his hair and the sweet, sexy sounds she made when his mouth found hers.

She was the first to look away. "The sofa would be a good place to set me, but the, um, powder room would actually be better."

He set her down outside the door of the bathroom just off the kitchen. "I imagine Simone's going to need to go out. I'll take care of that and then build up the fire in the woodstove again."

"Thank you." To his discomfort, she reached up and brushed her fingers on his cheek. "Thank you for everything. I'm really sorry I dragged you into this."

"You wouldn't have been hurt if not for me," he said in a low voice.

She dropped her hand and gazed at him in surprise. "What do you mean?"

"If I had admitted from the first that I knew who you were, you never would have been up on that ladder."

"This was *not* your fault, Brant. If anyone's to blame, I am. I lied to you and used you, only because I needed a place to stay for a few days and the Western Sky was convenient for my needs. I selfishly didn't think for one minute about you only having a few days of peace to yourself. I never considered you might have better things to do with your brief free time than entertaining me."

She looked sad suddenly, as bereft as she had on the way to the clinic when she had been in fear for her child.

"That's who I am," she said in a low voice. "Selfish, irresponsible Mimi Van Hoyt, who never thinks of anyone but herself. So now you know."

She closed the door between them firmly before he could reply. A few days ago, he would have agreed. But right now, Brant didn't know what to believe.

Chapter 8

"Oh!" Mimi exclaimed four hours later. "You are nothing but a dirty, rotten cheater!"

The louse in question raised an eyebrow. "Hey, I won that hand fair and square. Is it my fault you're a lousy poker player?"

"Oh!" Mimi grabbed a kernel of popcorn from the bowl beside her and tossed it at him. To her regret, it hit his chest and bounced off again. "Who ever would have guessed that the upright, honorable Major Brant Western cheats at cards?"

"I did *not* cheat." He gave her a long look, that sexy mouth of his tilted slightly at one corner. "I could have, about a dozen times when you weren't paying attention, but I opted to claim higher ground."

She sniffed at this with a dismissive gesture at the pile of toothpicks in front of him. Compared to her very tiny winnings, his stash of toothpicks looked like a beaver dam.

"When you asked me if I wanted to play five-card stud, it might have been fair for you to mention you're as relentless as an Atlantic City card shark."

"You mean I forgot to mention the three years I spent on the pro poker circuit?"

"I believe it. I'm curious, though. How did you fit the poker circuit in between deployments."

"It wasn't easy but I managed."

She shook her head at his teasing, though she had to admit she loved this lighthearted side of him. Except for those few dark moments after they returned from the clinic when he tried to shoulder the blame for her threatened miscarriage, he had seemed like a different man throughout the evening.

Every now and again she had seen a certain brooding look in his eyes but he took pains to keep everything between them light and easy.

"I'm just about down to my last toothpick so I guess that means you've cleaned me out," she said.

"I might be persuaded to stake you a little more if you want to keep going," he said.

"And end up having my kneecaps broken by your little toothpick loan sharks? I don't think so, Major."

He laughed a low, rich laugh she was quickly coming to adore.

He was doing his best to keep her mind off her lingering worry by distraction. So far it had been a remarkably effective strategy. Not perfect, but nearly so.

"Who taught you to play poker so well?" she asked him. "Did you learn from your Army buddies?"

He shook his head with a grin. "That would be Cisco.

He never met a game of chance he didn't like. Craps, dice, whatever. Our favorite game was called Bull, er, shoot. Have you played it?"

"Is that where you hold a card faceup on your forehead and no one can see his own card but you can see what everyone else has?"

He smiled. "Nope. That one is called Guts. The game I'm talking about is also called Cheat."

"Oh, that's appropriate. I can see why you liked it."

He gave her a mock glare. "I didn't cheat! Tonight, anyway. But the whole object of Cheat is to lie your way through. You deal the whole deck and then you take turns with every player discarding all their cards by rank in order from aces down. Whether you really have that number of cards or not, you BS your way through. Too bad it doesn't work very well with only two people. Cisco, Quinn, Easton and I would play for hours. Cisco could beat all of us, just about every time."

She adjusted to a more comfortable position on the sofa. "Why's that?"

"Well, Quinn was always too busy trying to count the cards so he could figure out who was lying and Easton had some really obvious tells. She would tug the ends of her hair when she was trying to bull us. To this day, she doesn't realize she does it."

Easton again. She swallowed her frown. She was growing tired of the other woman's name. "You must all have been good friends."

He shuffled the cards with great dexterity. "We were more than friends. I guess you could say we were more like brothers, or the closest thing to it."

"Easton's not a boy." She had to point out the obvious.

He smiled. "No, but she thought she was. She was a real tomboy and loved to follow us around. We didn't mind. She was a cute kid."

"The others—Cisco and Quinn—did they live close by?"

"Sort of." He was quiet for a long moment. "We all lived together at a ranch just down the canyon. Winder Ranch. We were in foster care there."

"Foster care?" She forgot all about the cards and her hands tightened so much on Simone that the dog jumped off her lap in a huff and moved to Brant's lap. "But you told me you grew up here."

"I said I lived here for the most part. That means until I was twelve. Then the neighbors took me in because of…problems here."

"Problems?"

He looked as if he regretted saying anything. "I told you about my brother dying. Nothing was the same after that. My parents both drank afterward and then my mom ran off and things got worse. I guess you could say things around here hit rock bottom and a neighbor couple took me in. They already had one foster son, Quinn Southerland. I was only there a few months before they found Cisco Del Norte living by himself in a stolen tent in the mountains after his dad died. After that, we were inseparable. The Four Winds, Jo called us, because of our names."

"Southerland, Del Norte, Western. Easton's the fourth?"

He smiled, even after Simone did her favorite little lap-hopping thing and jumped onto him. "Right. She was the Winders' niece who lived on the ranch with her parents since her dad was foreman. She was more like a little sister to us. Still is."

Sister. He considered Easton a sister.

"She's not your girlfriend, then?"

"Easton? No way!" He was quiet for a moment. "Truth is, I've always suspected she and Cisco have feelings for each other but neither of them has ever said anything about it and I don't want to go there."

Mimi suddenly decided she liked the other woman much better.

"The four of us got into so much trouble," he went on. "You wouldn't believe it. Sneaking out for midnight fishing trips into the mountains, taking the horses when we weren't supposed to, playing pranks on the home-coming dance committee."

"You hellions."

He flashed her a wry look. "We were. Though I will say, I usually tried to be the voice of reason and managed to talk the others out of almost everything immoral or illegal."

"So you were the boring one," she teased.

"True enough." He paused. "I probably tried a little too hard to be perfect so Jo and Guff wouldn't have any reason to change their minds about giving me a home."

Her heart ached for the boy he must have been. "But you didn't want to be perfect, did you?"

Her guess surprised another laugh out of him. "No. I wanted to be like Cisco. He wasn't afraid of anything. He could talk his way out of just about any kind of trouble that came along. Still can, for that matter."

"Does he live around here?"

His eyes clouded a little. "No. He hasn't since he was eighteen. He's in Latin America somewhere."

"What does he do there?"

"He's pretty closemouthed about it. I have a few guesses but I don't know for sure. To be honest, I'm not sure I want to know."

"Something illegal or immoral?"

"Possibly," he said, with wariness in his voice, and she didn't press him.

"And the other one? Southerland?"

"Quinn." He smiled with genuine affection. "Right now he's in Costa Rica on his honeymoon. Remember, we were talking about his wedding the other day with Easton? He married a girl we knew in high school, Tess Jamison. She's actually expecting a baby, too."

He made a face. "Sorry, I didn't mean to run on. I imagine life around here must seem pretty provincial compared to private Swiss boarding school and holidays in Monaco."

She sipped at the hot cocoa he'd brought her earlier, which was now, unfortunately, lukewarm. "The boarding school was outside Paris, actually, and we generally summered in Cannes."

"A far cry from Pine Gulch, Idaho. You must be bored to tears playing five-card stud and listening to my meanderings down memory lane."

"Not at all," she admitted. "If you want to know the truth, I've been thinking how lucky you are."

"Lucky?" He looked astonished. "Because my brother died and my mom ran off and my dad was a drunk who liked to use his fists a little too much on his surviving kid?"

"Not about that. That part is horrible."

She couldn't imagine it, actually. Though her father

had been arrogant and distant, she'd never worried he would physically hurt her.

"I just meant this place. Cold Creek. There's a serenity here. I can't explain it. And you had all these people you love to share it with."

"You didn't have anyone?"

She shifted restlessly on the sofa. "Of course. I refuse to play the poor little rich girl card. I had a life of privilege beyond what most people can even imagine. I know that. Yachts. Penthouse apartments. Private jets. I hate to admit this, but I didn't fly a commercial airplane until the first time I snuck out of boarding school when I was nine, after I bought my own plane ticket back to New York out of my allowance."

"You flew by yourself from Paris to New York when you were nine?"

She shrugged. "It was the Christmas holidays and I wanted nothing more than to be home. My father was newly married again. Number four, I think. Jemma, the wife before Gwen—and they were expecting a baby right after Christmas and they didn't want me there in the middle of the happy event. Turns out my half brother Jack was born on Christmas Eve, just a few hours before I showed up at our apartment in the city. My father wasn't pleased to see me. Neither was Jemma, needless to say, but I adored Jack. Still do, for that matter. Of all the half and step-siblings, he's my favorite."

She smiled a little, thinking of her half brother. He had inherited his mother's looks and their father's brain, a formidable combination.

He was going to be a wonderful uncle to her baby, if Jemma let him see Mimi. But then, he was almost eighteen and his mother wouldn't have much of a choice in the matter.

"You said the wife before Gwen. She was your step-mother? Why didn't she ever say anything?" He looked rather dazed at the idea.

"Gwen considered her brief marriage a huge mistake. She was the only one of my father's wives who voluntarily left him. He dumped all the others."

"Nice."

"If Jack is my favorite sibling, Gwen is my favorite ex-stepmother."

"How many do you have?"

She had to think about it. "Four exes and one current, who at least has longevity. Marta has been married to Werner for going on eight years, which is something of a record for him."

"What about your mother?"

"She died when I was three. I barely remember her. I'd like to think she was the love of his life and he married all the others to assuage his broken heart. But then, I'd like to believe strawberry cheesecake isn't really fattening, either."

She was quiet for a moment. The only sounds in the room were Simone's snuffly breathing on his lap and the low crackling of the fire in the stove.

"None of them was horrible, Cinderella-grade step-mother material or anything, but they mostly just tolerated me. Gwen was the best. She never once made me feel like I was in the way."

"In contrast to your father."

She looked away from that perceptive blue-eyed gaze. "I never said that."

"You didn't have to say it. I'm good at picking up

on the unspoken. It's a handy skill when you're dealing with military command."

"Well, I'm afraid you missed the target here by a mile, soldier."

"Did I?"

She made a big production of arranging the throw over her feet as she mulled how to answer him. Lying seemed silly, suddenly, when he already knew more about her than anyone else.

She had been raised to be cautious of talking about herself. After several so-called friends had turned out to be tipping off the paparazzi to her every move, Mimi had a tough time trusting people.

But somehow she knew Brant would never sell her out to the tabloids. He was a good man. If she had any doubt about that, he had proved his worth today at the clinic when he had sat by her side the entire time, despite his obvious discomfort.

She didn't know how she would ever repay him for that kindness.

"What do you know about Werner Van Hoyt?" she asked.

"Not much, really. Only that he's a brilliant real estate investor and the force behind most of the movers and shakers in Hollywood."

"He's also abrasive and overbearing and treats everyone in his life from his current wife to his various children to the damn pool boy with that same detached indifference, as if we were all interchangeable cuff links."

"And so you compensate by jumping from scandal to scandal in the hopes that you can ruffle his calm a little and make him notice that one of his cuff links doesn't quite match."

She had a wild urge to pull the blanket over her head to protect her psyche from that steady gaze of his.

"Aren't you the smart one?" she finally said. "It took me three years on a therapist's couch to pick that up."

"I've only known you a few days," he said, "but I think you're smarter than you let the world see."

She flashed him a look under her lashes, wondering if he was being sarcastic, but he only continued watching her steadily.

"About some things," she muttered. "Relationships, not so much. I'm pretty stupid about those."

He leaned back. "Does the little squirt's father fit in that *stupid* category?"

"He's right at the top of the list." She sighed, knowing she was going to have to tell him, if not all the truth, at least some of it. He deserved that much for standing by her all day.

"The baby's father won't be in the picture. He's… unavailable."

"Married?"

"Not yet, but soon. That doesn't make it better, I know."

He continued watching her steadily, and she traced a finger along the fringed edge of the afghan, avoiding his gaze. "When I told him I was pregnant, he automatically assumed I would take care of the *little problem,* as he termed it, so he could continue on with his big plans to live happily ever after with someone else. He was not very happy when I told him I wanted to keep the baby."

He was quiet for a long moment. "He's the stupid son of a bitch, then, not you."

She laughed a little but then saw by the hardness of his jaw that he was completely serious and something warm and sweet fluttered through her.

"He is. And you know what, he doesn't matter."

He didn't, she realized. Somehow, today, amidst her frantic fear for the child, Marco's harsh words, his fury with her, had become completely unimportant. Her priorities had shifted and rearranged themselves and now all she wanted was for her baby to be healthy.

"I want this baby. And I'm going to be a darn good mother."

He smiled. "I don't doubt it for a minute."

His words soaked through her like spring rains on a parched desert. She hadn't realized how desperately she had needed someone to believe in her until Brant spoke but she suddenly felt tears prickle behind her eyes.

"Hey. Don't cry."

"I'm sorry. It's just…been quite a day."

Before she realized what he intended, he moved beside her on the couch and pulled her into his arms. "You've been a trooper, Mimi. You've been strong and courageous and done everything the doc told you to do. You're going to be a wonderful mother."

He kissed her, something she sensed he meant only as a gesture of affection and maybe respect.

But as his mouth touched hers, firm and strong, she was astonished as tenderness surged through her. She felt surrounded by him, safe and warm and comforted, somehow.

She tightened her arms around his neck, eyes closed as she memorized the scent of him, masculine and enticing. She didn't want to move from this place. She wanted to stay right here beside him feeling each breath against her skin, with the heat of him soaking through her and this fragile tenderness taking root in the empty corners of her heart.

Eventually he pulled away, looking slightly dazed. "You need your rest. Come on, I'll help you to your room."

He would have carried her again but she insisted on walking.

"I'll put Simone out one last time and then bring her to you when she's ready to settle down," he said when they reached her door.

"Thank you."

"Good night, Mimi." He pressed his lips to her forehead again and she felt something dangerous shift and slide inside her heart.

After she closed the door, she leaned against it, her thoughts tangled.

She was in serious trouble here. Once on holiday in Sicily she had climbed Mount Etna and had stood teetering on the edge, her nerves jangling and her heart racing.

She felt exactly like that right now, as if she stood peering into the abyss. She was in grave danger of falling for Brant, tumbling headlong into love with a tall, serious Army Ranger with solemn eyes and a deep core of decency. She had thought herself in love before, but all those other emotions paled in comparison to what she feared she could feel for Brant.

She couldn't love him. Whatever it took, she had to protect her heart. Right now her focus had to be her baby. She couldn't afford to waste her energy and time on a man who was unsuitable and unavailable.

No matter how much she might want him.

Chapter 9

He had to get the hell out of here.

Two days after Mimi fell off the ladder, Brant stirred the coals in the woodstove, then tossed another log on the red embers.

Behind him, he could hear another Alfred Hitchcock movie starting on the movie channel they'd been watching all day and he closed his eyes, not sure if he was man enough to endure the temptation of sitting beside Mimi for another two hours, with her sweet, delicate scent teasing his senses and her famous green eyes sparkling brightly and her wide smile clutching at his heart.

For two days, they had played games, had laughed at Simone's antics, had pored through the stack of baby books Mimi had squirreled away in her stacks of luggage.

This morning, one of the movie channels was having a Hitchcock marathon. They had watched *The Birds* and *Psycho* and next up was *Vertigo*. He wasn't sure he was up for that one, since he was entirely too dizzy around her as it was.

He had been very careful not to kiss her again, fearful that once he started he wouldn't be able to stop.

He needed a little distance from her or he was very much afraid he would find himself slipping headfirst down some dangerous slope with her and be unable to clamber back to safe ground.

The trouble was, he didn't want to leave. He loved her company. Mimi was clever and fun and wholeheartedly embraced everything she did, whether that was playing Monopoly or throwing a toy for her dog or curling up, completely engrossed in an old movie.

Before he'd come to know her these past few days, he might have expected the tabloid version of Mimi Van Hoyt to be petulant and resentful at her enforced inactivity. He could easily have envisioned temper tantrums and hysterics.

Instead, she was sweet and funny and showed a surprising gratitude toward everything he did, whether it was handing her another pillow or bringing her a grilled cheese sandwich and bowl of canned soup for lunch or just putting her little furball outside when Simone had to take care of business.

He was entirely too drawn to this Mimi and for the first time he could remember, he wasn't looking forward to returning to duty. If he could have dragged this time out longer, he would have tried to figure out a way, but he knew he only had three days left here before he flew out.

He only needed a little perspective, he thought. He had spent just about every waking moment of the last two days with Mimi. Once he was away from her, he would be able to shift his priorities where they should be. The Army had been his life since he was eighteen years old, and a few magical days with a beautiful woman couldn't shake that.

Through the glass door of the woodstove, he watched the flames lick at the log and Brant decided this would be a good time to escape, while the opening credits of the next movie had just started to roll.

"Go ahead and watch this one without me. I'm going to go feed the animals and check on Gwen's place, then I'll come back inside and fix some dinner for us."

Mimi didn't answer him and he turned around to find she was asleep, her long dark lashes fanning those high cheekbones and one arm tucked around Simone, who was curled up beside her on the sofa.

The little white bichon frise opened one black eye when she felt Brant's scrutiny and he could swear she grinned at him.

Yeah, he figured he'd be grinning, too, if he were snuggled up against all that warmth and softness.

One of Mimi's dark curls had drifted across her cheek and he reached a hand to push it out of the way, then froze, his hand extended.

He had to get out of here. Now, before he did something inordinately stupid like sit down beside her, pull her against him and wake her by kissing that delectable mouth. He had to go, even if that only meant escaping to the barn for a while.

Leaving the television buzzing softly, he moved with as much stealth as he could muster to the mudroom off the kitchen, where his winter gear hung.

A few moments later, he was outside in the icy air.

The sun was setting in a blaze of orange and purple and the ranch glowed with that particularly beautiful slant of winter light that turned everything rosy and soft.

When he reached the barn, he turned back to look at the ranch house, sprawling and unpretentious in the sunset.

Even in the worst years, when his family life had been in tatters, he had loved the house and the ranch, with the creek running just a short distance away and the mountains a solid, reassuring presence in the background.

He had dreaded coming home during those years when his father had turned cruel and bitter but he had never blamed the ranch for that. Even in the worst of it, he still hadn't wanted to leave. Guff Winder practically had to drag him away and those first few months at Winder Ranch he had cried himself to sleep just about every night after Quinn was asleep in the room they'd shared.

Eventually he had settled into the routine of life with the Winders and having an instant older brother and then Cisco a few months later. The six years he spent at Winder Ranch were the most peaceful of his life.

Peace.

He remembered Mimi saying she felt peace and serenity at the ranch. As he gazed at his home, he realized that was the indefinable emotion that seeped through him when he was with her.

She soothed him, in a way he couldn't explain. He let out a long breath. That made absolutely no sense but here in the pure clarity of dusk, he didn't see how he could deny it.

He had come home for leave with an aching heart,

guilty and grieving at his own failures that had cost good men their lives. He knew he would always regret the ambush, that he hadn't trusted his instincts that something was wrong, but these days with Mimi had distracted him from brooding over it. When he was with her, he could release the pain of regret for a little while and focus on the gift of the moment.

He sighed. What good was it to get away from her physically by coming outside if he couldn't shake her from his mind? With renewed determination, he headed into the barn, resolved to focus on the mundane for a while.

An hour later, he had finished the regular chores and was busy at the woodpile, replenishing Gwen's supply of split logs, when he heard the sound of a vehicle approaching the house.

Easton had said she would stop by sometime tonight or tomorrow. Assuming it was her, he set the split log carefully on the stack, then headed around the corner of the house just in time to find Jake Dalton holding open the passenger door of an SUV and reaching inside to help his wife climb out.

The tenderness of Jake's concern for Maggie warmed Brant. She deserved a safe haven after the hell she'd been through and it looked as if she had found it.

He reached them just before they headed up the stairs. "Hey, Doc. Maggie," he said with a smile.

"Hey, you." Maggie smiled back. "How's our patient?"

"She's had a pretty calm time the last few days. No more cramps. She was sleeping when I came outside an hour ago."

"Just what she needs to be doing," Jake said. "I'll go check on her, if you don't mind."

"Go ahead," Brant said.

Before Jake went inside, he sent Maggie a look loaded with meaning that flew right past Brant.

"Come on inside," he said. "Do you need help up the stairs?"

She shook her head. "I get around pretty well these days. Stairs don't bug me nearly as much as they used to."

To prove the truth of her words, she moved up the porch steps with smooth, easy movements.

Inside, he expected her to follow her husband immediately to Mimi, but she grabbed his arm in the entryway.

"So Mimi's doing better. How about you?"

He flashed her a searching look, wondering at the concern in her eyes. "Fine. I'm not the patient here."

"Easton told me you've had a rough time in Afghanistan in the last month. That you lost some friends."

He sighed. He hadn't intended to say anything to anyone about the failed mission, but Easton had cornered him the night before the wedding and wiggled it out of him.

"Easton's got a big mouth."

"You know East. She worries about you. But she's not talking around town about you, I promise. She wouldn't have even mentioned it to me, I think, except we bumped into each other at the grocery store. I think she thought I might have some insight into the situation because of, well, my past. She was worried about you since you seemed more stoic than usual. Which is saying something, by the way."

He didn't want to talk about this right now, but he didn't know how to avoid it. He could understand why Easton would think Maggie had a special perspective on the situation after her own military experience and losing her leg in Afghanistan.

"I'm doing okay. Things have been...better the last few days." That was as close as he would come to admitting that Mimi had helped him, without even knowing it.

"What happened? She didn't know details."

"Ambush in a little village in the Paktika Province. I was supposed to meet a high-level contact who insisted on giving his information only to a high-ranking officer. We had intel that the village where the meet was supposed to take place was safe, so I picked twelve of my best men to come with me. The intel was wrong."

He had a memory flash of shouts and screams, civilians caught in the middle of what turned into an intense fight for their lives. "We drove straight into it. My team fought back but in the firefight, three good men died."

"Did you do anything wrong?" she finally asked.

He sighed. Trust Maggie to hit the heart of the matter. "Strategically and militarily, no. I followed protocol to the letter and we had duplicate intelligence that said the area had been cleared of insurgents and any IEDs. But I should have listened to my gut. My instincts were telling me the situation was off, that the contact wasn't trustworthy, and I ignored them."

Her features were soft with a compassion he didn't want to see right now. "And of course you're blaming yourself for the deaths of your men."

His throat felt tight but he ruthlessly crammed the emotions down. "Of course. Wouldn't you?"

She was silent for a long moment and then she reached between them and squeezed his hand. "My first month in Kabul, I cried myself to sleep every night, until you and Nate came to visit me. Do you remember that?"

"I do." He somehow managed a smile, though it wasn't easy. He and Nate Cavazos, a fellow Ranger and Pine Gulch native, hadn't been in the same company but both happened to be deployed in Afghanistan at the same time as Maggie and they'd been able to coordinate leave so they could all meet up a few times.

"Do you remember what you said to me? 'Mag, if being here doesn't scare the hell out of you, then something's wrong with your head.' And you told me only an idiot would be too afraid to talk to somebody when they were hurting or scared. I finally confessed to my commanding officer how terrified I was and he was able to say all the right things to help me through it. I never would have gone to him if you hadn't nudged me in that direction. So I'm going to throw your words back at you. Don't be an idiot, okay? I know you only have a few days before you head back, but if you need to talk, you know where I am."

"Right."

"Nate's here, too, you know. You could talk to him if you'd rather."

"Yeah, I drove past him the other day while he was shoveling snow out at the old Hirschi place but it was the day I brought Mimi to the clinic so I didn't have a chance to talk. How's he doing?"

Brant knew Nate's world had changed radically six months earlier when his sister and her husband had died, leaving him guardian of his two nieces. He'd left the military to take up his responsibilities and Brant had been meaning to catch up with him ever since.

"Did you know he's getting married?" Maggie asked.

"Really?"

"Yes, to a woman from Virginia who stayed at his guest ranch over Christmas."

"No kidding? I hadn't heard."

She grinned, looking very much like the girl he remembered from school. "Then you also don't know the truly juicy gossip."

"Do tell," he said dryly.

"Turns out his guest—and now his fiancée—is actually Hank Dalton's illegitimate daughter."

"Poor thing."

Just about everybody in Pine Gulch had hated Hank Dalton, Jake's father—Maggie most of all.

But instead of agreeing with him, she only smacked his shoulder. "Since Hank's been dead for years, Emery gets all the benefits of being a Dalton without having to ever deal with him. Wade, Jake and Seth are over the moon to have a sister after all these years. You should have seen them all yelling and carrying on when she and Nate came over with the girls on New Year's Eve to tell everyone."

"I'm sorry I missed that."

Instead of spending New Year's surrounded by neighbors and the scents of home, he had been in Afghanistan planning a mission that would end up taking his friends' lives.

Unexpectedly, as if sensing his train of thought, Maggie reached to give him a hug and he felt those emotions jumble together inside him all over again. "You'll be okay, Brant. Just give it time."

"Thanks, Mag."

"Anytime, Major." She stepped away. "Enough of that. Let's go see how your patient's doing."

As she walked toward the family room with barely a limp, he thought he would like to have even a small portion of Maggie's courage and strength to face his own battles.

Dr. Dalton removed his stethoscope from her abdomen and pulled Mimi's sweater back down to cover her skin. "A strong and healthy heartbeat. I can't make any promises, but so far everything looks normal. Perfect, even. I have high hopes that you'll have an uneventful pregnancy from here on out."

A weight she hadn't realized had been pressing down on her heart for two days seemed to lift at his words.

"Oh, thank you. Thank you so much," she exclaimed just as the doctor's lovely dark-haired wife walked in with Brant.

Mimi wasn't really aware of doing it but she must have reached for Major Western's hand. He was at her side in an instant.

"Brant, Dr. Dalton says the baby still has a healthy heartbeat," she said. "For now, everything is okay with the pregnancy. Since I've had no more cramping, he thinks we might be past the immediate danger."

Relief washed across his clean-cut, handsome features. "That's wonderful news."

To her surprise, he hugged her and she returned the embrace, giddy joy bursting through her.

As she lifted her head, she caught a raised-eyebrow sort of look pass between Dr. Dalton and his wife. With considerable chagrin, she realized she and Brant were acting more like a happy couple than the casual acquaintances they should have been.

Her heart ached with the knowledge that she didn't

want to be only casual acquaintances with him, especially after these magical few days. She wanted so much more from him, even though she knew the dream was impossible.

She eased away from the embrace and forced herself to turn back to the physician. "I can't thank you enough for coming out to check on things. I thought house calls went the way of rotary phones and beehive hairdos."

"We're still a little old-fashioned here in Pine Gulch when necessary," Dr. Dalton said.

"Well, I'm very indebted to you both."

She didn't know how she would repay them but she would figure out a way. Perhaps a generous donation to their clinic so they could continue the practice Brant told her about of providing free or reduced care twice a month to patients without health insurance.

"Thank you," she repeated, though the words seemed woefully inadequate.

"I was just about to heat up some lasagna from the freezer for dinner if you two have time to stick around," Brant said.

"We can't," Maggie said regretfully. "The kids have been at Caroline and Wade's all afternoon playing with their cousins and we need to get them home. Thank you for the offer, though."

"You're welcome. Thanks for stopping by. I owe you," Brant said.

"Remember what I said," Maggie murmured to Brant, piquing Mimi's curiosity. "Don't be an idiot."

His mouth lifted in a small smile. "More than usual, you mean? I appreciate the advice, Mag."

She hugged him tightly then kissed his cheek. "If

we don't see you again before you ship out, take care of yourself over there, Major."

"I'll do my best," he answered, then shook Dr. Dalton's hand before walking them to the door.

Everyone liked Brant, she realized. There was something so reassuring about him and that air of competence and quiet integrity about him. She wanted to just curl up against him and let him take care of all her troubles. Did others sense it, too?

"What was Maggie talking to you about so seriously?" she asked when he returned to the living room. "What did she think you were being an idiot about?"

The muscle worked in his jaw. "She thinks I'm on edge because of what happened to my men."

"Are you?"

"I'm fine," he said abruptly. "I'm going to go heat up the lasagna. I think I've got some rolls in the freezer. I'll grab some of those, too."

She didn't like the shuttered look on his features or the way he seemed so careful about avoiding her gaze, but if he preferred to confide in Maggie Dalton, Mimi couldn't do anything about it.

Dinner turned out to be an awkward affair, something she wouldn't have expected at all after the easy camaraderie they'd slipped into the past two days.

Brant was mostly silent, though he ate with the single-minded energy she had come to realize was probably characteristic of a battlefield warrior who wasn't certain when he would find his next meal.

After dinner, she played with Simone for a while, running through the little dog's limited bag of tricks. The dog seemed to have picked up on the tension between the two of them. She was restless, sniffing in all the corners of the room and insisting on going out three or four times until Brant finally picked her up and stood by the window, petting her and looking out into the night.

"Want to watch something?" Mimi asked. "Or you could give me a chance to win back my fortune in toothpicks."

He shook his head and returned to his window-gazing. When he finally turned back, his features were tight, his mouth a hard, implacable line.

She thought he was angry at something, until she saw his eyes and she had to catch her breath at the anguish there.

"I told you that a month ago three of my men were killed in a botched operation."

"Yes."

He let out a long breath, as if all the air in his lungs had turned sour. "I didn't tell you it was my fault they were killed."

"Oh, Brant. I'm sure that's not true. You were doing your job."

"I was. But I put them in that village. I ordered them there as my security detail. I should have sensed we were heading straight into an ambush."

She didn't know what to say, how to comfort him. What did she know about warriors and their demons? But she sensed he needed to talk and she could provide that, if nothing else.

"Maggie told me I should talk to someone about what I've been going through. She thinks that will help me work it out in my head. I want to just forget everything but…somehow it seems important that you know."

She held her breath as she heard the emotion behind his words. He was not a man who leaned on others willingly. She sensed it without any real evidence to back it up, yet he wanted to share his grief and sorrow with her.

Why? She was flighty Mimi Van Hoyt, jumping from scandal to scandal and crisis to crisis. What would he possibly think she could offer that might help him?

But he was trusting her with this. She was important enough to him that he wanted her to know the things that were troubling him.

The weight of that trust burned inside her. She mattered to him and she couldn't bear the idea of letting him down.

"I haven't been sleeping well since the ambush. Things have been…rough." He gave her a long look she couldn't quite interpret. "Until you came along."

"What do you mean?"

"I don't know why. There's no logical explanation. But since you've been here, everything seems…easier."

She stared at him, heat fluttering through her. How was she supposed to respond to that? She didn't have the first idea what to say. Acting purely on instinct, she crossed the room to where he stood by the window, looking out at the black winter night. She took Simone from his arms and set the dog on the carpet, where she sniffed her disapproval but trotted to the rug by the fire as Mimi took her place, wrapping her arms around him.

After a surprised moment, Brant yanked her against him and wrapped her tightly in his arms, burying his face in her neck.

"I'm so, so sorry, Brant. For you, for those men, for their families left behind. But take it from someone who has spent her life screwing up in one form or another, you did nothing wrong here. I don't know anything about it. But I know you and I'm certain you were doing your job to the best of your ability. I am also certain not one of those men who died would have acted differently if they had been the one making the decision."

He held on for a long time and she could feel his ragged breathing against her skin.

She didn't know how long they stood that way in a silence broken only by Simone's snuffly breathing and the fire's low crackling.

That tenderness she had first recognized earlier pulsed through her and she pressed her cheek against his chest, listening to his heartbeat while his warm breath stirred her hair.

She thought it the most natural thing in the world some time later when his mouth found hers, as inevitable as the tide and the moonrise and the spring thaw.

Chapter 10

His mouth was firm and strong on hers and she leaned into him, relishing the solid heat of him. He tasted of cinnamon and mocha and Brant, and she couldn't get enough.

The world outside the walls of this modest ranch-house could be a scary place, full of pain and war and betrayals, but right now none of that mattered. In Brant's arms, she was safe.

His hand caressed her cheek with a sweetness and gentleness that nearly had her bursting into tears. In all her twenty-six years, not a single, solitary soul had ever looked at her like Brant was gazing at her, as if she meant the world to him

"You're so lovely," he murmured. "More beautiful than any picture in any magazine. I sometimes look at you and can't believe you're real."

He cared about her. She saw the tenderness in his

eyes, sensed it in his kiss. He wasn't simply trying to claim bragging rights that he'd been with Mimi Van Hoyt, as so many other men had tried, for some kind of a notch in his holster or whatever weapon an officer in the Army Rangers would carry.

Brant had feelings for her. A soft, seductive warmth bloomed inside of her, like the ice plants along the shore unfurling at the first morning rays of the sun, and she wanted to stay here all night and bask in it.

"I'm very real," she murmured. It seemed vitally important that he understand. "Everything else, the magazine covers and everything, that's the illusion."

She wrapped her arms around his neck and pulled his mouth to hers. This was real too, his kiss and the emotions swirling around them, the tenderness that engulfed them.

She was vaguely aware of him moving back to the sofa and pulling her across his lap, of his hands warm and sure under her sweater, of the rasp of his evening stubble on her skin, the solid strength of him against her.

They kissed for a long time, until they were both breathing hard and she burned brighter than the flames in the woodstove.

"We have to stop," he finally said, his voice ragged.

"Why?"

He pressed his forehead to hers. "Two days ago you nearly lost a baby. As much as I want you right now, I don't think the timing is the greatest."

"Dr. Dalton gave me the green light to resume normal activities," she reminded him, trying to keep the pleading note from her voice.

His mouth quirked into that sexy smile she adored. "I think we both know that when this happens between us—and it *will* happen between us—it's going to be anything but normal."

Heat scorched her cheeks, even as his words sparked an answering tug of desire.

"You need to rest if you're going to take care of that baby."

His big, square-tipped fingers covered her abdomen and she felt the heat of him through the knit of her sweater as he touched her gently.

Just like that, the blasted pregnancy hormones kicked in and those ever-lurking tears pricked behind her eyelids.

Oh, how she wished she had chosen someone like Brant to be her baby's father. Someone good and strong and honorable. Not someone *like* him, she amended. There was no one like him. She wished she had waited for Brant himself, the kind of man who would treasure her and their child, who would be eager to step up and take responsibility for the life they had created together.

Marco's harsh words echoed in her ears. *"Your problem...take care of it... I won't let you ruin my life because you're too stupid to take a damn pill."*

He acted as if their brief affair had been entirely Mimi's fault, as if she had tied him to the bed and seduced him.

"Let me know when you've taken care of it," he had ordered. "I'm marrying Jess, Mimi. You know that. This little *oops* of yours changes nothing. What we had was thrilling and exciting, sure. You're Mimi Van Hoyt. But we both knew it was only temporary and that I always had Jessalyn waiting."

He wanted her to take care of it and she would, just not the way Marco intended. Mimi would raise her child and love her and never, *ever* make her feel overlooked or unwanted.

And she would always regret that she hadn't waited for a man like Brant, someone who would cherish their child, who would toss her into the air and read bedtime stories and teach her how to ride a bicycle.

But as usual, she had screwed everything up.

"What's wrong?" he murmured.

She couldn't tell him, of course. He would think she was ridiculous, or worse, that she wanted him to rush in and rescue her from her mistakes.

"Just tired, that's all. I feel like I'm always tired."

He kissed her forehead and stood up from the sofa with her still in his arms, a feat of sheer muscle she doubted any other man of her acquaintance could manage.

"You should be sleeping. Come on, then. Let's get you to bed."

She didn't want to leave the shelter of his arms, where she could pretend even for a little while that this was anything but a deliciously sweet dream.

She wrapped her arms around his neck as he carried her down the hall to her bedroom. He set her on the bed, then kissed her again with breathtaking gentleness. "You and I need to have a long talk in the morning, when we've both got clearer heads."

"About what?"

"I've got five months left in Afghanistan. I hope I'm back before the baby's born and then it's looking like there's a chance I'll be stationed at Los Alamitos on a special assignment for a while. That's not so far from L.A. We can figure this out, Mimi. We will."

Unease clutched at her heart but she ignored it and

forced herself to smile. Couldn't she let herself be carried along in the dream for a little while longer?

"Good night."

He gave her that rare smile she found so unbearably appealing then closed the door quietly behind him.

Mimi sat on the bed long after he'd left, her emotions a wild tangle and a hundred thoughts chasing themselves around her head.

One of those emotions clamored to the fore, drowning out all the others.

She was in love with Brant.

Completely. Irreversibly.

Of all her ridiculous stunts, the scandals and the gossip and the poor decision-making, falling for an honorable, decent man had to be right near the top.

How could she have been so foolish? She was in the worst possible place in her life to fall in love. She was pregnant and alone and scared, on the brink of the biggest publicity nightmare her father could ever imagine.

The father of her baby was marrying someone else first thing tomorrow morning, for heaven's sake.

And yet in typical Mimi style, somehow she had complicated everything by falling head over heels in love with a solemn special forces officer who had a deep core of honor running through him.

Worse even than her own insanity was the terrifying fact that this decent, honorable man was cracked enough to think he might actually want some kind of future with *her*.

How insane was that? The tabloid princess and the war hero. The paparazzi would be euphoric.

She flopped back onto the bed, palms pressed over her eyes as nausea slicked through her.

The moment her pregnancy started to manifest itself, the entire celebrity press corps would be orgasmic trying to figure out who the father was. If she and Marco had succeeded in squelching any rumors about their liaison— and she had to believe they had, since not even a whisper had come out—attention would then shift to whomever she showed up with next.

Maybe she could hide out here at Western Sky for the next six months and then just tell people she had pulled a Madonna and secretly gone to some third world country to adopt a baby.

Nobody would buy it. Every corner of her life would be scrutinized.

She couldn't allow Brant to be dragged into the ugliness of her world, into that morass of endless cameras and shouting questions and rampant speculation about every minute detail of her personal life.

She'd been in the spotlight since she turned sixteen, when some intrepid photographer with a long lens had first snapped a picture of her sunbathing topless on her father's yacht in the Mediterranean.

She despised the constant attention, though she had to admit she had utilized it on occasion to tweak her father about something or other. She'd been in car chases with the paparazzi, she'd found them digging through her garbage and peeking in her windows.

How could she drag Brant into that world? She would destroy him, would take all that was good and right about him and ensnarl him in the sordid circus of her world.

She couldn't do that to him.

She loved him too much.

Those damn tears burned behind her eyes again and this time she couldn't stop one from trickling down.

She would have to leave. What other choice did she have? If she didn't break things off with him in a way that left no doubt in his mind that she didn't want to further their relationship, she had a powerful suspicion he would stubbornly continue trying to rush to her rescue. That was the sort of man he was.

But if she extricated herself from his world now, he would soon forget about this little interlude in his life. He would return to his career, to his life, to his dedication in the soldiers who served under him.

No one would ever connect him to Mimi Van Hoyt and her baby with the mysterious paternity.

She hated the very idea of it. But wouldn't it be far better to make a clean break now rather than later, after she had sucked him into her world, exposed him to the paparazzi, tarnished all that goodness?

Something bright and hopeful in her heart seemed to shrivel as she picked up her cell phone.

She turned it on, the first time she had bothered since she arrived at the ranch and she found more than a dozen texts and voicemail messages waiting for her.

Probably the vast majority of them were from Verena, her personal assistant. She was too cynical to hope any of them might be from her father. She could drop off the grid for months and the most intense emotion Werner would allow himself wouldn't be worry for his oldest child's safety but probably relief that Mimi was keeping her wild escapades out of the public eye for a while.

She didn't listen to any of the messages before she went to her favorites list and hit Verena's cell phone number, right at the top, where Verena had programmed it for her since Mimi was apparently too stupid to do even that.

Her assistant answered before Mimi even heard a ring on the other end.

"Where are you?" Verena Dumond sounded as ruffled as Mimi had ever heard the hyperefficient woman. "I've been trying to reach you for days. You were supposed to call me when you reached Ms. Bianca's so that I knew you arrived safely. When I didn't hear from you, I tried calling both your number and Ms. Bianca's but have had no luck."

"It's a long story," Mimi said, a vast understatement if she had ever uttered one. Her life felt fundamentally changed from the person she had been the last time she saw Verena and she was exhausted suddenly just thinking about all that had happened.

"Listen, I've had a change of plans," she said. "I know I intended to stay for another few days but I've changed my mind. I need you to make travel arrangements for me to leave as soon as possible."

"Will you be returning to Malibu?"

Mimi mentally scanned her options. She absolutely didn't want to return to California until long after Marco and Jessalyn enjoyed their oh-so-romantic wedding. She couldn't go to New York, where her father spent most of his time.

She gazed out the window and saw that the snow was falling again, fluttery soft flakes that didn't look as if they would amount to much before morning.

"Some place warm," she decided. "Is the St. Thomas house available?"

"I'll find out."

"Do you know what, Verena? I don't really care where I go. Just somewhere without snow. And I want to take the Lear this time, if it can be arranged."

She had flown commercial on her way out to Gwen's because none of the private planes had been available and she hadn't wanted to wait. Beyond that, she'd had some silly idea about not letting her father know where she could be found—as if he wouldn't have wormed the information out of Verena if he'd genuinely cared to know.

"I'll see what I can do but it might take me a few hours to route the plane to Idaho," her assistant said.

"In the morning should be fine. Oh, and I'll need a car service. The rental vehicle you arranged had a bit of a mishap."

"Again?" There was only the slightest note of condemnation in Verena's well-trained voice but Mimi bristled. Okay, she was a little tough on rental vehicles. That's why one rented, wasn't it?

"This time I couldn't help it. I was caught in a blizzard and slid off the road into a ditch."

"Good gracious."

"I'm all right."

That wasn't necessarily the truth. Mimi had a feeling she wouldn't be all right for a long time. When she left this place, this man, she would leave behind a huge jagged section of her heart.

"You're still at Gwen's?"

"Um, not exactly. I'm at the ranch but Gwen had a gallery showing in Europe and she's not here. After my accident, her landlord was kind enough to let me stay at the main house. But the address is the same. The Western Sky in Cold Creek Canyon."

Verena was silent for a long moment. "I see," she finally said in a carefully bland voice that didn't fool Mimi for a second.

"It's not what you think," Mimi protested.

"I don't think anything. I'm not paid for that." Verena used her frostiest voice and Mimi frowned.

"V., cut it out. Major Western was kind enough to rescue me from a creek when the SUV slid off the road. He's been...really wonderful."

"Will we be compensating him for his trouble, then?"

She let out a breath. Brant would hate that. He was proud enough that perhaps offering him money in return for helping her just might be enough to turn that soft affection in his eyes into disgust.

"I haven't decided how I'll repay him yet."

"I'm sure you'll figure out a way."

Again, that slight, barely perceptible note of condemnation in Verena's voice scraped her nerves. What really sucked was that Mimi knew she deserved it. Verena reported directly to her father, who paid her salary, so Mimi had done her best over the years to exaggerate her misdeeds to the other woman. If she went on a date with a man, she turned her version of the evening into a three-day orgy.

At this point in her life, Mimi doubted anyone would believe she had only ever been with three men, including her first love when she was eighteen—a rookie pro basketball player who had been sweet and nervous, even after they had dated for several weeks, her one-time fiancé who turned out to be gay, and Marco.

No sense trying to undo an image she'd spent years creating. Not in one phone call, anyway. "I'd like to make an early start in the morning. No later than eight a.m."

"I believe I can make those arrangements."

"I have no doubt." Mimi paused, thinking of her years of resentment for Verena. Her handler, she'd always thought. Verena approved expenses, coordinated her schedule, worked with the rest of the staff at Mimi's Malibu and Bel Air houses, all while reporting every detail to Werner.

She might also have been a friend, if she hadn't been caught in the crossfire of the war between Mimi and her father.

"Verena, um, thank you. I…don't know what I would do without you."

After a long pause, Verena spoke, sounding uncharacteristically disconcerted. "You're welcome."

Mimi cut the connection and sat on the edge of the bed for a moment, her thoughts tangled.

If Verena, who knew Mimi probably better than anyone for the past five years, had such little respect and regard for her, how could she ever think she would be the sort of woman a man like Brant deserved?

She was right to leave, even if some small part of her was afraid she was making the biggest mistake of a life that had been chock-full of them.

Chapter 11

What ever happened to that pregnancy glow she was supposed to be enjoying right about now?

Early the next morning, Mimi frowned at her reflection in the round guest bathroom mirror of the Western Sky. Her eyes were puffy, her skin red and blotchy.

No big deal. She had concealer and foundation and a half-dozen pair of designer sunglasses she could wear to hide away from the world.

She hadn't slept more than a few hours in the night. Mostly she had lay curled up on the bed, cuddling Simone close to her and watching the moon shift past the window.

She had never wished she could be Maura Howard more than she did right now. Oh, how she wanted to be just an ordinary woman who went grocery shopping and bought her clothes at a chain store and filled her car with gas every payday.

Maura Howard was a school teacher or a nurse or a librarian. Someone kind and uncomplicated, with simple tastes and ordinary parents.

Brant deserved someone like that, without baggage like Mimi's, someone he wouldn't be ashamed to introduce around Pine Gulch, someone who would fit in with the other Four Winds as they sat around the kitchen table sharing memories and swapping stories.

But she wasn't Maura and she could never be. She supposed the real challenge ahead of her was to somehow learn how to be happy being Mimi, but right now she didn't know how that could happen.

She finished her makeup and pulled her hair back into a loose twist at the nape of her neck, then quietly packed the rest of her belongings.

Simone planted her little haunches by the suitcases and whined, giving Mimi a mournful sort of look.

"We have to go, baby," she whispered. "Staying longer will only make everything so much harder."

Simone yipped sharply as if she wanted to disagree and Mimi shot a quick, nervous glance toward the door, afraid Brant would knock any moment.

Her dearest wish right now was that they could slip away to avoid a confrontation with Brant. Yes, it was cowardly, but it would be far easier to just sneak out without having to provide explanations or excuses.

She held her breath as she heard steps outside her door and she prayed he wouldn't knock and see her suitcases piled by the door. To her vast relief, he walked away and a moment later she heard the outside door open and close.

No doubt he was heading out to take care of the horses. Judging by the past few days, she had a narrow window of less than an hour for the car service to come while he was otherwise occupied.

Verena had texted her that the car should be arriving close to eight, which was still ten minutes away, so Mimi let Simone out, keeping a careful eye on the barn while she waited and let the dog take care of her business.

As she stood on the backsteps to the ranchhouse, she soaked in one more view of the exquisite surroundings. She hoped so much that Brant would decide not to sell, despite the work she had put into sprucing up the place.

Whether he wanted to admit it or not, he needed the peace of this place. Even if he could only spend a few weeks here each year, this was his home. She had a powerful feeling that if he sold it, he would regret it for the rest of his life.

Simone finished up quickly and hurried back up the porch steps, as eager as Mimi to get out of the bitter cold.

She returned to the front room, keeping a nervous eye on the clock while she struggled to write some sort of note to Brant. Nothing seemed adequate so she simply wrote, "I had to go. We both know it's for the best. Thank you for everything. I'll never forget my time here."

She was just signing her name when she heard the approach of a vehicle and then the doorbell.

Oh, thank heavens. She propped the note on the kitchen table where he couldn't miss it and hurried to the front door, where her suitcases was already piled up.

"I have to put my dog in her crate but you can carry the rest of my luggage out—" Her words to what she thought was the car service driver died in her throat at the familiar strobe of cameras flashing, again and again and again.

Paparazzi, only a handful—maybe two still photographers and a couple of videographers. But here in the quiet of an Idaho winter's morning, it felt like a mass invasion.

Like an idiot, she couldn't think past her shock that they had found her, couldn't move as the questions started flying.

"Where you going, Mimi?"

"Is it true you had an ultrasound at a clinic in Pine Gulch? Are you pregnant, Mimi?"

"Who's the father, Mimi? Is it Prince Gregor?"

Panic flared through her, hot and bright. Jake and Maggie must have a leak in their office staff or one of their other patients must have seen her while she was there.

Whoever it was, someone had tipped off the rabid horde and thrown Mimi into the middle of a disaster.

Today was Marco's wedding. Couldn't they have waited one more day? Would some enterprising gossip columnist somehow make the connection she least wanted out?

Simone continued yipping. Mimi knew she needed to do something, say something, but she couldn't seem to make the connection work between her frenzied brain and the rest of her.

Just as she started to edge back into the house, a new unwelcome sound distracted her—the pounding of horse's hooves and harsh male voice rising above all the others.

"What the hell do you vultures think you're doing?"

Brant. She closed her eyes, fighting the urge to sit

on the steps and burst into sobs. He rode up like some kind of damned avenging angel, big and hard and dangerous, plowing the horse right through the middle of the small group of photographers, who had to quickly move out of his way before he mowed them all down. Of course, they didn't stop filming for a second, she saw with resigned dismay.

Brant looked furious, more angry than she had ever seen him. And a livid Army Ranger was a dangerous force to behold.

At the porch steps, he slid down from the horse, threw the rains around the top railing of the porch and bounded up the steps to her side.

"Everything past that gate you went through off the main road is private property. Every damn one of you is trespassing."

"Go away," she hissed to him, barely able to breathe past her misery. "You're only going to make everything worse."

He stared at her, confusion on his features, then his gaze narrowed. "No," he answered, his jaw tight and his eyes a deep midnight-blue.

Before she could argue, he threw one powerful arm around her shoulders and yanked her against him, then turned back around to the gawking photographers.

He was a formidable man, with his powerful build and his steely Army commando stare, and though she wanted him anywhere else in the world than right here beside her, she couldn't help appreciating how the paparazzi almost as one took an instinctive step back.

"You have got exactly three minutes to get into your vehicles and slither back to whatever slime spit you out. I'm calling the sheriff, who just happens to be a good friend of mine. He'll have no problem rushing deputies up here to haul every one of your asses into jail for trespassing and harassment. I'm sure he won't mind confiscating all that nice camera equipment, either."

"Who's the cowboy, Mimi?" one intrepid still photographer, she thought was named Harvey, yelled at her.

"Is he the father of your baby?" another shouted.

"Does Werner know he's going to be a grandpa?" another added.

She was hyperventilating. She could feel the panic attack swell at the edges of her subconscious and she did her best to fight it back.

Brant took one look at her and yanked her back into the house, slamming the door behind them.

To her horror, he reached into the coat closet by the door and pulled out a lethal-looking shotgun.

The sight of it managed to shock her back to reality. She would have time to freak out when she was on the way to the airport but right now she had to keep it together, for damage control if nothing else.

She grabbed his arm. "What are you doing? Put that away!"

He flexed his muscle to keep the shotgun out of her reach and she felt as if she were touching one of those giant slabs of granite peeking through the snow near the river.

"I'm not going to use it. But they don't know that, do they?"

She had to stop him. If the man had no sense of self-preservation, she had to do what she could to protect him. "You have no idea what you're dealing with here. You are way out of your league, Major."

He raised an eyebrow. "I've spent five of the last

seven years in heavy combat. I think I can take care of myself against a bunch of photographers with lip rings and ponytails."

"You can't!" she exclaimed but he completely ignored her and opened the front door and walked out onto the porch with the shotgun cradled in his arms.

Mimi let out a sob of frustration and covered her face with her hands.

"Two minutes," Brant barked and then he worked the pump action on the shotgun with that distinctive *ch-ch* sound no one could mistake for anything else.

The paparazzi had been milling around by their vehicles, probably wondering just how far he would go to kick them off or hoping they could squeeze in one last picture of her.

At the sight of Brant in warrior mode, aiming a firearm at them, they snapped a few more images and climbed into their vehicles.

Through the window, Mimi watched them head down the road in three SUVs, tires spitting snow and gravel behind them.

As soon as they were out of sight, Brant returned to the house looking as pleased as if he'd just fought back an entire contingent of enemy combatants single-handedly.

"They won't bother you again," he said with such confidence that she couldn't help herself, she curled up her fist and smacked his shoulder as hard as she could.

She hadn't had much force to put behind it but at least shock had been on her side. He stared at her. "What was that that for?"

"How could you be so stupid?"

"You don't really believe I called those bastards, do you?"

She raked a hand through her hair. "Of course not. You would never do that. Anyway, would you have chased them off with a shotgun if you'd been the one to call them in the first place?"

"How do you think they found you?"

She sat on the sofa and covered her face in her hands, wondering how she was going to explain all this to Verena, to her friends, to her father.

"Any number of ways. I'm guessing someone at the clinic saw me, despite Jake and Maggie's best efforts. Or perhaps someone on their staff wasn't as discreet as he should have been."

"I'll find out," he vowed, with enough menace in his voice that Mimi had to swallow a whimper.

"It doesn't really matter how they found me. The important thing is that they have."

She punched him again, furious all over again that he would step up to defend her, even if one tiny corner of her heart glowed at the gesture.

"You have no idea what a mess you just thrust yourself into. A shotgun, for heaven's sake. What were you thinking? You look like you just stepped off a damn wanted poster. They're going to be calling you Mimi's Outlaw or something absurd like that."

"You think I care about that?"

"Maybe not now, right this moment, in the heat of battle, as it were. But what about a few days from now when you can't walk outside without a dozen clicking cameras? Or when you return to duty and all your men start calling you Mimi's Outlaw, too?"

"You think I care about that? It worked, didn't it? They're gone."

She curled her hands into fists. "I don't believe this! Can you really be so completely naive?"

He aimed a measure of that menacing look at her. "Naive? I've been leading troops into combat for almost a decade. Naivete is in short supply on the battlefield."

"What else would you call it? You solved nothing with your little shotgun act. Who do you think is going to be camped out at the end of your driveway on public property until your leave ends?"

"So what?"

She picked up the still-yipping Simone and set her into her cage. "So they're cockroaches. You might stomp on a few and scare off a few more but they're only going to go call their friends. Before you know it, you turn on the lights of your kitchen at night and they'll be everywhere."

How could she have done this to him? Dragged him into the ugliness of her world?

She had to end this, now.

"Brant, you had no right to come charging in like that to my rescue. I didn't ask for your help and I didn't need it."

"My house, my decision." He glared right back at her.

Mimi let out a long breath, despising herself for what she knew she had to do.

She had no choice. The rumors were already flying about her pregnancy. *Is he the father?* one of the paparazzi had yelled. Everyone would be speculating about it and she couldn't allow Brant's name to be dragged through the mud and muck of her world, anymore than it already would be from those pictures.

She curled her hands into fists, digging her nails into her skin. "You had no right," she said again. "Now everybody will know I've been staying here with you. There's no way I can keep it a secret after you pulled such a ridiculous stunt."

As she had half-hoped, half-dreaded, she saw some of his anger at the photographers shift toward her. "I didn't realize keeping your presence here a secret was our priority," he said stiffly.

Of all the silly, foolhardy things she had done, all the mistakes and the scandals, she had never regretted anything as much as what she was about to do.

And she had never despised herself more.

"Of course I wanted it to stay a secret. Do you really think I want these few days to become public?"

"I don't know. You tell me."

She forced herself to give him her famous ditzy smile and spoke in a lighthearted tone, though the words cut her throat like razor blades. "Of course not. I'm Mimi Van Hoyt. As sweet as you've been, Brant, you're… well, not exactly my type."

A muscle flexed in his jaw but other than that, he went completely still. "Your type?"

"You know. Men like Prince Gregor or an A-list actor or one of the Kennedys. That's what I'm used to."

"Yes, I can certainly see why I would present a change of pace."

He was furious now. She could see the embers flaring to life in his eyes.

"I'm only thinking of you, Brant." That, at least, was the truth, but she twisted her tone to make it sound as if it meant the opposite. "You don't want your name linked with mine, either. You have your career to consider.

What would your commanding officers think if they found out you spent your leave cavorting with someone like me?"

He crossed his arms over his chest. "Was there cavorting? Somehow I must have missed the cavorting."

She shrugged. "Just like you're completely missing the point. Our lives exist on different planes, Brant. Surely you can see that. What do we possibly have in common?"

"I thought we were coming to care about each other."

His careful words and the intensity behind them stabbed at her and she forced herself not to sway.

"Sure, I kissed you a few times because you were here and, let's face it, you're hot in that cowboy/soldier, macho kind of way. I'm really sorry if you might have gotten the wrong idea and thought those kisses meant more than they did."

She saw hurt and disbelief in his eyes and she had to dig her nails tighter into her palms to keep from reaching for him.

She put on her fake Mimi smile again. "Look, I'm not sure things are finished with my baby's father, despite what I told you before. You've really helped me put things into perspective there."

The second part also wasn't a lie but Mimi had always been good at twisting the truth to suit her purposes. And right now her purpose was to end things with Brant, once and for all, despite the devastation to her heart.

"Until I know for sure it's really over, I just can't complicate everything by becoming entangled with someone else. Especially not someone so...unsuitable."

She heard the sound of a vehicle pulling up out front.

Either one of the photographers had a death wish or her car service had just arrived. Since Brant still wasn't looking quite convinced, Mimi decided she had no choice but to play her trump card.

She gave him her hard, polished smile and picked up the note she had begun to write for him. She smoothly pocketed that one—even as terse as it had been, it somehow seemed far too personal. Instead, she picked another piece of paper from the stack and scribbled a phone number on it.

"Look, here's my assistant's cell number. Her name is Verena Dumond and she's a pain in the you-know-what but she's frighteningly efficient. Just let her know how much you think your time and effort is worth for the few days I spent here and she can cut you a check for any expenses I incurred while I was here. Gas, food, whatever. And don't worry, I'll make sure to tell her to throw in a nice bonus for all your trouble."

Brant stared at the slip of paper in her slim hand that jangled with silvery bracelets.

Ah.

Here she was at last—the Mimi frigging Van Hoyt he had expected to encounter when he dragged her out of her SUV in the middle of a blizzard.

She was condescending and abrasive and right now he was pretty sure he despised her.

He didn't know what was truth and what was an act. Though her words sounded convincing enough—snobbish and bitchy though they were—there was something in her eyes, some shadow, that didn't mesh with what she was saying.

He was so busy trying to sort it all out that he almost missed the sound of another vehicle approaching the house.

When he caught it, he picked up the shotgun again and walked out onto the porch, just as a man dressed in a black uniform stepped out of an SUV with tinted windows.

The driver froze when he saw a man on the front porch holding a Remington but Brant had to give the guy credit for not crawling back into the limo and speeding down the driveway.

"I'm here to pick up a Ms. Howard. Do I have the wrong address?"

"No," Mimi answered briskly from behind him before Brant could get any words out. "I'm here. I've got a few more bags inside if you could be so kind."

"Not at all, Miss."

Brant caught the chauffer's quick double take when he recognized Mimi but he concealed it quickly, too well-trained to react more than that first flash of surprise.

"You're leaving," Brant said, flatly stating the obvious. If he hadn't been so angry, he might have perhaps noticed her luggage by the door.

"Yes. There's a plane waiting for me right now at the Jackson Hole airport."

"Were you going to say anything to me or just disappear without a word?"

Something flickered in her eyes for just a moment then she gave him that bright, fake smile again. "I was starting to write a thank-you note when the photographers showed up."

"A note. You planned to leave me a note."

"Well, yes. Along with Verena's phone number, of course."

He had never been so furious. The rage swept over him like an August firestorm and he had to draw in several deep breaths to beat it back.

"You're angry with me." She actually had the gall to sound surprised.

"That's one word for it," he bit out.

"I'm sorry for that. But since Dr. Dalton told me it's safe to travel now, I decided there was no logical reason to delay the inevitable."

"None at all."

Underneath the anger, lurking several layers down like a hidden reservoir under the desert, was a vast, endless pool of pain, aimed mostly at himself.

How could he have been such an idiot? He had actually spent the night dreaming about building a future with her. Raising her child somewhere away from the cameras and the craziness.

The lunacy of it just about took his breath away. How could he ever have thought Mimi might want that with someone like him?

As sweet as you've been, Brant, you're...well, not exactly my type.

The chauffeur returned just then and quickly picked up the rest of her luggage.

"Will there be anything else, Ms. Howard?"

Mimi handed him Simone's pink crate. For some crazy reason, the sight of that silly little dog gazing at him with big soulful eyes affected Brant more than he would have believed possible.

"That's everything," Mimi said. "Thank you. I'll be just a few moments more."

The man tapped the bill of his cap respectfully and then left the house. When he was gone, Mimi smiled at Brant but it wasn't the winsome smile he had come to adore these past few days.

"Well, thank you again for not turning me out that first night and for helping me through the last few days."

She used exactly the same tone she used with the chauffeur. Impersonal. Polite. Detached.

"So that's it."

"I suppose it is." She paused for a moment. "Be safe, won't you?"

Her voice caught, just a bit, on the words and he gave her a careful look to see if he could find a crack beneath her veneer but she was once more cool and remote.

"Don't forget to send your expenses to Verena. I'll tell her to be expecting your call."

She stepped forward, brushed her cool lips against his cheek, pulled down her sunglasses from atop her head and walked out of the house and out of his life.

Chapter 12

Brant didn't know when he had ever been so tired.

He'd managed to doze a little on the plane from the military hospital at the Ramstein Air Base in Germany, but except for that restive sleep, he had been awake for close to twenty-four hours. Right now, all he wanted was to crawl into his bed, pull the covers over his head and crash for the next twenty-four.

The pain from his arm and side growled at him and gnawed with sharp teeth. He had a bottle of pain pills in his duffel but he was doing his best not to rely on them. He had a feeling that after a full day of travel, he might not have much choice.

He was also painfully aware that his decision to drive from Idaho Falls might not have been the greatest idea he'd ever come up with. He hadn't been behind the wheel since the incident nearly three weeks earlier and he hadn't realized how difficult it was to drive one-handed, especially when he'd injured his dominant right side. He was learning more about ambidexterity than he ever cared to know.

But he had made it this far. Only a few more miles and he would be home. As his eyes scanned the road in Cold Creek Canyon, he was struck once again by the familiar rugged beauty of the place. He could think of nowhere more gorgeous than Cold Creek Canyon in July, with the mountains a deep, soothing green, the creek flashing silver in the sunset, the scattered patches of columbine and yarrow among the towering stands of pine and fir.

This was home and he had never been more grateful to be driving up this canyon road.

Something sweet and calming seemed to wash through him as he turned onto the Western Sky access road. He drove under the ranch's log arch with a little prayer of gratitude in his heart that he had reached the momentous decision to not sell the place.

He didn't know what had changed during his time here with Mimi but after he returned to Afghanistan, he hadn't been able to shake the strange assurance that he couldn't sell the ranch. Not now. No matter where he traveled, the Western Sky would always be his home and he couldn't think about someone else living here.

Some day he might have a family of his own—though that time seemed a lifetime away. If he sold the Western Sky, his children would never know their heritage, never know they belonged to such a place of peace in the world.

Besides, if he had sold the ranch, where would he recover for the next month? The impersonal base housing in Georgia, where he had nothing to do but sit and watch television all day?

Oh, he probably could have stayed in a room at Winder Ranch with Easton. The house there had eight bedrooms, after all, and she was living all by herself. But Easton would have wanted to fuss over him and he would have been obliged to let her. This way was much better, here where he could be on his own with only his memories.

The heaviest runoff was done this late in the year, he noted as he drove up the access road to the ranchhouse. The creek burbled along beside the road with cheerful abandon. He was definitely going to spend some serious time with a fly rod while he was here if he could get his blasted arm to cooperate.

In front of the ranchhouse, any thoughts of fly fishing flew from his head. He braked the rental vehicle and climbed out, frowning as he looked around.

What on earth?

This was *not* the same place he had seen in February— even discounting the fact that everything wasn't buried in the two feet of snow he'd left behind when he returned to Afghanistan.

The barn and sprawling outbuildings sported a bright new coat of rustic red paint, the fences had been repaired, the sagging spot on the porch roof looked flush and level. Two white rocking chairs graced the long front porch, angled to take in the best view of the mountains and instead of the weedy, barren flower beds lining the front porch, a riot of color exploded.

He climbed out of the rental car and leaned a hip against the door, trying to absorb all these small changes that combined to make a huge difference.

The Western Sky looked charming and well-kept, something he hadn't seen here in, well, ever.

Easton emailed him she had hired a new caretaker to replace Gwen but she hadn't said much about her, other than it was someone who had a background in renovation. At the time, he had been too busy planning a couple major raids and hadn't paid as much attention to her email as he should have. He completely trusted Easton to do what was best for him and for the ranch and he'd told her so.

She had come through, in spades. Easton had never mentioned his new caretaker was a genius. His home looked clean and cheerful, the kind of place where a man could kick off his boots and all his worries.

Except for the memories.

Brant let out a breath, trying his best not to think about that last miserable scene with Mimi, when the paparazzi had stood just off the porch there, flashing their cameras and shouting their questions and sending his foolish dreams of a happily-ever-after with her drifting away into the bitter February air like the smoke from the chimney.

He should have known she would haunt him here. He had half-expected it, he just didn't know those memories would be waiting to ambush him the moment he drove onto the ranch.

She was everywhere here. Sitting on the sofa inside watching Hitchcock movies, playing poker at the kitchen table, painting the guest room with those adorable little paint freckles dotting her face.

He closed his eyes and once more saw her heading down those very steps as she walked out of his life.

That last scene had played vividly in his head for

months. He had pored over the memory again and again, sifting through her words, her expression, her tone of voice.

What was truth and what was lie?

Once he had stopped reeling from the cold finality of their parting, he had begun to think maybe Mimi hadn't been exactly truthful with him in that last ugly scene. There had been something not quite right in the tone of her voice and the overbright smile.

Big surprise there, that she might have been less than honest with him, since she'd spent her entire time at the Western Sky weaving one lie or another. But he had reached the inevitable conclusion that she wanted him out of her life. That much had been abundantly clear.

Oh, he'd had to deal with some questions and some ribbing after those pictures of the two of them together had been printed. A few junior officers had tried to make tasteless, off-color jokes about it, but only once. Brant had cut them off with a steely glare and a few well-placed threats.

Then had come that brief, shocking statement a few weeks after he returned to Afghanistan where she announced to the world she was having a baby from in vitro fertilization and an unknown sperm donor. Even thousands of miles away in the middle of a war zone, he had seen a little of the controversy and doubt that announcement had sparked.

He had been watching for paparazzi coverage of her—pathetic on his part, he knew—but other than a few well-documented shopping trips for baby clothes and maternity things every so often, Mimi seemed to be keeping a low profile.

She would be due in only a few months. Not that he was counting or anything.

He wasn't going to think about her. Because of his injuries, he had nearly a month in Pine Gulch before he needed to report to his new assignment at Los Alamitos.

In that time, he planned to give his body a chance to heal while he rode horses and fished and savored the serenity here.

But first he needed to sleep for the next day or two.

He grabbed his duffel out of the backseat of the rental and started for the house, interested to see if the inside had received the same spruce-up. He had only taken one step up the porch stairs when he saw a big yellow Labrador retriever round the house with something pink and flowery in its mouth.

The dog barreled to a cartoonlike stop when he caught sight of Brant and then he dropped whatever was in his mouth and started barking—a deep, excited hey-we-have-company kind of bark.

Brant barely had seconds to react to that when another little animal rounded the corner of the house and he could do nothing but stare at the fluffy white furball with bright black eyes as it let out an ecstatic yip and headed right for him.

It couldn't be Mimi's silly little dog. He knew it couldn't be. But why would another bichon frise be wandering around the Western Sky?

The question was completely yanked out of his mind a second later when a figure—this time a human—followed the dogs.

She was pushing a wheelbarrow loaded with flowers and she was laughing, her green eyes bright in the long, stretched-out shadows of an early-July evening.

"Hey, come back here with that, you rascal. You think I'm going to want to wear my gardening hat now that it's all slobbery and gross?"

He couldn't think straight and for a moment he wondered if he was having some kind of pain-induced hallucination. He dropped his duffel and curled his good hand into a fist, not quite believing this was real.

Mimi must have seen the car then. He watched her do the same sort of double take as the yellow Lab and then she turned toward him.

She was hugely pregnant and ethereally lovely, with her curly dark hair swept up in a loose style on top of her head and her skin glowing with color and health.

Something tugged at his heart, something fierce and powerful. For one insane moment, he wanted nothing so much as to rush to her, sweep her into his arms and twirl her in the air again and again.

He saw the shock in her eyes, saw her features go a shade paler, and as he stood with one foot on the porch step, the whole wall of denial he had so carefully constructed tumbled down, brick by painful brick.

He was in love with her. Nothing had changed. All those months of trying to tell himself she meant nothing to him, that he could turn his back on what they might have had just as easily as she apparently could, were meaningless.

He let out a breath, furious with himself and with her. "What do you think you're doing here?" he bit out.

"You… You're not supposed to be home for another ten days."

"You're not supposed to be here at all," he snapped, wondering how she had known his travel schedule, the original one from before his injury. "What are you doing here, Mimi?"

She shrugged, still looking stunned and completely breathtaking. And nervous, he suddenly realized. She looked nervous to see him.

"Oh, you know. Just putting in some flowering annuals to help fill in the holes in your beds. The perennials won't really come into their full color until next summer but it will be glorious by this time next year."

"What are you doing *here?* At my ranch?"

She moved closer, the guilty expression on her features fading to one of concern. "Are you all right? You look a little pale."

He would never admit to her or anyone else that his knees were beginning to go weak at the pain screeching from his injuries. "Mimi! Answer me. What are you doing at Western Sky, planting annuals in my flower beds?"

She gnawed her lip. "Um, I live here. At least for another couple of days. I guess I'll be moving quicker than I'd planned. We really didn't think you were coming home until the week after next. What happened? Why did your plans change?"

He didn't want to explain to her that he'd spent the past two weeks in the burn unit at Ramstein. He hadn't told anyone, not even Easton, and it certainly wasn't Mimi's business that he had been injured while trying to yank two Marines from a burning Humvee hit by an IED while traveling directly in front of his vehicle in a convoy.

Nor did he want to explain that he was becoming light-headed from the pain and needed to sit down before he fell over. Wouldn't that be a kick in the butt?

"Plans change," he said.

"Well, it would have been nice to know your arrangements," she said with a slightly disgruntled tone. "I planned to move out of Gwen's cabin before you arrived. Easton and I both thought it would probably be best."

"Easton knows you're here." She would have had to know, yet she hadn't said a word to him in their frequent email correspondence, the little sneak.

"Yes," she said warily.

The truth hit him in a rush, then. Everything seemed to shift into focus—the flower beds, the fresh paint on the barn, the hundreds of little changes around the ranch.

"You're the caretaker she's been raving about. The one who has poured so much effort into the house."

Guilt again flitted across her features. "Yes."

None of this made sense. He didn't know what to think. "Why do I always feel like I've stepped into some alternate universe when you're around?"

"I'm sorry."

"No, you're not. You like leaving people off balance, making sure they have no idea what to expect next. It's part of the whole Mimi charm."

She looked as if she wanted to disagree but she only moved toward the porch. "I'm sorry," she said again. "But if you don't mind, I really need to sit down. My feet are a little swollen right now."

Since that matched exactly with his own hidden agenda that he'd rather be tortured than admit, he shrugged and headed up the stairs, dropping his duffel by the door.

"Before I sit down, I'm going to get a drink of water," she said. "I'm parched. Can I grab you one?"

He shrugged, not eager to accept anything from her

even though the thought of the pure mountain spring water that came from the tap here was undeniably enticing.

He waited until she went into the house before he sagged into one of the rocking chairs and let out the tight breath that had been holding in all the pain from his injuries.

Simone had apparently missed him, if no one else had. The minute he sat down, she jumped onto his lap with an eager yip and he carefully kept her away from the bandages wrapped around his abdomen.

The Lab, not to be outdone, curled up at his boots, perfectly at home there.

Brant didn't care, he was just grateful to have a moment to absorb the shock of finding Mimi here in real life when he thought he would only be encountering the ghost of her memory.

She bustled out of the house a moment later with a small tray with two tall glasses, a sliced apple and some crackers and cheese. Seeing her so at home in his house gave him an odd feeling, a tangled mix of consternation and contentment.

While he drank, she lowered herself carefully into the rocker next to him and he watched over the top of his glass, fascinated with the cumbersome process. She looked round and lush and beautiful.

Once she sat, she sipped her own water, then set it on the arm of the rocker.

As the silence dragged on, it occurred to Brant that she was watching him as warily as if he were an IED being disarmed by an explosives ordnance disposal team.

He wanted to ask how she had been feeling. How

was the baby? Did she know if she was having a boy or a girl and had she picked out names? Was she nervous about becoming a mother?

All those questions rattled through him but he forced himself to focus on the only thing that really mattered.

"Why are you here, Mimi?"

She chewed the corner of her lip again, and he remembered how delicious that mouth had tasted, how perfectly she had fit into his arms, how for one magical night he had allowed himself the most ridiculous dreams.

She finally sighed. "I convinced Easton to hire me. It's not her fault, honestly. Please don't blame her. I can be...persuasive when I set my mind to it."

"Why would you try to be persuasive?"

"I needed a place to stay away from all the craziness and... I like it here. It's peaceful and quiet and the people are so warm and kind to me. Easton and Maggie Dalton threw a baby shower for me last week. Isn't that great? And nearly everyone they invited showed up. I got the most darling clothes and toys you can imagine for the baby and you should see the crib quilt that Emery Cavazos made. It's a work of art that should be in a museum! You wouldn't believe how kind everyone here is to me."

She seemed so shocked and delighted that he didn't have the heart to tell her most of the people in Pine Gulch were kind to just about everyone.

"How long have you been here?"

"Since March, when Gwen moved to her house in Jackson Hole."

He couldn't seem to absorb it, even with the reality of her sitting beside him. How could she have spent five months in virtual seclusion out here, away from the crowds and the stores and the cameras?

"Why didn't the paparazzi mob you here? I haven't seen anything about you living on a ranch in eastern Idaho."

Not that he'd been looking, he assured himself.

"I made sort of a devil's bargain with them. I would show up once a month in California for a long weekend and go to a few parties, do a little shopping, strictly for their benefit, and in return they would leave me alone the rest of the time. Since my life here is pretty tame, there's not much to photograph except the occasional trip to the hardware store for paint and to the Gulch for lunch with Easton and Maggie and the rest of the friends I've made here."

He tried to picture her walking the crowded aisles of the hardware store and ordering greasy food at the café in town and pushing a cart around the grocery store and couldn't seem to make his imagination stretch that far.

"Why did no one in town happen to mention to me in those five months that Mimi Van Hoyt was living in my house?"

"Not in your house, technically. In Gwen's cabin."

He glared at her nitpicky correction and she sighed. "Easton knew you wouldn't like it so she purposely didn't say anything. Everyone else probably figured you already knew."

"You could have found a quiet place anywhere else on earth to hide out until you have the baby. There are other peaceful spots around the globe. Why did it have to be here."

"I like it here," she said again. "I really can't give you any other explanation than that. When Gwen told me

Easton was looking to hire someone to replace her as caretaker and continue the work I started fixing up the place, I called her right away and applied for the job."

He apparently had to have a long talk with Easton about hiding things from him and about keeping her busybody nose out of his affairs. But then Easton couldn't have known the whole story about what had happened between him and Mimi. He supposed he couldn't be too angry at her for allowing the one woman he least wanted to see to take over his ranch.

"I'm sorry it upsets you," Mimi went on carefully. "I honestly planned to finish everything up and be out of here before you returned."

"So you'll be moving out."

"Yes." She hesitated. "But I should probably tell you, in the interest of full disclosure, that I want Dr. Dalton to deliver my baby, so I'll be sticking around Pine Gulch until after the birth. Nate and Emery have offered me the use of one of the guest cabins at Hope Springs. Caroline and Wade Dalton also have been pushing me to stay at their guesthouse at the Cold Creek. I guess I have to choose now, don't I?"

Some petty part of him wanted to tell her she had to choose right now, tonight. But she was hugely pregnant and he couldn't just toss her out into the cold, as much as he would like to. "No rush," he lied. "Take a few days to make up your mind where you want to go."

The way he felt right now, he figured he wouldn't be crawling out of bed for the next day and a half so he likely wouldn't even run into her again.

Before he could rein it in, his wayward imagination flashed a picture of falling asleep with Mimi next to him in his big bed, all her warmth and softness curled against him, with her dark curls drifting across his skin, with his hands splayed across that fascinating round belly....

He caught the direction of his gaze and frowned, disgusted at himself. Amazing what kind of crazy images could play with a man's head when he was exhausted and sore.

"I appreciate that," she said, and it took him a minute to realize she was referring to his comment that she didn't have to leave immediately.

He wanted to tell her that was still his preference— that she go and take her little dog with her—but he decided to save his energy.

"Are you all right?" she asked after a long moment.

He blinked at her. "Why?"

"You seem...distracted."

Well, he couldn't take a deep breath because of the burns and he'd just endured three weeks of misery in a military hospital and he was pretty close to falling over from exhaustion.

Other than that, he was swell.

"Just surprised," he said, his voice coming out gruff. "I didn't expect to find you here—or anywhere, really, ever again. It's been a shock and I'm still reeling a little."

"Are you angry?"

Angry? That seemed a mild word when he thought of the heaviness in his heart these past four months.

No. *Angry* would imply he cared about her, that he had been hurt by what had happened between them.

"I would have to care to be angry," he answered. "Now if you'll excuse me, I've been traveling for a day and need to find my bed."

"Okay." She smiled but it wasn't the incandescent Mimi smile he remembered. This one was smaller and a little sad. "Welcome home, Major."

He inclined his head to answer her and pushed Simone onto the ground, then gripped the arms of the rocker and marshalled all his strength to rise.

He probably would have been fine and managed to go inside without her being any the wiser, but he misjudged the width of the rocking chair and his injured side brushed the wooden arm as he rose.

Pain clawed at him—fierce, unrelenting—and he couldn't contain one sharp inhale. His knees went weak and he had to sit back down, more carefully this time.

Mimi paled and was at his side in an instant. "What is it? What's wrong?"

"Nothing. I'm fine. Goodbye."

"You're not fine! You've been hurt, haven't you? That's why you're home early. That's why you're so pale and you're sweating, even here on the cool porch."

He didn't want her to know. She would probably rush right over to Winder Ranch and tell Easton, who was apparently her chatty new best friend.

"It's nothing," he repeated.

"Who's the liar now?" she snapped. "What happened? You might as well tell me. I can find out with a few simple phone calls."

She was right. With her father's clout, she could probably worm out any detail of his life she ever wanted to know.

Anyway, the truth was easier. He was pretty sure he didn't have the energy to stand here and make up some elaborate story.

"No big deal. I suffered a little injury in an incident a few weeks ago."

Her face seemed to leach out of what little color she had left. "How little? What kind of incident? Were you shot?"

He thought of the three weeks he'd spent in the burn unit of Ramstein and the surgeries and the skin grafts and the risks of infection he still faced. He almost thought he would have preferred a nice clean gunshot wound.

"No," he said shortly, hoping she would leave it at that. But of course, being Mimi, she didn't.

"What is it? Tell me, Brant." She spoke in a low, urgent voice, her eyes huge in her lovely face.

He was weak to let her affect him so much, but somehow her concern warmed a cold, achy corner of his heart.

"Burned. We were in a convoy traveling behind a Humvee that hit an IED. My arm and side sustained a little heat damage during the rescue effort." A nice way of saying second- and third-degree burns over a good portion of skin.

Chapter 13

Mimi closed her eyes, trying not to picture the scene in her mind, the screams and the flames and the smell of burning flesh. She could clearly envision Brant rushing to the rescue, taking charge of the scene with that sense of command that was so innate.

She fought down tears, wondering why she seemed to spend so much time blubbering around him.

"You need to rest. I'm sorry I've kept you talking out here when you should be sleeping."

He didn't look as if he had the energy even to argue with her, though she still saw a shadow of the anger she fully deserved in his gaze.

"I'll start making arrangements to find another place to stay," she said. She hated the idea of leaving the Western Sky, but she owed him that, at least.

"Fine," he said shortly, and she caught the message

loud and clear. He wanted her gone. Beyond that, he didn't care what she did.

"Do you need any help with anything?"

His short laugh sounded icy cold. "From you? No thank you."

He rose abruptly, picked up his duffel from the porch and stalked into the house.

She deserved that. Mimi curled her fingers, doing her best to ignore the ache in her chest. He had every reason to detest her after the things she said to him. What else could she expect?

He was injured. She pictured again that shock of pain in his eyes when he had brushed against the chair. Foolish man. He was hurt and he hadn't even told his foster sister. Easton would have told Mimi if she'd known.

How could she leave him alone here at the ranch when he was in pain and possibly needing help?

Brant didn't want her here. She had made sure he wouldn't by pretending condescension and disdain. She couldn't complain now when her efforts paid off.

In her mind, those few days she had spent here with him possessed a magical, dreamlike quality, and she had wondered if she might have imagined the intensity of her feelings for him. Seeing him again answered that question. She was still in love with him, perhaps more now than she'd ever been. She had had five months to think about his strength and his honor, to vividly remember the safety and peace she found in his arms.

Because she loved him, she would leave this place she also loved. He deserved to have his home to himself, especially since he was injured and in pain.

She pressed a hand on her abdomen, to the little life growing there. "We'll be okay, kiddo," she whispered, repeating the mantra that had sustained her for five months.

She had used the same mantra during those first heartbreaking days after she left the ranch, when she told her father the news of her pregnancy, when she and her extensive team of lawyers met with Marco to convince him to formally relinquish any claim of paternity for the child and never speak of it again, which he had been only too eager to do. As far as Mimi was concerned, while the public statement that she had conceived via in vitro wasn't technically true, Marco had only been her baby's sperm donor, nothing more.

Seeing Brant again made her wish once more with all her heart that she had picked someone like him to father her child. But she wouldn't regret the course her life had taken.

She had grown more these past five months than she ever could have imagined. Here at the Western Sky, she discovered she loved fixing up properties and she was good at it. She had learned she could be completely focused on something when she set her mind to it and she had learned to count on herself instead of a team of handlers to take care of her every need.

Most important, she had found inside herself a strength and courage she never would have imagined before she had been forced to rely on them. She had a suspicion she wasn't finished needing those attributes. Now that she had seen him again and realized she still loved him, she knew she was going to have many days and nights of sorrow ahead.

At least she would have her daughter to help her through.

"We'll be okay, kiddo," she said again, then levered herself up from the rocking chair, not an easy task these days.

"Come, Simone. Come, Hector." She spoke to her bichon frise and to the Lab mix Easton had talked her into a month ago. "We've got flowers to plant."

The dogs jumped up and Mimi walked down the steps after them.

Like the complicated process of maneuvering around with her pregnancy bulk, she would eventually learn how to live with this emptiness in her heart.

He awoke disoriented and with his side bellowing in pain.

Brant drew in a deep focused breath and then another and another until he could force the pain to recede enough that he could think.

He hadn't slept round-the-clock, as he might have hoped, only about ten hours. According to the lighted face of his watch, it was 5:00 a.m. At this time of year, just a few weeks after the summer solstice, the sun rose early. Out his window he could see a pale rim of light along the jagged mountain peaks, a clear indication that sunrise was an hour or so away.

He lay in bed for a long moment, catching his breath and his bearings. He was a lousy patient, as any of the nurses at the Ramstein hospital could have attested. He hated the feeling that his body could be vulnerable, that he wasn't at full fighting form.

The doctors told him he could expect a good two or three months of healing time before he felt like himself. He was ready for it to happen this minute.

He sighed. He would get over it. He was good at learning to live with things he didn't want.

Like his memories of Mimi.

He didn't want to think about her, so he swung his legs over the side of the bed and headed for the bathroom.

She had made big changes here. New light fixtures, new paint to replace the aging wallpaper, even the vanity was new.

Blasted woman. He washed his hands and headed for the kitchen for a drink of water, dressed only in low-slung sweats. He turned on the low light above the kitchen and frowned again at more evidence of Mimi's handiwork. The paint was new here, as well, and it looked to him as if the knotty pine cabinets had a new coat of stain.

He hoped like hell she hadn't paid for everything out of her own pocket, that Easton had taken care of the expenses out of the ranch maintenance account she was named on with him.

When he had his strength back a little bit, he planned to have a long talk with Easton to find out what she possibly could have been thinking to allow Mimi here.

Not that he could blame Easton for this mess. He knew from past experience that Mimi could talk her way into anything.

But why would she want to? Why was she here? None of it made sense. When she walked away that terrible last day, she had left him in no doubt that she wanted nothing to do with him.

As sweet as you've been, Brant, you're...well, not exactly my type.

She couldn't offer much more clarity than that. And yet she'd spent the past five months taking care of his ranch while she grew huge with child.

He shook his head as he turned on the faucet—a new brushed nickel one that looked complicated and expensive. After he filled his glass, he turned around and nearly spilled the water all over the floor when he found her standing in the doorway in a nightgown, with a blanket wrapped around her shoulders.

"Mimi! What the hell?"

So much for being a highly trained commando. Mortification swamped him that she could catch him off guard like this, sore and sleepy and wearing only loose sweats.

He also had an instant of painful awareness that seeing her like this, lush and feminine and lovely in her soft mint-green nightgown, while he was only wearing sweats, would show her quite clearly just how glad at least some of him was to see her.

"Sorry. I saw the light and wanted to make sure you were okay."

"You sure moved fast from Gwen's cabin," he muttered, willing away his response.

A delicate hint of color climbed her ivory skin. "I slept on the sofa," she admitted. "I know, nervy of me. But you seemed so shaky earlier that I thought maybe I better check on you. I stopped in around midnight and… you were moaning a little in your sleep and I didn't feel right about leaving you here by yourself."

Now it was his turn to flush. He hated that the pain he fought so hard to contain during the day could growl to life when he wasn't conscious of it.

"I don't need a keeper."

He started to say more but then he caught her expression of horror and realized she was staring at his bandages, the eight-inch-wide gauze wrapped around his middle and the corresponding size encasing his arm from mid-forearm to above his elbow.

One hand fluttered to her mouth and her big green eyes filled with tears. "Oh, Brant."

He shifted. "Come on. Cut it out. Don't cry."

She drew in a ragged breath then exhaled a sobbing sort of noise, those eyes swimming with tears now, and he groaned. Though a big section of his brain was calling him any number of synonyms for nutty as a fruitcake, he crossed the distance between them and pulled her against his uninjured side.

"Come on, don't cry. I'm okay."

"You could have been killed."

"But I wasn't." He was suddenly fiercely glad of that, that he had been given one more chance to hold her again, to feel her soft curves and smell that delicious scent of flowers and citrus and her.

"I told myself not to worry, that you could take care of yourself," she whispered. "But I think I've prayed more in five months than I have the rest of my life put together and I've completely devoured all the coverage I could on Afghanistan."

Something in her words tugged at his Mimi-dazed brain, but it still took a moment for the incongruity of it to click.

"Why do you care?"

She lifted her eyes to his and he saw embarrassment flicker there and something else, something deeper, before she shifted her gaze away. "I just do."

She was lying. He knew it. He lifted her chin to face him again and this time he read everything in her eyes and the truth reached out and coldcocked him.

He stared at her for a long time and then shook his head. "You are a big fat liar, Mimi Van Hoyt."

The corners of her mouth trembled a little but she quickly straightened it out. "I know," she said in a deceptively casual tone. "I'm so big I can barely fit through doorways these days."

"You know that's not what I meant. I think you're more beautiful than you've ever been. But you lied to me that last day. You stood here in my house and fibbed through your perfect little teeth."

She stepped away from him, taking all her heat and softness away and leaving him cold in the predawn chill. "I...don't know what you're talking about."

He thought of the five months of misery he had spent, how it had taken every ounce of hard-fought discipline he possessed to focus on the mission and not wallow in self-pity. "It was all an act to push me away, wasn't it? You didn't mean a word."

She wrapped her arms around her chest, which just made her nightgown stretch across her round belly.

"Yes, I did. I didn't—I don't—want you dragged into my world, Brant. You saw how ugly it could be and those photographers showing up here was just a small sampling of what it can be like. I love you too much to put you through that."

He stared at her, her words surging around and through him. *I love you too much.* Some corner of his mind had begun to suspect it, but hearing her say the words still stunned him like a percussion round.

"What did you say?"

"I can't put you through that. It's not fair. You're a good, honorable man. I'm Mimi Van Hoyt—stupid, rich, silly socialite. I'll ruin your life."

By the time she finished, she was nearly sobbing and he realized two things simultaneously—that she wholly believed her words, and that he had been a frigging idiot.

"It's my life. Don't you think I ought to have a say in whether it's ruined or not?"

"No." She looked as distressed as she was determined. "You don't know what it's like in the spotlight and I do."

"I don't care."

"You say that now. But you haven't had to live with it day in and day out your entire life."

"Poor Mimi." He couldn't help himself, he pulled her into his arms again.

"You don't want that, Brant. Please believe me on this."

"Hate to break it to you, Mimi, but you don't get to decide what I want and don't want."

She opened her mouth to argue, but he gave a long-suffering sigh and shut her up by kissing her. She stood rigid in his arms for a moment and then she melted against him, her arms around his neck and her belly pressing against him.

It was sweet and wonderful, better even than kicking off his boots after a two-week mission, and he never wanted it to end.

"I just spent four months missing you every single minute of every single day," he murmured against her mouth. "I fell asleep thinking about you and woke up thinking about you. It took all my concentration to do my job."

She made a tiny sound but he couldn't tell what it meant.

"I love you, Mimi. I love your stubborn streak and your funny sense of humor and your big green eyes. I love the way you chew her lip when you're concentrating and the way you pamper that silly little dog and how you shiver when I kiss you. You want to know what I want, with everything inside me? You. That's all. You. Today, tomorrow, forever."

When her eyes met his, they were dazed and a deeper green than he'd ever seen them.

"What about the media circus?"

"What about them? You said yourself they haven't bothered you much when you're living here. So we'll just spent the next fifty years being boring and they'll lose interest."

"I wish it were that easy."

He kissed her again. "Who said life was supposed to be easy? We can make it work, Mimi. I swear to you. Can't you trust me?"

This couldn't be happening. Mimi closed her eyes, wondering if this was another of those dreams where she woke up with a wet pillow and empty arms.

No. He was real. Big and solid and wonderful and claiming he loved her.

She wanted so desperately to believe him, to hold on to the delicious dream that they could actually build a life together.

If any man was strong enough to face off against the paparazzi, it was Brant. And he was right; they had quickly tired of her sedate pace of life here in Pine Gulch. What was the fun in shooting her when she wasn't doing anything outrageous, just living her life like Maura Howard would?

Could she dare believe him?

"I'm having another man's child. Are you okay with that?"

His mouth quirked up in a half smile. "The way I heard, it was in vitro fertilization."

"You know that's not true."

"As far as I'm concerned, it is." He kissed her again, leaving her no doubts that he meant his words.

A fragile hope began to quiver inside her. A life with him here in Pine Gulch or wherever his Army career took him. She wanted it, more than she'd ever wanted anything in her life.

"Are we having a boy or a girl?" Brant asked against her mouth, and just like that she started to cry again. He kissed away every tear.

She didn't deserve to be this happy, did she? As soon as the thought pulsed through her, she pushed it away. Why didn't she deserve a little happiness? Or huge bushels full of it?

"A girl." She gave him a watery smile, a smile that carried all the love in her heart for him. "I was thinking about naming her Abigail Sage. It was my grandmother's name."

"Abigail Western. Has a nice ring to it, don't you think?"

She stared at him for a long moment and finally had to force herself to breathe. A quiet peace seemed to eddy around them like the rivulets of Cold Creek, washing away all the pain, all the doubt, all the hurt. In his arms, she could believe anything was possible.

"Yes," she said softly. "I think Abigail Western sounds perfect."

Brant smiled and kissed her with a tenderness that

nearly made her cry again. "If she's anything like her mother, she will be."

Mimi shook her head. She wasn't perfect. Far from it. She was a work in progress—but now she had her own blue-eyed warrior to help her on the journey.

Epilogue

"You make a beautiful bride."

Mimi hugged Easton, thinking how lovely her maid of honor looked. No one seeing this fragile, feminine creature in the pale sage dress with the long blond hair in a graceful updo would ever guess she spent most of her days riding fence line and fixing tractors.

Easton was stunning, even with that hint of sadness in her blue eyes.

"I appreciate you saying that," Mimi answered, "especially since I'm bigger than one of your cows right now."

"You glow, just like a new bride—and mom-to-be—is supposed to. Brant can't take his eyes off you."

That particular feeling was mutual. Every time she happened to see him in his dress uniform with that chest full of medals, looking tall and gorgeous and commanding, she couldn't seem to look away.

Her gaze unerringly found him, speaking with his friend Quinn Southerland and Quinn's wife, Tess. Brant held their newborn son, Joe, only a month old, and he looked completely natural with a tiny bundle in his arms.

She smiled with anticipation, imagining him holding their child, and she suddenly couldn't wait.

"He's something, isn't he?"

"He is," Easton agreed. "Sometimes I want to wring his neck but I wouldn't change him."

Mimi thought of how dear the other woman had become to her in the six months since she showed up at the Western Sky, afraid and alone. Easton had become the true sister Mimi had always wanted and never found with every new step-sibling her father gave her.

When Easton turned to whisper in Mimi's ear over the noise of the music and the crowd, she leaned closer, expecting maybe a tidbit of gossip or words of encouragement.

Instead, Easton smiled for the benefit of the other wedding guests and murmured, "Screw him over, Ms. Van Hoyt, and I'll come looking for you with a cattle prod."

"I wouldn't dare," Mimi promised with a laugh. Though she knew Easton was completely serious in her threat, she also knew her friend was thrilled she and Brant had found each other. "And it's Mrs. Western now."

"Good. As long we understand each other." Easton smiled back, then changed the subject, her duties as loyal foster sister apparently discharged. "I can't believe the vultures haven't descended yet."

"Thanks for the reminder." Mimi winced. Even now, the press corps would be milling at the end of the access road to the Western Sky, where she and Brant had married a half hour ago next to the silvery creek she had driven into that first day.

She had hoped to keep the wedding a secret, but Pine Gulch was a small town. Even though their wedding was intimate, between the caterers and the band and the florist, word had somehow trickled out. The paparazzi had begun arriving the night before and some of them had even started camping out on the public right-of-way along Cold Creek Canyon Road.

"How did you keep them out?" Easton asked.

"Brant threatened them all with a shotgun again," she said.

"He did not!"

"Okay, he didn't threaten them. But he made sure he had his Remington with him and ever so subtly held on to it at his side when we went down to talk to them this morning. We promised if they wouldn't try to crash the actual ceremony, we would come down and pose for the cameras later."

She supposed it had been foolish to hope she and Brant might avoid the tabloids completely, especially since the public had avidly latched on to the story when rumors of her romance with Brant and the impending wedding started to trickle out. The pregnant society heiress and the gorgeous injured war hero made for great copy.

They would probably have to cope with paparazzi for a while, what with the wedding and her impending birth, but she had high hopes that they'd lose interest soon. Brant didn't seem to be bothered by it. In fact, he seemed to be finding great humor in their interest, for the most part—especially his new nickname, Mimi's Warrior.

She pressed a hand to her abdomen, hoping she could make it on her feet long enough for a photo session. The vague aches in her back had intensified over the past hour, but she was doing her best to ignore them.

"Uh-oh. Werner alert," Easton said. "Want me to distract him?"

Mimi shook her head. "Thanks for the offer, but I think I'll be okay."

To her shock, her father seemed as close as she'd ever seen to being pleased about something she was doing. He was actually happy about her marriage to Brant, something she never would have expected.

They both had such strong personalities, she never would have guessed they'd rub together so well. Brant hadn't tried to ingratiate himself in her father's graces. In fact, he'd been on the abrasive side, making it clear that while Werner might consider his daughter a bubbleheaded socialite, Brant had far different views. Instead of being offended, her father had treated him with respect and even admiration.

"You look just like your mother did on her wedding day," Werner said gruffly now, and she was aware that Easton, the traitor, had melted away into the crowd.

Mimi laughed. "Was she eight and a half months pregnant, too?"

"You know she wasn't. But she was almost as pretty as you are right now."

He looked at Brant, still holding baby Joe. "He's a good man. He's almost good enough for you."

"Thanks, Dad."

He paused for a long moment, and then he smiled—

a little sadly, she thought. "I love you, you know. I'm not always great at showing it, but I do."

Tears welled up in her eyes but she refused to let them ruin her mascara. Not on her wedding day.

She kissed his cheek, the first time in her recent memory she had initiated affectionate contact between them. Werner stood stiffly for a long moment and then he gathered her close in a clumsy sort of hug, made even more awkward by her belly.

She closed her eyes, smelling the cologne he had created exclusively for himself at a Paris fragrance house. In this moment, all the pain of the past and the silly power struggles between them seemed far away.

"He's a good man," her father repeated. "He'll take good care of you and the baby."

Once he recovered from his initial shock at her pregnancy, Werner had once more surprised her. He seemed to actually be looking forward to becoming a grandfather.

Marta, his current wife, gestured to him a moment later and Werner gave her another awkward squeeze then went to join her stepmother.

Mimi felt the heat of someone's gaze on her and turned to find Brant watching her. She smiled at him and headed toward him, but she had only taken a few steps when she felt something strange.

She froze and it took her a full minute to figure out what had happened. When she did, she started to laugh and couldn't seem to stop.

Brant met her halfway and pulled her into his warm embrace. "I never realized being married to me would be such a laugh fest."

This set her off again and she had to wipe her eyes

with the little lace-trimmed hankie Easton had given her, the something old that had belonged to Brant's foster mother, Jo Winder.

"Um, have you seen Jake?" she asked him between giggles.

He frowned. "I think I saw him and Maggie out on the dance floor a minute ago. Why?"

She wrapped her arms as tightly as she could manage around him with her bulk in the way. He obligingly leaned his head down so she could whisper in his ear.

"My water just broke."

He jerked back as if she'd punched him and she had to laugh again at his stunned expression.

"You're not due for three more weeks!"

"I guess Abigail was a little put out that we didn't wait for her to be the flower girl at her mommy and daddy's wedding. Either that or she's a bit of a prima donna and wants all the attention for herself."

He still wore that stunned expression but after a moment, it shifted to something else, a complex mix of nerves and shock, underscored by a deep joy. He pulled her into his arms again and she felt his lips on her hair for only a moment, then he loosened his hold.

"Okay. We can do this. Where's Jake? We need to get your bag from inside. It's still packed, right? I'll drive us to Idaho Falls. Or do you want to take the limousine?"

This man who could coordinate complicated troop movements and arrange logistical support to transport an entire company of soldiers across the world within a few hours looked more than a little panicked.

She smiled and squeezed his fingers. "Dr. Dalton. Let's start with him."

"Right. Jake." He stepped away to go after the doctor, then suddenly turned back to her and swept her back into his arms. He kissed her fiercely, eyes blazing with tenderness.

"I love you," he said.

She managed a smile, even as the first contraction hit. "I still don't know why, but I'm so glad you do. I love you, too."

"You're doing this just to get me out of the photo shoot, aren't you?"

More laughter bubbled out of her. "No, but I wish I'd thought of it. You know they're going to go crazy over this. Not every bride leaves her own wedding reception in labor."

"Let them go crazy. It will be a great story we can tell Abby someday." He paused. "You're going to be a fantastic mother."

"If we don't hurry, I'm afraid I'm going to become a fantastic mother in the middle of my own wedding reception."

He grinned, squeezed her hand and rushed away.

Mimi watched him go, her warrior. She thought of the journey that had led her here, the strange twists and turns. It was fate that had led her to run to Gwen that day, fate that had brought her to this ranch she loved so much. And to this man she loved more than she could believe possible.

She pressed a hand to her abdomen as she saw Brant return with Jake Dalton in tow. "We're going to be okay, kiddo," she murmured. "You, me and your wonderful daddy."

* * * * *

Books by Caro Carson

Harlequin Special Edition

Montana Mavericks:
What Happened at the Wedding?
The Maverick's Holiday Masquerade

Texas Rescue

A Cowboy's Wish Upon a Star
Her Texas Rescue Doctor
Following Doctor's Orders
A Texas Rescue Christmas
Not Just a Cowboy

The Doctors MacDowell

The Bachelor Doctor's Bride
The Doctor's Former Fiancée
Doctor, Soldier, Daddy

Visit the Author Profile page
at Harlequin.com for more titles.

NOT JUST A COWBOY

Caro Carson

For Barbara Tohm, my very own fairy godmother.

Chapter 1

Patricia Cargill was not going to marry Quinn Mac-Dowell, after all.

What a dreadful inconvenience.

She'd invested nearly a year of her life to cultivating their friendship, a pleasant relationship between a man and a woman evenly matched in temperament, in attractiveness, in income. Just when Patricia had thought the time was right for a smooth transition to the logical next step, Quinn had fallen head over heels in love with a woman he'd only known for a few weeks.

A year's planning, a year's investment of Patricia's time and effort, gone in a matter of days.

She tapped her pen impatiently against the clipboard in her hand. She didn't sigh, she didn't stoop her shoulders in defeat, and she most certainly didn't cry. Patricia was a Cargill, of the Austin Cargills, and she would weather her personal storm.

Later.

Right now, she was helping an entire town weather the aftermath of a different kind of storm, the kind that made national news as it made landfall on the coast of Texas. The kind of storm that could peel the roof off a hospital, leaving a town in need of the medical assistance that the Texas Rescue and Relief organization could provide. The kind of storm that let Patricia drop all the social niceties expected of an heiress while she assumed her role as the personnel director for a mobile hospital.

Her hospital was built of white tents, powered by generators, and staffed by all the physicians, nurses, and technicians Patricia had spent the past year recruiting. During Austin dinner parties and Lake Travis sailing weekends, over posh Longhorn football tailgates and stale hospital cafeteria buffets, Patricia had secured their promises to volunteer with Texas Rescue in time of disaster. That time was now.

"Patricia, there you are."

She turned to see one of her recruits hurrying toward her, a private-practice physician who'd never been in the field with Texas Rescue before. A rookie.

The woman was in her early thirties, a primary care physician named Mary Hodge. Her green scrubs could have been worn by anyone at the hospital, but she also wore a white doctor's coat, one she'd brought with her from Austin. She'd already wasted Patricia's time yesterday, tracking her down like this in order to insist that her coat be dry cleaned if she was expected to stay the week. Patricia had coolly informed her no laundry service would be pressing that white coat. This Texan beach town had been hit by a hurricane less than two days ago.

It was difficult enough to have essential laundry, like scrubs and bed linens, cleaned in these conditions. Locating an operational dry-cleaning establishment would not become an item on Patricia's to-do list.

Dr. Hodge crossed the broiling black top of the parking lot where Texas Rescue had set up the mobile hospital. Whatever she wanted from Patricia, it was bound to be as inane as the dry cleaning. Patricia wasn't going to hustle over to hear it, but neither would she pretend she hadn't heard Hodge call her name. The rookie was her responsibility.

Patricia stayed standing, comfortable enough despite the late afternoon heat. Knowing she'd spend long days standing on hard blacktop, Patricia always wore her rubber-soled Docksides when Texas Rescue went on a mission. Between those and the navy polo shirt she wore that bore the Texas Rescue logo, she could have boarded a yacht as easily as run a field hospital, but no one ever mistook her for a lady of leisure. Not while she was with Texas Rescue.

As she waited in the June heat, Patricia checked her clipboard—her old-school, paper-powered clipboard. It was the only kind guaranteed to work when electric lines were down. If Texas Rescue was on the scene, it was a sure bet that electricity had been cut off by a hurricane or tornado, a fire or flood. Her clipboard had a waterproof, hard plastic cover that repelled the rain.

She flipped the cover open. First item: *X-ray needs admin clerk for night shift.*

There were only two shifts in this mobile hospital, days and nights. Patricia tended to work most of both, but she made sure her staff got the rest their volunteer contracts specified. She jotted her solution next to the problem: *assign Kim Wells.* Patricia had kept her personal assistant longer during this deployment than usual, but as always, Patricia would now work alone so that some other department wouldn't be shorthanded.

Second item: *Additional ECG machine in tent E4.*

That was for Quinn, the cardiologist she wouldn't be marrying. She'd make a call and have one brought down from Austin with the next incoming physician. She could have managed Quinn's personal life just as efficiently, making her an excellent choice for his wife, but that concept wouldn't appeal to the man now that he was in love.

If there was anything Patricia had learned as the daughter of the infamous Daddy Cargill, it was that men needed managing. Since Patricia genuinely liked Quinn, she hoped the woman he married would be a good manager, but she doubted it. Fortunately for Quinn, he didn't need much direction. Cool-headed and logical—at least around Patricia—he would have been a piece of cake for her to manage after living with Daddy Cargill.

Third: *Set up additional shade for waiting area.*

The head of Austin's Texas Rescue operations, Karen Weaver, was supposed to be responsible for the physical layout of the hospital as well as equipment like the ECG machine, but Karen wasn't the most efficient or knowledgeable director to have ever served at the helm of Texas Rescue. Waiting for Karen to figure out how to get things done was hard on the medical staff and the patients. Patricia would find someone to get another tent off the truck and pitch it outside the treatment tents.

"Patricia." Mary Hodge, sweating and frowning, stopped a few feet away and put her hands on her hips.

"Dr. Hodge." Patricia kept her eyes on her to-do

list as she returned the curt greeting. The woman had earned her title; Patricia would use it no matter how little she thought of the doctor's lousy work ethic.

"Listen, I can't stay until Friday, after all. Something's come up."

"Is that right?" Patricia very deliberately tucked the clipboard under her arm, then lifted her chin and gave Dr. Hodge her full attention. "Explain."

Dr. Hodge frowned immediately. Doctors, as a species, gave orders. They didn't take commands well. Patricia knew when to be gracious, and she knew how to persuade someone powerful that her idea was their idea. But Patricia was also a Cargill, a descendant of pioneers who'd made millions on deals sealed with handshakes, and that meant she didn't give a damn about tact when a person was about to welch on a deal. Dr. Hodge was trying to do just that.

The doctor raised her chin, as well, clearly unused to having her authority challenged. "I have a prior commitment." Unspoken, her tone said, *And that's all you need to know.*

Patricia kept her voice cool and her countenance cooler. "Your contract specifies ninety-six hours of service. I haven't got any extra physicians to take your place if you leave."

"I'm needed back at West Central."

Patricia had recruited as many physicians as she could from West Central Texas Hospital. The hospital had been founded by Quinn MacDowell's father, and his brother Braden served as CEO. She knew the hospital well. It had just been one more item on the list of reasons why Quinn had been her best candidate for marriage.

Her familiarity with West Central gave her an advantage right now. "West Central is perfectly aware that you are here until Friday. If you went back this evening, people might wonder why you returned ahead of schedule."

The woman started to object. Patricia held up a hand in a calming gesture. It was time to pretend to be tactful, at least. "You have a prior commitment, of course, but some people could jump to the conclusion that you just didn't like the inconvenience of working at a natural disaster site. Wouldn't that be a terrible reputation to have in a hospital where so many doctors somehow find the time to volunteer with Texas Rescue? I do hope you'll be able to reschedule your commitment, just to avoid any damage to your professional reputation."

The threat was delivered in Patricia's most gracious tone of voice. Dr. Hodge bit out something about rescheduling her other commitment at great inconvenience to herself. "But I'm out of here Friday morning."

"After ten, yes." Patricia set Dr. Hodge's departure time as she unflinchingly met the woman's glare.

Dr. Hodge stalked away, back toward the high-tech, inflatable white surgical tent where she was supposed to be stitching the deep cuts and patching up the kinds of wounds that were common when locals started digging through rubble for their belongings. Patricia didn't care if Hodge was angry; that was Hodge's personal problem, not Patricia's.

No, her personal problem had nothing to do with this field hospital, and everything to do with her plans for the future. Every moment that Texas Rescue didn't demand her attention, she found her mind circling futilely around the central problem of her life: *How am I going to save the Cargill fortune from my own father?*

The radio in her hand squawked for her attention. Thankfully. Patricia raised it to her mouth and pressed the side button. "Go ahead."

"This is Mike in pharmacy. We're going through the sublingual nitro fast."

Of course they were. After any natural disaster, the number of chest pain cases reported in the population increased. It was one of the reasons she'd recruited Quinn to Texas Rescue; she'd needed a cardiologist to sort the everyday angina from the heart attacks. The initial treatment for both conditions was a nitroglycerin tablet. The pharmacists she'd recruited always kept their nitro well stocked, but a new pharmacy tech had freely dispensed a month's worth to each patient instead of a week's worth, and the hospital had nearly run out before anyone had noticed.

Patricia had recruited that pharmacy tech, too. She accepted that the shortage was therefore partly her fault. Even if it hadn't been, Patricia would've been the one to fix it.

She pressed the talk button on her radio again. "You'll need to make what you've got last for several more hours. I'm going to have to reach quite a bit farther out of town to source more."

She'd find more, though. *Failure is not an option* was the kind of cheesy line Patricia would never be caught saying, but it fit the mission of Texas Rescue.

Patricia started through the white tents toward the one that housed her administrative office. The Texas Rescue field hospital had been set up in the parking lot of the multi-story community hospital. The missing roof of the town's hospital had rendered it useless, and the building now stood empty. Its shadow was welcome, though, to offset the Gulf Coast's June heat. She noticed the Texas Rescue firefighters had moved their red truck into the shade, too, as they used their axes to clear debris from the town's toppled ambulances. The fire truck's powerful motor turned a winch, metal cables strained, and an ambulance was hauled back into its upright position.

There was a beauty to the simple solution. The ambulance had been on its side; the ambulance was now upright. If only her world could work that way...but Daddy Cargill had tangled the family fortune badly, and Patricia needed more than a simple winch to set her life back on track.

The shade of the damaged building couldn't be doing much to help the firefighters as they worked in their protective gear. Patricia barely tolerated the steamy heat by wearing knee-length linen shorts and by keeping her hair smoothed into a neat bun, off her neck and out of her face. There hadn't been a cloud in the sky all day, however, and the heat was winning. Thank goodness the administration's tent had a generator-run air cooler.

Unlike the surgical tents, her "office" was the more traditional type of structure, a large square tent of white fabric pitched so the parking lot served as the hard but mud-free floor. Before pushing through the weighted fabric flap that served as her tent's door, Patricia caught sight of Quinn at the far side of the parking lot. Tall, dark and familiar, her friend stood by a green Volkswagen Bug, very close to the redheaded woman who'd stolen his heart—an apparently romantic heart Patricia hadn't suspected Quinn possessed.

Her name was Diana. Patricia knew Diana's forty-eight-hour volunteer commitment was over, and her career in Austin required her return. Quinn was committed to staying the week without her.

Patricia watched them say goodbye. Quinn cupped Diana's face in his hands, murmured words only she would ever hear and then he kissed her.

Like the worst voyeur, Patricia couldn't turn away. It wasn't the sensuality of the kiss that held her gaze, although Quinn was a handsome man, and the way he pulled Diana into him as he kissed her was undeniably physical. No, there was more than just sex in that kiss. There was an intensity in the kiss, a link between the man and woman, a connection Patricia could practically see even as Diana got behind the wheel of her tiny car and drove away.

The intensity in Quinn's gaze as he watched Diana leave made Patricia want to shiver in the June heat.

It was too much. She didn't want that. Ever.

Nitroglycerin.

With renewed focus, she pushed aside the fabric flap and entered her temporary office, grateful for the cooler air inside. The generator that powered their computers also ran the air cooler and a spare fan. The tent was spacious, housing neat rows of simple folding chairs and collapsible tables. It was the nerve center for the paperwork that made a hospital run, from patients' documents to volunteers' contracts.

Her administrative team, all wearing Texas Rescue shirts, kept working as Patricia headed for the card table that served as her desk. Only a few nodded at her. The rest seemed almost unnaturally busy.

She didn't take their lack of acknowledgment personally. She was the boss. They were trying to look too busy for her to question their workload.

She was grateful, actually, to slip into the metal folding chair without making any small talk. She placed her clipboard and radio to the right of her waiting laptop, opened its lid, and waited for the computer to boot up—none of which took her mind off that kiss between Quinn and Diana.

The kind of desire she'd just witnessed had been different than the kind she was generally exposed to. Her father was on his third wife and his millionth mistress. He was all about the pet names, the slap-and-tickle, the almost juvenile quest for sex. Quinn had been looking at the woman he loved in a totally different way. Like she was important—no, crucial. Like she was his world.

That kind of desire would be demanding. Unpleasantly so. Burdensome, to have a man need her so completely. It would only get in the way of what Patricia wanted in life.

She didn't want the perpetual adolescence of a man like her father, but neither did she want the intensity of a soul mate. No, she just wanted a husband who would be an asset, who would efficiently partner her as she achieved her goals in life. A man who would slide as seamlessly into her world as one of her beloved sailboats glided through water, barely disturbing the surface.

"Coming through!"

A fireman crashed through the tent's door, dragging another firefighter behind him. He pulled off his friend's helmet and tossed it on the ground as he yelled "Water!"

No one moved. Lined up in their matching polo

shirts, Patricia's entire workforce froze with their fingers over their keyboards.

The next second, Patricia was on her feet, coming around her table toward the men. Clearly, the second guy was overheated and on the verge of passing out.

"There's cool air here," she said, stepping out of the way as she pointed toward the side of the tent where the blower was located.

The first man, a giant in his helmet and bulky uniform, hauled his stumbling buddy past her. He dropped to one knee as he lowered the man to the asphalt in front of the cooler, then took his own helmet off and set it lightly on the ground. He let his head drop as he took one long, deep breath. His black hair was soaked through and his own skin was flushed from heat, but then his one-second break was apparently over, and he was back in motion.

To Patricia, the two men were a heap of reflective tape, canvas straps, rubber boots, and flashlights tucked into more straps and pockets on their bulky, beige uniforms. It took her a moment to make out what the first man was doing. He'd zeroed in on the toggles that held his friend's coat shut.

His friend fumbled at his own chest with clunky, gloved hands. "S'my coat." His words were slurred. "I get it."

"Yeah, sure." The black-haired fireman pushed his buddy's hands out of the way and kept unfastening.

Patricia knelt beside him, ignoring the rough asphalt on her bare knees, and tugged off the overheated man's gloves. "Do you want me to radio the ER? We've got a backboard in here that we could use as a stretcher." She turned to speak over her shoulder to the nearest person. "Bring me my walkie-talkie."

"He'll be fine once he's cooled off." The black-haired man tugged the heavy coat all the way off his friend, then let the man lie flat on his back in front of the cooler. "You're feeling better already, Zach, right? Zach?"

He slapped the man's cheek lightly with the back of his gloved hand. By now, Patricia's team had gathered around. She took her walkie-talkie from her staff member, and the black-haired firefighter took one of the bottles of water that were being held out. He dumped it over Zach's hair. The water puddled onto the asphalt beneath him.

Zach pushed his arm away, still clumsy in his movements. "Stop it, jackass." His words were less slurred, a good sign, even if he spoke less like an admin clerk and more like a...well, like a fireman.

The black-haired man turned to Patricia. Their eyes met, and after a second's pause, he winked. "Told you. He's feeling better already."

Patricia kept looking at his impossibly handsome, cheerfully confident face and forgot whatever it was she'd been about to say. He had blue eyes—not just any blue, but the exact shade that reminded her of sailing on blue water, under blue sky.

He shook off his own gloves in one sharp movement, then shrugged out of his own coat. As he bent to stuff his coat under his friend's head, Patricia bent, too, but there was nothing for her to do as he efficiently lifted his friend's head with one hand and shoved his coat in place. She straightened up, sitting back on her heels and brushing the grit off her knees, but she stayed next to him, ready to help, watching as he worked.

As the muscles in his shoulders moved, his red suspenders crisscrossed over the black T-shirt he wore. A brief glance down the man's back showed that those suspenders were necessary; his torso was lean and trim, while the canvas firefighter pants were loose and baggy. The stereotypical red straps weren't just designed to make women swoon....

She looked away quickly when he finished his makeshift pillow and straightened, too.

Propping his left forearm on his bended knee, he extended his right toward her in a handshake.

"Thank you for your help, ma'am." His voice was as deep as he was large. Deep, with a Texas twang. "My name's Luke Waterson. Pleased to meet you."

He had cowboy manners even when he was under stress, introducing himself like this. She had to hand that to him as she placed her hand in his. His skin was warm and dry as she returned his handshake in a businesslike manner. He was still a giant of a man without his fireman's coat, broad-chested with shoulder and arm muscles that were clearly defined under his T-shirt, but he returned her shake without a trace of the bone-crushing grip many men used.

Patricia knew some men just weren't aware how strong their grip was, but others—including her father's cronies—used the too-hard handshake as a form of intimidation. If this fireman had wanted to play that game, Patricia would have been ready.

But he didn't hold her hand too long or too tightly. He let her go, but that grin deepened, lifting one corner of his mouth higher than the other as he kept those sailing-blue eyes on her.

Patricia looked away first. Not very Cargill of her, but then again, men didn't often look at her the way this young fireman did. A bone-crushing handshake? No problem. She could handle that. But to be winked at and grinned at like she was…was…a college coed…

As if.

She'd never been that flirtatious and carefree, not even when she'd *been* a college co-ed. In college, she'd come home on weekends to make sure her father's latest bed partner wasn't robbing them blind. She'd gone over every expense and cosigned every one of her father's checks before they were cashed.

Lord, college had been a decade ago. What was it about this fireman—this Luke Waterson—that made her think of being twenty-two instead of thirty-two?

He used his heavy helmet to fan Zach's face, a move that made his well-defined bicep flex. Frankly, the man looked like a male stripper in a fireman's costume. Maybe that explained her sudden coed feeling. When she'd been twenty-two, she'd been to enough bachelorette parties to last her a lifetime. If she'd seen one male review with imitation firemen dancing for money, then she'd seen them all.

Those brides had been divorced and planning their second weddings as everyone in her social circle approached their thirtieth birthdays together. Patricia had declined the second round of bachelorette weekends. Always the bridesmaid, happy to have escaped being the bride.

Until this year.

The real fireman used his forearm to swipe his forehead, the bulge of his bicep exactly at her eye level. Oh, this Luke was eye candy for women, all right. Muscular, physical—

There's no reason to be so distracted. This is absurd.

She was head of personnel, and this man was wiping his brow because he was nearly as overheated as the unfortunate Zach-on-the-asphalt. If Patricia didn't take care of Luke, she'd soon be short two firemen on her personnel roster.

She plucked one of the water bottles out of her nearest staff member's hand. The young lady didn't move, her gaze fastened upon Luke.

Annoyed with her staff for being as distracted as she'd let herself be, Patricia stood and looked around the circle of people. "Thank you. You can go back to work now."

Her team scattered. Patricia felt more herself. It was good to be in charge. Good to have a job to do.

She handed Luke the bottle. "Drink this."

He obeyed her, but that grin never quite left his face as he knelt on one knee before her, keeping his gaze on her face as he tilted his head back and let the cool water flow down his throat.

Look away, Patricia. Use your radio. Contact the fire chief and let him know where his men are. Look away.

But she didn't. She watched the man drink his water, watched him pitch it effortlessly, accurately, into the nearest trash can, and watched him resume his casual position, one forearm on his knee. He reached down to press his fingers against his friend's wrist once more.

"He's fine," Luke announced after a few seconds of counting heartbeats. "It's easy to get light-headed out there. Nothing some shade and some water couldn't fix."

"Is there anything else I can get you?"

He touched the brim of an imaginary hat in a two-fingered salute. "Thank you for the water, ma'am. You never told me your name."

"Patricia," she said. She had to clear her throat delicately, for the briefest moment, and then, instead of describing herself the way she always did, as Patricia *Cargill,* she said something different. "I'm the personnel director."

"Well, Patricia," he said, and then he smiled, a flash of white teeth and an expression of genuine pleasure in his tanned face. His grin had only been a tease compared to this stunning smile. "It's a pleasure to meet you."

He meant it, she could tell. He'd checked her out, he found her attractive, and that smile was inviting her in, inviting her to smile, too, inviting her to enjoy a little getting-to-know you flirtation.

Patricia couldn't smile back. She wasn't like that. Flirting for fun was a luxury for people who didn't have obligations. She'd never learned how to do it. She'd known only responsibility, even when she'd been twenty-two and men had been interested in her for more than her bank account and Cargill connections.

It almost hurt to look at Luke Waterson's open smile, at the clear expression of approval and interest on his handsome face.

She preferred not to waste energy on useless emotions. And so, she nodded politely and she turned away.

Chapter 2

So, the princess doesn't want to play.

He'd given her the smile, the one that had kept the woman of his choice by his side for as long as he could remember, whether at a bonfire after a high school football game or at a bar after a livestock show in Austin. Patricia-the-personnel-director, apparently, was immune.

That was a real shame. He couldn't remember the last time he'd been around a woman who was so...smooth. Smooth hair, smooth skin, a woman who handled everything and everyone smoothly. She spoke in a smooth, neutral voice, yet everyone ran to do her bidding as if she were a drill sergeant barking out threats. This Patricia was the real deal, a Texas beauty who looked like a princess but had a spine of steel.

It was a shame she wasn't interested. He watched her walk away, headed for the chair she'd been in when he'd first hauled Zach in here. He liked the way she moved, brisk and businesslike.

Businesslike. He should have thought of that. She was clearly the boss in here. The boss couldn't flirt in front of her staff. If they weren't in her office space, would he be able to get her to smile?

Luke switched his helmet to his other hand and kept fanning Zach. Maybe it wasn't that she wasn't interested. She'd been a little flustered when they'd shaken hands, not knowing quite where to look. Maybe she wasn't interested in *being* interested. That was a whole different ballgame.

She wore diamonds in her ears, discreet little studs, but none on her fingers. If she wasn't married or engaged, why not give him a smile?

When he reached for Zach's wrist to check his pulse, Zach shook him off. "I'll live," he said, managing to sound tired and pissed off at the same time.

Patricia picked up a clipboard and turned their way.

Luke ducked a bit closer to Zach and spoke under his breath. "Be a pal and lay still a while longer."

Patricia returned to his side of the tent. She didn't crack a smile, but she crouched beside him once more. Her arm brushed his, and she jerked a tiny bit, as if she'd touched something she shouldn't. It was the smallest of breaks in an otherwise excellent poker face, but Luke was certain: she wasn't totally immune to him.

He sure as hell wasn't immune to her.

"You can stop fanning him," she said. "Rest. I'll take over. You need to cool down, too."

Aw, yeah. Talk to me some more. Her voice fit her looks, sophisticated, assured. She had the faintest accent, enough to identify her as a Texan, but she was no cowgirl. She had the voice of a woman raised with Big Money, the kind of woman who'd gone to college and majored in art history, he'd bet.

She started fanning Zach with her clipboard, so Luke put his helmet down and studied her profile until she glanced at him. She had eyes as dark brown as her hair was pale blond. She didn't drop her gaze this time. Luke was torn between admiring her self-control and wishing she'd act flustered once more.

She kept fanning Zach with her clipboard in one hand. With her other hand, she handed Luke another bottle of water. "Here, drink this. You're as hot as he is."

He nearly laughed at that. Maybe she wouldn't flirt back with him in front of her staff, but he couldn't resist such an easy opening. "Well, ma'am, I'd say thank you for the compliment, but only being as hot as Zach isn't truly that flattering. He's just your average-looking slacker, laying down on the job."

Zach grunted, but didn't bother opening his eyes. Zach had always been a good wing man.

Luke gestured toward him with the bottle of water. "That eloquent grunt means Zach agrees."

Patricia looked away again, but not in a flustered way. Nope, now she just raised one brow in faint disgust and turned away, the princess not lowering herself to comment on the peasants' looks.

Luke chuckled, enjoying this brush with a Texas beauty queen, even if it led nowhere. It was something else to be in the presence of royalty.

She pointed toward the unopened bottle in his hand, but before she could repeat her order, he raised his hand in surrender.

"I'm drinking. I'm drinking." He had to stop chuckling in order to down the second bottle of water.

Princess Patricia stood abruptly, but she only stepped a foot away to grab a metal folding chair and then place it next to him. "Here, you'll be more comfortable."

Not quite royalty, then. Or at least, she was hardworking and considerate royalty.

"Thank you, ma'am." Before rising, he clapped Zach on the shoulder. "How 'bout you sit up and drink some water now?"

"I'll get another chair," Patricia said.

Then it happened. She turned away for a chair. He turned away to extend his hand to Zach. He hauled his friend to his feet; she set a folding chair next to the first. They finished at the same second, turning back toward each other, and collided. He steadied her with two hands. Her elegant fingers grasped the edge of his red suspender for balance. The rubber edge of her boat shoe caught on the rubber of his fireman's boot, tripping her, and she clung a little tighter. She was tall, but he was taller, and into the side of his neck she exhaled a single, awkward, warm and breathy "oh."

In that moment, as he stood solidly on his own two feet and held Patricia in his hands, Luke knew that a slender, soft woman had just knocked all two hundred pounds of him flat on his back.

She looked away, then down on the ground, flustered again. The diamond stud in her delicate earlobe grazed his chin. She let go of his suspender and pushed back a half step, turning to collect her clipboard off the chair she'd placed for him. "Stay as long as you need to," she said without making eye contact. "I'll let the fire chief know where you are."

She left, pushing the tent flap out of her way as impatiently as Luke had when he'd been coming in.

Luke sat heavily where her clipboard had been, frowning as Zach guzzled his water next to him. Patricia had felt every bit of electricity he had, he'd bet the ranch on it. He'd never had a woman who was so attracted to him be so eager to get away from him. There had to be a reason, but damn if he could guess what it might be.

Zach finished his water and started a second bottle. Halfway through, he stopped for a breath. He jerked his head toward the door flap. "Give it up now, rookie. You aren't getting a piece of that action. Ever."

"Not here," Luke silenced him tersely. There were too many people listening to the firemen who'd landed themselves in the middle of a bunch of paper pushers. Luke sat back against the cold metal of the chair and crossed his arms over his chest.

So, Patricia didn't want to flirt. He could understand that on one level, but he felt instinctively that it went beyond being on duty or in charge. She'd hightailed it out of there, if such an elegant woman could be said to move so hastily, yet they'd just experienced chemistry with a capital *C*. Chemistry that couldn't be denied. Chemistry that Luke wanted to explore.

"You ready?" he asked Zach. Without waiting for Zach's grunt of agreement, Luke stood, then started picking up coats, gloves, and his helmet. As the men headed toward the exit, they passed Patricia's table. Luke dropped one glove, kicking it mid-stride to land precisely under a chair. Her chair.

Zach noticed. "You gonna get that now or later?"

"Neither," Luke said under his breath. When they

reached the door, he bent to scoop up Zach's helmet. They stepped outside, into the blinding Texas sun.

Luke handed Zach his coat and helmet. "I'm gonna let her bring that glove to me when she's ready."

"You never leave your equipment behind, rookie."

"True enough." Luke wasn't going to argue that point. He was a rookie for the fire department, but he was a twenty-eight-year-old man who'd been running a cattle ranch for seven years. No cowboy worked without gloves, so he'd known to bring more than one pair. He could leave that one for Patricia to find. To find, and to decide what to do with.

Zach smacked dirt and grit off the polished black surface of his helmet. "For future reference, rookie, throwing a helmet on asphalt scratches it all to hell."

"Battle scars, Zach. We've all got 'em."

Luke didn't mind his engine's tradition of calling the newest member "rookie" for the first few months of service, but Zach was laying it on a bit thick, considering they'd gone to school together. They'd played football, suffered through reading Melville and hand-fed goats in 4-H together.

Zach shook his head. "You may have a way with the fillies on your ranch, but that woman isn't a skittish horse. She runs this whole place, whether it's official or not. I worked with her last summer after those twisters in Oklahoma. If you think she just needs patience and a soft touch and then she'll follow you around like a pet, you're wrong."

"We'll see." Both men started walking toward their fire engine, taking wide strides out of necessity in their bulky turnout pants and rubber boots.

"You're too cocky, Waterson. Go ahead and ignore

my advice. It'll be good for you when she shuts you down before you even make it to first base."

"First base? A kiss? High school was a long time ago, Zach."

"You won't get that much, I promise you. You aren't her type."

Luke remembered that moment of impact. Chemistry with a capital *C,* all right. He smiled.

Zach shook his head. "I know that smile. Tell you what. You manage to kiss that woman, and I won't make you repaint my helmet."

Luke's smile dimmed. On the surface, Zach's casual dare seemed harmless enough. They'd been through plenty of dares before. *You buy the beer if I can sweet talk that waitress onto the dance floor while she's still on the clock.* But this was different. Somehow.

"You're forgetting two things," Luke said. "One, my mama raised me better than to kiss a girl for a dare. Two, my daddy raised me that if I broke it, I had to fix it. I'll paint your damned helmet when we get back to Austin."

"Two more things," Zach said, laying a heavy hand on Luke's shoulder. "One, thanks for getting me out of the sun when I was too dazed to do it myself. Forget about the helmet. I owe you more than that."

"Don't worry about it."

Zach let go of his shoulder after a hard squeeze. "And two, that was my glove you left behind, Romeo. If your filly shies away from you, you're gonna have to go back and get it. Today."

Chapter 3

Darkness came, and Luke was glad that a strong breeze from the ocean came with it. Cutting vehicles loose from downed trees had been grueling in the motionless air the storm had left behind. When the order came to stand down, Luke was glad for that, too. He considered himself to be in good shape, working on the ranch day in and day out, but wielding an ax for hour after hour had been backbreaking, plain and simple.

The one thing he would have been most glad of, however, never came. Patricia never appeared, not in a flustered way, not in a collected way, not in any way. Whatever the beautiful personnel director was up to, she wasn't up to it in his part of the relief center. But since impatient Zach wanted his damned glove back, Luke was going to have to go and get it.

Determined to make the best of it, Luke had hit the

portable showers when the fire crew had their allotted time. He'd dug a clean T-shirt out of his gym bag and run a comb through his hair while it was still damp. Shaving was conveniently required of the firemen, since beards could interfere with the way a respirator mask sealed to the face. He'd been able to shave without drawing any attention to himself.

All he had to do was tell the guys to head off for chow without him, and then he could take a convenient detour that would lead him past Patricia's tent on his way to supper in the mess tent. He'd listen for her voice, and if she was in, he'd go in to retrieve his glove. Damn, but he was looking forward to seeing her again.

He was so intent on reaching her tent that he nearly missed her voice when he heard it in a place he hadn't expected. He stopped short outside the door marked "pharmacy," a proper door with a lock, set into a wooden frame that was sealed to an inflatable tent, similar to the kind he knew were used for surgeries and such.

"The rules exist for a reason." Smooth but unyielding, that was Patricia's voice.

"I thought we were here to help these people," another female voice answered, but this voice sounded more shrill and impatient. "These people have lost their houses. They've lost everything. If I can give them some free medicine, why shouldn't I? When I went to Haiti, we gave everyone months' worth of the drugs they needed."

There was a beat of silence, then Patricia's tone changed subtly to one of almost motherly concern. "It might help if you keep in mind that this isn't Haiti. Half of the homes in this town were vacant vacation homes, second homes for people who can well afford their own medicine. You don't need to give them a month's worth, just a few days until the town's regular pharmacies re-open."

"Then I don't see what the big deal is." The other woman, in response to Patricia's gentle concern, sounded like a pouting teenager. "Nitroglycerin is cheap, any-way."

"It's not the cost, it's the scarcity. I had to send some-one almost all the way to Victoria to get more. He was gone for nearly four hours. He used gallons of gasoline that can't be replaced because the pumps aren't running yet because the electricity isn't running yet."

Luke nearly grinned when he heard that steel slip back into Patricia's voice. He crossed his arms over his chest and tilted his head back to look up at the stars. She was right about the electricity being out, of course. When an entire town's streetlights were doused, the stars became brilliant. When all traffic stopped, the crash of the ocean surf could be heard blocks away.

It should be easy to set the right mood to explore a little physical chemistry, and he realized now he'd been hoping to find Patricia—and Zach's glove—alone. It would have been better if he could have waited until she'd had the time and the desire, or at least the curios-ity, to come and find him. But since he needed to get that glove, he'd half hoped she'd be happy to see him walk back into her tent tonight. He'd forgotten some-thing important: Patricia was still working. Still work-ing and still the boss.

He should get to the mess tent. He could stop by the admin tent an hour from now, or three, and he knew she'd be there, working. There was no need to wait for her right now.

Yet he lingered, and listened, and admired the way she stayed cool, alternating between logical and sympathetic until the other woman was apologizing for the trouble she hadn't realized she'd caused, and Patricia was granting her a second—or what sounded more like a third—opportunity to prove she could be part of the Texas Rescue team.

The door opened and Patricia stepped out. As she turned back to listen to the other person, the generator-powered lights inside the tent illuminated Patricia's flawless face, her cheekbones and elegant neck exposed with her pale hair still twisted up in that smooth style.

"The regular pharmacies will reopen, don't forget. This isn't Haiti. The buildings are damaged, but they didn't disappear into a pile of rubble. If they had, I promise you, we'd be working under a different policy entirely."

Luke hadn't thought of Patricia as a high-strung filly, and damn Zach for putting the thought into his head, but now he could imagine a similarity. Patricia was no ranch workhorse, though. Once, after a livestock show in Dallas, Luke had been invited by a trainer to spend time in the Grand Prairie racetrack stables. He'd found the Thoroughbreds to be suspicious and nervous around strangers, requiring a lot of careful handling. But once they were brought out to the track, once that starting gate sprang open and they raced down their lanes, doing what they were born to do, those Thoroughbreds had been a sight to behold. Unforgettable.

He'd just listened to Patricia doing what she was born to do. She kept people at their jobs, working hard in hard conditions, serving a community. Whether it required her to revive a pair of unexpected firemen or turn around a pharmacy tech's attitude, that's what Patricia did to make her hospital run, and she did it well.

The unseen pharmacy girl was still apologizing. In the glow of the lights, Luke watched Patricia smile benevolently. "There's no need to apologize further. I'm sure you'll have no problems at all complying with the policy tomorrow, and I look forward to having you here on the team for the rest of the week. Good night."

Patricia shut the door with a firm click. With his eyes already adjusted to the dark, Luke watched her polite, pleasant expression fade away, replaced by a frown and a shake of her head. She was angry. Perhaps disgusted with a worker who'd taken so much of her time. Without a glance at the brilliant stars, she headed down the row of tents toward her office space.

After a moment, Luke followed. He told himself he wasn't spying on her. He had to pass her tent to get to the mess tent, anyway. But when she stopped, he stopped.

She didn't go into her tent. She clutched her clipboard to her chest with one arm, looking for a moment like an insecure schoolgirl. Then she headed away from the tent complex, into the dark.

Luke followed, keeping his distance. When she stopped at a picnic table near a cluster of palm trees in the rear of the town hospital building, he hesitated. She obviously wanted to be alone. She sat on the bench, crossed her arms on the table, then rested her head on them.

The woman was not angry or disgusted. She was tired. Luke felt foolish for not realizing it sooner.

While she apparently caught a cat nap, he stood silently a short distance away. He didn't want to wake her. He'd look like an idiot for having followed her away from the tents. On the other hand, he couldn't leave her here, asleep and unprotected. Except for the starlight, it was pitch black. There'd been no looting in the storm-damaged town, but there were packs of displaced dogs forming among the wrecked homes, and—

Hell. He didn't need wandering pets for an excuse. He wasn't going to leave Patricia out here alone. Period.

He cleared his throat as he walked up behind her, not wanting to startle her, but she was dead to the world. He sat down beside her. She was sitting properly, knees together, facing the table like she'd fallen asleep saying grace over her dinner plate. He sat facing the opposite way, leaning back against the table and stretching his legs out. The wooden bench gave a little under his weight, disturbing her.

"Good evening, Miss Patricia."

That startled her awake the rest of the way. Her head snapped up, and she blinked and glanced around, looking adorably disoriented for a woman who carried a clipboard everywhere she went. When she recognized him, her eyes opened wide.

"Oh."

"It's me. Luke Waterson. The firefighter who barged in on you today."

"Yes, I remember you." She looked at the watch on her wrist and frowned.

Luke figured she couldn't read it in the faint light. "You've only been out a minute or two."

She hit a button on her watch and it lit up. Of course. He should have known she'd be prepared. She touched her hair, using her fingertips to smooth one wayward strand back into place. She touched the corner of each eye with her pinky finger, then put both hands in her lap and took a deep breath. "Okay, I'm awake. Did you need something?"

This was what her life was like, he realized. Everyone came to her when they needed something. She didn't expect Luke to be there for any other reason. Did no one seek her out just to talk during a work shift? To play a game of cards in the shade when they were off duty? To share a meal?

He didn't feel like smiling at the moment, but he did, anyway. She'd asked if he needed anything. "Nope. Nothing."

She tilted her head and looked at him, those eyes that had opened so wide now narrowing skeptically. "Then what are you doing here?"

I can't stop thinking about you. I want to feel you fall against me again.

His mother had always told him when in doubt, tell the truth, but he wasn't going to tell Patricia that particular truth. He settled for a more boring—but true— explanation. "I left a work glove in your tent. I was coming to get it when I saw you walking off into the dark. I was worried about you, so I followed."

"You were worried about me?" She gave a surprised bit of a chuckle, as if the idea were so outlandish it struck her funny. She got up from the table, then picked up her walkie-talkie and her clipboard, and held them to her chest.

Luke stood, too. As if he were handling a nervous Thoroughbred, he moved slowly. He stood a little too close, but unlike this afternoon, she didn't back away.

He hadn't imagined that chemistry. It was still there, in spades. Looking into her face by the light of the stars, he wanted to hold her again, deliberately this time. To kiss her lips, to satisfy a curiosity to know how she tasted.

But he wouldn't. Standing this close, he could also see how tired she was, a woman who'd undoubtedly been handling one issue after another since the first storm warnings had put Texas Rescue on alert. A woman so tired, she'd fallen asleep while sitting at a wooden table.

"Let's go back to the hospital," he said, when he would rather have said a dozen different things.

He took the clipboard and the radio out of her hand, then offered her his arm. She slipped her hand into the crook of his elbow immediately, and he suspected she did it without thinking. Her debutante ways and his cowboy etiquette meshed with ease for a second. Then she seemed to realize what she'd done and started to drop her hand.

He pressed her hand to his side with his arm. "It's dark. This way you can catch me if I trip."

"This way you can drag me down with you, more likely." But she left her hand where it was as they walked in silence.

When he started to pass her office tent, she pulled him to a stop. "You need to get your glove."

He turned to face her, and now it was easy to see every detail of her face in the light that glowed through the white walls of the hospital's tents. She was so very beautiful, and so very tired.

"I thought that was what I needed when I first followed you out into the dark, but now I know I need something else much, much more."

He moved an inch closer to her, and he felt her catch her breath as she held her ground. "What is that?" she whispered.

"I need to get you into bed. Now."

Chapter 4

He wants to take me to bed?

What a stupid, stupid suggestion. They were in the middle of a mission, in the middle of a storm-damaged town, not to mention that Patricia felt gritty and hungry and so very damned tired. How could any man think of sex when all she could think of was—

Bed.

Oh.

"You're trying to be funny, aren't you?" she accused.

That lopsided grin on his face should have been infuriating instead of charming. She drew herself up a bit straighter. It *was* infuriating. It was.

Luke had the nerve to give her hand a squeeze before she pulled it away. "There, for a few seconds, the look on your face was priceless."

"I hope you enjoyed yourself. Now, if you'll excuse me—"

He didn't let go of her clipboard when she reached for it.

"Nope," he said. "You go where this clipboard goes, so you'll just have to follow me if you want it back." He took off walking.

She was so stunned, he was several yards away before she realized he really expected her to follow. He turned at the corner of her tent and disappeared—but not before he looked over his shoulder and waved her own damned walkie-talkie at her.

Shock gave way to anger. Anger gave her energy. She caught up to him within a few seconds, her angry strides matching his slower but longer ones as they headed down the aisle between tents.

She snatched her walkie-talkie out of his hand. "You're being childish."

"I am." He nodded, and kept walking.

"This isn't summer camp. People are relying on me. On all of us. They rely on you, too."

"And yet, I can still respond to a fire if I hear the signal while I'm enjoying this romantic walk with you. It's okay, Patricia."

She yanked her clipboard out of his hand and turned back toward the admin tent. He blocked her way just by standing in her path, being the ridiculous, giant mass of muscle that he was. She felt twenty-two again. Less. Make that nineteen, handing a slightly altered ID to a bouncer who was no fool.

"It's not okay," she said, and her jaw hurt from clenching her teeth so hard. "I cannot do my job if I can't get to my headquarters. Now move."

Instead, Luke gestured toward the tent they'd stopped next to. "This is the women's sleeping quarters. Recognize it? I didn't think so. You were first on scene, weren't you? You decided where the first tent spike should be driven into the ground, I'll bet. So, you've been here forty-eight hours, at least. You were supposed to have gotten sixteen hours of sleep, then, at a minimum. You've taken how many?"

Patricia spoke through clenched teeth. "You're being patronizing."

The last bit of a grin left his face, and he suddenly looked very serious. "I just watched you fall asleep sitting up on a piece of wood. Forty-eight hours is a long time to keep running. Take your break, Patricia."

Patronizing, and giving her orders. She didn't know him from Adam, but like every other man in her life, he seemed to think he knew best. She was so mad she could have spit. She wanted to shove him out of her way. She wanted to tell him to kiss off. But she was Patricia Cargill, and she knew from a lifetime of experience that if she wanted to get her way, she couldn't do that.

She'd learned her lessons at her father's knee, and she'd seen the truth over and over as stepmamas and aunties had come and gone. If a woman got spitting mad, Daddy Cargill would chuckle and hold up his hands and proclaim a soap opera was in progress. His cronies would declare that women were too emotional to be reliable business partners. The bankers would mutter among themselves about whose turn it was to deal with the harpy this time.

No one ever said those things about Patricia Cargill, because she never let them see her real feelings, even if, like her father's discarded women, those emotions were justified now and again.

Luke was standing over her like a self-appointed

bodyguard. He'd decided she needed protecting. That was probably some kind of psychological complex firefighters were prone to. She could use that to her advantage.

She placed her hand oh-so-lightly on his muscular arm, so very feminine, so very grateful. "I've gotten more sleep than you think. That power nap was very refreshing. It's so very thoughtful of you to be concerned, and I'm sorry to have worried you, but I'm fine." She took a step in the direction of the admin tent.

"Where are you going?"

"Let's get your glove. It will only take a minute." She smiled at him, friendly and unoffended, neither of which she felt. She didn't give a damn about his stupid glove, but it gave her an easy way to get back to her office.

"Forget it. You're very charming, Patricia, but you're very tired."

For a fraction of a second, she felt fear. She'd failed in an area where she usually excelled. She'd failed to manage this man effectively.

Luke lectured on. "The rules exist for a reason. You've been working nonstop, and you're going to get sick or hurt."

The rules exist for a reason. She wasn't sure why, but that sounded so familiar.

"Who takes your place when it's your turn for downtime?" Luke tapped her clipboard. "I bet you've got a whole organizational chart on there. I'm curious who you answer to, because you seem to think the rules don't apply to you."

"Karen Weaver is the head of the Austin branch of Texas Rescue," Patricia said. She sounded stiff. That was an accomplishment, considering she felt furious.

"I bet you make sure every single hospital volunteer from the most prestigious surgeon to the lowliest rookie gets their breaks, but Karen Weaver doesn't make sure you get yours?" Luke used her own trick on her, running the tips of his fingers lightly down her arm, all solicitous concern.

"Karen is...new," Patricia said.

Luke laughed. The man laughed, damn him. "She's new and she doesn't know half of what you do, does she? You don't trust her to take care of your baby."

Bingo. But Patricia wouldn't say that out loud, not for a million dollars.

Luke's hand closed on her arm, warm and firm. "Karen isn't you, but she's good enough to handle the hospital while everyone's sleeping." He turned her toward the sleeping quarters and pulled back the tent flap, then let her go. "Please, take your break."

She wanted to object. She made all the decisions. She was in charge. But even her anger at his high-handedness wasn't sustaining her against her exhaustion. He'd brought her to the very threshold of the sleeping quarters. To be only a few feet away from where her inflatable mattress lay, empty and waiting...it was enough to make the most adamant woman waffle.

Luke's voice, that big, deep voice, spoke very quietly, because he was very close to her ear. "I'm not your boss, and you aren't mine. You answer to Karen, and I answer to the fire chief. But this afternoon, you gave me orders, and I obeyed them because they were smart. You told me to drink; I did. You told me to sit; I did. So it's my turn. I'm telling you to get ready for bed. I'm going to bring you a sandwich from the mess tent and place it inside the door, because it's a sure thing that you haven't taken time to eat. You'll eat it and you'll get some rest when you turn off that walkie-talkie, because you know it's the smart thing to do. You've worked enough."

Patricia had never had a man speak to her like that. Telling her to stop working. Telling her she'd done enough. It made her melt the way poets believed flowers and verse should make women melt. It made her so weak in the knees, she couldn't take a step for fear of stumbling.

Weakness was bad.

"You can't give me orders," she said, but her voice was husky and tired.

"I just did." With a firm hand in her lower back, an inch above the curve of her backside, Luke Waterson pushed her gently into the tent, dropped the flap and walked away.

Patricia felt strange the next day.

It should have been easier to focus on the relief operation after a full meal and a good night's sleep. Instead, it was harder. That sleep and that meal had come at the hands—the very strong hands—of a fireman who looked like—

Damn it. There she went again, losing her train of thought.

She checked the to-do list on her clipboard. The items that had been done and crossed off were irrelevant. Being at the helm of Texas Rescue's mobile hospital was like being at the helm of one of her sailboats. Congratulating herself on having handled a gust of wind two minutes ago wouldn't prevent her boat from capsizing on the next gust. Whether on a lake or at a relief center, Patricia looked ahead, planned ahead, kept an eye on the horizon—or in this case, on her checklist.

One unfinished item from yesterday jumped out: *Set up additional shade for waiting area.*

Patricia tapped her mechanical pencil against her lips. She had the additional tent in the trailer. She just didn't have the manpower to get it set up. According to the tent's manual, it would take three people twenty minutes. That meant it would require forty minutes, of course, but she didn't have three people, anyway. She could serve as one, although she wasn't good with the sledgehammer when it came to driving the spikes in the ground. At this site, the spikes had been driven right through the asphalt in many cases, and she knew her limits. Driving iron spikes through asphalt, even crumbling, sunbaked asphalt, wasn't her skill set.

An image of Luke Waterson, never far from her mind this morning, appeared once more. Appeared, and zoomed in on his arms. Those muscles. The way they'd flexed under her fingertips as he'd escorted her back to the tents in the dark…

Luke could drive a spike through asphalt.

Patricia went to her tent and fetched his glove.

Chapter 5

Being a rookie was everything Luke had expected it to be. He'd volunteered for Zach's fire department just for the chance to be the rookie. For the chance to shed some responsibility. For the chance to have a little adventure without having to do any decision-making. For a change, any damned change, from the endless routine on the James Hill Ranch.

He'd gotten that change on Sunday night. Their fire engine had driven through the still-powerful remains of the hurricane as it had moved inland toward Austin. They'd arrived at the coast only hours after the hurricane had passed through, and they'd had rescues to perform the moment they'd rolled into town.

The repetitive ladder drills they'd practiced for months had finally proven useful as they'd reached a family who'd been stranded on a roof by rising water.

Then they'd laid that ladder flat to make a bridge to a man who was clinging to the remains of a boat on an inland waterway. In the predawn hours, Luke had waded through waist-deep brackish water with a kindergartner clinging to his neck.

That experience had been humbling. He'd been seeking adventure for its own sake, but that rescue made him rethink his purpose as a part-time volunteer fireman. He'd been blessed with health, and strength, and in that case, the sheer size to be able to stay on his feet and not be swept away by a rush of moving water. Being able to carry a child who could not have crossed that flood herself had made him grateful for things he normally didn't give a second thought.

But it was Wednesday now, the water had receded substantially, and they'd "rescued" only empty, toppled ambulances yesterday. Today, they'd cleaned their fire engine. And cleaned it. And cleaned it some more.

He shoved the long-handled broom into the fire engine's ladder compartment, a stainless steel box that ran the length of the entire fire engine, then swept out dried mud that had clung to the ladder the last time they'd slid it into its storage hold. *Yeah, big change from mucking stalls.* At least this dirt smelled better.

Luke had looked forward to following someone else's orders, but being a rookie gave him too much time to think. He wasn't required to use his brain at all, not even to decide what to clean next. This gave him way too much time to relive the mistakes he'd made with Patricia last night. He'd been childish, she'd said, refusing to return her clipboard. He'd shoved her into a tent, like giving an unwilling filly a push into her stall. He'd slid a sandwich and a bag of chips and a Gatorade bottle under the edge of the tent door like he was feeding a prisoner.

Yeah, he'd been a regular Casanova.

He pushed the broom into the ladder compartment again, and hoisted himself halfway into the compartment after it, head and one shoulder wedged in the rectangular opening so he could reach farther.

Zach's whistle echoed in the metal box. Luke felt Zach's elbow in his waist. "Don't look now, but I think a certain filly is finally curious about the man who has been standing by the corral fence. You patient son of a bitch, she's coming over to give you a sniff, just like you predicted."

Luke backed out of the compartment, cracking his head on the steel edge in his haste.

Zach was leaning against the engine, one boot on the rear chrome platform that Luke would be sweeping next. Zach shook his head as Luke rubbed his.

"I just said 'don't look now' and what did you do? Jumped out of there like a kid to get a peek. You're losing it bad around this woman, Waterson. Don't look."

Luke looked, anyway. Patricia was walking straight toward them, no doubt about it. Her hair was piled a little higher on her head today and her polo shirt was white instead of navy, and God, did she look gorgeous in the sunlight, all that blue sky behind her blond hair.

Luke took a step toward her. "She's got my glove."

Zach put a hand in his chest. "I wasn't in a condition yesterday to fully appreciate the view. Now I am. That's my glove. I'll get it. You keep sweeping, rookie."

He took no more than two steps before Chief Rouhotas appeared from around the side of the engine. The chief was looking in Patricia's direction even as he stuck his hand out to block Zach. "I've got this, Lieutenant Bishop. Back to work."

Luke crossed his arms over his chest as he watched Chief Rouhotas walk up to Patricia and greet her with his head bobbing and bowing as if she really were the princess she looked like she was. Patricia nodded graciously. They spoke for a minute, then she offered him her hand. He shook it as if it were an honor.

The important detail, however, was in Patricia's other hand. When the chief had greeted her, she'd casually moved her left hand behind her back, keeping the glove out of sight. She could have given it to Rouhotas, of course. She could have asked for it to be returned to Luke—which would have earned Luke another round of hazing, he was certain, for leaving a piece of equipment behind—but she kept it out of sight as she concluded whatever business deal she was making with the chief. No mistake about it, an agreement about something had been reached. Luke recognized a deal-sealing handshake when he saw it.

He didn't have to wait long to have that mystery solved. Patricia walked away—without a backward glance for as long as Luke watched her—and the chief started bellowing orders.

"Waterson. Bishop. Murphy. Report to the hospital's storage trailer. Bring your sledgehammers. Looks like they need help setting up a tent to make an extra waiting room for the walk-ups."

Zach and Luke exchanged a look, but Murphy complained. Out loud. At nineteen, he still had moments of teenaged attitude. "Seriously, Chief? It's already a hundred degrees."

"That's why they need the shade, genius."

Murphy opened the cab door and retrieved his own work gloves, muttering the whole time. "We're not even part of the hospital—"

"They're feeding us and giving us billets, so you don't have to sleep in this engine," Chief cut in.

Murphy ought to know the chief heard everything his men uttered. Luke had figured that out real quick.

"So quit your whining and moaning," Chief said, "or I'll let Miss Cargill be your boss for the whole day instead of an hour. You'll find out what work is."

Miss Cargill, was it? Patricia Cargill. He liked the sound of it. They couldn't get to Patricia's job soon enough to suit Luke. He had no doubt that more backbreaking labor would be involved, but given the choice between sweeping mud here or getting an eyeful of Patricia, he'd take the hard-earned eyeful.

First, of course, they had to pack the engine's gear back in place. The engine had to be ready to roll at all times. Luke took one end of the heavy, twenty-eight-foot extension ladder as Zach gave the commands to hoist and return it to the partially swept compartment.

It was more grunt work, leaving Luke's mind free to wander, but there was only one place his mind wanted to go: Patricia. She'd kept the glove. She still wanted to talk to him later, then, maybe to chew him out for last night. That was all right with him. That gave him a second chance.

She was waiting by the trailer, no glove in sight, when he and his crew walked up in the nonflammable black T-shirts and slacks they always wore on duty, even under their bulky turnout coats and pants. They were big men, all of them, and they carried sledgehammers, so they were stared at openly as they hauled the several-hundred pound tent out of the trailer and carried it on their shoulders, following Patricia down the row of hospital tents.

When a nurse wolf-whistled at them, Luke grinned back. Whether working on the engine or on the ranch, a little female appreciation never hurt his spirits.

He wasn't getting any of that appreciation from Patricia, unfortunately. Or maybe he was, but her calm, neutral expression certainly gave none of it away.

They dropped the tent where she indicated, and Murphy and Zach started freeing the straps. That was a two-person job, so Luke kept himself busy by taking their sledgehammers and setting them aside with his, right at the feet of the woman who was pretending he didn't exist.

"I've been officially informed that you are my boss today," Luke said, giving her the smile she was so good at ignoring, but which he liked to believe she wasn't entirely immune to. "What do you want to do with me? Tell me to go to hell, maybe?"

She didn't say anything, but held a cell phone up in the air and squinted at its sun-washed screen. "The cell towers are still down."

"I think it's only fair that we reverse positions after last night. I was a bit overbearing, so now it's your turn. You should order me to get in bed. I'll be very obedient."

She lowered the phone with a sigh and gave him a look that could only be described as long-suffering martyrdom. "I assume you are, once more, enjoying yourself ever so much."

He smiled bigger. "Around you? Always."

She shook her head, but he caught the quirk of her

lips. He wasn't in the dog house, after all. Her next words confirmed it.

"Thank you for the sandwich last night." Before he could say anything, she smoothly changed the subject. "There's no cell phone service. The towers are usually fairly high priority after a disaster. Phones have really become essential to daily function—"

"You're welcome. What are you doing for dinner tonight?"

"Absolutely nothing. I'm your boss. I can't go on a dinner date with a subordinate."

"You're only my boss until this tent goes up. Twenty minutes, tops."

"It'll take forty," she countered.

"Twenty, and you have to eat dinner with me."

"You've made yourself a bad deal." But she held out her hand, and they shook on it.

After unpacking the tent, Luke drove the first spike into the earth around the remains of the town hospital building's shrubbery in a single, satisfying stroke. He glanced in Patricia's direction, ready to deliver some smack-talk that twenty minutes was all they'd need at his pace. But her back was to him, the walkie-talkie pressed between her shoulder and ear as she signed a form for one of her staff members who'd appeared from nowhere. She'd missed his fine display of manliness.

The heat was already broiling. Murphy and Zach shed their shirts to a few appreciative female whistles, but Luke, too aware of Patricia, kept his on. Call it instinct, but behind that neutral expression, he thought the wolf whistles from the women bothered Patricia.

Maybe she just thought others were being lazy. Actions spoke louder than words or whistles. While passersby slowed down to watch the men at work, Patricia helped. She didn't just give verbal directions, although she did plenty of that to get them started, but she also held poles, spread canvas, untangled ropes. She cast a critical eye at Murphy's first guy line, then crouched down, undid his knot, and proceeded to pull the line beautifully taut while tying an adjustable knot that would have impressed any lasso-throwing cowboy.

Since Luke threw lassos in his day job, he was impressed. "Where'd you learn to tie knots? Do you work the rodeo circuit when there aren't any natural disasters to keep you busy?"

"You're quite amusing." She didn't answer his question as she moved to the next line. "Once it's up, I want to be able to pull the roof taut. There's more rain in the forecast."

And since she wanted it taut, she did the work. Patricia Cargill, with diamonds in her ears, didn't stand on the sidelines and giggle and point at shirtless men. She worked. Luke thought he might be a little bit in love. He'd have the chance to explore that over dinner. They had half the tent up already, and only ten minutes had passed.

The spikes on the other side of the tent, however, had to be driven into asphalt. Although they adjusted the lines to take advantage of any existing crack or divot in the asphalt, their progress slowed painfully as every spike took a dozen hard strikes or more to be seated in the ground. The sun cooked them from overhead, the asphalt resisted their efforts, and then Patricia's walkie-talkie squawked.

"I'm sorry, gentlemen, but I'm needed elsewhere.

You're free to leave when you're done. I'll come back to check on things later."

"Doesn't trust us to put up a tent," Murphy grumbled.

Patricia was a perfectionist, Luke supposed, a usually negative personality trait, but if she wanted a job done just right, it seemed to him she had good reason for it. When she'd told him rain was in the forecast, she hadn't needed to say anything else. A tent that sagged could hold water and then collapse, injuring those it was supposed to shelter. Luke understood that kind of perfectionism.

He stepped closer to her. "Just take care of your other business. Don't worry about this shelter. That roof will be stretched as tight as a drum. I'll check all the guy lines before we go."

She looked at him, perhaps a bit surprised.

"In other words," he said, "I'll fix Murphy's knots."

She almost smiled. Luke decided it counted as a smile, because it started at her eyes, the corners crinkling at their shared joke, even if it didn't quite reach her perfect, passive lips.

"Thank you," she murmured, and she started to walk away.

"I know it's been more than twenty minutes," Luke called after her, "but you could still eat dinner with me."

She kept walking, but tossed him a look over her shoulder that included—*hallelujah*—a full smile, complete with a flash of her pearly whites. "A deal is a deal. No welching, no cheating, no changing the terms."

Zach interrupted Luke's appreciation of the view as Patricia walked away. "Hey, Romeo. It's not getting any cooler out here. How about we finish this up?"

Luke peeled his shirt off to appreciative cheers from

the almost entirely female crowd that had gathered, then spread it on the ground to dry. Without cell phones, TVs or radios, Luke supposed he and Zach and Murphy were the best entertainment around.

For all his talk about hurrying, Zach was going all out for the onlookers, striking bodybuilder poses and hamming it up for the ladies for the next quarter hour as they finished the job.

Luke double-checked the last line, then bent to swipe his shirt off the ground. The sun had dried it completely. He stuck his fists through the sleeves, then raised his arms overhead to pull the shirt on. Some sixth sense made him look a little distance away. Patricia was leaning against a tree, eyes on him, watching him dress, not even trying to pretend she was looking at anything else.

She was caught in the act, but long, gratifying seconds ticked by before she realized it. She was so busy looking at his abs and his chest, she didn't realize he was looking back until her eyes traveled up to his face.

Bam. Busted.

She ducked her head and stuck her nose in her clipboard instantly, as if the papers there had become absolutely fascinating.

Luke pulled on his shirt, tucked it into his waistband, picked up his sledgehammer and walked toward Patricia, who was conveniently standing in the path he needed to take to get back to the fire engine. Her paperwork was so incredibly absorbing, she apparently didn't notice that a two-hundred-pound man had come close enough to practically whisper in her ear.

"That's all right, darlin'," Luke said, giving her a casual pat on the arm as he continued past her. "I enjoy looking at you, too."

* * *

Patricia could not look up from her clipboard. She was simply incapable of it. A coward of the first degree, humiliated by her own weakness. She was so grateful she could have wept when Luke kept walking after telling her it was all right.

It wasn't all right.

He'd caught her looking. Caught her, and loved it, no doubt, as much as he'd undoubtedly loved that crowd of women feasting their eyes on him with his shirt off. Was every man on earth a show-off, so eager to be adored that they had to flash their cash or their fame or their looks—whatever they had that foolish women might want?

She forced herself to look up from the clipboard. The other two firemen had their shirts on now, too. Their little audience had dispersed and the men were headed her way, following Luke. She smiled thinly at them and said her thanks as they passed her.

Every man in her world certainly was after as much female attention as he could get, even her father, who'd long ago let himself go to flab once he'd realized his money would keep women hanging around. He wore tacky jewelry encrusted with diamonds as he drove a classic Cadillac convertible with a set of longhorns, actual longhorns, attached to the front. The sweet young things of Austin fell all over themselves to hitch a ride around town in that infamous Cadillac. It was revolting.

Now Patricia had been just as bad as Daddy's bimbos. She hadn't feigned a giggling interest in a fat tycoon, but she'd been ready to drool as a man showed off his body. And dear Lord, what a body Luke had. Not the lumpy muscles developed out of vanity at a gym, but an athlete's body, real working muscles for swinging a hammer or an ax with force. She couldn't imagine what it would be like, having that kind of strength, that kind of physical power, to be able to push an obstacle out of the way at will.

And yet, he shook hands like a gentleman.

What an irrelevant thing to think about.

The distinctive sound of an emergency vehicle's horn sounded in the near distance, three distinct tones that were repeated almost immediately. It must have been a signal from their particular fire engine, because Luke and the other two men broke into a jog. Luke slowed enough to look over his shoulder at her, catching her staring, again. He tipped the brim of an imaginary cowboy hat, then turned away to run with his crew, answering the emergency call.

Patricia had to admit it was all so appealing on a ridiculously primitive level. It was too bad she needed a husband, and soon, but a deal was a deal, and her father would never let her change the terms now. She couldn't attract the right kind of husband while she kept a pool boy, so to speak, which was her loss. Luke Waterson would have made one hell of a pool boy.

Her last lover, a Frenchman who'd sold yachts, had been less than satisfactory. Easy enough on the eyes, somewhat knowledgeable about sailing and a fair escort in a tuxedo, he'd nevertheless been easy to dismiss once she'd needed to set her sights on a suitable husband. She hadn't missed Marcel for a moment.

But Luke…

Luke, she had a feeling, would not be a lover one took lightly.

And so, physique and handshake aside, she couldn't afford to take him at all.

Chapter 6

Less than a minute after Luke's chief had used his engine's siren to call his crew back, another fire engine sounded three notes in a different sequence. Patricia guessed it was the larger ladder truck from Houston that was also stationed by her mobile hospital. Somewhere in town, a situation required urgent attention.

Patricia scanned the horizon, turning in a slow circle, but saw nothing out of the ordinary. Three days after the storm, floodwaters were subsiding. People had settled into shelters where necessary and repairs were underway, so Patricia doubted it was any kind of storm rescue. They still had a huge line of patients waiting to be seen at the hospital, but the life-threatening injuries of the first twenty-four hours had given way to more conventional complaints.

She heard the massive engine of the ladder truck

as the Houston firefighters pulled out of their parking spot by the hospital building. Perhaps a car accident required a fire truck's Jaws of Life tool to get an occupant out of a car.

Patricia's staff were lining up folding chairs in the new tent, so more of the waiting line could be moved out of the sun. All the fabric walls had been rolled up so that any passing breeze could come through. Patricia walked around the outer edge, inspecting the set up. She ran her fingers over the ropes, testing their tension. They were all correct, each and every one.

She paused on the last guy line, envisioning Luke's hand on the rope she held. She'd been watching him long before he'd caught her, mesmerized as he'd tightened this very rope. For once, his nonchalant grin had been replaced by concentration as he'd kept his eye on the roof, hauling hard on the rope until the fabric had been stretched perfectly taut. The muscles in his shoulders and arms had been taut, too, as he'd secured the line to its spike without losing the tension.

Then, shirtless in the Texas sun, he'd walked exactly as she just had, touching each line, checking every knot while she'd watched from a distance. He'd understood why it mattered to her. She'd known he was doing it because he'd given her his word that he would.

It was the sexiest sight she'd ever seen.

She let go of the rope. It was stupid, really, to take a volunteer fireman's attention to detail so personally, but an odd sort of emotion clogged her throat, like she'd been given a gift.

More sirens, the kind on a speeding emergency vehicle, sounded in the distance. Patricia started scanning the horizon again as she turned her walkie-talkie's dial to the town's police frequency.

Chatter came over the speaker immediately. She couldn't follow all the codes and unit numbers, but she heard enough to know a large-scale emergency was in progress. *All vehicles please respond....*

She'd almost completed her slow circle when she spotted the smoke, an ugly mass of brown and black just now rising high enough to be seen over the trees and buildings. Last summer, as she'd volunteered near the Oklahoma border after some terrible tornados, the dry conditions had caused brush fires all around them. That smoke had been white and beige, a hazy, spreading fog. This smoke was different. Concentrated. The black mass looked almost like a tornado itself, rising higher into the sky with alarming speed.

Patricia's stomach twisted. It was a building fire, and a big one. She'd seen building fires before, too. The variety of burning materials, from drywall to shingles to insulation, each contributed their own toxic colors of brown and yellow and black to the smoke. It looked almost evil.

Charming, carefree Luke was heading into it.

Clogged throat, twisting stomach—all were signs of emotions she'd prefer not to feel. All of it made Patricia impatient with herself. She had a hospital to run. If the structure that was burning in the distance was an occupied building, then her mobile hospital's emergency room might be put to use very soon.

And if it is an abandoned building, firemen could still be hurt.

A useless thought. Regardless of who might be hurt, the emergency department needed to be put on alert. Patricia started walking toward that high-tech tent, ready to find out if they needed extra personnel or supplies. She'd be sure they got it.

"Oh, Patricia, there you are." Karen Weaver stopped her several tents away from Emergency. "I couldn't reach you on the radio."

"I'm on the police frequency."

"Oh." For whatever reason, Karen seemed inclined to stand still and talk.

Annoyed, Patricia gestured toward the emergency facility. "Let's walk and talk. What do you need from me?"

"Well, I was hoping you could tell me where I could find—"

"Wait." Patricia held the walkie-talkie up, concentrating on making out the plain English amid the cop codes. "Seaside Elementary. Isn't that the school that was turned into the pet-friendly shelter?"

"I don't know," Karen said, frowning. "Is there a problem with it?"

Patricia stopped short. "Have you not heard all the sirens?"

The question popped out without the proper forethought. Fortunately, they'd reached the entrance to the emergency room, so her abrupt halt could be smoothed over. "I'm here to be sure the ER knows there's a fire. Their tent is sealed, so they may not have heard the emergency vehicles, either."

There, she'd given Karen an easy excuse for failing to notice blaring sirens in an otherwise silent town.

"You think there's a fire?" Karen asked.

Silently, Patricia pointed to the north, to the dark funnel of smoke.

"Oh, I see."

Patricia waited, but Karen didn't seem inclined to say anything else.

So Patricia did. "This will impact us. We may have injured people arriving with pets in tow. We just put up a new shade tent outside the primary care. That could be a designated pet area. You could assign someone to be there with extra rope in case a pet arrives without a leash. We'll need water bowls of some sort."

"Yes, but we can't keep pets here."

"Of course not." Patricia tempered her words with a nod of agreement. "The Red Cross has responsibility for relocating the shelter, but expect them to call you for support. Transportation, probably. We could loan the van, but let's keep our own driver with it. Food, definitely. You may want to head over to the mess tent now for a quick inventory. Better yet, see if there's anyone in that hospital building at the moment. They've been pretty good about letting us raid their pharmacy. There should be usable stores in their cafeteria."

As soon as she said it, Patricia thought of a better idea: put the town hospital CEO and the Red Cross directly in touch with each other, leaving Texas Rescue out of the food supply business altogether. She didn't suggest it, because Karen was looking overwhelmed already, and Patricia had a feeling Karen hadn't made contact with the hospital they were temporarily replacing. In Austin, Karen had seemed adequate, pushing paper and calling meetings, but here in the field, it was obvious that she was in over her head.

"I'll get you the van driver and someone to act as unofficial pet-sitter," Patricia said. "I need to take care of the ER now. You get rope and water bowls."

"Okay, that sounds good." Karen turned her walkie-talkie to the police frequency and left to start her assigned task.

Patricia entered the multiroomed ER tent, stopping in its foyer to pull paper booties over her Docksides.

Rope and water bowls. Pitiful that a simple task like that would keep a grown woman busy. Patricia couldn't coach incompetence. It was easier just to handle everything herself.

She took a breath and composed herself before entering the treatment area that she hoped would not see heavy use this day. At least she could be grateful to her supervisor for one thing: she'd managed to prevent Patricia from thinking about Firefighter Luke Waterson for two whole minutes.

Patricia no longer thought Luke or any fireman had any sex appeal whatsoever. It had been a moment of temporary insanity when she'd had the crazy idea that Luke Waterson could have made a memorable lover.

Hours had passed. Darkness had settled in. Information was scarce, and the reports they received were inconsistent and sporadic as sooty and smoky patients arrived at her hospital, telling conflicting tales. The school had burnt to the ground; only a small part of the school was damaged; the top story had collapsed into the ground floor. Everyone had evacuated the building on their own; firemen had gone in to carry out injured people; a fireman had died while saving a pet—that one had made Patricia's heart stop—but no, a pet had died but a firefighter had brought its body out of the building.

Patricia heard enough. Luke with the sailing-blue

eyes and the unfunny wisecracks was fighting a fire that could cost him his life. And Patricia cared, damn him.

She told herself the knot in her stomach wasn't unusual. She always cared for the people who were her responsibility, and although the fire crews were not technically part of her hospital, they'd made her relief center their home base, and she'd gotten used to seeing them around. Heck, she'd used them to get her extra waiting room erected today. But when she heard a firefighter was injured, she didn't think of Zach or the Chief or the other guy—was the name Murphy?

No, she thought of too-handsome, too-carefree Luke.

She kept her walkie-talkie set to the police frequency nearly the entire time. The fire was burning itself out. Austin Rescue, *Luke,* was still on the scene, along with the Houston ladder truck, something from San Antonio and the town's own fire department. Patricia's emergency room hadn't treated any life-threatening injuries, thankfully.

The Red Cross had opened a new shelter—also thankfully, because the patients were starting to hurl accusations at each other about who had been burning forbidden candles. Patricia didn't want to break up any fights tonight. She just kept loading people in the van, round after round, smiling reassuringly and ignoring her growing ulcer as they were driven away to their new shelter.

Food might have helped settle her stomach, but she wanted to be sure her staff got to eat first. All of her staff, including the temporarily assigned fire crews. Still, she could get coffee. She refused to have so weak a stomach that she couldn't tolerate coffee.

She entered the mess tent just as Karen was scoop-

ing mashed potatoes from the steam tray into a portable
plastic container. "The Red Cross called, just like you
said they would. We're giving them our leftover food."

"These aren't leftovers. We need this food."

Karen stopped in mid-scoop, surprised. "Dinner
hours are over. Everyone's eaten."

"No, they haven't. The fire crews are still out there."
Patricia wanted to yank the giant spoon out of Karen's
hand. She clenched her clipboard tighter instead.

"Oh, that fire might go until dawn. You never know."
With a plop, Karen dumped more mashed potatoes into
the plastic container.

"Don't do that." Patricia's tone of voice made Karen
and the cook both look at her oddly. She realized she'd
stretched out her hand to physically stop Karen.

She snatched her hand back. "I haven't eaten yet.
How about emergency? Has anyone checked with them
to be sure they've all had their break?" Feeling clumsy,
she switched her radio back to the hospital channel,
ready to call the ER.

She had to wait. Others were talking on the channel,
but she shot Karen a look that made her wait, too. *Don't
you dare give away one more scoop of those mashed
potatoes.* What kind of supervisor gave away her own
people's food?

Patricia was being a little irrational, and she knew
it. The rules of safe food handling wouldn't allow them
to keep food warm until dawn, but Patricia couldn't let
go of this idea that she had to have dinner with Luke.
He'd wanted to eat a meal with her, and she'd made a
big deal out of saying no, although he'd been thoughtful enough to bring her a sandwich the night before.

The radio traffic caught her attention. The ER had

definitely been too busy to eat. A firefighter had fallen from a ladder. Too many bones broken to treat here; no MRI facility on site to be certain organs weren't perforated. A medevac helicopter was on its way to transport him to San Antonio. Patricia had been listening to the town's police radio when the real news had been right here in her own hospital.

"Don't touch that food," Patricia ordered, and she threw open the door and left the tent. Her neat and orderly complex seemed like a maze in the dark, and she nearly tripped on a tent's spike as she tried to take a shortcut to the emergency room.

A fireman fell from a ladder. His arms must have been tired. Luke's arms were tired. I made him swing a sledgehammer. A sledgehammer! After he'd come into my tent exhausted from cutting down trees with an ax the day before. He fell from the ladder. His arms were tired.

She didn't know which firefighter it was, of course. There were firefighters in town from all over Texas. She just wanted desperately to get to the ER to find out, because she was being irrational and weak and she hated herself for it.

The helicopter sounded close. Patricia started running.

Chapter 7

She was too late.

The lights over the emergency room's door were bright enough for Patricia to see a stretcher being rolled to the waiting helicopter by personnel in scrubs. They had a distance to go, because the helicopter had landed as far from the tent city as possible. Wind from the blades still beat rhythmically at the complex. Strands of Patricia's hair came loose from her bun and whipped painfully at her eyes.

She cleared them away and blinked twice at the group of firemen who were walking past her. They were absolutely filthy, their heads uncovered, their coats undone. Underneath, they wore polo shirts instead of black Ts. *Houston,* their coats read.

Patricia, breathing a bit hard from her short run, counted them silently. Six. Were there usually six people manning a ladder truck? Was there a seventh being wheeled into a helicopter? She felt like an awful person for half hoping so.

She stopped an exhausted-looking female firefighter. "Have you seen the Austin truck?" she asked, trying to control her panting.

The woman, probably too tired to talk, as well, stuck her thumb over her shoulder and kept walking with her crew. Patricia looked, but didn't see another truck, just the stretcher being loaded onto the helicopter. Did the woman mean someone from Austin was on the stretcher? Patricia stood helplessly, staring at the little hum of activity around the distant helicopter. In mere minutes, the nurses in scrubs ducked as they ran with the empty gurney back toward the ER from under the helicopter's downdraft.

His arms must have been so tired....

She was responsible. If the injured firefighter was Zach or Murphy, she was to blame, as well. But Luke— if it was her fault Luke had been hurt—her mind kept focusing on Luke.

Stop it. This was useless conjecture. She needed to find out the patient's name, now. Determined, she spun toward the ER's door, and crashed right into a man. A very solid man in a black T-shirt.

"Luke!"

He steadied her with a hand on each of her upper arms. One of his cheeks was black with soot, his hair was a crazy mess and he reeked of smoke.

"Oh, it's not you," she sighed, then took in a gulp of air.

Even tired and dirty, he looked a little amused. "Actually, this is me."

The helicopter was taking off behind her. She gestured in its general vicinity and raised her voice a bit. "I mean, that's not you. I thought, you know, with your arms being tired and all... I thought..."

He said nothing at all, but stood there with a ghost of a grin on his face, watching her intently. Even in the glow of the ER's artificial light, she could see how blue his eyes were.

"They said a fireman fell off a ladder," she explained. "His arms must have been tired, and I thought..."

Realizing it still could be an Austin crew member on that flight, she glanced up at the rapidly receding helicopter. "That's not one of your friends?"

"No. We're all present and accounted for."

Luke was here. He was fine. The wave of relief was a palpable thing, as physically painful as the worry had been. She was unprepared for it and the uneven emotions crashing inside her.

She shook one arm free of him and poked him in the chest. "That could've been you. You realize that, don't you? You shouldn't have let me boss you around. You shouldn't have done all that work for me today. I mean, sledgehammers are not easy—"

"Patricia." He gave her arms a friendly squeeze as he chuckled.

Her poke became a fist. She gave him one good thump on his uninjured, healthy chest. "You can't let someone wear you out like that. It's dangerous. I shouldn't have made you do it."

He caught her fist to his chest and held it there, pressing her hand flat against his cotton T-shirt and the muscle underneath. "You didn't make me. You can say Chief Rouhotas made me, if it makes you feel better. And that guy in the helicopter got hurt because his ladder collapsed, not because his arms were tired. It was their mistake, a bad one. They didn't secure their ladder properly. I'm okay."

"You're okay this time." The relief was coursing through her, an adrenaline rush she didn't welcome. "But let me tell you something. I do not ever want to do this again. It is sickening and awful. I don't even like you anymore, if I ever did."

"I can tell." He was smiling openly at her now.

"I'm serious." She jerked her hand out from under his and took a step back. "But I saved you some dinner. There's mashed potatoes in the mess tent for you. Go eat."

"So we're on for dinner after all?"

"I would never, ever date a fireman. Especially not you."

"Patricia, come here." He tugged her with him out of the light, around the side of the tent. In the darkness, he stood very close, too close, the way he always did. Then he took it further, and put his arms around her.

She shuddered. All her muscles shook with that relief, and she put her arms around his chest, needing to hold something solid, just for a second, until that shudder passed. She rested her head against him a little bit, her cheek on the top of his shoulder.

"You were worried about me," he said.

"You smell like smoke," she said, an accusation spoken into the side of his neck.

She felt his rib cage expand, felt his breath in her hair. "And you, thank God, do not."

"I didn't know what your call sign was. They kept calling for squad this and unit that, but I couldn't re-

member what number was painted on your truck." She
picked her head up and glared at him. "I could hardly
understand anything on that police radio. How can that
be efficient communication in a situation that involves
so many different agencies?"

"Patricia," he said, and he kissed her forehead. The
bridge of her nose. Her cheek. "You were worried about
me, and it's about the sweetest damned thing I've ever
heard. Now quit yelling at me."

He kissed her mouth, fully, gently, his lips covering
hers as if he had all the time in the world. She felt his
hand smooth up the nape of her neck to cradle the back
of her head just below her pinned-up hair. His other arm
stayed around her waist, holding her firmly against his
body—as if she weren't holding him tightly enough herself. Then his mouth lifted away for a breathy whisper
of a second, and came back a little harder, at a different angle, nudging her mouth open to kiss her more
intimately.

Her knees gave way. Truly weak, she fell in a tiny dip
of a curtsy, but his arm must not have been tired at all,
because he kept her secure against his body. Still in no
rush, he tasted her, tested the way their tongues could
slide, teased her by lifting away again, just far enough
to toy with her lower lip. He planted small kisses at the
corners of her mouth.

She wanted him to kiss her deeply again, to take all
her weight against his body. It was beyond reason. She'd
never needed a kiss before, but she had this terrible
want. When he didn't kiss her right away, she opened
his mouth with hers and took the kiss she wanted.

She could have cried at his perfect response, and she

could have cried again when he broke off the kiss, the best kiss of her life.

"Patricia, Patricia." He murmured her name and lifted her against him so only her toes touched the ground. He hugged her, hard, then set her down again and stepped back, looking her over and reaching out to tug the hem of her shirt into place and brush some dust or dirt off her sleeve.

She missed his kiss already, sorry it was over, because it could not be repeated. There was no place for this kind of helplessness in her life. There never would be. It served no purpose. She felt a little fuzzy about the exact reasons why, but she knew she had things to do, responsibilities to other people. Business entanglements. Family obligations.

She gestured between the two of them. "This can't be a thing between us."

He quirked one eyebrow at her. "A thing? Sweetheart, this is most definitely a thing."

"I mean, I can't… I can't be kissing you. I'm working. I've got things…"

Luke stepped closer again, but he only rested his forehead to hers. "I know I'm filthy dirty, and I know you're worn out from worry, so we're going to call it a night. I know you're always working. You are the boss around here, and you don't want to be caught sneaking away to kiss a boy like this is summer camp. I respect that, but darlin', do not kid yourself that I'm never going to kiss you again.

"Now, take off while I'm being good and keeping my hands to myself. I'll see you in the mess tent in a few minutes, because I could eat about a hundred pounds of mashed potatoes right now, and we'll pretend we're just pals and this never happened. For now." He kissed her once more, a firm press of his mouth. "You're beautiful. Now go."

Patricia went, looking back just to catch another glimpse of him, wanting to see him standing safe and sound in the middle of her hospital, but he'd already disappeared in the shadows, leaving her faster than she could leave him.

There was good, and then there was good enough. When it came to preparing the fire engine for another run, good enough was all Luke had patience for tonight. They'd been on the fire scene almost six hours. He wanted to get cleaned up himself, and he wanted to sleep, but mostly, he thought as he mindlessly executed the chores that came with a fire engine, he wanted to leave good enough and get back to what was great: Patricia Cargill. More specifically, kissing Patricia Cargill. He wanted to do it again, for far longer, until he lost himself completely in her cool beauty and forgot the black destruction he'd just lived through.

Luke gave the pry bar a cursory swipe with a towel before returning it to its assigned place on the engine.

"Heads up." Zach sounded impatient.

Luke turned and caught the pike pole Zach threw his way. Tempers were short because they were all tired. Even with full stomachs, they were snapping at each other. That hot meal was probably the only reason they hadn't killed each other yet. Thank God Patricia had done that smooth-talking thing she was so good at, persuading Chief that the men needed to eat immediately so the rest of the food could be sent on to the new shelter.

Patricia had eaten dinner with him, after all. In a way. She'd stood just a few feet from his table, eating precise forkfuls as Karen asked her questions about handling requests from sister agencies. Patricia had dished out instructions in a way that had Karen nodding and agreeing as if she'd always planned to do things Patricia's way. Luke had been content to listen to his Thoroughbred race down her lane, but as the Houston and Austin fire crews rested and ate, they'd gotten louder and more raucous and ruined his ability to eavesdrop. Patricia had slipped away before Luke could invite her to sit down and get off her feet, too.

He didn't know when he'd see her again.

Luke unpacked hose as Zach ran it to the overfull pond on the edge of the hospital parking lot. While the engine sucked in hundreds of gallons to refill its tank, Luke lifted the pike pole and slid it into its place along the ladder. Every muscle in his body protested.

The pole wasn't that heavy. Its fiberglass handle was the lightest in the industry, the best available, like everything else on this brand new engine, but Patricia had been right. His arms were tired. Damned tired. He'd ended days on the ranch with his body aching like this, but not many.

His head wasn't in the best place, either. No lives had been lost in the fire, but it had been harrowing to enter the building repeatedly, first to get all the people out, then again to retrieve pet carriers with terrified animals in them. Each trip in had gotten darker, smokier, hotter.

The chief had been about to call it off, but a child's high-pitched voice had carried right over the roar of fire and the growl of the vehicle engines. "Is it our cat's turn? The firemen get our cat now, right?"

Luke had heard the question, and all the faith in it, loud and clear. The bullhorn was in the chief's hand, but he hadn't given the command to stay clear yet. Luke had headed back in, tank on his back, pulling his mask on as he went. It had been bad, though. He'd lumbered in upright, but he'd ended up crawling out on his hands and knees, shoving the last two cat carriers in front of him as he went.

Zach had met him at the egress point and grabbed the carriers. As Luke had struggled to his feet, the chief had practically lifted him by his coat collar and given him a hard shake by the scruff of the neck, the only condemnation Luke had received. He'd skated a fine line, but he hadn't technically disobeyed an order, because Chief hadn't spoken the words yet.

The families had stayed behind the yellow tape the cops had put up. They'd peered in their pet carriers and wept tears of gratitude and called out to Luke and the rest, thanking them and calling them heroes.

Luke hadn't felt like a hero. The only normal emotion in that situation was fear, and he'd felt it. He'd used that fear to keep himself going in the growing inferno, crawling as fast as he could while trying to control his breathing in the mask. He'd managed to keep the correct wall to his right and not lose his bearings, and he'd made it out. But hell, he was no hero. He was lucky.

He wasn't a man to stake his life on the whim of luck, not if he could help it. Just when he'd been feeling darkest, watching another fireman who was less lucky being wheeled away to a waiting helicopter, he'd run into Patricia. Her feelings for him had been transparent, all of her unflappable cool stripped away by worry. For him. And her kiss…

Well, that had soothed his soul. Whatever it took, Luke planned on running into her again. Soon.

Chief's handheld radio squawked as they packed the last hose away. The voice that came over the air was feminine and cultured, extending an invitation as graciously as if she were inviting them to tea. "Chief, I'm reopening the shower facility for you and the Houston crew. The generators would wake our inpatients, but if you could bring flashlights and tolerate the inconvenience of unheated water, I think the noise will be minimal."

Chief keyed his mike to answer. "As long as the water's wet, ma'am, we'll be there."

Luke felt his mood lift. He wasn't going to have to wait until morning to scheme for a chance to see the woman he couldn't stop thinking about. It looked like his very near future included soap and water and Patricia.

How lucky could a man get?

Patricia knew he'd be here any moment.

She was sitting on a plastic chair at the entrance to the field showers, waiting with the female firefighter for the men to finish so the women could take their turn. Still, when Patricia saw Luke's large frame emerging from the shadows, striding toward her with a towel slung over his shoulder, she felt a little flutter, like she wasn't ready for something.

The shower facility was, of course, a specialized tent, with a locking wood door set into a wood frame at each end. Six vinyl shower stalls and a common area of tub sinks and benches were inside. Water from an external tank could be pumped in by hand, but lights and heated water were provided by generators. The showers were available to men and women in alternating hours during the day, but they closed every night at nine. There was a reason for that rule: in order to reduce noise when the majority of the staff and patients were sleeping, the mobile hospital ran only vital generators at this hour of the night.

Patricia hadn't bothered consulting her supervisor for permission to break the nine o'clock rule tonight. These showers weren't a luxury for the firefighters. They wouldn't wake the sleeping staff as long as they didn't run the generators, so Patricia had made the decision and retrieved the keys from the admin tent. Besides, Karen was already in bed. Why wake her up only to tell her what she was going to agree to?

Chief Rouhotas hurried ahead of Luke to greet her first. He was very appreciative. So much so, it confirmed Patricia's earlier suspicion that he knew exactly who she was. The daughters of Texas millionaires were spoken to in a different way than non-profit personnel directors. Judging from his men's antics while putting up the tent this morning, however, Luke and Zach and Murphy had no idea that Patricia Cargill was *that* Cargill.

Her eyes strayed to Luke. He was watching Rouhotas kowtow to her as if the chief had lost his mind. The chief was starting his second round of thanks. Patricia held up the keys in her hand and gave them a jangle. "I did nothing daring. The keys were already in my office. I'd appreciate it if you and your men keep it quiet, that's all. No locker room antics, please."

The chief chuckled, but that didn't mean she'd actually said anything amusing, of course. It only meant she was a Cargill.

"Got that, guys?" the chief said, turning back toward Luke and the guys. "No towel snapping."

If he said anything after that, Patricia paid no attention. The sudden image of a nude Luke having a towel snapped at what was undoubtedly a muscular backside made that fluttery feeling return in force.

Luke lingered as the rest of his crew entered the facility, but Patricia didn't get out of her chair for a private word. It would be too obvious that she knew him better than the others. She stayed next to the woman from Houston, knowing—hoping—Luke wouldn't say anything inappropriate in front of his peer.

"So we have you to thank for providing the cold shower," he said.

"It is June, and this is Texas, so I don't think the water will be that cold." She tried to make her voice cold, though. He couldn't expect her to fall to pieces like she had earlier.

"Cold is fine with me," Luke said, sounding perfectly sincere. "After the heat we dealt with earlier, a cold shower is just what I need."

As he walked away, he took the towel off his shoulder and started spinning it into a loose whip, which he cracked at the handle just before he opened the door and walked into the showers.

"Men," said the woman beside her.

Patricia closed her eyes, willing herself not to envision Luke stark naked, just a few feet away.

"Men," she agreed.

Chapter 8

Patricia was the first woman to finish her shower. She combed out her wet hair and twisted it up with a clamshell clip. The Houston firefighter and the cook who'd made the late night run to the new pet-friendly shelter were still showering, as well as an ER nurse. How the cook and the nurse had found out the showers were open was a mystery, but Patricia knew from previous missions that word traveled fast when everyone worked together in a confined community like the mobile hospital.

The exit from the showers was at the opposite side of the facility from the entrance. Patricia gathered up her toiletries bag, her towel and her deck shoes. She'd wear her shower flip-flops back to the women's sleeping quarters. Although she'd have to wait for the others to finish so that she could lock up, she'd rather wait in the open air. The forecasted rain was threatening, but

Patricia knew she'd be able to hear the ocean in the quiet of the night. She could listen, and dream of something that had nothing to do with Texas Rescue and hospitals and firemen.

She could dream of sailboats. Large, oceanic ones. The kind that went somewhere. The kind she would own someday soon, when her money was her own.

The exit door had just shut behind her when a man's voice quietly said, "First one out. I knew that high-maintenance look was just an act."

Patricia squealed in surprise and whirled to face Luke.

"Shh," he said, and he took her shoes out of her hand and pulled her deeper into the dark.

"What are you doing?" she hissed.

"Making sure no one sees you running off to kiss a boy, remember? You wanted to keep this a secret."

Luke stopped when they reached a tree, a multi-branched oak that had survived the hurricane. There was enough light to see his smile. There was enough night to make it feel like they were alone.

Patricia kept her voice to a near-whisper as she set the record straight. "That's not what I said. I said kissing you wasn't going to be an ongoing thing."

"Why not? It's fun." Luke dropped her shoes and looped his arms around her waist, then leaned back against the tree and pulled her to stand between his legs.

"Because…but…*fun?* What does fun have to do with anything?"

He was wearing a T-shirt again, but his uniform slacks had been replaced by some kind of athletic track pants after his shower. They were probably what he slept in. Their nylon fabric slipped over her freshly-shaved legs when she shifted her weight, restless in the loose circle of his arms. Her own cotton T-shirt and draw-string shorts were meant for sleeping, too. They felt too flimsy for staying outdoors like this.

"You told me this wasn't summer camp," Luke said, "but you're sure making it as fun as one. The one year I actually went to a summer camp, I didn't have the cour-age to stand outside the showers to steal a girl. I wish I had. Right now, I need a little bit of courage again, because you are looking mad as a hornet, but I want to kiss you pretty badly. I don't want to look back on this moment and say I wish I had."

Patricia held her breath in the moonlight. The coming storm clouds sent a gust of wind through the branches above them. Luke's grin faded, and the look in his eyes was intense as he pushed off the tree and stood over her. He moved his hands to hold her waist securely, one warm palm above each hip. She had all the time in the world to back away.

But she didn't.

She held on to her towel and her toiletries, but she lifted her chin, making it easy for him to dip his, and for their mouths to meet. It was the sweetest thing, al-most tentative, two kids learning how to kiss at sum-mer camp.

Except, this was the man she'd been worried about all day. It was scary to be so concerned for one person. It was achingly good to have him here now.

Then his hands were sliding up her rib cage, and she recalled watching them tying knots, just for her. Hands so strong and sure then, hands so strong and sure now. She wanted those hands on her, everywhere, but he kept moving slowly.

And still, their lips touched lightly, closed and soft, the kiss almost chaste.

She let her arm relax, extending it toward the ground and dropping her towel and the zippered bag. Luke's hands traveled just a little higher, and his thumbs grazed the sides of her breasts. She was wearing an athletic bra, the stretchy one-piece kind that pressed a woman's breasts flat against her body. She felt suddenly self-conscious, like the teenager she'd once been, afraid she wouldn't measure up to a boy's expectations.

But Luke's warm hands slid around to her back, not her front, and began a slow descent. He didn't stop at the curve of her lower back, but slid farther down, warm palms smoothing over the curves of her backside, until he cupped her to him. With strength.

Summer camp was over. As one, their mouths opened hungrily and the kiss became adult. Patricia pressed against him, pushing him back against the tree. He took her with him, lifting her to her toes, her soft body sliding up his hard body. She raised her arms to circle his strong shoulders, burying one of her hands in his thick hair, which was clean and still damp from his shower.

She kissed him with abandon. It was just the two of them in the dark. There was no one to see, no one to judge her, no one to remind her of who she was and what she needed to do.

When the first pattering of rain came, she didn't care. Neither did Luke. But when the first lightning strike cracked the sky, they let go of each other.

Everyone at summer camp knew not to stand under a tree in a lightning storm.

Luke bent to scoop her belongings up from the ground, then took her hand and ran with her through the rain, which was falling harder by the moment. They reached the exit door of the showers quickly. Patricia opened the door and leaned in. "Ladies? Are you dressed?"

The inside was dark.

She stepped inside and held the door open for Luke. "There's no one here."

He stepped inside and the door banged shut in its wooden frame just as the skies opened and the rain came down, full force. The sound of it was like a roar against the tent. She couldn't see in the dark, so the sound was all she had to focus on. That, and Luke.

"It's lucky you hadn't locked the door yet," Luke said. "If you'd spent one second finding the key, we'd be soaked through."

It was unnerving, not being able to see to move away. The moment under the tree had passed, and she needed space. "If you'll hand me my bag, I've got a flashlight in it."

Immediately, a flashlight lit the night. Luke had it aimed at the floor so she wouldn't be blinded, but now she could see his face. He looked friendly, not as hungry as she felt. She cleared her throat. She should be friendly, too.

"You had a flashlight in your pocket this whole time?" she asked. "I thought you were just happy to see me."

The rain thundered down for a second more, and then Luke laughed. "Why, Miss Cargill, you find yourself ever so amusing, don't you?"

Patricia took her shoes and towel from him, unable to stop her own smile. She'd just told what was quite possibly her first crude joke. Luke had laughed, and not because she was a wealthy benefactor. He just thought she was funny.

What does fun have to do with it?

She slid the deadbolt on the back door and walked away from him. The tent was only about twenty feet long, so the glow of his flashlight gave her enough light as she went to the front door and opened it an inch. There was nothing to see outside except a deluge of falling water.

"Looks like we'll be here a while," Luke said. "We might as well be comfortable."

The light careened around the space as he moved to the long bench that ran the length of the common area. He rubbed the towel over his arms, then spread it on the double-wide bench.

Patricia shut the door and hung her towel on the hook by the nearest shower stall. "Maybe you should turn that light off. Anyone walking by will wonder why there are people in the shower at this time of night."

Instantly, the tent was plunged into darkness. "Wouldn't want the camp counselors to walk by and see us in here," Luke said.

Patricia couldn't take a step, the darkness was so absolute. "Okay, point taken. Turn it back on."

He did, and then he reached to set it on the edge of one of the tub sinks, pointed away from the bench so it gave the space an ambient glow. "No one in their right mind is walking outside right now, Patricia. You aren't about to get caught doing anything. In fact, you *aren't* doing anything. Come sit down."

She did, sitting next to him on the wooden bench, knees together, facing forward, prepared to wait for the storm to die down.

After a moment, Luke leaned forward and stuck his face in her line of vision. "Seriously? You're killing me. We might as well be comfortable. Come here."

He kicked off his flip-flops and swung one leg onto the bench, sitting sideways, knee bent. With an arm around her waist, he slid her closer, turning her so that her backside securely fit in between his thighs and the warmth of his chest was at her back. Trying not to sigh at the futility of resisting him, Patricia kicked off her flip-flops and put her feet on the bench, then hugged her bent knees.

"You could lean back against me," Luke said into the nape of her neck.

She reached forward to brush leaves off her feet. "It's been a horribly long day. You must be exhausted by now."

"The day that I'm so exhausted that I can't stay up-right when a beautiful woman leans against me is the day that I turn in my spurs and hat and walk off into the sunset without a horse."

Patricia laughed a little. "You're too much, Luke Wa-terson."

"Am I?" He slipped his fingers under the short sleeve of her cotton sleep shirt. With agonizing patience, he slid his fingers and her sleeve up over her shoulder. He bent forward and kissed her bared shoulder. "Funny, but it seems to me that you can handle anything I dish out."

As if they'd choreographed it, he released the clip in her hair, and she leaned back to rest her head on his shoulder. He set her clip on the bench, then smoothed his hand down her arm. He kissed her temple. The shell of her ear.

She drew her knees in a little closer, afraid of the spell he was casting, afraid she wouldn't say no.

Afraid she wouldn't say yes.

Afraid he wouldn't ask her at all.

Luke was a patient man. Any good cowboy had to be. Horses weren't trained in an hour. Grass didn't grow overnight and steer didn't fatten in a day.

But, like any good cowboy, Luke stayed alert for the signs that things were about to change. He looked for steer that drifted farther to forage. Trees that started to bud. Horses that twitched their ears in confusion before they got spooked and tried to bolt.

Patricia, who'd been open and bold outside in the rain, was on the verge of being spooked right now. Luke wasn't sure what had caused the change. He was fairly certain she didn't know, either, so he didn't ask her. He just touched her, starting with another kiss on her bare, rounded shoulder.

She responded with a small shudder, reminding him of her reaction when he'd touched her for the first time, after she'd learned he was not the injured man leaving in a helicopter. Was that shudder a sign of relief? A release of tension?

She held a lot of tension in her body, her posture always perfect, her arm always flexed with a clipboard or handheld radio in her grip. She shouldered a lot of responsibility with Texas Rescue, just as he shouldered responsibility for the James Hill Ranch. He knew bosses were people, too. Patricia wasn't just a director; she was a woman. He wanted to know what made this woman relax. What made her tension disappear. And, perhaps selfishly, what made her aroused.

Luke ran his hand down her arm again, going slowly, putting gentle pressure on her muscles even as he savored the perfection of her skin. Her hand was resting on her knee, curled up as she was in front of him. He passed his hand over hers, then slid his palm down her impossibly smooth shin to hold her ankle in his hand.

She leaned back, turning her face to cuddle into the area between his shoulder and neck, making herself more comfortable. Relaxing. She liked this slow, thorough touch.

Luke's body was already hard as hell, but there was nothing he could do about that, and no way to hide it. He didn't have to act on it, though, and he didn't intend to, not with a woman who couldn't decide whether to kiss him or sit a foot away from him. He was a patient man, he reminded himself. He enjoyed simply touching her.

"What are you doing?" she whispered after long moments of silent caresses.

"I'm learning you. You like this." Luke ran his thumb down the front of her shin. "But you love this."

He slid his cupped hand up the underside of her bent leg. She breathed in on a little moan of pleasure. It felt incredibly intimate to him. The curve of her calf and the bend of her knee were his to know.

"But I was very sincere," she said, "that I didn't want to date a fireman."

He kissed her jaw near her ear. "Luckily for us, I'm just a cowboy."

She shivered as she laughed. Laughter was good. Luke caressed her from her thigh to her waist to her breast, kissing her neck again as he kept his hand still on her breast, letting the heat from his skin penetrate her damp shirt.

"I'm wearing a sports bra." Her words came out in a rush as she placed her hand over his. Luke thought she sounded almost defensive. She couldn't be insecure about her gorgeous body. She just couldn't be.

"I don't want to boast or anything," he said, "but I do know the difference between a sports bra and the other kind. I'm grateful this job calls for you to wear athletic gear and polo shirts. You'd kill me with cleavage."

In the soft light, he saw her smile. She tilted her head so he could nuzzle her neck more easily. "I do have a little black dress that could possibly knock you out."

"You could send me straight to my grave, I'm sure."

Her leg was warm where it settled against him, her body heat reaching him through the thin nylon he wore. Relaxed by their nonsense talk, languid under his caresses, she let her other leg fall open to the side.

The feast wasn't only one of touch. It was visual, as well. The sight of her thighs, parted before him in the dim light, was so arousing Luke stopped talking. He could only breathe for long, painful seconds. He'd already been hard, but there was aroused, and then there was *ready*. Ready could get damned uncomfortable.

He tore his gaze from her thighs, but looking at her foot resting delicately next to his was no help. Her foot was incredibly feminine compared to his, so yin to his yang with her polished, pedicured toes. The sight only drove home the fact that she was his opposite in the best, most feminine way.

The storm outside was relentless. He spoke beneath the low rumble of thunder. "Even your damned toes are sexy."

He hadn't meant to curse, or make it sound like an

accusation, but inside his body, pleasure was losing to pain.

Patricia stretched her leg out and flexed her foot in response. "Do you know what that color of polish is called? Fire-engine red."

She was killing him, no cleavage required, reclining against him trustingly, head resting on his shoulder as she spoke against his neck. She smelled clean, like she'd used shampoo and soap in girly scents. Her body looked ready and waiting, her open thighs forming a triangle. He was going to have to get up and walk away to regain some command of himself, yet he didn't want to move.

His hand wrapped around her upper arm. "You're strong. I noticed that today when we were putting up the tent. What do you do when you're not running a mobile hospital?" It was a pretty blatant attempt to change the subject. Clumsy, but necessary.

If their bodies hadn't been so close, he would have missed the way she stiffened almost imperceptibly. She'd been tempting him intentionally, then, wanting him to want her.

I'm not rejecting you, I'm just slowing things down.

He stroked her arm again, so that she'd see that he loved touching her. "I can't picture you doing something as mundane as lifting weights at the gym scene. My guess is that you play tennis."

"When I must."

That was an unusual answer. He tucked his chin to kiss her temple, then smoothed her hair with his hand. He twisted one long, damp strand around his finger. Watched it unwind as he let go.

Into the intimate quiet, she said, "I sail."

"Boats?" he asked, surprised. Then immediately, "Never mind, stupid question."

"Do you sail?" she asked.

"I never have."

She sat up a little higher and turned toward him. For the first time since they'd run in here, they made eye contact as she talked.

"You should try it sometime. Out on the water, speed is a beautiful thing. When you've caught the wind just right, you slice through the water without disturbing it. It's quiet. Fast and quiet. I think you'd love it."

"I think I would." He rested his hand on his bent knee, ready to listen all night, because she settled back into him and started explaining more about what was clearly her life's passion. He looked down at her body. Her bare feet and bare legs were no longer artfully arranged, yet they were all the sexier for being casually nestled against his.

She made little boat gestures with one hand as she talked, slicing this way and that through imaginary water. Her other hand rested on his.

"You can't control the wind," she said. "You have to work around it, tacking at different angles. Even if the wind doesn't cooperate, you can use it to get where you want to go. You just have to be clever about it."

He turned his palm up, and she slid her fingers between his. "Have you been sailing your whole life?" he asked.

"Since I was a very young teen. I first learned how at…" She twisted toward him once more. "At summer camp."

For a moment, they laughed. Then she kissed him as she had by the ER and as she had under the tree, full on, burying both her hands in his hair. It was a relief to meet her need, to plunge into her warm, wet mouth. To hold her with hands that weren't steady or slow or particularly gentle.

Greed ignited greed. She turned toward him fully, climbing into his lap and straddling him as best she could, but the bench was too wide and their position too awkward.

Luke's thoughts were reduced to two-word bullets that tore through his mind. *God, yes. Too soon. Not here.*

"Please," she said, straining against him, frustrated. Patricia was begging him. All he could think was, *She shouldn't have to beg me for anything.*

She took his wrist and moved his hand from where he cupped her cheek, dragging his hand over her collarbone, down her breasts, until his palm was spread on the impossible softness of her stomach. "Please," she repeated, "you've touched me everywhere else."

He was a patient man, but if she wanted to set the pace faster than he did, then maybe he didn't know best. Her belly button was an erogenous indentation. He ran his fingertips over it, lightly, then slipped his fingers so easily under the drawstring of her loose cotton pants. She inhaled in anticipation. Luke realized he was controlling his breathing like he was wearing a mask in a fire.

The angle was wrong for his hand to do what she wanted. They were chest to chest, breathing heavily, able to kiss one another, but…

"Stand up," he said quietly, "and turn around."

They stood together, Luke behind her, and Patricia reached for the flashlight on the edge of the sink and turned it off. With her back to his chest, he pinned her in place against him with one arm across her middle. With his free hand, he lifted the edge of her shirt and let his fingertips find the smooth skin of her stomach once more. He slid his hand lower, under the drawstring of her shorts. A few inches under the drawstring was the elastic of her panties, and underneath that, his fingers slid into curls.

She groaned, and he hushed her gently. His fingers explored, wanting to find what made her feel best, but it was difficult to tell when his every stroke brought a response. He pressed in small circles, and she put her hand out to the edge of the sink to steady herself, tension building until her body gave in to sweet waves of shudders, one after the other. Then she sagged against him and he held her, savoring every aftershock and the little tremors that shimmied through her.

The rain had stopped. Their breathing was loud in the new silence. The words in Luke's mind were crazy and intense, *only you* and *perfect,* but again he heard *too soon, not here,* so he and Patricia panted into the silence until their breathing slowed.

The distinctive sound of wood on wood sounded nearby, a door opening and swinging shut on a tent across the way. There were voices outside.

The change in Patricia was immediate. All the tension returned to her body as she whirled to face him. "Security," she breathed, nearly silent but completely petrified.

"They won't come in here," he assured her, speaking low.

"Yes, they will. They make rounds."

She was so nervous, Luke swiped his towel off the

bench and pulled her with him into one of the shower stalls. If the main door opened, they would be hidden from sight. They were both dressed but damp from the earlier rain, so he wrapped the towel around them for warmth and an extra layer of modesty that she seemed to need.

She clung to him under the towel as they listened. Several people were talking, murmuring as they walked to wherever they needed to go. The mess tent wasn't far away; Luke was certain the night shift was taking advantage of the break in the weather to get one of the cold sandwiches that were available twenty-four hours a day.

Gradually, he felt Patricia relax.

"The camp counselors didn't catch us," she said.

He smiled, but he cupped her cheek in the dark, tilting her face up to his and resting his forehead on hers. He wished he could see her eyes. "We weren't doing anything wrong. There's no law against two adults kissing."

Patricia was silent.

"Is there some Texas Rescue regulation I don't know about?" Luke asked.

"Not that I know of," she said, but only after a pause so long, he was willing to bet she'd mentally reviewed the rule book first. "We should get to our sleeping quarters while the rain's stopped. I'm, uh, I'm sorry I didn't…you know."

An insecure Patricia was an adorable Patricia. "No, I don't know."

"I didn't reciprocate."

"I love the way you talk dirty."

That made her gasp, a tiny, indignant sound. She

was so fun to tease, it almost took Luke's mind off the pleasure-pain of his body.

"If you'd reciprocated, I'm pretty sure I wouldn't be able to stand right now, let alone walk you to your quarters," he lied. "Tonight has been plenty of fun. Have breakfast with me tomorrow."

"I can't. I can't be doing this."

"I've got no intention of doing this to you over breakfast, darlin'. Some things should be private. I'm just asking you to share a table and some soggy scrambled eggs."

"It's not that easy. People will wonder how I've come to know you so well, don't you see? Murphy and Zach would wonder what's happened between putting up the tent this morning and us having breakfast tomorrow morning."

Luke didn't like it. A little romance between adults should be no big deal, but Patricia was acting like it would be the end of the world. "You just trusted me completely, but being seen with me would destroy your reputation?"

In the dark, she reached for him, her palm cool against his jaw. "Don't you see? It's nearly impossible to be a female boss without being labeled as a bitch, but I think it would be even more difficult to be labeled a bimbo who chases after a cute fireman when she should be working. I'm trusting you to be discreet. Please."

The "please" undid him. A woman like Patricia shouldn't have to beg, not for completion, not for discretion. She was so very serious, and that bothered him, too. He wanted her to be happy, so he kept his answer light. "Well, since you pointed out how cute I am, I can see the potential problem. Your reputation is safe with me. Sneaking around will be fun, anyway."

The rain started falling again, pelting the tent sporadically. She stepped out of the shower stall. "I'm not going to lock up. The other women think I left with the keys, so it would look odd if it were locked now. There's nothing to steal here, anyway."

Luke had to admire her attention to detail. He was also going to have to be truly creative when it came to hiding places, if he expected her to relax enough to kiss him again. They left together, but when they reached the main aisle, she stopped him a full tent away from the women's sleeping quarters.

"You're beautiful," Luke said. "Sleep tight."

He thought she'd leave him easily, but to his surprise, she reached for his hand. "I'll only sleep well if I don't hear any fire engines going out. Be safe."

Then she squeezed his hand, let go and walked quickly and gracefully to the women's tent, head held high. She could have been in high heels instead of flip-flops.

She was a rare kind of woman, and she cared about him.

Luke decided not to question his luck.

Chapter 9

Patricia woke feeling strange once more. She'd slept like a baby on her air mattress with her sleep mask over her eyes.

Not like a baby. Like a satisfied adult.

Because of Luke Waterson. It had been vain to try to push him out of her mind yesterday morning. Today, it was impossible. He was so vivid to her now. No longer a handsome man viewed from a distance or a person with whom to match wits at an arm's length. Now he was strong hands and warm skin. They'd been so close, she'd felt the bass of his voice through her body while they talked.

Luke was the reason she'd had another night of sound sleep. At this rate, she was going to finish this Texas Rescue mission more rested than she'd begun. The thought made her smile to herself. That would be a first.

Rain was falling. She listened to its steady patter on the fabric roof of the sleeping quarters. Last night, it had thundered and poured. Today, it was gentle, constant, almost comforting in a way, like the difference between sex and cuddling. She'd never been much for cuddling. King-size beds were her preference if she anticipated spending an entire night with a man.

But this morning, she could imagine Luke beside her, and she felt a little pang of longing for the way she envisioned him. She didn't have a word for it. Close? Almost…welcoming? Or comforting, like the sound of this morning's rain.

Rain. Patricia yanked her sleep mask off. Rain wasn't comforting on a Texas Rescue assignment. Rain meant floods. Rain meant mud and the challenges of keeping patients and equipment both clean and dry. Lord, she needed to snap out of it. A firefighter's warm hands were making her brains turn to mush.

She blinked as light hit her eyes, impatiently squinting at the watch on her wrist without waiting for her eyes to adjust. Good lord. She'd slept so long, all the other cots and air mattresses that stretched the length of the tent were empty. The mess tent would soon end its hot breakfast hours. She'd miss her chance to see Luke, even if they were only going to nod politely at one another like distant acquaintances.

She pulled her navy polo shirt on over her stretchy sports bra and swiftly started brushing her hair. With an elastic band and a dozen bobby pins, she began twisting it up, rushing against the clock.

Why rush?

Missing Luke at breakfast would be for the best. She'd dismissed Marcel so easily when she'd needed to focus on securing Quinn MacDowell as a husband. Now that Quinn had fallen through as the man who could defeat Daddy Cargill's demands, she needed to find a new candidate for a husband as soon as possible. She shouldn't be rushing into a relationship with another Marcel.

Luke is nothing like Marcel.

True, and that made it worse. If she couldn't dismiss Luke easily, then he was a liability. He'd distract her from her husband hunt, and she'd fail to win her fight against her father. She let her hands fall to her lap, bobby pins resting in one palm like a child's game of pick-up sticks.

Little girl. Her father's voice grated even in memory. He'd always called her "little girl," and he still did. It had taken her years to realize it wasn't a term of endearment.

Little girl, you can't expect me to release millions of dollars to a spinster. You've got no one to take care of. You don't need the money.

Father, you know perfectly well the reason we have money in our trust fund is because I invest it wisely. I'm not a spinster. I'm single by choice.

Prove it. Land yourself a suitable husband within the year, and half the trust fund is yours. I'll cosign a money transfer to your personal account. You won't have to wait for me to kick the bucket.

She'd stood, prepared to leave the bank president's private office, insulted beyond the high tolerance she usually had for Daddy's nastiness.

Daddy Cargill had stood, too, blocking her path to the door. It was an old trick and one of his favorites: negotiating while standing up. His height, a fluke of DNA he'd done nothing to deserve, gave him a psychological advantage over nearly every opponent. She'd had no choice but to stand there and wait as he dared her to disagree with his description of a suitable husband for a Cargill heiress.

Patricia had been seething inside. His games would never end. Cargill men had lived well into their eighties generation after generation. She had decades of this ahead of her, an entire life that was going to be spent cajoling and bargaining, dealing with him and his mistresses and enduring his whims.

I could call his bluff and marry a man like he's describing. It wouldn't be hard.

None of his fanciful ideas had ever offered her an out before. She could taste the freedom.

You have yourself a deal, Father. The look on his face when she'd held out her hand had been priceless. It hadn't lasted for a full second, but she'd seen it. He'd been forced to shake on his own deal, because their bankers had been avidly watching, eager to witness a living example of Texas lore. Everyone knew once a Cargill shook on a deal, there would be no welching, no cheating, no changing the terms. For two Cargills to shake hands was a once in a generation event.

The deal was set. All she needed was the husband.

Luke Waterson, young and sexy and unpaid as a volunteer fireman, did not meet the criteria. He was, in other words, a waste of Patricia's time. Daddy Cargill himself might as well have put him in her path to distract her from gaining her financial independence.

Patricia stopped rushing. Very carefully, she placed each pin in her hair. A French twist took a few minutes longer than a chignon, but it was just as practical. In the end, underneath the elegant veneer expected of a Cargill heiress, Patricia was a practical woman.

She never ate breakfast, anyway. Coffee would do.

The mess tent was not empty. Patricia had donned her yellow boating slicker and taken the time to stop at administration. She needed her clipboard and a fresh battery for her walkie-talkie. Even so, when she walked through the wood-framed door, Luke and his two buddies were still sitting at one of the tables. A deck of cards was being dealt.

Patricia experienced another annoying clash of emotions. Irritation, that her plans to avoid him had failed. Pleasure, because the man was beautiful to look at, and he was looking at her. A quick wink, and his attention returned to his hand of cards.

It was raining, and she realized the fire crew had no assigned place to be except the cab of their engine—or at a fire. At another table, a cluster of women in nursing scrubs were chatting over coffee. They didn't look guilty or jump from their chairs when Patricia entered, which was how Patricia knew they must have finished the night shift, and were unwinding before going to sleep for the day.

Unwinding apparently entailed gazing at the firemen quite a bit. Murphy seemed equal parts interested and embarrassed, making eye contact and then ducking his head to fiddle with the radio attached to his belt. Zach was eating it up, stretching his arms over his head and flexing as the women looked his way. And Luke, well, every time Patricia glanced his way, their eyes met. Either they had perfectly synchronized timing, or he was staring at her.

Please don't be too obvious.

The day shift cook was pulling empty metal bins out of the steam table's compartments. He seemed to enjoy making a terrific clatter. "Miss Cargill, you missed breakfast."

"Good morning, Louis. Coffee's fine." Patricia started to pour herself a cup from the army-size container that held coffee for her team, twenty-four hours a day.

"I'll get you a biscuit with some gravy."

"Please don't go to any trouble. I'll grab a sandwich if I get hungry later."

Please don't make me stay here longer than I have to.

"You know the biscuits and gravy are the only tasty thing we get out of these prepackaged rations." He began his usual tirade against the food that kept for years in plastic bags while he opened a warming drawer and produced a plateful of white cream gravy. "Lunch will be tasteless. Eat while you can."

Patricia was unable to refuse. When someone was being gracious, she was too well trained to be anything but gracious back. "Thank you, Louis. I'll see if I can get access to the hospital building's cafeteria for you. They might have some produce that didn't go bad with the power outage."

She sat alone. She kept her back to the fire crew and her profile to the nurses. It was, she had to admit, exceedingly uncomfortable. She didn't belong. It was like being in the sixth grade all over again, the new girl at Fayette Preparatory Boarding School.

Unwelcome childhood memories killed her appetite. Still, she ate, bite after bite, at an unhurried but steady pace. She'd risen to the challenge at Fayette, keeping her chin high the way her mother did when she returned home from one of her equestrian events to find a party of bathing beauties in her swimming pool... with her husband.

At eleven, Patricia had sat at the marble-topped table in the refined prep school dining hall, frightened and lonely, and imitated her mother. She'd raised one brow at anyone who dared to approach her. At breakfast, girls had scoffed at her and loudly asked each other who she thought she was. By lunch, they'd whispered that she was Daddy Cargill's one and only child. By dinner, Patricia had been holding court, requesting her fellow students' surnames before granting them permission to sit at her table.

It was nothing to sit alone this morning. Truly nothing a grown woman couldn't handle.

"Patricia!" Luke called. "Come be our fourth, so we can play hearts."

So vividly had she been reliving her Fayette Prep School awkwardness, Patricia felt shocked that someone had dared to speak to her. She turned to face Luke while keeping her chin high and one brow raised.

He raised one brow right back as he shuffled the cards. "Hurry up. I'm dealing."

He was serious. She was the director. She didn't play cards on duty. "I'm sorry, but I was just leaving to check on something."

"This will be over fast. First one to a hundred points. Ten minutes, tops." He pushed a metal folding chair out from the table for her with the toe of his boot.

Zach twisted in his seat to face her. "You know how to play hearts, don't you?"

She nodded, surprised he was seconding Luke's invitation, such as it was.

"Then you know it sucks with three people. Help us out. We helped you out yesterday."

The nurses were silent, watching her. Louis was whistling, rain was falling, and Patricia couldn't see a way out without appearing churlish. She sat at their table, Luke to her right, Zach to her left, and Murphy, who failed to make eye contact with anything but his cards, seated directly across.

She started enjoying herself, especially after she stuck Luke with the queen of spades, the card that caused the most damage in the game.

"Ouch," Luke said, scooping the cards toward him with the same hand that had trailed its way up her bare leg last night.

Patricia pressed her lips together to cover her smile.

"Glad you're so amused," Luke said.

Apparently her attempt to hide her triumph hadn't been totally successful.

The radio on his belt sounded an alarm. The volume was multiplied as all the men's radios sounded the same three tones. She remembered that sound. Her heart jumped into her throat as the men around her came to their feet.

"Oh, no." The words escaped her in genuine dismay. Murphy was practically out the door already, but Zach and Luke both turned to her. "I didn't think you could have a fire in the middle of a long rain like this one."

"Lightning," Zach said. "It can set stuff on fire even when it's wet." He shrugged into the bulky beige overcoat they wore to fight fires. All three men had been using them as raincoats, she guessed.

Patricia set her cards down and put her hands in her lap. "Be safe, gentlemen."

Luke stood with his coat slung over his shoulder. "Don't let Zach here impress you too much. It's probably nothing. A cat in a tree. A false alarm, like ninety percent of our calls are."

Zach started toward the door, stopping to bid a flirtatious farewell to the nurses on his way out.

"Engine thirty-seven," Luke said quietly. "But it's probably nothing."

"Thirty-seven. Thank you."

Then he turned away, gave Zach a push toward the door and left.

Patricia gathered the cards up. She supposed she could keep them with the glove at her desk, all to be returned as soon as possible.

"Could we borrow those cards?" a nurse asked. "We'll give them back to the guys."

"Certainly." Patricia gave them the cards, knowing full well the nurses were less interested in playing cards now and more interested in having a reason to seek out the fire crew later.

Zach seemed like the kind of guy who'd like to keep them all entertained. Murphy might overcome his shyness. And Luke, well, Patricia could imagine him turning on that lazy grin as the nurses suggested they have a little game of cards. But what Patricia wanted to imagine was a Luke who was too interested in her to notice a table full of nurses.

The way he treated me this morning.

Patricia stood and snatched up her walkie-talkie. She knew better. Men were men. For her to even begin to wish for something different with one man in particular was a sure sign that she was losing focus. She had long-range goals, short-term plans and an immediate job to do. Nothing in her life required the devotion of a cowboy.

It was time to get to work. She refilled her coffee as she thanked Louis again for the breakfast, then she headed back to her admin tent, pulling the hood of her yellow raincoat up as she walked. As she passed the new waiting room tent, her hand itched to trail itself along the guy lines. She kept it in her raincoat pocket.

The door to the admin tent had been zipped shut against the rain. She opened it, then kept her chin raised as she entered the admin tent. A few people nodded at her. Most just kept themselves looking very busy.

Patricia sat at her laptop after setting down her clipboard and walkie-talkie neatly to the right. No one dared to approach her table. She told herself she liked it that way.

Discretion sucked.

Luke wanted to stop by admin to let Patricia know he was fine. The call had been to a traffic accident that hadn't required the use of any of their tools. They'd basically shown up, met the local police, hung around for half an hour and returned. Luke had joined the fire department to find adventure, but this was the most common kind of call they responded to. He wanted Patricia to know it, because she worried about him.

She was concerned for the other guys, too. Hell, she worried about every aspect of this hospital. But mostly, Luke knew she was worried for him, and he'd gotten the kiss to prove it. It seemed like the least he could do, to let a woman who'd kissed him know he was okay.

Right now, Luke couldn't spare Patricia from any worries, however, because he was supposed to be sparing her from…hell, he wasn't sure. In the light of day, it seemed hard to recall just why she'd been so adamant in the dark that their new relationship be a secret. He'd made a promise, though. He'd keep it.

It was painful to watch Patricia at lunch time. The moment she got herself a lousy salad, she had to set it down to write something on her always-present clipboard that the cook had asked about. When she picked her food up and turned toward the tables, Luke knew she wouldn't sit with him, but he willed her to sit with someone else. Anyone else. She'd been such a lonely princess this morning, sitting with her perfect posture at a table meant for ten.

"Ah, Patricia, there you are." A woman in a white lab coat approached her.

Good. Someone was seeking her out. Luke relaxed a little and took another bite of the brown meat patty that passed as a preserved hamburger. He'd been concerned that Patricia wasn't eating enough when she'd taken that salad, but now he had to acknowledge her greater experience with Texas Rescue food. She'd probably known the salad would taste better than the hamburger puck.

"Dr. Hodge," Patricia greeted the woman. "Did you need something else?"

"Yes."

Not a friend, then.

Patricia put her salad down once more to consult her clipboard and answer a question. Apparently satisfied, Dr. Hodge stepped away. Patricia stopped to speak to another physician, chucked her coffee in the trash can by the door, and left the mess tent alone, carrying her Styrofoam bowl of lettuce leaves.

Luke managed two more bites of the hamburger before he tossed it onto his plate and stood up. "I'll see you back at the engine," he said to Murphy.

Zach checked his radio. "Did I miss a call? Where are you going?"

"It's time for me to get your glove."

Chapter 10

The rain had stopped, so Patricia had walked slowly enough that Luke caught up to her easily. Maybe too quickly. He only had a half-formed plan. He wanted to talk to her about how dangerous his job usually *wasn't*. He also hated seeing her eat alone, and he thought it had something to do with her assumption that everyone resented the boss. She'd said something along those lines last night. And speaking of last night, he wanted to change this agreement that they'd pretend they barely knew one another.

Luke wasn't sure how he was going to say all that, but he was within a step of her already. "Hey, beautiful."

She stopped to let him join her, but he watched her brown eyes dart left and right, looking for eavesdroppers. "Just call me Patricia, please."

"I've been thinking." He paused, weighing his next words, wondering where to begin.

"I assume that's not an unusual activity," Patricia said after a moment.

Luke smiled. "No, but it's more fun when I've got you to think about. I've had a lot of time to think this morning because we've only been on one call, and that call was a boring one."

She started walking again, and he fell into step beside her.

"Every time you hear the engine go out, I don't want you to worry. You've said a couple of times that you don't want to date a fireman, but it's really not that big of a deal. Most calls are very boring."

They were walking a little distance apart, but he felt her sincerity when she said, "I hope you have many boring mornings like that."

"It is pretty nice to know a pretty woman cares, and you sure are pretty."

"Of course I care."

Yes, she did. After her passionate kiss when she'd learned he wasn't the injured firefighter, after their intimacy as they'd waited out the rain—

"I care about all the Texas Rescue personnel," she added.

He felt the sting of her words. She was trying to say she cared no more for him than for the cook or that Dr. Hodge. That was bull, and Luke couldn't let that statement stand.

He stopped in front of her and crossed his arms, if only to prevent himself from reaching for her. With a kiss, he could remind her just how much they meant to each other. *Not now, not here.*

He strove for outward calm, aware that they weren't the only people outside. "Why would you say that? We practically made love last night, Patricia. I would hope you'd spare me a little more concern than the average person on your roster."

She looked very controlled. Too controlled, like all the muscles in her face were very carefully being held in a neutral expression. Her words, however, were fierce. "I do not like when you do that."

"Do what?"

"Block my way. You are forcing me to stop walking by blocking my way. Physically."

"I'm what?" Luke was baffled. They were talking about attraction, or lying about attraction, or something like that, and her change of subject made no sense. "I'm not blocking you."

She said nothing but stepped around him. Like one of the sailboats she'd described last night, she stepped diagonally to pass him, then diagonally back to her original path, marching on with her clipboard in one hand and her salad in the other.

Luke turned in place to watch her continue walking in a straight line. By God, he had been standing directly in her way. He uncrossed his arms and caught up to her in a few strides.

"I didn't realize I did that." And he wasn't sure what the significance was, but it obviously meant something to Patricia. "I'm sorry."

They were at the entrance to her tent. He was careful not to stop between her and the door.

"I can't stand here and talk to you." Patricia hitched her clipboard under one arm and placed her hand on the zipper of the tent door. "People will start to wonder."

Two of those people happened to pass by them at that

moment, a man in jeans and a woman in scrubs. They barely glanced at Luke and Patricia.

Luke began to cross his arms again, then stopped himself. He didn't want to do anything to spook Patricia further. She was already dying to bolt into her tent.

He nodded toward the couple that had just passed them. "What do you think those people thought of you just now?"

Judging by the confusion in her expression, it was Patricia's turn to be thrown by the turn of the conversation.

"Last night," he continued, "you said they'd think less of you as a boss if you were seen flirting with a fireman. Do they think you are a bimbo for having a normal conversation with me in broad daylight?"

"No, of course not."

"I'm glad to hear that. Then we can be friends during the day."

"I have friends," she said.

It was a lie. She couldn't meet his gaze as she said it, and he wanted to call her out on it. *Name them, tell me.* She'd have no answer, because she hadn't made any friends here. With her head bent, avoiding his gaze, she looked just lost enough that his heart wanted to break for her.

"Darlin', haven't you noticed that every day, people are becoming friends around here? Playing cards, lingering over delicious meals. People talk. They make friends. We can act like that, too."

She let go of the zipper to reposition her clipboard. "That always happens, on every mission. Wait until the cell towers are up and running. People will be absorbed in their phones so fast, your head will spin."

"In the meantime, Patricia, I want to be your friend, not your secret."

She looked up at him quickly. "That's very sweet of you, but we made a deal. I didn't think you were the kind of man who'd try to change the terms. It will be my misfortune if you do. Now, if you'll excuse me, I need to get back to my desk. This salad is wilting in all this humidity."

She unzipped the door, and slipped inside. The sound of the zipper going up again infuriated him. It wasn't raining any longer. She wasn't shutting the weather out. She was shutting him out.

He scrubbed a hand over his face. This woman had him tied up like one of her nautical knots. He felt sorry for her. He was furious with her. Through the tangle of feelings, he grasped onto the one thing that seemed black and white: she was accusing him of trying to welch on a deal. That was an assault on his manhood if he'd ever heard one.

It was absurd. He'd proposed being friendly. Talking to each other, not gossiping to other people about what had transpired in the dark.

On that point, at least, he wanted to be perfectly clear. He'd get that glove back in front of her little platoon of clerks, and he'd give nothing of his feelings for her away. Actions spoke louder than words.

He unzipped the tent. The air inside was almost cool, and the light was considerably less bright, but his eyes adjusted quickly. He saw the panic on Patricia's face as she looked up from her desk in midbite and saw him.

"Afternoon, Patricia. I came to see if I might have left a glove in here from the other day."

"Oh." She set her plastic fork down. "Yes, you did. I have it right here."

As she unzipped a briefcase bag at her feet, Luke looked around and realized there was only one other volunteer in the tent, a young woman who was typing furiously fast on her computer. One clerk was witness enough as he demonstrated that he was keeping Patricia's secrets.

Patricia stood and walked around her table, glove in her hand, keeping up appearances herself. "Here you go. Is there anything else you need?"

His poor princess. What a normal question for her to ask any of the personnel she claimed to be so concerned about. Of course she had no friends here; they were too busy bringing her all their needs, their shortages and their problems. He'd thought it was sad that she didn't sit with friends to eat her meals, but he'd rather eat alone if he were in her shoes, too. If she'd stayed in the mess tent, her to-do list would have grown longer than it already was.

"No, we're doing fine on engine thirty-seven."

He couldn't think of any way to say he understood. He could only wait until dark, and hope she gave him a second chance to explain.

"Finished." The young woman stood as if she'd just won a race. "I'm going to take my break now before lunch closes, if you'll be here for a while, Miss Cargill?"

"Go right ahead, and please call me Patricia," she said, but the young girl was already heading through the door. The sound of the zipper going up after she left was music to Luke's ears.

He didn't have to wait until dark to steal her away.

They could speak privately right now. He just didn't know what to say.

"Patricia," Luke said. He got no further.

"Thank you for not making a scene." She tossed the glove on the table and then turned to perch in a half-sit on the table herself. "I thought you were charging in here to make some kind of point."

"I was. I just can't remember what that point was. Something to do with showing you that you can count on my discretion."

"Why did you follow me out of the mess tent in the first place? You wanted to tell me I had no friends?"

She was direct, his Patricia. Luke scrubbed his jaw for a moment. "I think I wanted to tell you the opposite. Last night, you said that it was easy to be labeled as a bitch when you're the boss. I'm guessing you sat alone at breakfast and you didn't sit at all at lunch because you assume that everyone thinks of you that way."

"I don't put that much thought into it, I assure you."

"It's just a reflex with you, an automatic assumption. But I don't think it's true."

"You don't?"

Those two words gave so much away. Luke realized his intuition had been right. Patricia, deep down, assumed no one liked her.

"What I see is that everyone has a great deal of respect for you. They bring you all kinds of problems, and you never roll your eyes or act like they've wasted your time. I've watched you, Patricia. Not once have you made someone feel foolish for asking for your help."

"And yet, plenty of their requests are absurd." She crossed her arms over her chest as if his words didn't particularly interest her, but she was listening. She stayed exactly as she was, waiting for him to go on.

"You may think that when you take charge, people resent your abilities or your assertiveness. I think the truth is, they're glad you're on their team. You know what you're doing, and you don't let anyone fail. That is not a bitch. People are glad you're part of this hospital, more than you know."

He moved to take a spot next to her, leaning against the table like she was, hip to hip. She glanced at the door immediately.

"It's zipped," he said. "You'll have plenty of notice before anyone barges in. Even a couple of firemen would have to stop for a second to undo that zipper."

She smiled a bit, then she moved her arm toward him an inch or two, just enough to pretend she was digging her elbow into his ribs. "I do have friends, by the way."

"I'm sure you do. You also have me now." If he'd hoped to see her smile at that, he could only be disappointed at her small frown.

"You are hard to be friends with," she said. "I couldn't stand it while you were at the fire. I couldn't... not care."

He kept his arms folded like hers, wondering why a woman would be so set against caring for a man. *What happened to someone you cared for?* There would be time for questions like that, as long as he was patient and didn't push too soon.

Job safety was a simple issue to address. "It's not as dangerous as you think."

In a flash, the memory returned. *Keep the wall to my right. Trust the mask. Get out of the building.*

He wasn't lying to her, really. He'd made it out without a scratch.

"You should come and check out engine thirty-seven. We've got the best equipment available, and I know we might not seem that impressive, but we are well trained. Come and see, and then maybe you'll have a little more confidence."

"That will seem just a tad suspicious, don't you think? Me, coming to inspect a piece of equipment that isn't technically part of the hospital? Chief Rouhotas would have a fit."

"People love fire engines. They look all the time. Come and see it for fun, on a break. Talk to Murphy the whole time. No one will suspect a thing."

That did get her to smile a bit, if only at the idea of Murphy being sociable.

Luke pressed his luck. "This being discreet thing has its limits, you know. You're right that it would seem odd if we were suddenly close today, but our public relationship has to evolve. A week from now, if we still aren't speaking and you're still avoiding me like I've got mange, that will set people talking. It's not natural in this situation. We've only been here a few days, and I can see bonds forming all over this relief center."

"They don't last." She stood and walked away a step. "This is an unreal situation. People get close too fast, and then when the situation is over, the relationship is over. Friendship or otherwise."

He stood, too, close but trying not to crowd her. The need to touch her was strong, so he placed his hands on her upper arms and tried not to hold very tightly.

Her breathing was unsettled, her arms flexed and still crossed over her chest. "It really is like a summer camp. Friendships seem so real, but they don't last after everyone goes back to their regular lives."

Luke rested his forehead to hers. A minute ticked by, but their silence made it feel like a long and lazy time. Patricia uncrossed her arms and placed her hands on him, palms against his chest. He drew her in close, and she slid her hands up his chest to wrap her arms around his neck.

"It's nothing but a summer romance," she whispered against his lips.

"If that's what you believe—"

"It's what I know. It will only last a week."

"If that's what you believe, then I believe we should make it the best week of our lives."

The zipper was loud. And fast. Luke only had time to drop his arms as Patricia whirled to the desk to snatch up the glove.

One male clerk came in, followed by another.

"Here it is," Patricia said, sticking the glove nearly into Luke's stomach, because he was standing a shade too close.

"Thank you." Luke took the glove and turned to the two men. "Don't bother zipping it. I'm leaving."

He had one foot out the door, literally, before he realized that he wasn't certain if he'd see Patricia at dinner—and if she'd sit with him or anyone else. If she'd come by to see the engine. If she was committed to a week of romance or an indefinite relationship. Anything.

"Do you happen to know what's for dinner?" he asked.

She shook her head the way he'd seen her do when

she'd so graciously, so regretfully, been unable to help someone. "I'm sorry, I'm really not sure."

"Then I guess I'll have to wait to find out. Good afternoon."

He stepped out of the tent just as three distinct tones sounded on the radio at his waist. He hoped Patricia hadn't heard them.

Chapter 11

It's not that dangerous.

Right. Easy for Luke to say, hard for Patricia to believe. She'd turned her handheld radio to the town's emergency frequency and deciphered enough to know there was no fire. The rain had caused some already-damaged buildings to collapse. Power lines that weren't downed by the hurricane were down now. It sounded like Luke and the rest of the crew were being called upon to use those axes and sledgehammers. Not that dangerous.

Patricia sat at her desk, resolved to put firefighters out of her mind. She had a hospital to run—or rather, to help Karen to run. Updating her records for Texas Rescue hadn't taken very long, so Patricia didn't mind reviewing the areas Karen was supposed to manage, too.

The hurricane had come through Sunday night. It was now Thursday, and the hospital was running nicely on autopilot. Outpatient, inpatient, emergency: all shifts were covered, all equipment functional. Supply lines had been established. Personnel were departing and arriving as scheduled.

In other words, she had nothing to do. There were no Texas Rescue problems to solve at the moment. There was no firefighter to distract her.

Patricia had time to work on her personal problems, then. She'd left Austin with a banking issue unresolved. Specifically, money was disappearing from the trust fund she shared with her father. Since neither one could withdraw money without the other one's signature, it had to be a banking error, one she'd caught and reported on Friday. It should have been resolved when the banks opened on Monday. Patricia had been running a hospital in a town with no cell-phone service, so she had no way to verify it.

Out of habit, she checked her cell phone again. Nothing.

She looked over to Karen Weaver's desk. The hospital had one phone that could make outgoing calls by a special satellite uplink. It was not for personal use. Patricia repeated that rule to others regularly.

Still, it was tempting. Patricia couldn't have a conversation with the bank, not with clerks coming and going, but she could dial the automatic teller and check the balance on her account. That would tell her if the problem had been rectified. One quick call. Karen would never know, because she never asked for itemized bills. She'd never see the number that had been dialed.

Disgusted with herself for even thinking of misusing Texas Rescue resources, Patricia left the tent. The

Cargill fortune had survived through one hundred and fifty years of Texas history. It would survive this week.

The original Cargill millionaire, her several-greats grandfather, had made sure of that. Cliff Cargill had set up all kinds of rules to protect his money, and generations later, most of those rules still held.

The entire fortune was tied up in trust funds. Perhaps he'd done it to keep his children together, but Cliff had set up the trust fund so that no one family member could spend a dime. Three legal signatures were required to disperse any funds. His descendants had to sink or swim together.

Decades after his death, Cliff's grandchildren had spread across Texas in what Patricia thought of as clusters of legal-signature siblings. There were now three branches of the family. The Dallas, the Houston and the Austin Cargills each held their own trust fund, but each fortune still required multiple signatures.

For generations, the Austin Cargills had been the richest, because they'd been the stingiest. Not with their money, but with their *seed,* for lack of a better word. Having few children meant fewer people among whom to share the money, of course. Fewer combinations of siblings and cousins existed, so the Austin Cargills didn't experience episodes where one group would gang up and sign money away from other cousins who didn't want it spent or invested the same way. Those episodes were part of a saga that had provided fodder for Texas lore for generations.

Daddy Cargill had continued the Austin tradition, fathering only one child, and that one only because Patricia's mother was no fool. Patricia had been born exactly nine months after her parents' wedding. If her father had paid more attention to his inheritance before his young marriage, he would have realized he had to share his money with his progeny. Patricia doubted she ever would have been conceived.

Afterward, he'd certainly taken steps to ensure he'd never have any more children. There were only two living Austin Cargills, Patricia and Daddy. Only two possible signatures on every check. Lord, how she envied those Dallas Cargills. There were so many of them, they probably ran into a co-signer every time they went to the grocery store.

Not her. She had to persuade the same obstinate man to agree to every investment, every expenditure, every time.

Patricia sat at her picnic table, the one that was just far enough away from the mobile hospital to prevent people from passing by. The one where Luke Waterson had found her sleeping. He said he'd been coming to get his glove. In retrospect, it had been much simpler. Boy had met girl. Boy had wanted to get to know girl.

I'm that girl.

She felt the most sublime shiver of satisfaction. Luke Waterson had found her at this table because he'd come looking for *her,* not a glove.

If she sat at one particular corner and perhaps craned her neck in an unladylike way that would never have passed muster at Fayette Prep, Patricia could see two fire engines from her picnic table. The Houston ladder truck was parked in its usual spot. Engine thirty-seven was still gone.

Her pleasure dimmed.

She didn't want to sit alone at this table any longer.

I have friends, she'd assured Luke.

Not many. She'd recently damaged the one friendship she'd relied on the most: Quinn's.

She couldn't fix any other problems right now. The bank was unreachable. She couldn't snap her fingers and produce a qualified husband. With engine thirty-seven out on a call, she couldn't even enjoy a summer romance that wouldn't last a week.

But she could apologize to Quinn MacDowell. Then, when Luke asked her if she had any friends, she could look him in the eye the next time and say yes.

Patricia found Dr. Quinn MacDowell in the mess tent at a crowded table, eating his supper. She paused behind the chair across from him, summoning her poise. It took a lot of summoning. Not only might Quinn reject her overture of friendship, but so might everyone else at the table. *I was saving this seat for someone else* was polite-speak for *I don't want you to sit with me.*

Luke thought people were glad she ran the hospital. She didn't believe him, but she was going to risk that he was right. Right now.

"May I sit here?"

There, she'd said it.

Quinn hesitated for the briefest moment. "Of course."

She sat down, but he said nothing else. They ate in silence for a few minutes, until the two people next to them got up and left. Patricia told herself not to take it personally. Besides, now she could talk to Quinn in relative privacy.

He didn't seem inclined to talk. He didn't even glance up from his plate.

She'd been hard on his girlfriend, she knew. Cold, shutting her out of their social circle, hoping that Quinn would see Diana didn't belong. Diana had nothing to do with the medical world. She volunteered at dog shelters, of all things.

Patricia started there. "Did you see the dogs I had to corral yesterday because of the pet-shelter fire?"

Quinn didn't answer, but he did meet her gaze. He was gauging her, she knew, wondering where the conversation was headed. He no longer trusted her. He no longer found her conversation amusing.

Her heart sank. He'd been her closest friend every other time they'd served together with Texas Rescue. He'd never been intimidated by her, and there were very few people in her world who treated her like she was normal, not like her DNA came from a Texas legend. She wanted her friend back.

"Your girlfriend would have been a real asset in that situation," Patricia said. She had to call on a considerable reserve of Cargill confidence to keep chatting as if he weren't staring her down.

Quinn stopped eating and sat back, watching her warily.

"Dogs are her specialty, right?" Patricia asked. "If your girlfriend is interested, she could come back. I could get her—*Diana*—in touch with the pet-friendly shelter. Diana would be a huge help with them."

It could have been her imagination, but Quinn's expression seemed to soften. "Patricia Cargill, are you trying to apologize for something?"

She looked around a little, making sure their conversation was private. "How much humble pie would you like me to eat? I can do it. I hate having you not speaking to me."

Quinn picked up his fork, digging back into his meal

casually. "What, exactly, made you so set against the idea of me dating Diana?"

"I wanted to get married."

"To me?" He looked very concerned, like she was telling him she was experiencing some terrible medical symptom.

"I still need to get married." She sighed, wishing she didn't need to explain anything at all. "It's a long story, but Daddy Cargill's involved, so it's no joke. You were the man I thought would be the least horrible to be married to."

"Least horrible. I was supposed to jump at the chance to be your least horrible option?"

She felt defensive. "I would have made you an excellent wife."

"In a terrifying way, you probably would."

"I couldn't get you to see me as a potential wife as long as Diana was in the picture."

"That's true. Although you've made it clear your heart isn't exactly broken over me, I'd like you to hear something from me before you hear it from the grapevine. I intend to ask Diana to marry me as soon as I get back to Austin."

So soon? Patricia stopped herself from saying it out loud. She wanted to be Quinn's friend again. He knew his own mind—or rather, his own heart. If he wanted to marry a woman he'd known a month, she could support him.

"You know," she said, "I heard the power is back on at a McDonald's on the other side of town. Karen Weaver came back from an errand with a milkshake today. You know what that means."

Quinn set his fork on his plate with a bit of a smile.

"It's the surest sign we won't be needed much longer. Once a town gets their McDonald's up and running, our days are numbered."

"We've seen it before, haven't we?" She consulted her clipboard, flipping through her rosters. "I don't see why I should keep you past Saturday morning, if you had something in Austin you'd rather do."

Quinn started to smile.

"Congratulations in advance," she added, and then forgot the rest of her friendly, no-hard-feelings sentence, because Luke walked into the dining area. He spotted her immediately and winked, but rather than pretend he barely knew her, he started to walk straight toward her.

Patricia felt her heart beat a little harder. She directed her attention back to Quinn, summoning a smile while she wondered what on earth Luke was doing, coming right up to her table. They had an agreement. They were discreet. He couldn't just walk up and say hello like this.

"How's it going?" Luke clapped Quinn on the shoulder.

Quinn looked up at him. "Hey, Luke. Long time, no see. How's it going with you?" He extended his hand and they shook hands like old friends.

"Same old, same old," Luke said. "How's your mom?"

"Better. Thanks for fixing that light for her."

"No problem." Luke nodded politely at Patricia as if she were an acquaintance with whom he played cards, then left to get in line for the food.

Quinn resumed eating, like nothing was out of the ordinary.

It took Patricia a moment to find her voice. "Do you know that fireman?"

"Who? Luke? He's a good kid. I used to ref his Pee Wee football games. Why do you ask?"

She and Quinn were the same age. Thirty-two. Quinn had been a referee while Luke was in Pee Wee football. How old were children in Pee Wee football? Six years old? Luke's boyish charm suddenly took on more significance.

Good lord, I'm a cougar.

Patricia studied Luke's back as he waited in line. She'd been lusting after a man far too young for her, following in her father's footsteps, chasing an outrageously young piece of eye candy. It was so unfair, though, to be expected to resist those blue eyes and those kisses. The man could kiss.

Quinn squeezed her hand. "Why Patricia Cargill, you think he's cute, don't you?"

She jerked her gaze back to Quinn. Alarm made her stiffen her spine. She couldn't give herself away. She couldn't stand for everyone to make fun of her for being just like her father.

"Who?" She raised her chin, prepared to brazen it out. Patricia Cargill was never teased, not about anything.

"Luke. You think he's cute."

"Cute?" She flicked her fingers dismissively. "That word isn't in my vocabulary. I wouldn't describe a puppy that way, let alone a man."

"No? How do you describe puppies, then?"

"Très charmant."

Quinn laughed, but he wasn't deterred. "You think Luke Waterson is cute. You can't take your eyes off him."

Caught staring at Luke again, Patricia cut her gaze

back to Quinn and leveled her most condemning look on him, the one where she didn't so much as blink. It made bankers and businessmen squirm.

Quinn didn't squirm. "What is this, a staring contest? I was great at this in fourth grade."

She only narrowed her eyes at him, boring a hole right through his eyeballs into his tiny, man-size brain.

Quinn leaned in to speak conspiratorially. "Can you see what he's doing? Is he coming this way, or is he going to sit with another girl? Aren't you dying to take just a quick peek? Maybe he's checking you out right this second."

Patricia gave up and sat back, disgusted that Quinn was laughing at her. "Oh, do be quiet."

"Well, you have my blessing. Have some fun for once in your life. Those sharks you call your girlfriends are blessedly scarce around here, so I'll have to fill the role." Quinn affected a high-pitched voice. "*He's a total hunk.* No, wait. *He's a total hottie.* I think that's the going term."

"I'm leaving. Honestly, I thought we could be friends, but you're just a pest."

"Like a brother."

"Yes, a pesky brother."

She tossed her napkin on the table and stood, ready to make good on her threat to leave, but Quinn caught her hand. "But even pesky brothers are still brothers. Remember that."

She paused and looked down at him. Patricia had no brother, of course. Her father had made sure she had no siblings, unless she counted Wife Number Two's daughter from a previous marriage. Yet Quinn was telling her she had him.

Just when she softened, just when she wasn't sure how to handle the lump in her throat, Quinn smiled devilishly and very softly started chanting, "Tricia and Lukey, sittin' in a tree, k-i-s-s-i-n-g."

"Oh, for the love of God. I can't believe I ever wanted to marry you."

"Is this seat taken?" Luke said, standing right beside her.

Oh, the timing.

Quinn stood immediately, grinning like a fool. "Have a seat. This is my friend, Tricia. Keep her company for me, would you? I was just leaving." Before he left, he made a big deal out of raising Patricia's hand and kissing the back. "*Au revoir,* Tricia dear. *Très charmant.*"

"Go away."

He did.

Luke skipped Quinn's chair and sat next to Patricia instead, shoulder to shoulder. He began eating his prepackaged, reheated meatloaf with gusto.

Patricia knew her cheeks were burning. She picked up her fork and spun a cherry tomato around her plate for a moment. The suspense of waiting for Luke to say something was too much, so she decided to go first. "I gather you know Dr. MacDowell?"

"Apparently not as well as you do, Tricia dear."

She stabbed the tomato and watched the juice drain out around her fork.

He tore a ketchup packet open with his teeth and squirted it directly onto his meatloaf. "Were you two engaged?"

She hadn't wanted to give Quinn a hint about her deal with Daddy Cargill. She didn't want to tell Luke that she knew Daddy Cargill, period. Luke didn't know she was an oil baron's daughter. He liked her just for being Patricia, the personnel director who had no friends in the dining hall.

Luke pressed her for an answer. "I'm asking because that was a mighty interesting comment I heard as I walked up. You wanted to marry him?"

"Does it matter? He's madly in love with someone else. Or is there some guy code, and you can't date his sloppy seconds?" She stared straight ahead, looking at the door.

"Since Quinn was nice enough to introduce us, I believe you can look at me without anyone thinking twice about it. Look at me, so I can casually smile at you and pretend I'm not about to say something important."

She looked at him.

He smiled, but his eyes didn't quite crinkle at the corners as they usually did. "If you told me that you'd married and divorced Quinn MacDowell, it wouldn't change the fact that I can't get enough of you. You're in my thoughts all day. I can't wait for night to come, so I can touch you again. Just so you know, of all the women I've ever met, you are the least likely to ever be sloppy, and no man could ever look at you and think 'seconds.' You are first quality, Patricia. The finest."

She ignored his smile for the public and looked into his serious eyes. He meant what he said. She didn't think she'd ever heard a more sincere compliment. She doubted she'd hear one like it again. It had taken her thirty-two years to receive this one.

"Since we are supposed to be making small talk," Luke said, "why don't you smile politely and say something?"

"I'm the same age as Quinn," she blurted. "Thirty-two."

"Okay." He shrugged. "Why are you looking like you just confessed a murder to me?"

Patricia stole a look around the tent. Most people had cleared out, thankfully, because she was having a hard time pretending this conversation wasn't engrossing. "How old are you? Quinn said he refereed your Pee Wee football games."

"I don't remember that, but it's not hard to believe that he did."

"So, how old are you?"

"Afraid you're robbing the cradle? I'm twenty-eight. Twenty-nine come November, if you'd like to throw me a party."

She was four years older. A woman in her thirties befriending a man in his twenties sounded a little desperate, maybe, but a four-year age difference wasn't so bad.

No daughter of mine will get a dime for marrying a man who's not of the right age. You want to prove you're not a spinster, then don't marry a doddering old man with one foot in the grave, and no college boy, either. Believe you me, it's a piece of cake to get a sweet young thing half your age to marry you for money. And you're getting old enough for a man to be half your age, aren't you?

Her father had failed to set a specific age. Twenty-eight wasn't all that young.

Patricia stopped herself short. Luke didn't meet any other criteria, anyway.

She stabbed another tomato. "I'll kill Quinn for lying to me about that. When he said Pee Wee football…"

"Pee Wee isn't as young as it sounds. I played when

I was twelve, so he was probably fifteen or sixteen. I reffed a few times in high school myself. Got twenty dollars on a Saturday morning to spend on a girl Saturday night. Please pass the salt."

Patricia reached for the plastic shaker and slid it down the table, feeling stiff and self-conscious.

Luke salted his green beans like this was just any old dinner. "Do you like me more or less, now that you know I'm younger than you? I think I like you more. The idea of dating an older woman is hot. When we're done being discreet, can I tell everyone you're much, much older? It'll make me seem like a gigolo."

"You just keep amusing yourself, Waterson." She didn't have any fresh tomatoes to stab, so she pricked the first one again. "So, if you don't remember Quinn from being a Pee Wee—" she paused to cast a skeptical look at the man who looked like he couldn't possibly have ever been a Pee Wee anything "—then how do you know him?"

"Ranching, mostly. We spent school vacations rounding up steer. Branding calves."

"Really? But he's…he's a cardiologist. And you're…"

"Still branding calves."

He didn't sound happy about it.

How could he be? Cowboys weren't any more glamorous than firemen, and probably were paid less. "A cowboy paycheck" was a daily wage, paid in cash. The last time Patricia had fancied herself in love with a cowboy, the standard rate had been one hundred dollars a day.

She'd just turned eighteen and didn't think her father could control her anymore. Daddy had found out about the cowboy, who'd worked on the ranch of a girl

from Fayette. Daddy had offered him ten times his pay
to leave her. One thousand dollars, spread like a fan in
his hand. The cowboy had turned him down, and Patricia had felt the thrill of being valued.

She was better than the dollars that had made her
family so famous.

Then her father had offered the cowboy one hundred
times his pay. Ten thousand dollars. The cowboy had
taken it and left. Proof that at the age of eighteen, Patricia had been worth ten thousand dollars.

She supposed she ought to be pleased with this year's
upgrade. A suitable husband for the Cargill heiress
would hold at least a million dollars in liquid assets,
in addition to owning land in the great state of Texas.
Her father now thought she was worth a million. How
fast would a cowboy leave her if Daddy Cargill offered
him a million dollars?

Patricia knew, suddenly, that was exactly what her
father planned to do when she produced a prospective
husband. She was the real Cargill, the one who had the
Midas touch. She could turn money into more money.
Daddy Cargill was just the front man in his white suit
and his longhorn Cadillac. She hadn't thought he realized that—but he knew. Daddy wouldn't let her go. She
was worth too much.

Still, they'd made a deal. They'd shaken hands, with
witnesses. He couldn't welch on the deal. He couldn't
cheat. He couldn't change the terms—but he would
surely try to offer a millionaire of the right age a better deal to leave her. And he'd surely never offer her
another chance to escape again.

Luke patted her on the arm as he got up, a friendly,
"nice seeing you" type of gesture for the dining public.

"I don't know what has you looking so sad, but hang in there. It will be dark soon, and I'll help you chase away the day's worries."

He threw his paper plate in the industrial garbage can and walked out the door.

Chapter 12

She did not need a handsome fireman to make her forget her worries.

She needed to focus on them. If it hadn't been for this hurricane, she'd be making the rounds to all the right events in Austin, perhaps branching out to Dallas, putting herself in the path of the right type of men, inquiring discreetly into their financial and marital backgrounds.

Instead, she was at a hurricane relief center where the only man who kept crossing her path wore a close-fitting black T-shirt and called her *darlin'*. The only thing she had to do discreetly was purely physical and involved sneaking around after dark.

She wondered if it was dark yet. One of her clerks left the tent, and Patricia watched the door as he unzipped it. It was still only dusk outside.

She returned her attention to her laptop. Local medical personnel had been walking up to the relief center and volunteering to work with Texas Rescue, a typical occurrence in this kind of situation. Patricia appreciated their willingness to help, but she still required them to fill out the application forms. Just because people introduced themselves as nurses or doctors didn't mean they were. Her clerks had been verifying licenses and running background checks all day.

Another Dr. MacDowell could have been entered into the system. Patricia slid a glance to the satellite phone. Reviewing personnel files wasn't really abusing Texas Rescue resources, not like making a call to check her bank balance would be. Personnel files were at her fingertips, right here in her laptop. It was her job to verify physician's applications. And if she found a man who fit certain criteria while she did it…

She scowled at her fingers and the way they just rested on the keys, refusing to type. The average family doctor was almost never a millionaire, she knew. Having a medical degree did not mean one owned land, either. The doctors who had the time to volunteer tended to be the older ones, retired or semiretired.

Still, she should look. It was possible the right man was right here, right now.

Or, I could take a week off from the husband hunt. Quinn even said I ought to have a little fun for once.

She could be blowing a golden opportunity here. All she had to do was open the first file of a local volunteer and check the date of birth. Just take that one, tiny step.

Her fingers wouldn't move. Disgusted with herself and afraid the two night-shift clerks would notice her lack of activity, she opened a game of hearts on her laptop.

This did not take her mind off Luke in the least.

"I've never heard of a horse named Pickles."

Patricia froze, finger poised over her touchpad, as Luke's voice carried through the fabric wall of the tent.

Feminine giggles followed. "'Pickles' was my idea. He's my horse, so I got to name him."

"I could've guessed that. You don't think any man would ride the open range on a horse named Pickles, do you?"

More giggles. "If you're a cowboy, what's your horse's name?"

"Only manly names are allowed on the ranch. We've got Killer, T-Rex, and his son, Ice-T."

"You do not."

"We do have a horse named Ice-T. That's the honest truth, and he looks like a badass, too, just like the actor. Ice-T glares at a cow and it's too afraid to move. That's why he's my favorite mount. Cows are much easier to rope when they're not moving."

The peal of feminine giggles snapped Patricia into action. She killed her game and closed her laptop's lid. Like a fool, she'd started listening to Luke's tall tale as if she was one of the girls he was telling it to, but the sound of a real horse snuffling and chewing on a bit was unmistakable. The girl or girls Luke was wasting his time charming were on horses in Patricia's hospital.

"If the cattle heard me call a horse Pickles, I'd lose their respect as fast as that."

The answering giggles were like fingernails on a chalkboard.

Patricia headed out of the tent. The door, naturally,

was on the opposite wall of the tent from where she was hearing Luke's voice. She had to go out the front and then walk around to the back side, where the tents backed into one another.

When she rounded the corner, she saw the rear of a large, brown horse. Luke was standing at its head, stroking its muzzle as he kept entertaining the young ladies who were sitting on the horse's bare back. No wonder Patricia had been able to hear him so clearly through the fabric walls. The horse's flank was practically touching the tent.

Two young women, riding double and riding bareback, had attracted the attention of a cowboy. Had Patricia seen it anywhere else, she would've turned to an acquaintance and made a cutting quip about the predictability of such a thing. She was at her hospital, though, and the cowboy was Luke. It was hard to deny that there was something distinctly unpleasant about it all.

Lord, it was jealousy she was feeling. The young women, despite being on a horse, wore denim cut-offs and no shoes. Their legs looked long, but their feet were filthy, Patricia noted with a sniff. She doubted Luke or any other man would notice such a thing, because the girls were also wearing bikini tops. They were as tanned as only girls who lived in a beach town could be.

And they were definitely girls. Perhaps they were teetering on the edge of adulthood, but they were still teenagers. Surely Luke could see how painfully young they were.

Patricia was accustomed to seeing older men with much younger women, but generally that didn't occur until the men of her acquaintance were on their second wives, and then those women were generally no more than two decades their husband's junior. Only men like her father pushed the boundaries further. It went without saying that he'd slept with women younger than Patricia while Patricia was in college.

Are you quite sure she's eighteen, Father? Think of the negative press. The cost of a good legal team. Yes, twenty-one is a much safer age.

Patricia would have bet a million dollars that Luke was nothing like her father, and yet before her eyes, he was enjoying a long and silly chat with pretty young girls on a horse. She shouldn't have been surprised. Men were so predictable.

The real issue here was that there was a horse in the hospital. Once more, she'd lost her focus around Luke.

From a good five yards away, she broke into their party of giggles. "Good afternoon, ladies. I'm sorry, but you need to take your horse out of the tent area immediately. It may not look like it, but this is a hospital. The horse presents sanitation and safety issues."

At the sound of her voice, the horse stepped in place, dangerously close to the guy lines. The girls on its back twisted around to glare at Patricia, causing the horse to shift more nervously.

Luke kept his hand on the horse's muzzle. "Don't walk up behind the horse, Patricia. You'll get kicked." He sounded perfectly calm.

"I know that," she said. Basic equestrian skills had been a mandatory part of her schooling. Besides, she'd once been in love with a cowboy, back when she'd been young like these riders.

"Then stop doing it." Luke sounded quite firm, although his posture was very relaxed, and all his attention was on the horse. Patricia had thought she was walking toward them at an adequate angle for the horse to see her coming, but she stepped farther to the side at the tone of Luke's voice.

"We're not hurting anything," one girl said, clearly feeling her oats. "You can't make us leave."

"Actually, she can," Luke said. "This is a restricted area, and she's the boss lady."

The girls, who moments ago had seemed on the verge of womanhood as they'd practiced their feminine wiles on Luke, became petulant children. "Fine, we'll leave. What a bitch."

The horse whinnied, bobbing its nose under Luke's hand.

"Now look there," Luke said. "Pickles doesn't want to hear such an ugly word coming from his owner's mouth. I know you love this horse, but look at his feet. You've got him ready to trip over a tent spike, and he's going to have to step around a half-dozen more to get back out to the main walkway. There's a difference between someone being bitchy and someone enforcing a rule to save your horse, isn't there? Hand me the reins, and I'll walk you out."

And that, Patricia realized in a flash, was why Luke had been talking to those girls in the first place. He must have spotted the horse and had stepped in to prevent it from getting hurt. How easily it could have tripped on a rope and torn down part of the hospital, possibly hurting itself or others. Luke had been talking to the girls in order to keep the horse in place, giving the horse time to smell him, then more time to adjust to his touch as he petted it.

The horse, relaxed and trusting Luke, willingly followed him out of the tangled danger into which its young owners had placed it. Patricia drifted along at a little distance, watching Luke as he coaxed the giant horse to take delicate steps over and around the guy lines. Luke needed nothing more than his calm voice and a gentle tap of the reins on a foreleg that needed to be lifted higher before he would let the horse proceed.

Patricia didn't want to feel the emotions he was stirring in her. Her fireman clearly had the horse sense of a cowboy, for example. It was easy enough to fool herself that her admiration wasn't really lust for a man who tamed a beast.

It was easy to admit that she felt gratitude, too. He'd stepped in to take care of a potential problem for her, after all. But it was the relief that worried her most, because she clearly felt relief, damn it, that Luke wasn't the kind of man who chased anything female in a bikini.

It shouldn't matter so much to her. After this week, she wouldn't care what he did with girls who wore bikinis or anything else. Patricia needed to stay detached, but he was making it so very difficult.

In the morning, Patricia woke feeling wonderful.

Luke Waterson was an excellent kisser. He'd come for her after dark, taking her back to the picnic table near the hospital building. He'd made her lay on top of the table with him. She'd felt silly, a grown woman reclining on wood planks, but he'd said he wanted her to look at the stars. They were brilliant in the black sky, undiluted by civilization's usual glow of street signs and restaurant marquees.

Even in June, the night air had felt a bit cool, and Patricia had stayed warm by keeping herself tucked by his side, her head on his chest, leg along leg. They'd kicked off their shoes and let their bare feet tangle, and they'd talked about stars they could see from horseback and stars they could see from boat decks.

Then, they'd kissed. Long and lazy, knowing the whole night stretched before them. She'd enjoyed the slow build-up. When he hadn't pushed for more, she'd enjoyed it a while longer, but eventually, she'd been confused. They'd taken things pretty far in the shower facility. Surely, he'd expect things to go further this time.

Men wanted sex. That was a fact of life. They wanted it, they appreciated the woman who gave it to them for a short while, and then they moved on, wanting it again from the next woman. Patricia excelled at keeping sexual relationships civilized, as did her friends. It was the height of bad taste to weep after a lover or to be enraged over a divorce.

Yet last night on the picnic table, Luke had kept things surprisingly PG. Maybe he'd lifted the elastic of her sports bra and let his thumb slide over her full breast. Maybe she'd let her hand slip over the nylon of his track pants, just to get a hint of the size and the shape of him. But mostly, it had been a starry night of kisses and whispers.

Surely, that meant he was enjoying her company, if he was delaying the sex. He was in no rush to be done with her and then move on to another woman. She felt dangerously pleased about that.

He won't be easy to leave.

She wouldn't think about that now. Fortunes and husbands and fathers could wait. She would work through this day, and live for another precious night.

* * *

Not touching a man was an aphrodisiac.

There could be no other explanation for it. Patricia was dying as she ate lunch sitting to the left of Luke. Others surrounded them, eating and talking, oblivious to the way Patricia tried not to stare at the man with the blue eyes and lazy grin. A nurse sat down to debate sci-fi movies with Murphy. Some of the Houston fire crew sat there, too, eating quickly and leaving. Quinn stopped in for a bite and stayed awhile.

Patricia found that being polite to an acquaintance so no one would guess he was really a man who'd caressed every inch of her body required concentration. She couldn't be too aloof, but she also had to be careful she didn't laugh any louder at Luke's jokes than Quinn's. When Murphy asked if anyone else had noticed how many more stars there seemed to be in this part of Texas, she turned her face away from Luke and brushed imaginary crumbs from her lap, not daring to meet his eyes and share a memory.

Lunch could have been horrible hot dogs or heavenly foie gras, so little did Patricia pay attention to her food. Instead, she was exquisitely aware of every move Luke made. She deliberately didn't watch the muscles in his shoulders move when he turned to toss a bottle of ketchup to Zach's table. She was aware when he casually placed his left hand on the table, perhaps four inches away from her right, and kept it there. She didn't move her hand away, either. They talked to other people while they didn't hold hands.

When his radio sounded its alert tones, though, she forgot not to look into his blue eyes. He didn't look away, either.

"Guess lunch is over," Luke said. *Don't worry about me, darlin'.*

"I hope your crew gets back before dark this time," she answered. *Because I'm dying to touch you tonight.*

And then he was on his feet and out the door, and she was looking at her plate, vaguely surprised to see lunch had been neither hot dogs nor foie gras. She'd apparently chosen mashed potatoes and vanilla pudding, a gourmet combination the elegant Cargill heiress would never have touched before a hurricane had put her plans on hold.

She looked at the silly lunch on her disposable plate and started to smile to herself. She wouldn't let herself laugh. She had her limits. But then Quinn began whispering his chant about kissing in a tree, and Patricia got a bad case of the giggles.

Laughing must have been an aphrodisiac, too, because when she left the mess tent and saw engine thirty-seven pulling out of its parking space, she forgot to worry. She was too busy imagining a certain fireman touching her tonight.

She checked her watch to see how many hours it would be before the world went dark and the fun would begin.

Chapter 13

Patricia hid behind a tree, listening to the locker room sounds of men taking showers. The world was wonderfully, gloriously pitch black, and Luke would soon emerge, damp and clean. Then finally, finally, he'd come find her.

Patricia planned to make that the easiest of tasks. He hadn't come to find her when his truck had returned from its call. She'd monitored the police radio, so she knew engine thirty-seven had been called to yet another car accident. Luke hadn't been kidding when he said they rarely were called to fires.

This time, a car had rolled over on the main road out of town, triggering a series of smaller accidents with minor injuries her ER could handle. Only one person had been taken straight from the scene to San Antonio by helicopter, and that person had been a car driver, not an emergency responder.

She hadn't had to worry about Luke's safety. With nothing to dampen her spirits, she'd waited to catch another glimpse of him before darkness fell. He must not have been able to detour past her office after he'd grabbed a sandwich from the mess tent, although she'd managed to linger by the unzipped door flap. When Karen had stopped in the middle of the main thoroughfare to let Patricia know the permanent hospital's roof repairs had begun, Patricia had not kept walking as her supervisor talked. She'd stood still and listened, hoping Luke would pass by and send her a covert smile.

He hadn't. People or duties were keeping him from her. Since he couldn't get clear to come see her, she was going to come to him. Any moment now. It was late and the showers were closing.

The bark of the tree felt hard and intricate under her palm. Her whole body felt sensitive, every summer breeze making itself felt as it passed over her exposed arms and legs. She was even aware of the strands of hair that had come loose from her chignon to tickle the nape of her neck. With her drawstring sleep shorts, she'd worn an oversize shirt, easy for a man's hands to push out of the way. She intended to entice him to do just that.

It wouldn't take much doing. He wanted to touch her as much as she wanted to be touched. *What a perfect pair we make.*

The wooden door opened, light poured out. Luke stepped out, hair damp, towel around his shoulders, and Patricia stepped from behind the tree, ready to dart forward and snag his hand. Then Zach stepped out, and Patricia could have stamped her foot in frustration. In fact, she did.

Zach nodded at something Luke said and walked

away. Patricia feared Luke would follow, but he paused to lift the towel from around his neck to give his hair another rub. Patricia seized her moment, stepping lightly over the ground to grab a corner of his towel and give it a tug.

"Shh," she whispered. "It's me."

In the half-light, he half smiled. "It *is* you."

She took his hand and pulled him into the darkness. She found the tree where they'd first kissed within a minute. Funny how it had seemed farther away that first night.

She turned and stepped into Luke, body fitting against body effortlessly. Her leg stepped in between his and her back arched as she raised her arms to wrap around his neck. The movement was smooth, as if she'd done it so often, it was part of her muscle memory. She tilted her face up, just so. Luke gave his head a little shake and closed his eyes before his mouth came down on hers.

Lord, he tasted good. He felt good. After a day of discipline and denial, it was like melting, a release of everything strict and straight. He ended the kiss, but he didn't let go. For a long moment, he just breathed in the dark with her, his mouth an inch away from hers.

Luke didn't want the kiss to be too sexual yet, perhaps. But he wasn't letting go of her, either.

She let one hand drift from his neck up to his wet hair. "What was that head shake for? What were you thinking?"

"Nothing," he murmured. "I'm just a lucky man."

And then he kissed her again, and this time there was less restraint. Less control. More hunger. More tongue, more heat, more strength in his hold.

This time, when he ended the kiss, they were both panting. His hand had messed up her chignon as he'd cupped the back of her head, keeping her where he wanted her as he kissed her. He'd controlled her during that kiss, deciding what angle, how deep, when to stop. Patricia felt a little thrill of discovery. *So this is what it's really like to belong to a man.*

That had been a taste. She wanted more. She wanted to lose herself, to let go and let Luke lead her somewhere she'd never been. She trusted him. She could turn her mind off and focus only on this craving that every touch satisfied and stoked simultaneously.

She felt the tension in his arms as he let go, almost like he was forcing himself to step back. "Not here. I don't think I should—it's not the right—not here."

Patricia was drunk on her taste of desire. If this wasn't private enough, she could fix that. She took his hand once more and pulled him deeper into the darkness. Silently, she led him out of the trees toward the hospital. She'd found this shortcut earlier. In moments, they stopped beside their picnic table.

He'd found her sleeping here that first day he'd crashed into her tent. He'd talked to her here last night for hours. Tonight...

Patricia didn't try to hide her smile. She pointed at the sky. "Stars."

She pointed at the table. "Talk."

Then, smiling and sure, loving the way his eyes were eating her up, she stepped into him again, thigh between his, arms around his neck. "Let's fast forward past all that tonight."

He didn't smile back. For a moment, her confidence faltered. She'd misread something. Could a kiss like that

be one-sided? He didn't want her. Then he had a fistful of her shirt and his hand cupped under her thigh to
lift her body so he could press against her intimately.

She read that message loud and clear.

The hospital building loomed over them, offering
protection, offering privacy. Luke took it, lifting her
off her feet as he leaned her back against the building,
looming over her.

She wrapped her legs around his waist. He said, "I'm
not going to make love to you up against this wall, out
in the open," and then he kissed her as if he was making love to her.

He kept her secure with one arm around her waist.
He pressed the palm of his other hand into the wall by
her head, keeping their balance as he rocked his hips
into hers. She closed her eyes, loving the way he would
move when they didn't have a paltry few pieces of clothing between them.

Her chignon caught in the stucco, tugging strands
free a little painfully, but she didn't care. She pressed
her head back as he kissed his way down her throat,
giving him easy access.

She couldn't have been more willing, more open,
more wanting.

Abruptly, Luke stopped. He froze in place, holding
her against his waist, head bent into her neck, breathing like he'd just run five miles.

She felt, once more, like she'd made a terrible mis-
calculation. It was a very cold feeling.

"Patricia, Patricia." Luke pushed off from the building, holding her tightly to his chest, as she kept her legs
wrapped around his waist, but then he found her knee

with his free hand. He pressed gently, until she lowered her leg to the ground.

"I can't make love to you like this."

"You can't?"

She disentangled herself the rest of the way and stood on her own two feet. Aching with physical need, shaky with confusion, she held her chin high, long years of practice not failing her, even now. "It seemed like you wanted to."

"I want to, darlin'. I want to. But this would be a lousy first time." Luke didn't let her take another step back, but reached for her and pulled her into his chest. He pressed her cheek against the side of his neck and stayed like that, one hand cradling her head, pushing pins into her scalp, for long moments.

Patricia had no idea what Luke was objecting to. Being out of doors? Standing up? Those details were trivial. It was the desire that had been key.

"My head's not in the right place," he said, answering her unspoken questions. "The call we went on today was bad, and I can't forget it."

"You stopped because you were thinking about a traffic accident?"

"I stopped because I was using you to forget it, and that's a lousy reason to make love for the first time." He stopped squashing her, letting go of her head and holding her more loosely around the waist, so they could face each other.

Patricia felt so raw inside. She'd never had a man turn her down cold before. She'd never had a man with whom her desire had burned so hot.

"Isn't that what sex is for?" she asked. "To blot everything out for a moment?"

Luke frowned, so very unlike him that it helped Patricia refocus. Her head was clearing from its descent into passion.

Luke cupped her cheek with a warm palm. "I suppose people have sex for a million different reasons. I can only speak for myself, and the way I feel about you. There's a difference between wanting to make a new memory and trying to blot out an old one. When I have sex with you, I'm not going to want to forget a thing."

"But not tonight." Patricia said it calmly, confirming his timeline, feeling like a child being told her mother would come to visit her, but not this week. "I didn't realize you were bothered by anything. The accident didn't sound bad over the radio."

This time he was the one who took her by the hand, tugging her to the picnic table. They sat down on it, side by side.

"Do you know why they call fire engines out to car accidents?" he asked.

"In case the car catches on fire?"

"It's to free trapped people. Our engine carries the hydraulic Jaws of Life tool to cut through metal."

"Did you have to operate that today?"

"I'm just a volunteer fireman. I don't have certification on that yet. Rouhotas and Zach handle that piece of equipment." After a moment of silence, Luke leaned against Patricia's side. She put her arm around his back. Drew soft circles on his shoulder blade.

"The driver was a young mother. Unconscious. Helicopter standing by while they worked."

"That sounds awful. If you didn't operate the power tools, what did you do?"

"We know she was a mother because she had a little

daughter in the back seat. She's this many years old."
Luke held up three fingers, like a child would. "Thank
God she was in a child safety seat, because that car was
upside down, and she was upside down, too, but safely
strapped in that five-point harness. While Rouhotas
and Zach cut the car apart, my job was to keep the little girl from looking at her mom. You didn't like when
I blocked your way the other day, but I crawled in the
backseat and blocked her view."

"Oh, Luke." Patricia turned toward him and tried to
hold him in her arms, pulling him to her chest, a little
like the way he'd held her on the bench when they'd
hidden from the rain.

"Three-year-olds don't understand why their moms
won't answer them, you know. I kept telling her everything was okay, even the noise of the metal was okay.
We don't carry ear plugs small enough for a kid that
tiny, so I had to cover her ears with my hands."

"Oh, Luke," she repeated helplessly. Patricia couldn't
remember the last time she'd cried. She honestly
couldn't remember. A decade? Twenty years? Had she
been eleven years old the last time she'd dashed a cheek
against her shirtsleeve like this, aware that boarding
school was her new life, aware that she'd never live
with her mother again? There'd been no point in crying after that.

"It was a piece of cake to get the little girl out once
her mother was removed. She had no injuries at all.
When I have a kid, she's going to be buckled into a
seat like that before I put my key in the ignition. Every
single damned time."

He was going to have kids someday. It was a cer-
tainty, the way he said it. Those kids would have a

daddy who protected them. Patricia didn't want to identify the emotions that thought stirred up.

"I just hope her mother made it. That woman never came to, never even moaned."

The mother had been the one patient airlifted to San Antonio, of course.

"Come with me." Patricia wiped her cheeks with the heel of her hand. She took Luke by the hand and started for the admin tent. "You know that phrase 'better than sex'? I think I've got something better than sex right now. I've got access to a satellite phone, and I can call San Antonio."

"You don't have to do that. Rouhotas will get on the radio tomorrow. Firemen relay info like that."

Patricia sniffed. "That's rumor. I'm going to get you the facts, so you can sleep tonight."

She stuttered to a stop. Luke nearly crashed into her. "If that would help you. Maybe you'd rather wait until morning? The facts might not be good. I can't stand not knowing, but maybe that's just me."

He rubbed his jaw, and it took her a moment to realize he was exaggerating the indecisive move. "Let's see. I could hope for info tomorrow and have Murphy to talk it out with, or I could find out tonight while I've got a beautiful blonde by my side who's being very kind. She's very soft, too, I might add, and a thousand times more fun to kiss than Murphy. Gee, this is a tough one."

"You are just a barrel of laughs, Waterson." Patricia couldn't quite hit her usual acerbic tone. Everything seemed more hopeful now that Luke was teasing her.

They continued walking to the admin tent. "This may not be a great idea, Patricia. Your hair is a mess. People will definitely talk."

Without stopping, she pulled a few pins out, held them in her teeth, made a quick twist of her hair, and stuck them back in.

"Okay, that's distracting. You know men are amazed at how women do that stuff, right?"

Luke stayed outside the tent while Patricia nodded coolly to the night clerks, used her laptop database to find the hospitals in San Antonio that had major trauma centers, and started dialing. No one questioned her right to pull the satellite phone from its orange case.

She'd refused to abuse Texas Rescue resources for her personal benefit, but when it came to Luke, she found it easy. Should Karen ask, Patricia could explain that Texas Rescue personnel had made the rescue, and she'd needed the patient's status for the follow-up report. Or, the emergency responders needed to know if their efforts had been successful in order to refine their training. Or—oh, hell. Patricia would just buy her own satellite phone and bring it next time.

She left the tent to find Luke and tell him the good news. The mother was already out of surgery and had awakened from anesthesia. She was under observation because she'd lost consciousness at the scene, but it was only a routine precaution. She was expected to be moved to a regular bed after twenty-four hours.

"The charge nurse was in a chatty mood, so I got her chatting about how patients fared better when family members were present. I asked her what kind of accommodations her hospital had for out-of-town families."

Luke pulled her into the shadow between the tents. "I heard some of that. You are one smooth talker, Patricia Cargill. What did the nurse tell you?"

"The husband is there, and the nurse says it's the

sweetest thing, how he won't let his daughter out of his sight. The nurse was very proud to tell me how she'd arranged a room for them in the hotel next door. They're going to be okay."

Luke didn't say anything. In the dark, Patricia couldn't read his expression.

"Are you going to be okay?"

He answered her with a kiss that made her go weak in the knees. Patricia didn't worry that she'd fall. She didn't worry about anything at all. Luke was happy, and so was she.

Chapter 14

Patricia couldn't wait for night to come again, but first, she had to face the day. She took her sleeping mask off and rolled onto her back, raising her wrist to squint at her watch out of habit. It took a moment for her mind to register the sounds coming from a few cots away. The distinctive *whoosh* sound that meant a text message had been sent. The chime of an email coming in.

Phones were working. The cell towers had been fixed.

As eager as everyone else, Patricia grabbed her cell phone and turned it on, then laid back on her air mattress to wait for the miracle of technology to begin.

It began slowly. Images of circles spun slowly, loading, loading, as Patricia's phone competed with every other phone in the city to claim space on the network. Thousands of people were undoubtedly trying to download four or five days' worth of information and updates.

Impatient, Patricia sat up and started brushing out her hair, keeping one eye on her phone screen. This mission had pulled her out of her normal life in the middle of so many issues. There'd been that unauthorized withdrawal from her bank account, which should have been fixed. Patricia pressed the app for her bank account. Its circle started spinning.

She waited for it to open, hoping against hope to find that her father had finally signed the last series of checks she'd written. He'd been sitting on them, doing nothing, as usual. She hadn't had time to cajole him into signing before Texas Rescue had been activated.

She knew her father was busy with his new mistress, but the old one was pouting and getting in his way. Patricia could use that to her advantage. She'd handle the old mistress, if he'd sign her checks. It was a deal she'd made with him a dozen times.

From the cot across from Patricia's, Karen made a little squeal of excitement. Patricia closed her eyes briefly, her only outward show of her inward disgust. Her supervisor shouldn't have already been in bed if Patricia wasn't up and on duty.

Karen smiled at her and waved her phone. "Level eighty-nine, and I got an extra sprinkle ball, too."

"How lovely."

Honestly, what was the polite rejoinder to nonsense like that? *Get the hell off the network. I'm trying to verify that the Cargill donation to Texas Rescue went through. Your paycheck depends on it.*

That would be so satisfying to say. Her father would have said it in a heartbeat, and loudly, which is why Patricia did not. She'd been trained to be twice as classy to make up for his bluster.

Patricia glanced at her own phone. Half the screen had loaded, so she could see the trust fund's balance. Her father must have signed those checks, because the balance was considerably lower than she expected. Millimeter by millimeter, her bank statement appeared, but it froze before loading more than half the screen.

She read the two entries that appeared. The first was Wife Number Three's quarterly allowance, a hefty seven figures. Number Three and Daddy had never legally divorced, and the seven figures hurt less than alimony might have, so Patricia was relieved to see she'd been paid. *Keep her happy with her polo ponies in Argentina, where I don't have to deal with her.*

The second entry was an electronic funds transfer to a jewelry store, the one from which Daddy Cargill liked to buy baubles for his "girls." Patricia had long ago agreed to a standing order that pre-authorized a certain amount every month, so that her father could practice his largesse without consulting his daughter in public.

The two expenditures blurred before her eyes. Money for women, so he could have more women. A family fortune, a Texas legacy, squandered to appease one man's appetites. Patricia had to negotiate for every donation to Texas Rescue. He'd made her crawl before they'd donated an MRI machine to West Central, and then he'd shown up to cut the ribbon and flash his diamonds.

The humiliation would be over soon. She'd been foolish to place all her hopes on Quinn, but she'd find the right husband, and she'd find him before her year was up. She'd win his bet, take her inheritance and start her own branch of the Cargill family. Things would be different.

The first step in winning her freedom was simple: give up Luke Waterson.

The phone screen stayed stuck, half loaded. The jeweler's amount taunted her. Daddy had hit the spending limit already, and it was only early June. She supposed she'd have to call him, but a more unpleasant chore didn't exist.

Someone else in the tent didn't feel the same. Patricia heard a chipper "Hi, Daddy" spoken with such delight, it was startling. The new pharmacy tech was sitting cross-legged on her inflatable mattress, speaking happily into her phone. "Daddy, it's so good to hear your voice. I'm doing great. How are you?"

Patricia closed her eyes, blindsided by a sudden wave of emotion. She had no idea what it would be like to want to hear her father's voice. The joy in the young woman's words speared right past every defense Patricia had, painfully showing her what her life might have been like, had she been born to a different kind of man.

"Oh, Daddy, this has been the best week of my life."

The best week of her life. Patricia knew it was almost over. The cell towers were up. The McDonald's had reopened. The best week of her life would soon end, and her crucial hunt for the right husband would resume.

Patricia let the cell phone slip from her fingers. There was no contact in her directory, no family member, no friend that she wanted to call. The only person she wanted to see right now was a fireman named Luke. She wanted to see him right away, because soon, she wouldn't be able to see him ever again.

Her dearest Daddy—every Texan's favorite Daddy—had made sure of that.

* * *

"The rain was good for the grass, but it was bad for the dirt. The herd can't eat the green stuff without getting stuck in the mud."

Luke had been dreading this phone call, with good reason. He'd left the James Hill Ranch in the competent hands of his foreman, Gus, but he'd known Gus wasn't going to have any rosy news for him when Luke called. This morning, when everyone's cell phones had started to work, Luke had known he had to check in, anyway.

"How much feed have you laid out?" Luke asked.

"Hay every day."

Luke saw dollar signs going down the figurative drain. His herd ought to be grazing from pasture to pasture right now, but the mud was making him buy them dinner. The year's profits were literally being eaten up by the day.

"No way around it," Gus said apologetically. "That was a lot of damn rain."

"Yep. We drove through it on the way down here." Luke opened the door to the fire engine's cab and climbed in. He might as well sit while Gus hit him with bad news. "Move as much of the herd to the high hundred as you can. I know they ate it low already, but there should be enough left that you can put out less hay."

"Will do. And boss, I know this is a sore subject for you, but those free-range chickens are running out of dry places to do their free-range thing."

The damned chickens. Luke called them something else out loud, and Gus echoed it heartily.

Luke's mother had fallen in love with the idea of organic chicken-raising the last time she and his father had decided to come home from their endless travels and play ranchers for a while. They'd stayed a month longer than usual, all the way through Christmas. Then his father, one of the generations of James Watersons for whom the James Hill Ranch had been named, had suddenly realized that if he was going to the southernmost tip of South America to see penguins, he needed to do it in the winter. "Because when it's winter in Texas, it's summer near the South Pole."

Thanks for the tip, Dad. When it's winter in Texas, you work every day. How about we talk about penguins while we drive some hay out to the dogleg pasture?

He hadn't said anything out loud, of course. He loved his parents, and they'd raised him to be respectful at all times. But as they'd been doing since he'd turned twenty-one, they'd packed their suitcases and left him to care for the cattle, and a bunch of chickens to boot.

Luke had been born on the JH Ranch, because his mother had been in love with the idea of organic homebirth at the time. He'd been raised on the ranch. He was trapped on it.

His older brother, another James Waterson, owned a third of the JHR. He hadn't been home to the ranch he was named after in years. Their parents owned a third, which funded their world travels. Luke owned a third, but ran the whole damned thing, of course. By default, because everybody else was older and had left first, Luke was a rancher, tied to the land for better or worse.

The fence line penned him in as surely as it did his cattle. He felt it keenly enough that he'd joined Zach as a volunteer fireman. A man had to be stir-crazy for certain, working natural disasters just for the change of pace.

Still, when this job was over, Luke would return to the JHR. He knew every square mile. He'd touched every new calf this spring. He was a cattleman.

But he wasn't dealing with someone else's left-behind chickens any longer.

"I'll tell you what we're going to do with those chickens, Gus. Sell them."

As Gus agreed heartily over the phone, Luke looked toward the tent hospital and saw a sight that wiped all his thoughts of mud and hay and obligations clean out of his mind. Patricia Cargill was walking toward him, looking the same as always in polo shirt and knee-length shorts and boat shoes, yet looking completely, utterly different.

Her hair was down.

Luke knew it was long. He'd twisted it around his finger in the dark shower tent, when the strands had been wet and straight. But he couldn't have known how it would look in the sun, full and golden, framing her face and tumbling over her shoulders with every step. Patricia wasn't a princess. She was a movie star.

Luke had never before felt a woman was so incredibly out of his league. He could only stare for a moment. Then his brain began to work again, and he realized that for Patricia to come to him like this, something must be wrong.

"Boss, you there? Which way do you want to get it done?"

"Sure, Gus, that's fine."

Luke hung up and jumped out of the cab. He started walking toward Patricia, since she was clearly heading straight for him, discretion be damned. Luke might have to play it cool for both of them right now.

"What's up?" he asked, stopping a decent foot away from her. They were only a few yards from the engine, and Luke didn't know exactly where his crew were and who was watching.

"Cell phones are working now," she said.

"Tell me about it."

She looked like she had more to say, but she only clasped her hands together. And unclasped them.

Luke realized she wasn't carrying her clipboard or her radio. "Patricia, what's up?"

The sound of air compressors and nail guns filled the air. A construction crew had been on the hospital building's roof since yesterday.

"They're fixing the roof," Patricia said, stating the obvious, and she almost wrung her hands together. "It's only a matter of time now. Our work here is through."

Since she seemed to be sad about that, Luke tried to offer her some hope. "The power's still out."

"That hospital has generators. They only shut the place down because of the roof. If they hadn't lost their roof, we never would have been called down here." She didn't sound like herself. Her voice was shaky. "Your fire engine might have been called down, but they wouldn't have needed my mobile hospital. We're just temporary, you know."

"I know. Would you like to take a walk with me?"

"No, I might cry."

It was the most surprising thing Luke had heard in a long, long time.

"I just wanted to see you," she said, and she unclenched her hands and stuffed them in the front pockets of her crisply-creased long shorts.

"Because the cell phones came on?"

"It's silly, isn't it?"

Luke had a hunch that, like him, she wasn't eager to return to her normal routine. He was also pretty certain that whatever she was returning to was far worse than what he faced.

"Chief Rouhotas is coming," she said, looking over his shoulder. She started speaking quickly. "Tonight could be our last night. We could start breaking down as early as tomorrow."

"Then we'll make the most of it."

And I'll find out what you're afraid to go back to.

"Good morning, Chief," she said, and the smile on her face was almost as politely pleasant as usual. "I wanted to see the fire truck while I still could. Breaking the hospital down will be a twenty-four-hour operation like setting it up was. I better play hooky while I can."

The chief was as dazzled by the waves of blond hair as Luke, but he managed to speak with his usual *un*usual courtesy, offering to show her the engine personally.

"Thank you, Chief, but Luke has already promised me a tour," she said, using her perfect manners to neatly force the chief to bow out. Whatever had upset her so badly this morning was a mystery, but Luke was glad to see she was back on her game, at least verbally.

He led her over to the red engine. "Here she is, engine thirty-seven."

Zach and Murphy paused in the middle of wiping down the smooth red side of the vehicle. After they grunted their "good mornings," Luke walked Patricia around the vehicle, opening doors and sliding open compartments, showing her the array of tools and ladders. She seemed impressed at how compactly they stored two thousand feet of hose, so Luke kept talking as the other guys kept cleaning, giving her the same spiel he'd give an elementary school class.

"What are you going to do today?" she asked.

"Murphy's already doing it. We clean. We clean every day."

"Can I help?"

Murphy and Zach didn't hide their surprise any better than Luke did. "It's grunt work."

Patricia picked up a polishing cloth from Murphy's stack and started wiping down the bottom row of gauges on the side of the trunk. They measured hose pressure, foam pressure, even air pressure to the horns. She began wiping down their cases and lenses as if it were routine. She did it well.

All three of the guys shrugged at each other. Zach announced that he was going to clean the other side, since the two of them had this. "C'mon, Murphy."

"Do you call this brightwork?" Patricia's demeanor didn't change although they were relatively alone. "That's what we call it on a boat. You have to polish all the brass, all the time. Of course, on a boat it's not really made of brass anymore, but everyone still calls it that." She kept polishing, methodically moving from lens to ring, from left to right. She obviously found "brightwork" soothing.

Luke kept one eye on her as he picked up a rag and started polishing a higher row. "I hope you'll get some sailing in, when you get back to whatever you're dreading going back to. I assume 'dread' is the right word."

"Is it that obvious?" she asked quietly.

"Can I help?"

She shook her head slowly. He'd never seen her look so sad. They kept polishing gauges, wiping away every trace of sea salt left by the coastal air.

"Why don't you want this mission to end?" he asked, when they came to the end of their rows.

She folded and refolded the cloth in her hands. "Do you know what the problem is with sailing? The lakes in Texas are huge. I can run full sail for miles, outsmarting the wind, using it for speed. But at the end of the day, I'm still stuck on a lake in the middle of Texas. I haven't gone anywhere."

He took the neat square of cloth out of her hands. "Do you know what the problem is with being a cowboy? On a good horse, you can ride for miles without seeing another soul as far as the eye can see. But at the end of the day, you're still stuck on a ranch in the middle of Texas."

"Come see me tonight."

"Leave your hair down."

Without looking around to see if anyone was watching, she kissed him on the lips, and then she was gone.

Chapter 15

Luke heard Zach's whistle, but he didn't take his gaze off Patricia's receding figure.

"I guess you don't have to paint my helmet when we get back," Zach said.

"I wasn't painting your helmet because I saved your sorry hide from heatstroke."

"That, too. But damn. You got her to kiss you."

Patricia disappeared among the tents. Luke chucked the polishing cloth she'd folded into the bin where they kept the rest.

Zach gave a swipe to an already-shining gauge. "You're not as happy as I would be about getting kissed by a woman with some sexy friggin' hair."

"She's from Austin, right? She must be. We're all part of the Austin branch of Texas Rescue. So answer me this. Why does she act like she'll never see me again?"

Zach was silent, which meant he was actually giving it some thought. "I can't help you there. Be careful these last few days. I wouldn't want to see it go bad on you."

Murphy came around the side of the truck. "Are you guys going to talk all day? You got time to lean, then you got time to clean."

Zach deliberately leaned against the engine. "No one says that in real life, Murph."

Chief Rouhotas walked up, too. Luke thought they might as well be livestock. A beautiful female had scattered them, and now the men were huddling up, ready to regroup. Luke would've found that amusing, if he'd felt better about the whole situation.

Chief spoke first. "I didn't expect to see Miss Cargill cleaning a fire engine, I'll tell you that."

Murphy's laugh sounded suspiciously like a snort of disgust. "I guess it's fun when it's not your real job. Right, Luke?"

Luke was in no mood for surly remarks. He felt too surly himself. "Your panties are in a wad because I'm an unpaid volunteer? Feel free to share your paycheck."

"I'm just saying it must be nice to stop and chat when you feel like it. No one can tell you to get to work, since no one is paying you. Miss Cargill shows up and wants to flirt, then you get to stop and flirt."

Zach made a great show of banging his forehead on the red metal of the engine. "Murphy, Murphy, Murphy."

The chief just shook his head at Murphy. "I've got a life lesson for you, son. Be nice to money."

"Whose money? Hers, or Luke's?" Murphy jerked his chin at Luke. "At least you work on your ranch. She just sits around and gets her nails done."

The unfairness of his assumption hit Luke in the gut. Sure, Patricia had money. She looked like money, from her yacht-club clothes to the way she carried herself. Murphy had noticed that much, but he didn't recognize the work Patricia did. That required a correction. Luke was in the mood to give it.

He stepped forward. "Did you like your warm, dry bed last night? She's the reason you had a place to sleep. You enjoyed having a hot meal and a shower after that fire, didn't you? Guess who you have to thank. Before you get pissed off that she's got diamonds in her ears, you better be thankful she's got a mind as sharp as a diamond, too. Are we clear on that?"

"All right, okay, enough." The chief backed Luke up a step with a hand on his shoulder.

Zach tried for a joke as he backed Murphy up. "You can't get mad every time a woman likes Luke better than you. It happens for no good reason, now and then."

But Murphy shook Zach off. "Of course she likes him. He owns a goddamn cattle ranch."

Luke didn't like the way this whole morning was going. He tried to follow Zach's lead and laugh it off. "She must just think I'm pretty. She doesn't know I own a ranch."

"Sure, she doesn't."

Back off. Luke rested his hands on his hips. No fists. No fighting stance. But aggressive enough that thick-headed Murphy ought to get the point. "Unlike some men, I don't go around bragging to women about the size of my acreage."

"You got oil wells on your ranch, don't you?"

Obviously, Murphy didn't know when to stop. Equally obviously, he had a chip on his shoulder when it came to money from some past slight. Luke wasn't going to knock that chip off since he hadn't been the one to put it there. He turned away.

"You think a Cargill doesn't know about an oil well?" Murphy said to his back. "Hell, they smell it miles underground. Maybe she's not after your body. Maybe she's after your land."

Luke opened the cab door, prepared to climb up to get the phone he'd left on the seat. Chief's next words gave him pause.

"The kind of oil the Cargills go after is too big for them to concern themselves with a few wells on ranches. If you're going to talk out of your backside, at least know your facts."

Luke turned back around. "She's related to those Cargills?"

Chief was just getting warmed up as he laid into Murphy. "You like this engine, son? Her father bought it. That's right. For years, we struggled to find enough in the budget to maintain the old engine. Then one day, out of the blue, Daddy Cargill himself just writes us a check. Six hundred thousand dollars. And while he was at it, threw in a hundred thousand more so we'd have all new equipment on the shiny new truck."

"Daddy Cargill?" Luke asked. He'd seen him once in Dallas, showboating at an NFL game. He'd walked down the sideline, a rhinestone cowboy, filling his arms with cheerleaders as the crowd took photos.

He was nothing like Patricia.

"This engine was a gift from the oil baron himself. He was wearing a white suit when he came by the station in his Cadillac. Why did he throw nearly a million our way? It's because his daughter works for Texas

Rescue, that's why. So you're not going to piss her off, understand me, Murphy? If Miss Cargill likes the fire department, then the fire department gets money. She wants you to put up a tent in hundred degree heat, then you put up a tent, and you smile at her while you do it, understand?"

"Chief." Luke spoke his name firmly, but the chief was on a roll.

"She can come by as often as she wants, and she can touch anything or anyone she wants."

"Chief, that's enough."

"If she wants to talk to Luke, hell, if she wants to sleep with Luke, you get them a bed and you plump the goddamned pillows for them."

"*Chief.*" Now it was Luke backing the chief up a step. "That's out of line."

The chief shut his mouth abruptly. He ducked his head. "Sorry. No offense."

"For God's sake, you have a daughter yourself."

"You're right. Forget I said that, Murphy."

There was nothing else Luke could do. Nothing to say. He could barely think straight.

Patricia was the daughter of Daddy Cargill.

Luke repeated that to himself a few times, but it didn't sound real. To hell with waiting until dark. He wanted to talk to Patricia now.

"I'm going to get coffee." He slammed the cab door shut as he passed it.

"Me, too." Zach ruined his show of solidarity by turning around to holler at the chief. "If any Rockefeller ladies are looking for someone to bat their eyelashes at, let me know. I'm happy to help out the department."

* * *

"Hello, Daddy."

There was a long pause. Patricia waited patiently, sitting at her out-of-the-way picnic table, staring at the nearby stucco wall of the hospital that would soon put hers out of business. She'd waited for a break in the construction on its roof to place her call. The smell of hot tar was wafting down, pungent enough to make her consider moving, but while the workers were applying it, the construction noises were minimal.

She listened to the quieter sounds of fumbling on the other end of the phone line. Rustling sheets made such a distinctive noise. Her father had grown so heavy in the past twenty years, he grunted when he tried to sit higher on his satin pillows. Patricia closed her eyes, but it didn't help erase the visual image.

"Hello, sugar. Give me just a moment—don't go anywhere—"

There was no caller ID on the phone by his bed. Last time Patricia had been in that house, the phones throughout had been oversize Victorian abominations of gold and ivory. In what Daddy thought was true Texas fashion, the old-fashioned ivory handsets were made from the horns of steer. Patricia never used them. She didn't have to; she and Daddy had a deal. The tacky palace was his. The lake house was hers.

"All right, sugar, tell Daddy what you need that couldn't wait until tonight, but make it quick. I've got company, but I just sent her to fetch me a snack."

Wait until tonight? Good Lord. Her father thought she was one of his women. He must have already lined up an even newer mistress while he was seeing the new mistress, and the old mistress hadn't been paid off and put out to pasture yet.

"Daddy, it's me. Patricia."

The change of tone was immediate, and defensive. "How am I supposed to know it's you if you call me 'Daddy'?"

"I'm your daughter. Who else would I call 'Daddy'?"

"You're not cute. Get down to business, little girl."

"You haven't signed the checks I left. Only Melissa's." Melissa was Wife Number Three in Argentina. Patricia had checked her banking app once more and gotten a full screen this time. Only Melissa's check and the pre-authorized withdrawals like the jewelry store were listed.

Her father's chuckle was transparently forced. "That's the most important one. Keep the women happy, that's what I always say."

"I'm a woman. It would make me happy to be able to pay for maintenance on the lake house. The staff deserve their paychecks on time. One of the boats needs a new furler and they are all due for bottom jobs—"

"You know I don't like all those fancy boating terms."

"Paint, Daddy. The bottoms of the boats need painting every year. It will cost less than a tennis bracelet, and you give those out like candy."

"No one sees the bottom of a boat, sugar. You should spend the money on yourself. Get your own topside spiffed up. That's the way to get a man."

The insult stung like a slap. Patricia was tallish, and slender, but she had breasts. She just wasn't an inflated stripper. Her father's view of women was distorted after decades of keeping the company he did. He didn't know what a good figure was, and that was all there was to it.

It shouldn't have mattered. Yet, after shedding tears over Luke's experience at the car accident last night, her eyes watered now. How rotten, to have remembered how to cry.

"Your year is almost up." Daddy's reminder was malicious.

Patricia couldn't stand it a minute longer. "I'm sorry, the connection is really bad here on the coast. You're breaking up. I'm going to have to go."

"The coast? What are you doing there?"

"The hurricane. There was a hurricane last Sunday, remember? Never mind. Sign the checks. Please."

She ended the call. Very carefully, she placed the phone on the picnic table, face down. She'd slept so well last night, feeling good because she'd made Luke feel better after a tough accident scene. It was still morning, but already Patricia felt as tired as she'd ever been in her life. She folded her arms on the table and put her head down.

I cannot live my life this way. I will do anything. I will marry anyone I have to.

She felt the bench give next to her.

She only knew one man who was big enough to rock her like that.

An arm brushed her arm. A hip pressed against her hip.

She only knew one man who was confident enough to sit so close to her.

She picked up her head and blinked at the sunny day until her vision cleared.

I will say goodbye to anyone I have to.

"Hello, Luke."

* * *

He had no idea what to say.

Nail guns fired high above them on the hospital roof. Patricia was sitting properly at the table, of course, with her hair pinned up properly, too. Luke was facing the other way. He stretched his legs out and leaned back against the table. He knew he ought to say something, but his mind was drawing a blank.

This was getting to be a bad habit of his, chasing after Patricia with no more than a half-baked plan in mind. He'd done it the first day he'd laid eyes on her, when he'd come back for the glove at night. He'd found her right here, and he'd cared enough to make her eat and sleep. In return, she'd cared about him so much that when he'd fought a fire, she'd worried herself nearly sick.

Ah, but that had made for a great night, hiding out from the thunderstorm. Not a bad outcome for a man with no plan.

He'd chased after her again after that, after watching her work alone through lunch, on some half-baked hunch that she might need a friend during the day as well as a secret lover during the night. She never ate alone now, and it was a helluva lot of fun to tease her in broad daylight. That chase had turned out all right.

Here he was without knowing what he wanted from her. Again.

"Since I said 'hello, Luke' and you haven't said anything, I can only assume you are about to tell me you've had a thought. Perhaps two, given this long silence."

The words were right, a classic Patricia zinger that should have made him grin, but she seemed fragile today.

"I'd say it's less like I'm thinking and more like I'm wondering. For one thing, I'm wondering what it is you're dreading going back to. For another thing, I'm wondering why you didn't tell me you were Daddy Cargill's daughter."

He was watching her closely, but she gave no indication that he'd surprised her at all. Not the smallest flinch.

"Chief Rouhotas told you?" She immediately answered her own question. "It wouldn't have occurred to Quinn to tell you. It had to have been Rouhotas. I could tell that he knew, although he's never said so."

"If he's never said so, then how do you know he knows?"

She laughed, but it sounded as brittle as she appeared. "It's obvious in the way he looks at me." She turned her chin, not her shoulders, just her face, and looked him in the eyes. "Look at how you're looking at me now. Money changes everything."

"I'm not looking at you like Rouhotas."

"No, not quite. It hasn't occurred to you yet to ask me to buy you something."

That shocked him. He was already edgy and frankly angry that he'd been blindsided by Rouhotas. "I don't ask women for gifts. Cash has nothing to do with what I need from you."

"Then what do you need from me, Luke?"

From the roof above them, more nail guns fired away. Their private place had been invaded. Their summer romance was ending.

Not like this. Not here. Not now.

"What I need is more time with you. Have Karen take over at supper, like she's supposed to. Eat dinner early. I'm not waiting until dark to see you again."

Chapter 16

Luke barged into Patricia's admin tent, hauling his bulky, beige turnout coat and pants with him. "Ready, Patricia? It's quitting time."

Patricia froze right along with her clerks. He'd been serious about not waiting for dark. She hoped she looked less surprised than she felt as she stood up from her desk. She grabbed a bottle of water, said good-night to everyone in general and no one in particular, and left. Even with his arms full of his uniform, Luke held the tent flap open for her as if it were a proper door and he was the perfect gentleman.

"Where are we going?" she asked, when Luke headed away from both the permanent and mobile hospitals. He walked with energy, a man who knew where he was going. Gone was the scowl from this morning.

She wished she didn't have to bring that scowl back.

"I borrowed a ride from one of the firefighters in town. It's part of the code. If your fellow firefighter has a beautiful woman and no way to take her to the beach, then you must loan him your pickup truck. We're going to go gaze at the waves and think deep thoughts—"

"Oh, dear. More thinking?" Her soft-spoken barb came automatically.

Luke grinned, as she'd known he would.

Immediately, she felt guilty, like she'd led him on, letting him believe this would be a fun evening and not a hard goodbye.

"And we're going to watch the sunset," Luke finished.

Tomorrow, Texas Rescue would begin breaking down the less essential tents at eight in the morning. The town hospital was anxious to have them leave. Every day that the mobile hospital operated was a day the town's hospital lost its usual income. It was another sure sign that a town was recovering, when their gratitude for the emergency help turned into calculations of lost revenue.

Money changed everything—except the compass points on the earth.

"There's a small problem with your plan," Patricia said. "If we're watching the waves, we're facing east. I do believe the sun sets in the west."

"Annoying, isn't it? There's an obvious solution. We'll turn our backs on the shore and watch the sunset over the town."

That was exactly what they did. It wasn't as romantic as either of them might have hoped. The buildings on the beach had been hit the hardest. The pink and orange sky was beautiful, but it was viewed over a tattered sky-line. They had the apocalyptic scene all to themselves.

"You know, I didn't plan to go riding off into the sunset any time soon, anyway," Luke said. "Let's look at the waves."

As easily as that, Luke turned his back on the negative, and changed their plans. Patricia wished she could be as carefree.

He'd brought his uniform and radio in case there was a fire call. He'd have to drop her off and then meet the engine at the site, but Patricia soon learned that the thick fire uniform also made a good cushion for the bed of the borrowed pickup truck.

Luke made an even better cushion. She hadn't objected when he'd pulled her into his lap. He lounged against the metal wall of the truck bed, facing the gentle waves of the ocean. She felt so safe, curled against his chest, head on his shoulder. It felt like nothing could hurt her when arms as strong as his were wrapped around her.

It was a lovely fantasy. The whole week had been a lovely fantasy. But just as the placid waves of the Gulf of Mexico could turn into the crashing danger of a hurricane, this was only the calm before her personal storm. She couldn't delay it any longer. She had to say goodbye.

"We start breaking down tomorrow," she said.

But Luke had spoken at the same moment. "I let you down today. I'm sorry for it."

"You did?" She looked up at his face, his short hair tousled by the strong ocean breeze, his eyes a beautiful gray in the dwindling light. But his gaze was narrowed as he looked over the abandoned beach, and there was a serious set to his jaw.

"You were upset this morning, so upset that you came to find me. Then I found out that you were related to Daddy Cargill, and I came to find you for the wrong reasons. I asked you the wrong questions."

Patricia tried to think back to exactly what had been said. "I don't remember."

Luke bent to kiss her lightly on the lips. "I asked you why you didn't tell me you were a famous heiress. What I should have asked you is why don't you want this week to end?"

It was just the opening she needed. *I don't want this week to end, because I'll miss you forever.* It seemed so strange to her that she should end it in his arms, feeling cared for, feeling safe. It would have been better to say goodbye this morning amid the noise of construction and the horrid smell of hot tar, to walk away as he scowled at her.

She had to say it now. "I'm going to miss you. Terribly. You're a good man, in every way. You are very hard to say goodbye to."

"Luckily for us, we don't have to say goodbye."

"This is our last night. We live in different worlds."

"Patricia, we live in Austin. My ranch is about an hour out of town. I mean, sure, that's a little inconvenient, but it's hardly—"

"I can't have you!" Her voice was loud in the metal truck bed. The fact that she'd nearly shouted at him made her feel disoriented. And then, once more, the cursed tears were blurring her vision.

There was no need to shout. Ever. She lowered her voice, but then it came out a whisper, which wasn't right, either. "I can't have you. We had our week, and I loved it. I loved it. But this is our last night, and that's the way it has to be."

"Or else…what will happen?"

"Daddy Cargill will make my life a living hell."

If he'd been serious before, he was ten times that now. "What do you mean? Are you in danger?"

His entire body went on alert. The muscles holding her were suddenly charged, ready to take action.

"Not physically in danger, no. It's being a Cargill. He makes it hell to be a Cargill. It's hard to explain."

"I want to hear it. Please."

"You mean, what's it like to be the daughter of Daddy Cargill?"

"No. What's it like to be *you?*"

The facts were the facts. Whether she told Luke or not, it wouldn't change anything. But just once, Patricia wanted somebody to know the truth. And so, safely tucked in Luke's arms, she started talking. She told him about the money and the signatures, and how they weren't a Cargill myth. She told him about the begging and the negotiating, day in and day out.

"When did you start dealing with this?"

"I was eighteen when I cosigned the first alimony check for my mother. She's Wife Number One. Then I had to sign a check for Wife Number Two. I didn't mind too much, because she'd brought a little girl from a previous marriage into the mix, and I'd kind of liked having another kid in the house. I figured little Becky deserved to go to college and have nice things, since my dad had cheated on her mom. It seemed fair."

Patricia fell silent. She'd forgotten how painful it had been when Number Two and Becky had suddenly disappeared from her life. They'd gone from being part of her life to a check she signed quarterly.

Luke began rubbing her arm with slow, deep strokes. "Go on. I'm listening."

"Fair or not, there was a lot of money going out, and nothing coming in. I started moving our investments around, changing the balance of high-risk stocks and low-yield securities. Daddy didn't care, and the money started growing. Once I started managing the portfolio, though, it became apparent that if I was going to protect my inheritance, I needed to manage the mistresses, as well.

"Daddy was always buying his girlfriends a bracelet or a necklace or what have you. When he was ready to move on, I'd hear him say, 'Take the bracelet with you, honey. It's so you.' It never made a woman happy. Not a single one, and the drama would start. But at this point, I was getting to be around the same age as the mistresses, so I asked myself—"

"How old were you for this?"

"This was when I was about twenty."

Luke stopped his caress and held her tightly for a moment, like a reflex had made him squeeze her a bit. She stole a look at his profile again. He was still alert. Tense.

"I asked myself, what do girls my age really want?" Patricia tried for some levity. "Do you want to guess? Test your knowledge of young bimbos?"

He looked at her, and his eyes, for the first time that she could remember, looked sad. "I probably would get it wrong. There aren't many twenty-year-old girls hanging around the JHR."

Patricia knew that ranches were sometimes referred to by their brands. As cute as names like "the Rocking C" sounded, most ranch brands were a rancher's initials.

"The JHR? Is that that ranch you work on?"

"Every day, unless Texas Rescue calls."

"What does JHR stand for?"

"The James Hill Ranch." He watched her as he said it.

"I don't know if I've heard of that one in particular." Patricia rolled the name over in her mind. "Is there a man named James Hill, or is it a corporate holding?"

"There's a James or two, but the Hill is because the main buildings are built on a hill. It's mostly a cattle operation, but there are two oil rigs on the property."

"And as I'm a Cargill, you expect me to know all the ranches that have oil rigs." Her family's lore was common knowledge in Texas. Luke's assumption shouldn't have tasted so bitter.

"Wasn't Daddy Cargill born on an oil rig?" She heard the amusement in his voice. The bitterness grew.

Luke rubbed her arm briskly. "There's no insult intended. Just the opposite. You're so sharp, Patricia. If Daddy Cargill can smell oil a mile away, then I expect you can smell it two miles away."

That was the story, all right. That was the reputation her father worked so hard to maintain. Lifestyle came with being a legend. He was welcomed everywhere, from horse races to the governor's inaugural ball. He was the kind of man everyone wanted to believe had made Texas the great state it was, a self-made millionaire who could smell oil under the ground.

"He's never discovered a drop of oil. He spent one day working on an oil rig because his grandfather made him. Then he threatened to never sign a check for his grandfather, and he never had to work another day in his life."

She probably sounded like an awful person, trashing her own father like this. "The right answer is 'cars,' by the way. Twenty-year-old girls like cars. Not very expensive ones, either, which is lucky. A Mustang will do the trick."

"Lucky. That's what you call lucky? Where was your mother for all of this?"

"Oh, she stuck it out until I was old enough to go to boarding school. Then she moved to Argentina. She loves the polo ponies. Ironically, she and Wife Number Three move in the same circles."

"At what age does an heiress go off to boarding school?"

"I was eleven. It's hard when you are a pimply pre-teen and you know darned well that you sure as heck can't smell oil. But when everyone thinks being near you gives them a certain *cachet,* you learn to play along. You pretend your life is charmed. You pretend you are an American princess."

"And the next thing you know, you really are?"

"Something like that."

He'd been caressing her arm and dropping kisses on her temple or her cheek, but now he shifted, setting her next to him and turning to look at her fully, face-to-face. "You really are an American princess, Patricia, but it doesn't sound like a good life. If you are tired of it, you can decide to be something else now."

He looked so confident. He sounded so certain.

"Like what else?"

"Like the well-loved woman of a cowboy like me."

If only that were possible, because right now, in the bed of a truck parked on the edge of a dark ocean, she wanted nothing more in life than to be loved by a man like Luke. His words made her heart hurt. She could feel the contraction in her chest.

I still have tonight.

The strong, salty breeze made her eyes sting. Strands of her hair were pulled loose from their pins, whipping her cheeks.

You could be the well-loved woman…

Calmly, Luke tucked the strands of her hair behind her ear. "This wind is too much for that twisty thing you do with your hair."

"It's a chignon," she said, sitting up straighter when she wanted to melt under his touch.

Luke raised an eyebrow at her term, or perhaps at her posture. One corner of his mouth lifted in a bit of a grin, as if she were still amusing despite the ugly tales she'd just told about her own family.

"When you go to school at Fayette," she said severely, to counter his mockery, "it's a chignon."

"Take it down for me."

She shivered.

Luke kissed her, gently, his mouth covering hers for a warm, summery moment. "Take it down for me."

She moved to her knees. With trembling fingers, she lifted her hands and started pulling out pins. Each one fell to the truck bed with a metal ping, a little noise that sounded clearly over the sweep of the waves. When all the pins were gone, she shook her hair out, then turned her face into the wind.

"You are so very, very beautiful."

Luke laid her down, the beige uniform thick and dry beneath her, and then he stretched out beside her. He propped himself on one elbow and smoothed her hair outward, fingertips touching the skin of her forehead and chin as he pushed her loose hair away. The sides of the truck bed shielded them from the wind, so her hair stayed where he smoothed it.

"I enjoy looking at you, too," she said.

He laughed, and she tried to laugh with him, but it might have sounded a bit like a sob. He kissed her, lightly, playfully, like it wasn't the last day of summer camp, and they still had time.

But they didn't.

Patricia reached for him, trying to tell him with her kiss and with her hands in his hair that she wanted him, all of him, before time ran out. Hands and mouths were not enough. She wanted to touch him, everywhere, anywhere she pleased.

She grabbed a fistful of his black T-shirt and pulled, jerking it free from his pants. When she tried to yank it over his head, he helped, sitting up to grab the hem and pulling it off over his head in one beautiful, masculine movement of muscle.

She exhaled at the sight, then sat up, eager to press herself against his bared skin. Her polo shirt was coarse and covered too much of her body, so she imitated him, grabbing the hem and pulling it over her head, leaving her bared except for her sports bra. She barely had time to shake the hair back from her face before he was on her, spreading his hands flat on her back and pressing her body into his. The sensation of skin meeting skin overrode her thoughts, making her melt.

They lay down again, together. Horizontal was where they both wanted to be, pressed together, kissing, kissing. Luke broke the kiss as he rolled to his back. Patricia rolled with him, lifting herself on one arm over him. Before she could start kissing him again, he pulled her

bra's shoulder strap down, the firm elastic pinning her
arm against her side but freeing her breast.

His mouth was hot and moist, a sure sweep of tongue,
a greedy taste of her body. Patricia knew she would not
stop this. She wanted to make this memory, like he'd
said they should. She'd take the passion now; she could
have regrets in the morning.

Oh, she would have regrets.

Just a few days ago, when she'd been so happy to see
him after the terrible fire, she'd been afraid he would stop.
She'd hugged her knees as she sat on that bench, so afraid
he wouldn't touch her as she'd longed to be touched.

She wasn't afraid anymore, because now he knew
who she was. If she decided *yes, you may,* then men did
not say no to Daddy Cargill's daughter.

Luke shifted positions again as he laid her back and
pulled her bra down further, freeing both breasts, sliding her arm out of the strap. He ran his hand gently
over her body, making her arch her back, seeking more.

"Did you bring protection?" she whispered.

He hesitated, and she knew he had, just in case.
Daddy Cargill's daughter, what a prize. But he would
be discreet, just like Marcel and the rest she'd so carefully chosen over the years. He wouldn't brag after
they'd gone their separate ways.

Luke held himself over her, studying her face in the
starlight. "In a truck?" he asked. "On a beach?"

She knew what he was really asking. *Are you sure?*

She smiled at him. *Yes, you may.*

But as his mouth came down over hers, she said, "I
won't want to forget a thing."

And then, she started to cry.

Chapter 17

"I can't make love to a woman who's crying. Talk to me, darlin'."

Luke watched Patricia's expression closely. Her poker face was gone. Her hair was a pale blond tumble around her face, her throat tan in contrast, her eyes dark and huge as she stared up at him. She was exposed to him for once, her cool and haughty veneer gone as she lay beneath him, her naked breasts pressed beneath his chest.

She wiped her tears with a single swipe of her hand. "It's nothing. The wind."

Incredibly, she seemed to think she could hide from him, still, but he could read her like he'd never been able to read any other woman. She was aroused, but she was feeling desperate about more than just his body.

"It's something. Tell me."

"We've talked enough. I don't want to talk. I want to make love to you."

"That makes two of us."

As she blinked up at him, more tears trickled from the corners of her eyes, rolling into her hair.

Sexual frustration combined with true concern. He shifted to the side, but her body, bare from the waist up, was too hard to ignore. He grabbed his T-shirt and bundled it over her. Maybe she'd feel more secure if she was less exposed. He didn't know. She was complicated, but by God, he was into her. This was so much more than sex.

She pulled his shirt aside and pulled his head down for a kiss. "This will still be great," she said, and then kissed him again, rebuilding their passion to where it had been a minute before. "It will still be great."

"Even though...fill in the blank for me, Patricia." The physical demands of his body clamored for him to forget it. Take what she offered. He commanded himself to control the need. "This will be great, even though what?"

She blinked up at him, perhaps surprised he wasn't giving in to her seduction. "It's just..."

Then she closed her eyes, and he looked at her dark lashes on her smooth skin as she whispered what sounded like a fervent wish. "It would have been so nice if you hadn't known. Just once, to have a lover who didn't know."

He could feel her heartbreak. What must it be like to live as she did, always with her father's legend over her head? Never knowing at age eleven or twenty or thirty-two if someone wanted to be with you because they liked you, or because they wanted a taste of that Cargill *cachet*.

He wished he had a blanket to cover her for this conversation, but since he didn't, he interlocked his fingers with hers, and brought their joined hands to rest between their hearts, hiding her nudity with their arms. *Cuddling.* It wasn't a word he ever used, but he sure didn't mind having Patricia close.

"How soon you forget," he said. "When I asked you if you'd known Quinn, didn't I make it clear that nothing in your past mattered to me? Nothing changes the fact that I can't stop thinking about you, every minute of the day."

"Now that you know I have money, I bet that's about a million times more true."

Her words were tough, but she looked so vulnerable beneath him, her words only made him more aware of the lifelong depth of her pain. "Patricia, Patricia. Money has hurt you so badly. I don't want to talk about money. Let's talk about love."

"Love?"

That cooled her ardor. Luke was sad to feel it, the little recoil in her body.

"Love me, love my money, it's all the same," she said. "You can't separate one from the other."

"But I did. Until this morning, I had no idea whose daughter you were. So all week, I've been kissing you, not your money."

He kissed her again. "Does that feel like I'm kissing money? You must know what it feels like when a man kisses the Cargill heiress. Go ahead. Close your eyes. Remember some other man for a moment."

"You want me to think about another man?"

"Yes."

"You're crazy. Men don't like to be compared."

"It's for a good cause. Close your eyes. Remember him. Remember the guy before him."

He studied her closed eyelids once more, waiting until it looked like she was concentrating as he'd asked.

The jealousy was worse than he'd thought. He controlled his breathing, like he was wearing a mask. Waited another moment, and then he kissed her. He kissed her to make her forget. He kissed her as if he could draw all that pain and uncertainty from her.

He kissed her as if she were his one and only. She was the only woman in his world, the only woman who really touched his heart.

My God, that's who she is.

She began kissing him back, passion for passion, until she made a little whimper of need that nearly sent him over the edge.

He tore his mouth away, ending the kiss abruptly and panting as he concentrated on controlling this lust that was more than lust.

"Do you see it?" he said into the warm space filled by their mingled breaths. "Do you see the difference? This is a man who is kissing Patricia, only Patricia, not an heiress. I kissed you in the rain under a tree, do you remember? The night when I came back from the fire, we kissed in the rain. Close your eyes and remember that. Then lightning struck, and we hid in the showers, and we kissed some more. Remember those kisses."

He kissed her again, remembering the rain himself, and the surprising, soothing sweetness of knowing she cared about him. This kiss, he ended gently.

"It felt like that," he said. "It doesn't matter if you have a billion dollars, I'm kissing my beautiful, mysterious Patricia when I kiss you."

She opened her eyes, humbling him by looking at him as if he'd hung the stars above them. Another tear ran down from the corner of her eye, but this time, Luke understood. This tear was different. He could kiss it away.

They began removing their remaining clothes, anticipation tempered by a near reverence at what they were about to do. Luke lowered himself over her, pausing one last time to whisper in her ear.

"And when we make love, you'll remember the night of the fire and the rain, and you'll know that the first time I brought you release, you were Patricia to me. You are Patricia to me still. Always."

The next meeting of the Texas Rescue and Relief leadership team was uneventful for everyone except the daughter of Daddy Cargill.

The meeting started inauspiciously in one of the conference rooms at West Central Texas Hospital. Karen Weaver droned on, attempting to disguise her incompetence with long-winded explanations. Impatient with Karen's nonsense, Patricia opened her email on her phone. The message from the bank stopped her heart.

Please be advised that there will be a maintenance fee assessed this month due to a low account balance.

Impossible. The daily interest on the trust fund was enough to keep the account above the minimum balance. This insanity had to stop. The balance hadn't been stable since the hurricane. As soon as Patricia challenged one expenditure, another unauthorized one would appear.

She preferred to call on the bank by appointment. Appearances were everything with her father's cronies, so she usually ensured they were assembled and waiting for her entrance. Then she would arrive wearing the appropriate attire for negotiation, a severe suit with the length of the skirt tailored precisely to midknee.

This email was the last straw. She was done with their games. The bank wasn't far from the hospital. She could use the element of surprise to her advantage. Besides, although her tailored slacks were gray and her silk blouse was pink, their pastel colors were icy, not to be mistaken as weak. She would remove the string of pearls, though. They might be seen as feminine. Weak.

She felt weak.

Darlin', you do not look like a woman who was well-loved last night. You're more worried this morning than I've ever seen you. I have to ask you again, when you return home, are you going to be in any danger?

The mobile hospital had broken down and packed up in a record fast forty-six-hour stretch, but engine thirty-seven had been sent home early in the process. Luke had had no choice but to go. The engine had to carry its full crew. Patricia had used those regulations to prevent Luke from persuading her to extend their romance beyond its week's limit.

I told you the truth last night, Luke. I'm going to miss you. This was a week of summer-camp romance. So very real, but unable to last. I just can't see you anymore.

Karen droned on. Patricia stole a look around the conference room at her fellow directors. She apparently was no longer the only one who could see through Karen's act. Things were going to change, and soon.

I remember the day after our first kiss. You tried to deny that we meant something then, too. This is no sum-

mer romance, darlin'. You're going to have to get used to being loved for more than a day or a week.

Don't be so kind, the daughter of Daddy Cargill had said, chin in the air, spine straight.

Give me your number. We have the rest of our lives to sort this out.

She'd pronounced each digit precisely. He'd typed them in his phone. Looking her square in the eye, he'd held his phone up and hit the green call button. Her phone hadn't rung.

He'd taken her phone from her hand, dialed his own number, and let his phone ring twice before silencing it. In equal silence, he'd kissed her on the cheek, then just as chastely on the lips, and he'd climbed into the cab of engine thirty-seven.

"I'm sure the operational expenditures will be counterset by the financial expenditures of the host city," Karen said.

Patricia jerked her attention back to the issue at hand. Karen was speaking accounting gibberish. If she stayed at the helm of Texas Rescue, she'd run its finances into the ground as surely as Daddy would if he didn't get her approval on every move.

She studied the phone in her lap again, refreshing the screen for the banking app. The door to the conference room opened. Out of the corner of her eye, she saw the polished leather of a cowboy's boots stop by her chair. Dark blue jeans. Slowly she lifted her head. Pale blue Western shirt.

Sailing blue eyes.

"I'm sorry I'm late," Luke said. "Is this seat taken?"

Chapter 18

The meeting was adjourned.

Luke stood and got Patricia's chair. She looked so achingly familiar, yet different. Her boat shoes had been replaced by high-heeled silver sandals, impractical but sexy. He'd gotten used to seeing her trim calf muscles at the mobile hospital, but now her legs were hidden by immaculate creased slacks. She looked more like a beautiful, off-limits princess than ever.

He spoke to her as if she wore shorts and ate in mess tents. "I thought that would never end. You actually volunteer to sit in these meetings?"

She didn't quite look at him. "You actually volunteer to go into burning buildings?"

"Ah, that's the Patricia I know and love. It's good to see you."

"Thank you." She snuck a peek at him. He noticed,

studying her as he was. She wasn't immune to him, but she sure didn't want to be attracted to him.

It made no sense. They should be openly in love, holding hands and making goo-goo eyes at each other until everyone was sick of them.

She picked up a purse with leather that was dyed so close to the shade of gray of her pants, it nearly disappeared. It was hard to imagine this woman living on his ranch. He had to remember the hard worker who'd tied knots in tent ropes. *That* Patricia would be at home on the JHR.

Which Patricia did Patricia prefer to be?

For once, he hadn't pursued her with a half-baked plan. He'd come determined to bring her to her senses. She hadn't called him, and he'd been certain that meant her life was miserable. He'd come to save her. They belonged together.

Seeing her in this environment gave him pause, he had to admit. She looked incredibly affluent in her pearls and silk clothing, a woman of leisure who chose to volunteer her time. She didn't look like someone whose life was a living hell.

Her cell phone vibrated, still on mute from the meeting. She glanced at the screen. "Excuse me, I need to take this. It was lovely seeing you again."

She walked briskly toward the door as she answered the phone in her cool and cultured voice, leaving him behind.

The pain of being dismissed was sharp. It simply wasn't *normal* for her to act that way toward a man she'd shared so much with. Was this some high-society game, a test to see if he'd come to heel?

Luke wasn't in the mood to play games. If she wanted

to know if he'd follow her like a puppy dog, then she'd find out. He'd follow her, all right. But when he caught up, they were going to talk.

In the hospital hallway, she turned right, walking at a steady clip as she spoke. "No, I will not pay for an after-market paint job. I'm sure the Mustang is available in at least one color that she will find acceptable. The sunroof option is fine. Randolph, I would appreciate it if you could limit any further requests from this one. Perhaps tell her everything else is standard, or that the order has to be placed by noon. Whatever it takes. Please."

The please was Luke's undoing, as always. Patricia should not have to beg him for anything, and she sure as hell shouldn't have to beg a car dealership to run interference between herself and one of her father's castoffs. His irritation toward her softened; his disgust with her father grew.

"Patricia."

She was startled by the sound of his voice, jerking her hand a bit as she dropped her cell phone into her purse. Not normal behavior for the confident personnel director, again, and Luke hated to see her this way. He slowed his steps, taking his time to cover the polished linoleum between them. He stopped just a little bit too close to her. She didn't move away.

He'd missed her so much. *I love you* would have been so easy to say. It was close to frightening, the way he had to consciously not speak the words.

"You shouldn't have come," she said, and then the chemistry took over, and she was kissing him at least as hungrily as he was kissing her.

"You two should get a room." Quinn's voice boomed in the sterile hospital corridor.

Patricia pushed away from Luke as if she'd been caught doing something forbidden, darting looks down the hall like a nervous bird. Something was wrong, and Luke needed to find out what it was.

"Do you have a room we could use?" Luke turned to Quinn. The look on his own face must have been intense, because Quinn's expression turned sober.

"Most of the conference center should be unlocked. Help yourself." Quinn stepped back as Luke took Patricia by the hand and led her back the way they'd come.

The second door Luke tried was unlocked. He pulled Patricia in with him, then turned and shut the door. Neither one of them hit the lights. A week without contact had left them starving for one another. It wasn't just him. She felt the same, her need obvious in the dark as she wrapped her arms around his neck and pressed her body to his.

The high heels changed the angle that their mouths met. The silk of her shirt was nothing like the cotton of her Texas Rescue polo. She was new, she was familiar, she was his.

After long moments of physical communion that filled Luke's soul, Patricia backed away. Her voice was less than steady in the artificial darkness, like she was on the verge of bolting. "I've got to get to the bank."

Luke tried for humor. "It's a sad thing when a woman would rather go to a bank than keep kissing."

"You make it so hard."

"Well, thank y—"

"Damn you, why do you have to make everything so hard for me? I have to go to the bank. I have to do a lot of things, and I have to do them quickly, and you are making it so hard."

Luke fumbled for the lights. In the sudden brightness, Patricia looked just as upset as she sounded.

"Then we'll go to the bank," he said. "Together."

"No, we will not. I have a life that cannot include you. I told you that."

"Or else Daddy Cargill will make yours a living hell. I remember. It's apparently already a living hell. Let me help."

She put her hand out to stop him when he tried to step closer. With distance between them, she took a deep breath. She stood taller, graceful in her high heels. "I explained that incorrectly. I should have said that my life is a living hell now, but if I leave you and keep my focus on what I have to do next, I can be free of Daddy Cargill forever. I will have my own life. I want, more than anything, to stop living his."

"I want that for you, too. I'll do anything I can to help. I'm all yours, all my time, all my energy."

"Oh, Luke." She looked at him, finally, with an expression more like the one she'd had in the pickup truck, under the stars. A tightness in his chest eased. She was still his Patricia.

"You cannot help me at all, my darling."

He put his hands in his jean pockets, because she so clearly didn't want his touch. "What is it you have to do that I can't help with?"

"I have to marry another man."

The hit was hard, like hitting the ground after being bucked off a stallion.

He saw red. "Who?"

"I don't know yet. I have to find him. There's a set of criteria that must be met for the terms of the deal. My time is running out to find someone suitable."

"Terms of the deal? No one can make you marry anybody. You know that. You must know that."

"It's a personal bet between Daddy and me. We shook hands on it. You've heard of Cargill handshakes. If there's one thing he has, it's pride in his own legend. He started offering me a deal, my financial freedom if I could prove that I was single by choice, not because I couldn't land a man. He was running off at the mouth in front of his friends, but I saw my chance. He was forced to shake when I agreed to his terms."

"You don't really think the man is going to honor this deal, do you? I assume you're talking about serious money. A million dollars? More? Your deal is unenforceable by law. He won't follow through."

"He loves his own legend. A Cargill deal must stand. No welching, no cheating, no changing the terms."

She was actually excited about this. As she spoke, she looked more animated. She looked like a woman who could run the world, so confident was she that she could win this bet.

It was a sick bet, made with a sick man. Luke had to find a way to show her that, before it was too late.

She actually placed her palm on his arm, a soothing gesture, as if so little could fix this mess. "You can see why you are a terrible distraction. I only agreed to a week's romance with you. I need you to stick to that deal, so that I can stick to mine. Please."

A week's romance? He ought to throw her over his shoulder and take her back to his ranch. That week hadn't been long enough. Not nearly long enough.

She was begging him, *please,* but it hadn't been long enough, because it hadn't been a full week. Zach had passed out while they'd been flipping those ambulances on a Tuesday. Engine thirty-seven had been sent home on Sunday. Six days.

"You expected me to take that week literally?"

"Yes, of course. Please, Luke."

"You can stop begging me. First, I hate to hear you beg for anything. But second, you owe me one more day."

"But…"

He could practically see her counting the days on a calendar in her head. "You owe me one more day," he repeated. "No welching, no cheating, no changing the terms of the deal."

She was all offended dignity, the princess drawing herself up to stare down her peasant.

Luke could finally find it in himself to laugh. "Forget the bank. Today is my day. Don't bother glaring at me." He kissed her lightly on the lips. "I'm going to show you a good time, princess, and it starts right now."

He hit the lights, and took her in his arms, and let chemistry do the rest.

Patricia couldn't deny it. She'd never been happier to be forced to obey a man. Luke wanted to remind her of what the truly good things in life were, he said. So far, they'd involved kissing her senseless in a hospital conference room and feeding her Mexican vanilla ice cream with candy crushed in it.

He handed her up into his truck, for she'd needed a boost to climb into the pickup's cab. It seemed to be a ranch vehicle, meant for pulling horse trailers, because it had a significant hitch on the back. It was hardly her style, but when Luke swung into the cab and settled behind the wheel in his denim and boots, he looked almost as sexy as he had in his red suspenders. A fireman cowboy. Lucky her.

For one day.

Then she'd get back to the real world.

They didn't drive far, just from the hospital to Lady Bird Lake, the wide part of the Colorado River which Austin's downtown was centered around. Luke parked in front of a humble chain hotel, the kind found at interstate exits across the country.

"Really?" she asked him.

They were going to spend the rest of the afternoon in a hotel room. Her body said *yes*. Heck, her mind said *yes,* too. But her heart knew that passion was fleeting, even destructive. She'd seen three marriages die passionate deaths, and her childhood die with them. If Luke thought she'd give up her chance at lifelong freedom from Daddy Cargill because he'd shown her that an afternoon of sex was fun, then Luke didn't know her as well as he thought. Maybe not as well as she'd hoped.

Have I been hoping for him to change my mind?

He paused to kiss her in the lobby. He paused to kiss her by the elevators, and then he pushed through the glass doors to go out the other side of the hotel, and Patricia realized he knew her very well. Oh, so very well.

The park between the hotel and Lady Bird Lake was littered with sailboats on trailers. Little two-man boats with colorful sails were just waiting to be rolled into the water. They were nothing like her sailboats, her twenty- and thirty-five-foot beauties moored at her house on Canyon Lake, but they were sailboats all the same, designed to catch the wind and race across water.

Patricia looked to the sky, automatically checking

the sunny weather. The lake was perfectly calm. Luke came up behind her and pulled her to his chest.

She sighed. "We're not dressed for this."

He kissed her ear. "I only have a day. No time for wardrobe changes. If you feel a wardrobe malfunction is imminent, though, be sure to get my attention first."

"You're really not as funny as you think you are, Waterson."

She wanted to smile as she said it, but she suddenly felt very, terribly sad. Sad enough to cry, and there was something about Luke that seemed to make her want to cry. It was a weakness around him.

"Are we going to go sailing?" she asked. Weakness made her impatient.

Luke spread one arm wide, gesturing toward the variety of sailboats before them. His voice was strangely serious when he spoke.

"Choose your destiny."

Chapter 19

The two-man sailboat skimmed with surprising speed along the water. Luke recognized that there were expert hands on the reins, to put it in cowboy terms, so he reclined next to Patricia as she perched at the rear of the boat and handled everything with ease. He practically had his head in her lap, so he could look up at her and enjoy her pretty face. She looked completely and utterly at home, focused and yet relaxed. His Thoroughbred was doing what she'd been born to do.

"He has to be the right age," Patricia said quietly.

Luke almost asked *who?* because he'd been so content to watch her blond hair in the sunlight. The pins had lost their battle as soon as Patricia had captured the wind.

"Not too young, not too old," she said. "At least average-looking, although my father and his cronies are strange people to judge male beauty."

"So far, so good."

She looked down at him and smiled, but she didn't seem happy. Maybe resigned was the right word for her expression.

"I think you're too good-looking. Daddy wouldn't like that."

Luke thought back to the NFL game where he'd seen Daddy Cargill. He was an imposing figure. Patricia shared his bone structure. It bothered Luke to be reminded that the bastard was truly her father.

"He must own land. Texas land, of course, and not just a little suburban house plat. Oil fields would be best, but Daddy didn't technically say there had to be oil on the land. He must have a million in liquid assets. Cash he can get his hands on, not something like a vacation home that's appraised at a million."

Luke recognized himself. He felt unnaturally calm. His emotions were neither hot nor cold. He just existed for a moment, letting Patricia's words sink in.

He was the perfect candidate for her husband hunt. The liquid assets were high, and he thought only a fool would keep that much ready cash or stocks on hand, but Luke could sell off his cattle early in the season, if a man really needed a bank balance to read a certain number on his wedding day.

He thought this all through in a detached way. Then one clear emotion broke through his neutral review of facts: outrage.

There was no way on God's green earth that he was going to play any game by Daddy Cargill's rules. If Patricia realized he was not just a cowboy—and God, he hadn't meant to deceive her so thoroughly, but now he was glad he had—then he'd end up with a wife who'd married him for his money. He'd marry Patricia Cargill if she asked, but only when she realized how much she loved him, not how much land he owned.

My God, I would marry Patricia Cargill.

The truth of it was obvious, now that he'd thought the words. He rubbed his jaw, wanting to file away these sudden revelations before they showed on his face. From now on, he was a cowboy, and nothing more as far as Patricia Cargill could know. A cowboy who loved her.

"The last requirement is fairly easy. He has to have a job. How many men would meet the other requirements without working? People who just slip into an inheritance are very rare."

"Present company excluded." He congratulated himself for coming up with a rejoinder when his mind was still reeling.

"I am very rare."

"But you do work, and hard, for Texas Rescue."

"Thank you. It's a pretty unfair parameter for my father to place, though, considering Daddy's never worked a day in his life. His cronies probably believe the oil-rig story. Everyone does."

"Except me."

"And my mother. I wonder if she always saw through him, or if her first year of marriage was a crushing disappointment."

"You could ask her."

"That would imply that we have some kind of regular communication."

His poor princess. Such a hard life she'd been handed on her silver platter. But she didn't have to keep living it. This day was meant for him to show her a better option.

"This is the good life," Luke said. "Is there really anything more that you need?"

The sail began to deflate. Patricia loosened a rope and wind pulled the nylon taut immediately. "Why do I think this is a loaded question?"

"Can you sail and kiss me at the same time?"

"That's definitely a loaded question."

She made him wait for it, but she finally bent over and kissed him. She even slipped him a little tongue, shy and quick. Funny how she could be shy after they'd made love out in the open, under the stars.

"You're making the sailing tricky by lying on my side of the boat," she said. "I have to compensate for the uneven weight."

"You like the challenge."

She quirked her lips a bit. "You could just move over to the other side and lay down there."

"That would put the rudder between us. I don't want a rudder in my face. I like what's in my face right now just fine." He settled his head more firmly in her lap and looked up at her face. Of course, he had to look past her boobs to get to her face.

When she looked down at him, he wiggled his eyebrows and was rewarded with a laughing roll of her eyes. She was so beautiful when she laughed. She was beautiful when she didn't laugh, too. And she was most beautiful when...

"Can you make the boat stop?" he asked.

"Stop? We're cruising perfectly."

"Yes, we are. Make the boat stop, darlin', and then lay down here with me. We haven't had enough chances to make memories."

She made him wait again, an eternity this time as

she tacked the boat, but when she had them in an un-crowded spot, the sails went slack and she started tying things off.

"When I wonder if there is anything more I really need in life," he said, as she settled beside him, "my answer will always be more of you."

She didn't answer him in words, but her responsive body gave him the answer he wanted to hear.

They turned the boat in as the sun was setting. Luke didn't want Patricia to see the color of his American Express card as he paid for the extra time they'd kept the boat. He'd be damned if she chose him now for being rich.

He just wanted her to choose him.

So before he gave the rental attendant his card, he gave Patricia the keys to his truck, knowing full well she'd go dig out the cell phones he'd left in the glove box. What he hadn't expected to find when he joined her in the truck cab was a white-faced, shell-shocked Patricia.

"What's wrong? What happened?"

"My mother called. She never calls." Patricia held out her phone and played a voice mail.

Hello, Patricia. I hope you're well. I did hear the most interesting news today, and I wondered if you'd heard it, as well.

The voice sounded distinctly like Patricia's. Bone structure from her father, vocal chords from her mother—he wondered if Patricia realized she shared more than a famous name with her family.

The Houston Cargills got a ruling on their trust fund. It seems the court decided that Cargills by marriage can sign the name as legitimately as Cargills by birth. Of course, it doesn't matter to me, but I did wonder if dear Melissa's divorce had ever gotten filed. She's been missing from the club for the last few days. You might want to check into it, dear. Everything's fine here, give your father my love. Or better yet, don't. Ciao.

Luke looked at Patricia's white face, and he knew someone named Melissa had a legal marriage to Daddy Cargill.

Patricia tapped one particular app on her phone. "I noticed a strange charge the Friday before the hurricane."

He wasn't sure what a man was supposed to do in this situation. Commiserate with the heiress? He tried. "And then you were at the disaster site without any way to check."

Her phone screen changed color, and she looked into it like she was looking into a crystal ball.

What the heck. He might as well ask. "How bad is it?"

"About a million so far."

He was struck silent. The one aspect of the Cargill legend that was apparently true was the income.

Her crystal ball must have shown her something awful. She literally backed her face away from what she saw on the phone. "Half a million dollars just cleared today. Today."

Her gaze locked on his, her eyes extra dark in her unnaturally pale face. "I was on my way to the bank. You stopped me."

He said the first thing that came into his mind. "I'm sorry."

She was chillingly calm. She even leaned back into

the seat as she gazed out the windshield at the humble cars of the hotel patrons. "Half a million dollars today, while I was sailing. We had half-a-million-dollar sex. I am my father's daughter, after all."

The truck cab seemed huge. Patricia was too far away physically. He was afraid she was growing un-reachable, mentally, but he tried. "If this Melissa is a legal second signature, then they could have authorized that half-million right in front of you. You would have watched it happen, and you wouldn't have been able to stop it. Are you listening to me? I'm glad you were sailing. You couldn't have stopped it."

"You're right, of course. The sailing was very nice."

Yeah, she was not in a good place mentally. Luke walked around the truck to her side, yanked open her door, and bodily lifted her out of the cab. It was enough to snap her out of her daze.

"What are you doing?"

"Are those sandals comfortable? Good, because we're going for a walk."

They hadn't gone far when Patricia suddenly snapped her fingers and stopped on the hotel's sidewalk. "It's not legal. In Dallas and Houston, you need three signatures for every expenditure. The only reason Austin requires two is because there are only two Cargills in Austin. If Melissa is now the third, then all three of us needed to sign. I'll phone the bank first thing in the morning. It's going to be a mess, but it can be undone."

Luke looked her over. Her color was returning to normal. "Honestly, I don't know whether to be appalled or impressed."

But she was still rolling with her train of thought, dollars and legalities on her mind. "I need to make this marriage happen more than ever. Every time Daddy gets married, I'm going to have to convince both him and his wife to sign for every expense. That will be a nightmare. I've got to get out while I can."

The woman he'd just made love to was planning to marry a stranger as soon as she could. It made Luke's stomach turn.

"Listen to me, Patricia. Walk away from the money. It's making you miserable."

"My inheritance is not making me miserable. Daddy Cargill is."

"That's the problem. If this marriage takes place, and if your father honors his deal, you still won't be free of Daddy Cargill. His share of the money will still require your approval."

"I'll have to sign his checks, but I won't care how he spends his half."

Luke laughed, because otherwise he'd break down. He knew she didn't see the absurdity of her claim. "You will care. You can't stand to see Cargill money wasted. You say he has pride in the Cargill legend, but you're the same."

She stepped back. "Don't say that. Don't say I'm like him."

"How long do you think it will take him to lose his last penny?"

She pressed her lips together.

"You've already calculated it, haven't you? You know exactly how fast he'll lose it. You're looking forward to proving that you can handle your half better. It's poison, don't you see? That money has owned you for thirty-two years."

"Do you think I don't know that?" She looked so

fierce, standing there with her arms crossed over her chest and her hair hanging wild. Fierce, and all alone.

"Choose to walk away."

"The law won't let me."

"The law can't force you to be rich, Patricia. You're choosing the money, and you're choosing it over me, damn it."

They'd raised their voices at each other. They were facing off like fighters, not lovers.

"Don't tell me what to do. *Don't tell me what to do.* You cannot possibly imagine what it's like to be me. Money hasn't destroyed my family. Passion has. Passion like this. I never raise my voice. I never cry. This is what rips marriages apart. This is what destroys families. Don't tell me to choose this."

"You can't decide not to feel passion." Luke remembered, suddenly and too late, how she'd been so distressed when she couldn't *not* care about a firefighter. About him.

"Darlin', passion can be a bond, too. It can hold two people together."

She looked away from him, impatient. "It does not. Sex is fine. People get together, they have a few laughs, someone moves on. But passion is different. People yell, and they cry, and they leave without letting you say goodbye.

"You think I'm crazy to choose a marriage without passion, but I'm not going to be like my father. He loves the drama and the ups and downs, and he forgets what's important. He'll remember now. For the rest of his life, he'll remember that the spinster he laughed at for not knowing passion turned out to be the best Cargill of them all."

Luke let her words sink in, trying to imagine the little girl she'd once been. "Your father has done a lot of damage to you. I can see why you want your revenge."

"Revenge?" She frowned as she repeated the word.

"I imagine that after thirty-two years, it would be very hard to be this close and then deny yourself your revenge."

"That's such an ugly word."

"I can't tell you what to do. I'm hoping you decide to forgo it, though, because I love you."

She looked up at him then, eyes wide. Alarmed, perhaps.

"It's not a crazy kind of love. It feels very solid in here." Luke pressed his fist to his chest. "I know I came into the game at the last minute, but I want to offer you a choice. You can finish your game, and be Patricia Cargill, the heiress who saved the family fortune from Daddy Cargill's ruin, or you can be Luke Waterson's woman. Loved and valued and cherished."

"I can't be that and Patricia Cargill, too?"

"You can. You are. But it seems to me that Patricia Cargill doesn't particularly enjoy her life. You could be Luke Waterson's girl, and you could relax your guard, and you could—"

"Lose my inheritance." She said the words adamantly. "I had no childhood because of it. I've spent my entire adult life fighting my father to keep it. It's not revenge, Luke. It's justice. I deserve to have the life I want. I want to spend money on what is important to me. To me, do you understand? Without sweet-talking and wheedling and begging any man for permission to do what I want to do. I'm thirty-two. I will have my own life, and I will stop enabling his. I will."

She was so angry, she was crying.

Luke held open his arms. It was her choice. If she wanted his comfort she had only to walk forward.

She did. Luke closed his arms around her, and she clung to him while she tried so pitifully to not cry.

"I know Patricia Cargill is unhappy," she said, not sobbing, "but I am her, and I will get free of my father no matter what it takes."

Luke stroked her hair. "Then you be her, and this cowboy will love you, anyway. I just pray you choose to let go of the poison. The money is poison. The revenge is poison. I don't want to lose you."

Chapter 20

The night of the annual Cattleman's Association black-tie gala would be the night Patricia Cargill found the right man to marry. It was her last chance. She could not fail.

It had been two weeks since she'd gone sailing with Luke, two weeks of using cold logic to choose the course of her life. She'd spent a sleepless night imagining marriage to Luke. As Mrs. Waterson, she would remain in her current financial situation. She'd be no worse off than she'd been for the past thirty-two years, with the positive addition of living with a man who loved her.

Daddy, Melissa, I need an allowance established at the feed store. No, more than that. Luke needs a new saddle. Yes, I know he got new bridles, but these things wear out when you're a cowboy.

Luke would not have taken a dime of her money. She

could not have bought him a gift, because her money was always half Daddy's. Children would be an issue. One child would bring the amount of Austin Cargills to four, depending on Daddy's marital status. Two children would mean five Cargills. When they turned eighteen, her two children could help her overrule Daddy and his wife *du jour.*

That possibility, more than any other, decided Patricia against marrying Luke. She would not curse his children with the Cargill fortune.

She did not return his calls. He left her messages several nights a week when he could get away from the JHR. He'd wait in the Driskill Hotel's famous bar, knowing she'd be comfortable in that elegant atmosphere, in case she wanted to talk. In case she needed a friend. She did not show up, not the first time he did this. Not any of the nights he did this.

She cried a lot, but she made her list of eligible men. There were only three. Unsurprisingly, they all owned ranches. They would be at the Cattleman's Ball.

How perfectly convenient.

Her limousine entered the last set of gates at the breathtaking estate that was owned by one of the members of the board of directors of the Cattleman's Association. She'd timed her arrival so that she could make an entrance. The candidates should all have arrived. In a sea of black tuxedos, her brilliant blue dress would stand out without being tacky or showy. She was looking to be chosen as a wife, not a one-night stand, after all.

Get your own topside spiffed up. That's the way to get a man.

She hated that there was truth in her father's words. She had a black dress that showed her cleavage to per-

fection. It would have been the smart choice this evening, a way to short-circuit a man's brain and skip ahead
a few levels of intimacy. But she'd mentioned the black
dress to Luke, just once, and he'd said it would probably kill him to see her in it. That was enough to make
her not want other men to see it first.

Foolish.

The blue dress was elegant, a single column of cloth
that fell from a collar around her neck, but its sex appeal
was more subtle. Feeling desperate in the limousine,
she'd carefully picked out the stitches in the long skirt's
side seam, extending the slit from mid-thigh to upper
thigh. She couldn't take chances. Tonight was the night.

Her entrance went brilliantly. The main entertainment area was on a flagstone terrace that had sweeping
views of the sunset. Patricia passed through the house
and paused on the steps that led down to the terrace.
The pause had been no more than a few seconds, carefully timed to not be obvious. Carefully timed to let one
man after another nudge each other and nod her way.
Then she'd descended the stairs, the conservative dress
revealing nearly the entirety of her leg—but only one
leg, and only every other step.

By the time she reached the bottom, she didn't have
to look for her three candidates. They'd already clus-
tered around her.

She hadn't known Daddy Cargill would be in atten-
dance, but when his white suit caught her eye, she had
a moment of sweet revenge. *Yes, Father. It's me. Look
how easy it is to catch a man.*

The moment was brief, because she heard Luke's
voice in her head. *The revenge is poison. I don't want
to lose you.*

She accepted a glass of champagne from an admiring candidate. He proposed a toast, and she laughed appropriately, doing her best to sparkle like the elegant, golden bubbles as she clicked her flute gently against one man's, then another's.

Then she looked directly into a pair of sailing blue eyes.

Luke Waterson turned his back on her and walked off the terrace, into the sunset.

Patricia hid in the bathroom.

She tugged on her dress, but the damage had been done. Because she'd snipped the first thread, the seam kept unraveling. The slit was so high, she was going to have to remove her underwear.

Then I really will be the kind of girl Daddy Cargill approves of.

Too late, she realized this hadn't been about Luke. It hadn't been about independence. It hadn't even been about revenge. It had been about Daddy, and trying to win his approval. Finally, after thirty-two years, she realized that he only approved of one type of woman, and she was not and never would be that type.

Her father would never love her.

The real tragedy was that Luke would never love her now, either. He'd witnessed her triumph, which had come at the cost of lowering herself to her father's standards.

She'd have time to regret this for years to come. She couldn't cry about it in her host's bathroom much longer. She pulled her compact from her purse and leaned forward to powder her nose in the mirror. The seam opened another notch higher.

There was a tap at the door. "Occupied," Patricia called, her voice sounding shockingly normal.

"Patricia? It's Diana. Quinn sent me to check on you."

Quinn. He was present as one of the owners of the MacDowell's River Mack Ranch, of course. He was one of her least favorite people right now, because he must have brought Luke as a guest.

"I'm fine, Diana. Thank you. I'll be out in a minute."

Another tap. "Would you let me in?"

Patricia looked at herself in the mirror. She deserved this. She really did. Why not let Diana have her moment of triumph? Patricia had tried to marry her man, after all, and had been rather nasty about it.

She unlocked the door. Diana stuck her head in, all cheerful smiles. Immediately, her eye dropped to Patricia's dress. "Oh, I see the problem. Here, I've got a safety pin. It will be tricky but if you turn the dress a little, you know, like this, you can pin it from the inside and no one will see it. Do you want me to do it for you?"

"No, thank you."

Lord, how did Quinn stand so much sunshine?

In a flash, she realized Luke had been her sunshine, too. Patricia and Quinn needed that balance in their lives. They would have stifled one another in a perfectly proper marriage.

"Okay," Diana said, setting the safety pin down on the counter and stepping back. "Well, if you need anything else, just come find me."

She put an extra safety pin on the counter and turned to go.

"Diana? Is Luke looking for me?"

She wrinkled her nose in a way Patricia imagined Quinn found adorable. "Luke who?"

"Luke Waterson. Didn't he come with you and Quinn?"

"I don't know the name. Do you want me to ask around?"

"No. Please, no. It's nothing. Thank you again for the safety pins. And… I just wanted to say, I think you and Quinn make the perfect couple. He's very happy now that he has you."

Diana's smile was radiant. "Thanks. Pin your dress and come on out to the party."

Luke waited on the edge of the terrace, wearing a tuxedo but having nothing to celebrate. He placed one polished black boot on a planter. He idly repositioned his formal black Stetson on the table beside him. He'd kept his hat handy. He wouldn't be staying much longer. Patricia would find him soon.

He'd chosen a spot that was quiet and shadowed, appropriate for a private conversation. He would spare Patricia from a public humiliation, if he could, but that was the kindest thought he had for her right now.

Only a few hours ago, he'd still believed there was nothing he wouldn't do for her. He would offer his friendship. He would sit alone at a bar, holding vigil, just in case she needed him. But now he knew there was one thing he wouldn't do.

He would not watch her sacrifice herself to please her father.

She walked up to him, a vision of elegance and sensuality in one. His body tightened in response, but then again, so had every other man's, earlier tonight. She'd made sure of that. *I'm available,* she'd announced with every sultry step down the staircase. *Let the bidding begin.*

Nausea could kill desire, Luke now knew. Nausea at

seeing such a worthy woman still trying to earn her father's approval. That's what it had come down to. Her father would never love her, but Patricia would never stop trying to earn affection he didn't have in him to give.

"Hello, Luke. You look so very handsome."

He wore black tie, of course. In Texas, however, the bow tie was often replaced by a Western bolo, something Luke felt more comfortable wearing. The silver slide on his string tie had been in his family for generations.

Patricia noticed it, with her eye for quality. She adjusted it for him, moving it an imaginary centimeter to the left. She was using it as an excuse to touch him, obviously, but whether she hoped to entice him or she just missed him, he didn't know.

He didn't care.

"Are you representing the James Hill tonight?" she asked.

"Yes."

He watched her dark eyes drop to the silver slider at his neck once more. She touched his family's crest. He could tell the moment she made the right guess.

"Do you own the James Hill?"

"One third."

"Do you still love me?"

That one was harder to answer. But he looked at her, so beautiful, so vulnerable, so stubborn, and he told the truth. "I imagine I always will in one way or another."

"But not enough to marry me and help me defeat this Cargill curse?"

Her question was the answer he'd been looking for tonight. It was not the answer he'd wanted to hear. Resigned, he picked up his formal black Stetson and set it on his head.

"Don't try to defeat poison by swallowing more poison. Good night, beautiful."

He didn't allow himself to touch her, and he didn't allow himself a backward glance. Sometimes, a man had to know when to walk away.

August was a helluva time to have a practice run-through, but Texas Rescue ran on a strict schedule. Although they'd run a real, full operation in June, they still had to do their annual practice scenario every August.

It was scheduled for a Saturday, and it would be hot. They'd pitch a third of the tents in the parking lot next to the new Texas Rescue headquarters building, and they'd run a few mock scenarios. All personnel were supposed to report to the admin tent to check in, verify their contact information and receive fake orders.

The physicians were routinely sent home immediately after verifying their information, so Luke was surprised when Quinn MacDowell called early on Saturday to ask for a ride. He was at the River Mack, next to the JHR. They were miles apart, but in ranching terms, he lived just around the corner.

Luke couldn't refuse to pick him up.

"I wasn't planning on attending," Luke said, as they pulled into the parking lot.

"She's no longer the personnel director."

"Ah." Luke told himself he was relieved.

"I'm heading to the hospital after this, so I don't need a return ride. Diana will pick me up."

Luke pulled his firefighter's uniform out of the back of his truck and headed for the admin tent. It took him one second to realize Quinn was a liar.

Patricia Cargill was checking in the personnel.

He had way too long to stare as she checked in each person ahead of him in line. She was beautiful. She always had been. In his memories, she was beautiful. But now, to see her again, he was bowled over by her beauty.

"Name, please."

She couldn't be serious. "Luke Waterson."

"You are assigned to engine thirty-seven."

"No kidding."

"And the director of Texas Rescue would like to see you in her office as soon as you're available. The fire crews are dismissed for the day, so I can walk you over now. Have you seen the new headquarters building?"

"I can't say that I have."

She stood and came around the table that served as her desk. "I'll show you where her office is."

"I'm sure that's not necessary."

"Please?"

It was the please that did him in.

Patricia thought she might faint, she was so nervous. Her plan was working so far, but the early stages had been all logistics. Now came the hard part.

Now she would try to win Luke Waterson back.

He was here, big and real, carrying his heavy helmet and overcoat, so close she could have reached out to touch him. He might have offered her his arm, if they were walking in the dark. They might have held hands, if they were dashing through a thunderstorm. But they were simply crossing a parking lot on a routine Saturday morning, and he was no longer her friend.

He'd said he'd always love her, though. She was counting on that.

The building was nearly empty. She led him down

the air-conditioned hall to the office of the director of all of Texas Rescue. There was a little outer office for the secretary, but it was empty on a Saturday morning.

"Wait here," Patricia told him. "Let me go tell the director you're here. You can set your uniform down on that chair."

She went into the inner office and shut the door. Her hands were shaking as she took a seat behind her new desk.

"Come in," she called.

Luke walked in and stopped short when he saw her sitting there, alone.

She waited.

"I don't get it," he said, in a voice so flat her heart sank.

"I'm the new director. Karen Weaver was fired, and I applied for her position. I beat out three other candidates."

Seconds ticked by. "Congratulations."

She leaned forward and clasped her shaking hands on the desk top. "It's a paying position. I'm drawing a salary."

"And this makes you happy?"

Patricia hoped Luke was just thick-headed. She prayed he hadn't changed his mind about all the things he'd told her on a rented sailboat in the month of June.

"It makes me happy, because I need to pay my bills. I walked away from the trust fund. It wasn't as easy as you made it sound. The law does want you to do something with your money, but I filed a formal declaration that I would not authorize any expenditures for the indefinite future. Any attempt by the bank to get me to do so is considered harassment."

He put his hands on his hips as he loomed over her desk, but otherwise, he gave no indication that he was anything but a giant hunk of a firefighter statue.

"Do you know what happens to the money? Nothing. It just sits there, earning interest indefinitely."

"Where does this leave your father?"

"He couldn't win a job like this if he tried. He doesn't want to work, anyway. I believe he's moved to Houston, to mooch off some cousins there. I really don't care. He's never loved me."

Luke stared down at her.

"But you did."

Luke did not confirm this in any way.

So much for Plan A. He was supposed to be so amazed by her new independence that he'd sweep her into his arms, tell her that he loved her, and then quite possibly have sex with her in her new office.

Patricia stood and took a set of papers from her drawer. She set them on the edge closest to Luke. Plan B.

"I really do have an issue to discuss with you." It was so easy to slip into her role as the boss. She needed to function on autopilot like this, because her heart was breaking with disappointment. "I must transfer you to the Dallas branch of Texas Rescue. As a paid employee of Texas Rescue, I can be sued for sexual harassment if I attempt to seduce any volunteer. If you'll kindly sign these transfer papers, your reassignment will take effect immediately."

She held out a pen. It trembled in her fingers, but there was nothing she could do about that. No way to hide it.

She looked into Luke's blue eyes. "After you sign, I can seduce you. I'm quite determined, and I've planned a very long campaign. I intend to remind you of all the reasons we should be together, and none of them has anything to do with money and everything to do with—"

She finished her sentence in a yelp as Luke lunged for the pen. He dashed his name across the bottom of the paper, and practically vaulted over the desk to sweep her into his arms. He held her like she was a bride being carried over a threshold.

She was crying and laughing, both at the same time, which made it very hard to kiss. "I love you, Luke Waterson, with all the passion I have. It's the kind that keeps a couple together, if you'll let me prove it to you." When she said the words, her laughter faded at their importance.

Luke took advantage of her more serious demeanor to kiss her properly. She loved every taste of him, but she finally broke off the kiss. She was the boss, and she was a Cargill, so she wanted to be sure everything was handled properly.

"I have a deal for you," she said. "You love me for the rest of my life, and in return, I'll love you until the day I die." She held out her hand.

He had to set her down to shake her hand properly. "Mrs. Luke Waterson, you've got yourself a deal."

* * * * *

We hope you enjoyed reading

A COLD CREEK SECRET
by *New York Times* bestselling author
RaeANNE THAYNE and

NOT JUST A COWBOY
by
CARO CARSON

Both were originally **Harlequin**® series stories!

Discover more heartfelt tales of family, friendship and love from the **Harlequin Special Edition** series. Romance is for life, and these stories show that every chapter in a relationship has its challenges and delights and that love can be renewed with each turn of the page!

HARLEQUIN®

SPECIAL EDITION
Life, Love and Family

When you're with family, you're home!

Look for six *new* romances every month from **Harlequin Special Edition**!

Available wherever books are sold.

www.Harlequin.com

He hopped down and walked around to her side, but she was already out.

She gazed up at him, her expression tender. "I do believe you. And you're right about the beard. I like you better without it. Lead the way."

He took off before he did something stupid and kissed her. As he climbed, he monitored his pace so he wouldn't wear her out getting to the top.

"You can go faster. I'm in shape. I go for a run every morning."

He turned around so abruptly they almost slammed into each other. "You run? Is that okay?"

"My doctor says it's fine unless I notice any problems after a run. She's in favor of women exercising throughout their pregnancy. It's just the horseback riding she cautioned me about. And the bungee jumping."

His stomach lurched. "Bungee jumping?" The mischievous

twinkle in her eyes clued him in. "You've never bungee jumped in your life, have you?"

"Nope. Just teasing you."

No kidding. Standing inches away from her, he was teased by a whole bunch of things—the scent of her shampoo, the curve of her cheek and the sound of her breath. He knew the pleasure her kiss could bring and he craved that pleasure again. But he'd promised that wasn't why he'd brought her up there.

"We'd better get a move on." He turned around and started back up the trail. "We want to get there before the sun hits that rock."

Fortunately it was still shaded when they reached the end of the trail. He should have thought to bring a blanket for her to sit on, but then she might have questioned his honorable intentions.

She walked out onto the rock and sucked in a breath. "Gorgeous. Thank you for bringing me up here. Now I wish I'd brought a camera, or at least my phone."

"We can come back another time."

She turned toward him. "No, we can't, Zeke. It'll be better for all three of us if we make a clean break."

"I don't want a clean break." He dropped to one knee. "I don't have a ring to give you, but I'll get one today. Tess Irwin, will you do me the honor of becoming my wife?"

Don't miss
SAY YES TO THE COWBOY by Vicki Lewis Thompson,
available July 2017 wherever
Harlequin® Special Edition books and ebooks are sold.

www.Harlequin.com

HARLEQUIN®

SPECIAL EDITION

Life, Love and Family

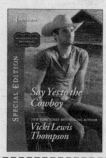

Say Yes to the Cowboy

NEW YORK TIMES BESTSELLING AUTHOR

Vicki Lewis Thompson

Save **$1.00**

on the purchase of ANY

Harlequin® Special Edition book.

Available wherever books are sold, including most bookstores, supermarkets, drugstores and discount stores.

Save $1.00

on the purchase of any Harlequin Special Edition book.

Coupon valid until September 30, 2017.
Redeemable at participating outlets in the U.S. and Canada only.
Not redeemable at Barnes & Noble stores. Limit one coupon per customer.

52614789

5 65373 00076 2 (8100)0 12276

® and ™ are trademarks owned and used by the trademark owner and/or its licensee.

© 2017 Harlequin Enterprises Limited

NYTCOUP0617